The TALE *of the* INCOMPARABLE PRINCE

With love and best wishes,

Beth Newman

THE LIBRARY OF TIBET

The TALE *of the* INCOMPARABLE PRINCE

MDO MKHAR
TSHE RING DBANG RGYAL

Translated and with an introduction
by Beth Newman

General Series Editor, John F. Avedon

HarperPerennial
A Division of HarperCollins*Publishers*

The emblem of the Library of Tibet is the wind horse (Lung da), a beautiful steed that brings happiness and good fortune (symbolized by the jewel on its back) wherever it goes. The image of the wind horse is painted on prayer flags in Tibet, which are then affixed to houses and temples, on bridges and at mountain passes throughout the land. The movement of the flag by the wind sets the wind horse in motion, carrying prayers for happiness and good fortune to the ten directions.

A hardcover edition of this book was published in 1996 by HarperCollins Publishers.

THE TALE OF THE INCOMPARABLE PRINCE. Copyright © 1996 by Beth Newman. All rights reserved. Printed in the United States of America. No part of this book may be used or reproduced in any manner whatsoever without written permission except in the case of brief quotations embodied in critical articles and reviews. For information address HarperCollins Publishers, Inc., 10 East 53rd Street, New York, NY 10022.

HarperCollins books may be purchased for educational, business, or sales promotional use. For information, please write: Special Markets Department, HarperCollins Publishers, Inc., 10 East 53rd Street, New York, NY 10022.

First HarperPerennial edition published 1997.

Designed by Caitlin Daniels

The Library of Congress has catalogued the hardcover edition as follows:

Tshe ring dbang rgyal, Mdo mkhar Zhabs drung, 1697–1763.
   [Gzhon nu zla med kyi gtam rgyud. English]
   Tale of the incomparable prince / by Tshe ring dbang rgyal ; translated with an introduction by Beth Newman.
      p.   cm.
   ISBN 0-06-017400-5
   I. Newman, Beth, 1955– . II. Title.
PL3748.M38G9813   1996
895' .43—dc20   95-42523

ISBN 0-06-092784-4 (pbk.)

97 98 99 00 01 ❖/RRD 10 9 8 7 6 5 4 3 2 1

This book is dedicated to my parents and teachers

CONTENTS

ACKNOWLEDGMENTS

Many people deserve thanks for their help on this book.

This translation first appeared as a portion of my doctoral dissertation in South Asian Languages and Literature at the University of Wisconsin-Madison. My thesis adviser, Venerable Professor Geshe Lhundup Sopa, first brought *The Tale of the Incomparable Prince* to my attention. His suggestions, advice, and encouragement gave me the impetus to begin work on the novel, and his skillful instruction provided me with the skills necessary to complete the project.

Two Tibetan teachers patiently worked with me in colloquial Tibetan to explain the intricacies of the novel's archaic style: Venerable Professor Jigme Dawa of the Central Institute of Higher Tibetan Studies, Sarnath, India, and Professor Drakton Jampa Gyaltsen of the Tibetan Medical Institute, Dharamsala, India. Professor Gyaltsen also generously shared his expertise in Tibetan poetics and literary history.

The staff of the Library of Tibetan Works and Archives, Dharamsala, helpfully directed me to valuable historical works in the LTWA collection and took the time to discuss those texts. Financial support for my dissertation research in India came from the American Institute of Indian Studies.

Finally, I am grateful to John Newman who offered editorial assistance, encouragement, and advice throughout this project.

INTRODUCTION

The Tale of the Incomparable Prince is unique in world literature: it is the sole example of a Tibetan novel. Written in a classical style in the early eighteenth century, Tshe ring dbang rgyal's story combines intrigue, romance, war, and religion in a rousing tale of adventure within the context of a traditional Buddhist worldview. The story is designed to entertain and to teach the reader about Buddhism. Long the most popular work of fiction in Tibet, this book is a stimulating addition to books about Tibetan culture and religion available to Western readers.

Although telling a good story in beautiful language has a long tradition in Buddhist literature, Tshe ring dbang rgyal felt a need to justify his work because in his cultural milieu religion was virtually the sole subject of belles lettres. Religious topics were elucidated with an attention to stylistic detail not displayed in historical, scientific, or other didactic works. In both the prologue and epilogue of the novel, Tshe ring dbang rgyal paraphrased the words of the first-century Buddhist author Aśvaghoṣa to substantiate his claim that the novel is meant to lead the reader toward virtue. Tshe ring dbang rgyal rationalized that through satisfying his readers' desire for a story of politics and love he could surreptitiously increase their sensitivity to religious principles.

Tshe ring dbang rgyal wanted to show that religion is not just for the cloistered clergy: his descriptions of court life illustrate the right and wrong ways to govern, relate to one's peers, find a spouse, and raise a family. One of his main points is that staying active in the world is compatible with Buddhist virtue. The novel's entrancing story has a subtext;

it is a parable showing the practice of Buddhism for the layperson. In today's busy world, where few can dedicate themselves full-time to religious pursuits, Tshe ring dbang rgyal's illustration of the practice of Buddhism as a part of secular life is all the more valuable. Even contemporary readers can find a few hints regarding the Buddhist way to handle daily situations in this eighteenth-century fantasy.

Tshe ring dbang rgyal wrote *The Tale of the Incomparable Prince* for his highly educated Tibetan peers. He and his intended audience shared a cultural and religious heritage that provides the foundation for the novel. Although *The Tale of the Incomparable Prince* can be enjoyed on its own, it will be helpful to the modern reader to have some of the assumed context explained. To that end, a brief biography of Tshe ring dbang rgyal, a discussion of the literary sources and style of the novel, and an outline of the traditional Tibetan Buddhist worldview follow.

Biography of the Author

mDo mkhar Tshe ring dbang rgyal (1697–1763) was an important political figure in eighteenth-century Tibet who contributed greatly to cultural life. For approximately a quarter of a century, he was the second most powerful man in the country: his influence on the events of his time as well as his literary works continue to affect Tibet and Tibetan culture. A biography of Tshe ring dbang rgyal depicts a man of letters who was devoted to his country, religion, and the literary arts.

In the eighteenth century, Tibetan society was feudal. There was a strict and fundamental division between a large class of common people and a relatively small landed nobility. The commoners—predominately laborers, farmers, and herders—were tied to the land, and land ownership was concomitant with control of the resident populace. Land ownership was the key to social prominence, wealth, and political power. The landed nobility filled the ranks of the secular arm of government and strove to protect and increase their personal landholdings, wealth, and power. The monasteries and the government also had significant property. Thus, the majority of the population owed their primary allegiance and a portion of their labor to a particular noble family, a monastery, or a noble granted temporary land rights in his role as a government minister.

The Tibetan nobility had hierarchical ranks determined primarily by land-based wealth. Most of the landed families controlled relatively little territory, whereas a few extended families held almost all the land and political power in the central government. Tshe ring dbang rgyal was born into the mDo mkhar family, one of the five wealthiest and most influential noble families in Tibet. His family had vast landholdings, and their political power can be traced as far back as the Tibetan dynastic period, circa 600 to 840 C.E.

Tshe ring dbang rgyal was given the best education available so that he could follow the family tradition of government service. In eighteenth-century Tibet, practically all intellectual and cultural activity was anchored in the monasteries. Monastic universities provided training for both the religious community and the lay nobility preparing for careers in government and commerce. A major part of this education focused on the science of language, including poetics and the product of the poetic process, literature. The poetic tradition studied in the monasteries was inherited from India. Sanskrit stylistic prescriptions, prosody, and literature were the main contents of Tibetan literature textbooks and courses.

Tshe ring dbang rgyal entered the monastic school system at Sera Monastery when he was five years old. However, when he was nine, his father took personal control of his education, and for the next five years Tshe ring dbang rgyal was placed under the tutelage of two men, a monk from the monastery of sMin grol gling and the Dalai Lama's private astrologer.

When he was fourteen, Tshe ring dbang rgyal faced a career decision. The wealthy monastery of sTag glung, which had long and close ties to the mDo mkhar family, asked him to become their chief abbot. Monastic officialdom was an alternate path to prominence in Tibet; however, Tshe ring dbang rgyal was determined to remain a layman and pursue a political career. He declined the monastery's offer and went to study at sMin grol gling, the best monastery school for aspiring lay officials, for the final three years of his formal education.

In 1714, when Tshe ring dbang rgyal was seventeen, he obtained his first official position. This was not an auspicious time to begin a government career, for the beginning of the eighteenth century was a period of extreme turmoil in Tibet. During Tshe ring dbang rgyal's lifetime, six different governments ruled. These were not peaceful transfers of power; a wrong step or misplaced alliance often meant death.

The political climate in 1714 was an uneasy peace: various unresolved religious and political issues from the recent past were ready to explode once again. Tibetan politics was complicated by eager Mongolian and Chinese attempts to gain political and economic influence in Tibet. Two powerful Mongolian tribes, the Qoshots and Dzungars, and the Ch'ing emperor of China offered military support to

Tibetan factions vying for power. The internal Tibetan power struggles, compounded by foreign involvement, centered on control of land, commerce, and the succession of the Dalai Lamas.

Tshe ring dbang rgyal's first position was as a tax collector under Qoshot Mongol military rule. He was an efficient worker and a popular figure, and he had the social connections critical to career advancement. As in every country, a great deal of government activity in Tibet was conducted during the social gatherings of the ruling class. Tshe ring dbang rgyal possessed every requisite social grace: polished amiability, athletic prowess, and genius in composing literary pieces. His noble peers highly valued literary and verbal ability. All trained in the same Indo-Tibetan literary tradition, the ruling class placed a high value on participating in speech competitions and circulating self-penned manuscripts on classical religious topics among friends. Tshe ring dbang rgyal's varied accomplishments led to his appointment as district commissioner of Shigatse in 1717.

Soon after he took up his new position, war broke out. The Dzungar Mongols invaded Tibet, promising to return secular power to their Tibetan allies. For a few years the Dzungars seemed invincible; they annihilated the Qoshot Mongol forces as well as a large army sent by the Ch'ing emperor. Tshe ring dbang rgyal advanced his career by shifting his allegiance to the new Dzungar court in Lhasa. He obtained a position of his own choosing, district commissioner of lCags rtse gri gu, and for a few years he was the chief chamberlain of the Dzungar's puppet Tibetan ruler. It was during his tenure at lCags rtse gri gu that he began to write *The Tale of the Incomparable Prince*.

In 1720 the Ch'ing emperor sent another large army to Tibet in the company of the Seventh Dalai Lama. The Dzungars fled, and most of their Tibetan supporters were executed. However, Tshe ring dbang rgyal was spared through the intervention of Pho lha nas bSod nams stob rgyas, the leader of the Tibetan resistance against the Dzungars. Tshe ring dbang rgyal and Pho lha nas were close friends: they had both studied at sMin grol gling and worked in the finance department under the Qoshot Mongols.

This close call resulted in a short hiatus in Tshe ring dbang rgyal's career. He returned to one of his familial estates and completed *The Tale of the Incomparable Prince*. After a year, he reentered government as a tax collector. But with Pho lha nas as his promoter, he quickly advanced to second in command in the finance ministry and was given the important responsibility of handling the Seventh Dalai Lama's travel and court protocol. Pho lha nas also arranged a marriage for Tshe ring dbang rgyal. (Unfortunately, we have no additional information about Tshe ring dbang rgyal's personal life and relationships; even his wife's name is omitted from his autobiography.)

A coup d'état led to civil war in 1727. The coup leaders formed a government and incarcerated all of Pho lha nas's associates in Lhasa except Tshe ring dbang rgyal. Although Tshe ring dbang rgyal had apparently broken with his old friend to support the coup leaders, it seems likely that subsequent to his capture and release by Pho lha nas's forces he secretly worked for the other side. This assumption seems safe given the fact that at the end of the war, when Pho lha nas became ruler of Tibet, he appointed Tshe ring dbang rgyal governor of the central province of dBu, making him second only to Pho lha nas in secular power.

The ensuing twenty relatively peaceful years allowed Tshe ring dbang rgyal to hone his skills as a negotiator and writer. He mediated the Tibetan-Bhutanese wars, conducted trade talks with the Dzungars, and eased the often difficult relationship between Pho lha nas and the Seventh Dalai Lama. During his later years, Tshe ring dbang rgyal turned from fiction to write history and biography. His works in these genres are the most important Tibetan sources available to contemporary scholars for the history of early eighteenth-century Tibet. The events of this tumultuous period are cited frequently in the Tibetan-Chinese dispute over the independence of Tibet, so Tshe ring dbang rgyal continues to play a significant role in shaping our understanding of this crucial geopolitical conflict.

The death of Pho lha nas resulted in immediate turmoil, and Tshe ring dbang rgyal was in imminent danger of execution. Only the timely assassination of the new Tibetan ruler by the Chinese ambassadors prevented Tshe ring dbang rgyal's death. The Tibetan government was restructured once again, and it lasted from the time it took power in 1750 until the Chinese invasion of Tibet in the 1950s. Tshe ring dbang rgyal was appointed the first prime minister of the ruling council. For the next seven years he worked closely with the Seventh Dalai Lama to manage Tibetan-Chinese relations.

Tshe ring dbang rgyal's last major official duty was as a member of the team appointed to locate the Eighth Dalai Lama. In 1762 he retired from government service, and he died one year later, at the age of sixty-seven.

The two major interests in Tshe ring dbang rgyal's life, politics and religion, are both clearly reflected in his writing. He was a consummate politician, able to negotiate, serve, and prosper under each of the six violent changes of government during his lifetime. He appears to have relished the complex politics of his time; his descriptions of the Machiavellian twists of court politics in *The Tale of the Incomparable Prince* are some of the liveliest and well-drawn passages in the novel. In the text, the hero's trusted companion engages in subterfuge and strategic maneuvering that only someone skilled in the political arena could conceive. At the same time, Tshe ring dbang rgyal was a deeply religious man; throughout his life he made a point of attending religious ceremonies, studying religious texts, and engaging in a daily practice of Buddhism. For him, religion and politics were inextricably mixed; he states in his autobiography that his most worthy role was to assist the Seventh Dalai Lama in his religious-political duties. The blending of religion and government is a theme throughout the novel. The prince, the novel's main character, makes an initial unsuccessful attempt to rule his kingdom according to Buddhist precepts, and eventually, after religiously inspired introspection, he establishes a happy rule of religious law.

Sources of the Novel

Tshe ring dbang rgyal's *Tale of the Incomparable Prince* is unique: there is nothing similar preceding it in the Tibetan literary tradition. However, Tshe ring dbang rgyal did not create this work in a vacuum. The elite aristocracy wrote for one another as a form of entertainment. This aristocratic literature was virtually always religious, consisting of poetic biographies of the Buddha, retellings of *Jātaka* stories describing the Buddha's lives prior to enlightenment, and stories about bodhisattvas. Tshe ring dbang rgyal's innovation was to shift the primary focus of writing from religion to romantic adventure: the excitement of the story took prominence, with religious themes as a subtext.

Tshe ring dbang rgyal did not depart from accepted traditional sources for literature in his work. He drew from the usual corpus of *Jātaka* stories and the Buddha's and bodhisattvas' biographies. However, in contrast to his predecessors, he relied heavily upon the Hindu *Rāmāyaṇa* epic for a large portion of the plot structure of the novel. The story line of the *Rāmāyaṇa* was familiar to many members of his social class because it was among the Indian literary materials translated into Tibetan and also preserved in Sanskrit. It had been used mainly to illustrate Indo-Tibetan grammatical points, poetic structures, and secular aphorisms; although occasionally given a literary treatment in translation, it never became popular, perhaps because of its inescapable Hindu references. Tshe ring dbang rgyal's creative step was to transform the epic, cloak it in Buddhist sensibilities, and thus create a romantic adventure story while remaining within the confines of acceptable literature. He succeeded in writing a novel that could be enjoyed by both the aristocracy and the educated clergy. The traditional Buddhist sources were represented, so the text could be read by the devout without guilt for indulging in frivolous activity. Yet this was a major development in Tibetan literature because it made a new type of literary pleasure available to readers.

A brief synopsis of the plot of *The Tale of the Incomparable Prince* will provide a context for the subsequent discussion of the influences on the novel. But readers who wish to be surprised by the twists of the plot may choose to skip this section.

The king and queen of the kingdom of Joyous Groves are unable to have a child. This lack of a successor is dangerous for the realm, so the king's ministers advise the royal couple to make offerings to the gods and ask for progeny as a boon. In response to the nation's prayers, the couple have a son, Prince Kumaradvitiya.

Everyone is overjoyed, but no one can agree on the best way to rear the prince. The controversy revolves around whether to educate the boy to become a religious figure, since he was born as a result of prayer, or to prepare him to lead his country. The faction desiring that the prince grow up to rule the realm triumphs, and the elders arrange to bring up the boy in a secular fashion.

When the prince reaches marriageable age, the only suitable bride is Manohari, a princess already betrothed to the unprincipled Prince Devatisha of Myriad Lights. Prince Kumaradvitiya unsuccessfully attempts to win the princess by diplomacy, and in the end he resorts to subterfuge. Unfortunately, a clever kidnap attempt fails, and Manohari and Prince Kumaradvitiya's best friend, Bhavakumara, are taken captive by the evil Prince Devatisha.

While Prince Kumaradvitiya prepares a large army to rescue them, Manohari is forced to marry Devatisha. But with clever strategies, she tricks him into postponing consummation of the marriage. Bhavakumara also is able to hoodwink his captors and convince them that he has joined their cause. Bhavakumara carefully plans his activities to cause dissension in the court of Myriad Lights, weaken the cohesion of society, and destroy the physical defenses of the realm.

Prince Kumaradvitiya's army arrives and wins a bloody battle. The prince finally is united with Manohari; however, her long stay in Myriad Lights as Prince Devatisha's wife makes him doubt her virtue. Manohari defends herself, and eventually the prince is convinced of her purity. The two are married and enjoy conjugal bliss. They remain in Myriad Lights to reconstruct the kingdom after the depredations of years of bad rule and warfare.

During this time, back in Joyous Groves, Prince Kumaradvitiya's father has fallen in love with a very young woman, Lavanya Kamala. The girl's father, the lowest of the king's retainers, is wily. As a bride-price he extracts a number of promises from the king, most significantly that if Lavanya bears a son, the boy will inherit the kingdom. The old queen, the court, and all the upper nobility are aghast but powerless to intervene. As they feared, the young queen promptly conceives and delivers a boy.

Despite the change in succession, when Prince Kumaradvitiya returns, he and Manohari befriend the child. While Manohari visits her parents' realm, Prince Kumaradvitiya feels the first stirrings of interest in a religious life. He attempts to leave the kingdom for a religious hermitage but is prevented by his father and the court. Prince Kumaradvitiya agrees to rule as regent until his half brother comes of age. He governs according to his concept of morality, but his grandiose efforts to perfect the practice of charity nearly bank-rupt the realm. The old king must quell the unrest led by Lavanya's father.

The young queen Lavanya becomes infatuated with Prince Kumaradvitiya. He rejects her amorous advances, and she, terrified that he will expose her impropriety, which might block her son's inheri-tance of the throne, tricks the old king into banishing Prince Kumaradvitiya. Only Bhavakumara, Prince Kumaradvitiya's loyal friend, follows him into exile.

Manohari returns from her visit and finds her husband gone. The court attempts to persuade her to marry her young brother-in-law, but she decides to follow her husband into exile. She traces his route but loses her way in the forest, and her two companions are devoured by wild beasts. Fearing for her life, Manohari is in despair when she finds the men in religious retreat in a forest hermitage.

After Prince Kumaradvitiya fulfills the terms of his exile, he decides to return to civilization to share the joy of his spiritual knowledge. On their way back to the city, Kumaradvitiya saves Bhavakumara's life through sacrificing one of his own limbs. This selfless act brings the prince to the stage of a bodhisattva. Out of love for his fellow men, he survives his self-inflicted injury and resumes his journey home. There he explains the meaning of Buddhism to all who will listen, thereby bringing happiness to his friends, family, and former enemies.

Tshe ring dbang rgyal drew from four primary Indian sources for *The Tale of the Incomparable Prince:* the biography of the Buddha, the *Rāmāyaṇa* epic, *Jātaka* stories, and textbooks of Indian poetics.

On the most general level of analysis, the plot of *The Tale of the Incomparable Prince* can be said to be based roughly on the life of the Buddha. The Buddha was born a prince, and his father's court debated whether he should follow a religious or a secular life. The importance of polity won out, and the prince was trained to rule. The young prince had religious inclinations, but every attempt was made to keep him in the realm. Eventually he escaped the palace and entered the religious life. After years of meditation, he attained the state of enlightenment and shared his message with the world. Prince Kumaradvitiya's life follows the same outline, with a lot of deviation in the middle for a love story and a war.

The novel's plot most closely parallels the *Rāmāyaṇa.* A number of recensions of the *Rāmāyaṇa* begin with the king making offerings to the gods to receive an heir. The primary queen gives birth to Rāma, a miraculous prince who appears destined to reign. However, a secondary queen wants her son to inherit the kingdom, and her jealous plotting sets in motion the dramatic tension of the epic. Rāma, an older and more deserving prince, is exiled as a result of the conniving of his step-mother, who wants to ensure her own child's inheritance.

A major portion of the *Rāmāyaṇa* revolves around the kidnap of Rāma's wife, Sītā, the ensuing war to rescue her, and her reunion with Rāma. Sītā is captured by a demon king and sequestered in his palace. There, against all odds, she remains faithful to Rāma and refuses to remarry. This is clearly reflected in *The Tale of the Incomparable Prince* by Devatisha's kidnap, imprisonment, and unsuccessful seduction of Manohari. Likewise, the war fought to liberate Manohari follows the same pattern as the war in the Hindu epic, where the initial work of weakening the enemy is accomplished by trusted assistants. The monkey general Hanuman of the *Rāmāyaṇa* is the model for Tshe ring dbang rgyal's character Bhavakumara. Like Hanuman, Bhavakumara goes alone into the enemy realm. When he is captured, he tricks the enemy court and ruins their defenses by destroying their infrastructure.

The reunion of the main protagonists does not result in immediate happiness in either the epic or the novel. Both heroes voice their suspicion that the beloved wife or fiancée, voluntarily had sexual intercourse with her captor. In both works such a lapse in feminine virtue would be a reason to terminate their relationships, so Sītā and Manohari must prove their virtue.

Although from the outset the novel's plotline follows the *Rāmāyaṇa,* Buddhist doctrine permeates *The Tale of the Incomparable Prince* and provides the explanation or motivation for events. For example, although the central section of the novel superficially appears to glorify the warrior ethic exemplified in the *Rāmāyaṇa,* a closer reading proves that the adventure is used to illustrate the Buddhist doctrine of karma, the moral law of causation. The characters in the novel all begin with a worldly, aristocratic, and military outlook on life, but gradually the vicissitudes of life lead them to ponder why and how events occur. As the hero and heroine come to understand reality, the reader also learns to view the world from a religious perspective. Even more specifically, the basis for Prince Kumaradvitiya's near bankrupting of the kingdom through generosity is found in the stories about the bodhisattva princes in the "King of the Śibis" and the "Viśvantara" *Jātaka* stories. The novel neatly paraphrases the moral adages regarding charity and morality found in these traditional Buddhist stories. Finally, the friction between renunciation and family life is a familiar theme in Buddhist biographical literature. The families and friends of religious aspirants often attempt to prevent them from leaving home for religious pursuits by graphically describing the difficulties of a religious life. In response, the religiously inclined outline the disadvantages of the secular world and the joys of religious life. This type of interchange occurs at three points in the novel: when the prince is convinced to rule the realm as regent, when he experiences joy at being banished, and when Manohari follows Prince Kumaradvitiya into exile.

In both the *Rāmāyaṇa* and this novel, the heroes eventually decide to return to the city. In *The Tale of the Incomparable Prince,* this decision springs from the prince's desire to spread the liberating knowledge gained during his exile. From this point on, the novel is drawn solely from Buddhist literature. On the journey home, Prince Kumaradvitiya voluntarily undertakes an extreme physical sacrifice to benefit Bhavakumara. Buddhist biographical literature is filled with similar examples of altruism. Before his enlightenment, the Buddha gave away parts of his body in various human rebirths, and he sacrificed his life for others when born as a fish, hare, elephant, lion, and tortoise.

In the prologue of *The Tale of the Incomparable Prince,* Tshe ring dbang rgyal states that his work is meant to accord with the traditions of

Indian dramatic literature. He wants readers to come away from his novel with a deeper understanding of all four classical Indian aims of life: *dharma* (virtue or duty), *artha* (wealth and power), *kāma* (love and pleasure), and *mokṣa* (renunciation and liberation). The novel's colophon lists how and where each topic was treated in the body of the work.

Character development in the novel is also clearly within the Indian tradition. In classical Indian literature, characters tend to be idealized types rather than individualized personalities. Characters are portrayals of the perfect hero, villain, or woman. Explication of the characters' natures illustrates positive (or negative) qualities, such as filial devotion, familial responsibility, and feminine charm. Character development does not entail transformation in the Western sense. As the story progresses, the nature of each character is more clearly revealed, but no one essentially changes. For example, Bhavakumara and Prince Kumaradvitiya typify the quintessential warrior-hero. They engage in deception, trickery, and violence to vanquish their enemies; yet because they are inherently heroic, both are applauded for their behavior. When these men turn to religion, their piety comes as no surprise because they have always been pure in heart. In contrast, if a villain employs similar military tactics, he is roundly condemned because he is evil by definition. Further, since everything about a villain is reprehensible, even a positive act passes without comment. Prince Devatisha is portrayed as a selfish fool for respecting Manohari's wish to refrain from consummating their marriage. In short, the reader's judgment about an event is determined by the preordained nature of the action's protagonist.

Stylistically, *The Tale of the Incomparable Prince* is a standard Sanskrit literary form called a *campū*, a mixed verse and prose composition. Tshe ring dbang rgyal uses prose to move the plot, for short descriptions, and for brief dialogues. Lengthy speeches and recapitulations of action are in verse. Tshe ring dbang rgyal employs all the Sanskrit figures of speech (metaphor, analogy, and so on) that can be mimicked in Tibetan.

The Buddhist Worldview

Tshe ring dbang rgyal's readers were all members of an elite class with a shared worldview. A synopsis of some of the beliefs that shaped the eighteenth-century Tibetan's perception of the world will provide the contemporary reader with a context that Tshe ring dbang rgyal assumed his readership shared.

Tibet inherited from India a number of ontological concepts that form the basis of Tibetan Buddhism; among them reincarnation, samsara, nirvana, and karma. Reincarnation is the process of rebirth. According to this belief, when one dies the body becomes a corpse but a portion of one's mental continuum transmigrates into another form of existence. We have been and most likely will be born a multitude of times as each of the six types of sentient creatures: humans, gods, demigods, animals, hungry ghosts, and denizens of hell. These realms of existence and the process of cycling through them in various rebirths are termed samsara.

Samsara is synonymous with misery. On the most basic level, suffering is the obvious physical and psychological wretchedness associated with each realm of existence. Birth, sickness, aging, dying, not getting or losing what one wants, and coming in contact with unpleasant circumstances are all unpleasant physical or mental states. Pleasure is merely a masquerade for a slightly more subtle form of suffering, change. Worldly happiness is also a kind of misery because it is transient, always changing to a neutral or unpleasant sensation. On the most sophisticated level of examination, the mere experience of rebirth and every moment of existence are inextricably bound up with misery.

There is, however, a state that is beyond the suffering of samsara: nirvana is the cessation of all suffering and liberation from the cycle of rebirths. It is a state of immutable bliss and extraordinary mental powers. Nirvana exists completely separate from samsara.

Even though one seems trapped in samsara, the situation is not hopeless. Rebirth into a particular realm of existence is not a matter of fate, the whim of a more powerful being, or an unaccountable circumstance. Causation is a universal law: each rebirth, and even escape from the cycle of rebirths, comes about as a result of specific causes.

The causes which determine rebirth are the moral quality of one's actions. Actions, or karma, are physical, verbal, and mental activities—the exercise of one's body, speech, and mind. The positive or negative quality and intensity of one's actions yield definite pleasant or miserable results. In other words, one's present physical and mental circumstances are the culmination of one's prior virtuous or nonvirtuous actions. Every aspect of one's life—internal, external, physical, and emotional—is the result of specific physical, verbal, or mental karmas created in the past. Karma is fundamentally a mental process, because every type of action leaves an impression upon one's mind. These mental imprints, like seeds, come to fruition as the events and circumstances in future lives. Thus, what one does, says, and thinks now condition one's mind to experience a specific future rebirth.

Logically then, one can control one's experiences by creating the appropriate causal sequences. A rebirth is conditioned only by the mental imprints of one's own actions, so deliberate positive actions will improve one's future destiny. In contrast, evil actions will propel one's future births in terribly unpleasant circumstances. We all have it within ourselves to improve our situations, we just need to know how. One of Tibet's great contributions to the world is a systematization of Buddhist doctrine and practice into a series of logically related self-improvement steps. Starting with simple instructions, one is gradually led through increasingly complex and sophisticated practices designed to help one reach the state of a completely enlightened Buddha.

Buddhism employs human psychology in its organization of the religious path. It recognizes that the most basic aspiration of all living beings is to experience happiness. This basic desire leads one first to strive for the most pleasurable rebirth possible within samsara. As one's religious knowledge deepens, one realizes that true happiness can only be found by escaping samsara completely. The motivation to become a fully enlightened Buddha, rather than just to attain nirvana, is formed through transferring the focus from oneself to others. Seeing that all other beings are as miserable and desirous of pleasure as oneself leads to compassion—the desire to alleviate others' misery and see them experience happiness. Because only a Buddha with extraordinary teaching abilities truly can help others, the ultimate religious goal is enlightenment.

Despite the existence of written instructions on these meditation practices, Tibetan Buddhism stresses the need for a teacher. Texts can be variously interpreted; it is easy to become confused or misled through solitary study or casual discussions with others who are equally unlearned. For any progress to be made along a religious path, a long-term personal relationship with a spiritual guide is necessary. This teacher must be someone who has already accomplished at least some of the stages of practice, at a minimum exhibiting mental control gained from moral discipline and concentration, and possessing wisdom derived from an understanding of the nature of reality. Such a person can be a true friend, someone who can lead a disciple along the path of virtue.

The story of The Tale of the Incomparable Prince is told within the matrix of these ideas. However, Tshe ring dbang rgyal did not blindly accept this framework of reality and unknowingly reflect it in his work; he deliberately wove the practice of the Buddhist path to complete enlightenment through the novel. In his own words, his purpose was to "clearly explain the marvelous qualities of the four aims of men so that religious instructions would arise from a tale enjoyed by ordinary beings."

The status of *The Tale of the Incomparable Prince* as an imaginative novel with a religious subtext has recently been placed in doubt. Some Chinese commentators have stated that the novel is a realistic description of eighteenth-century Tibetan society. Perhaps because of the significance of Tshe ring dbang rgyal's historical and biographical writing, these critics assert that the novel is an accurate account of a political marriage alliance between the Qoshot and Dzungar Mongols. However, a close reading of Tibetan and Mongolian history, the *Rāmāyaṇa,* the life of the Buddha, and some *Jātaka* stories leaves no doubt that *The Tale of the Incomparable Prince* depicts purely imaginary events.

Tshe ring dbang rgyal was one of Tibet's foremost men of letters. He wrote a number of important books that were well received at the time of their composition and have proved to have lasting value. *The Tale of the Incomparable Prince* continues to be the most popular work of Tibetan fiction. It has been printed and reprinted both in Tibet and by the Tibetan exile community. Even those unable to appreciate the complex language of the original know and relish the story.

The Tale of the Incomparable Prince has long been unknown outside Tibet. I hope that this translation will increase Western understanding and appreciation of an important aspect of Tibetan culture. My aim has been to give Western readers at least some of the pleasure and edification the novel has provided Tibetans over the years.

Translator's Note

Tshe ring dbang rgyal's heavy reliance upon the Indian tradition of literature posed an interesting problem for translation into English: how to handle the names of characters and places. Tshe ring dbang rgyal did not employ real Tibetan proper names. Instead he invented elaborate Sanskritic Tibetan names. Each name has a meaning that illustrates an important aspect of the character's personality; for example, the hero's name, gZhon nu zla med, is Incomparable Youth and his father, Nyi ma'i blo gros, is Wise Sun. Even ordinary names in Tibetan have meaning, so these exotic inventions furthered the author's evocation of a quasi-mythical atmosphere for Tibetan readers. However, except for place names, translations of names into English seemed cumbersome and contradictory to Tshe ring dbang rgyal's attempt to create a majestic milieu for his story.

I rejected transliteration of Tibetan names as an unsuitable option. Tibetan orthography and sound combinations are very different from those in English. An accurate spelling of the hero's name, gZhon nu zla med, would be an impediment to the reader. A phonetic rendering of the Tibetan name, Zhunnu-dahmay, is only slightly better. In contrast, the sound combinations of the Indo-European language Sanskrit seem mellifluous and regal to Western readers. Therefore, I decided to go back to Sanskrit sources for Tshe ring dbang rgyal's names. The names used throughout the text are my translations into Sanskrit. The Sanskrit has been simplified: no diacritics appear to confuse readers. For those interested, a glossary of names with literal English translations and the Tibetan transliterations follows this introduction.

The Tibetan text of *The Tale of the Incomparable Prince* is a continuous narrative. Because that is a format not often used today, I broke the story into chapters in this translation. I hope that this change makes the novel easier to read.

GLOSSARY OF PROPER NAMES

The Kingdom of Joyous Groves

PLACE NAMES	TRANSLATION	TIBETAN
Kingdom	Joyous Groves, also known as Gem of the World	Kun dga'i tshal Srid pa'i rgyan
Capital city	Open Lotus	Pad ma rgyas pa
Palace	Gem of the World	Srid pa'i rgyan

ROYAL FAMILY

King Suryamati	Wise Sun	Nyi ma'i blo gros
Queen Kundaladhara	Earring Wearer	rNa cha 'dzin
Queen Lavanya Kamala, second wife of Suryamati, daughter of Padmankura	Lovely Flower	mDzes sdug me tog
Prince Kumaradvitiya, son of Suryamati and Kundaladhara	Incomparable Youth	gZhon nu zla med
Prince Ananda Lalitasaras, son of Suryamati and Lavanya Kamala	Ocean of Joy	dGa' ba'i rol mtsho

MINISTERS OF STATE

Jneyavan	Holder of All Objects of Knowledge	Shes bya ldan
Vidyeshvara	Lord of Knowledge	Rig pa'i dbang phyugs
Atulyamati	Unequaled Intellect	mTshungs med blo gros ldan
Parambhasvaramati	Supremely Clear Intellect	bLo gros mchog tu gsal ba

MINISTERS OF THE ARMED FORCES

Virendra	Lord of Heroes	dPa ba'i dbang
Abhayabalahanta	Destroyer of the Enemy Host	'Jigs med dpung 'joms
Laksaikadvitiya	Worth a Hundred Thousand Comrades	'Bum phrag do zla gcig pa
Abhayavrati	Fearless Discipline	'Jigs med brtul zhugs ldan

COURTIERS

Bhavakumara, companion of Kumaradvitiya	Young Hero of the Universe	dPa' bo srid pa gzhon nu
Chetadasa	Abject Servant	'Bangs khol
Padmankura, father of Lavanya Kamala	Lotus Sprout	Pad ma'i myu gu

The Kingdom of Myriad Lights

PLACE NAMES	TRANSLATION	TIBETAN
Kingdom	Myriad Lights	sNang ba 'bum ldan
Capital city	Flowering Estate	Me tog ryas tshal
Palace	Myriad Lights	sNang ba 'bum ldan

ROYAL FAMILY

King Chandramati	Wise Moon	Zla ba'i blo gros
Prince Devatisha, son of Chandramati	Victor over the Gods	Lha las phul byung

MINISTERS

Pravadivadhaka	Ferocious Executioner	rGol ba gshed ma
Sattvavati	Courageous One	sNying stobs cen
Brahmadhimat	Intelligence of Brahma	Tshangs pa'i blo ldan
Viradhiman	Wise Hero	bLo ldan dpa' bo
Uddhatamanas Mokshabhadra	Laughing Mind of Liberation	bLo rgod thar legs

The Kingdom of Radiant Array

PLACE NAMES	**TRANSLATION**	**TIBETAN**
Kingdom	Radiant Array	bKod legs 'od snang
Province	Jewel Field	Man ni di pa

ROYAL FAMILY

King Dyutimat	Clarity	gSal ldan
Queen Chandraprabha	Moonlight	Zla 'od ma
Princess Manohari, daughter of Dyutimat and Chandraprabha	Allure	Yid 'ong ma

PROLOGUE

All Buddhas are nurtured by one father:
Manjushri, the lord of speech in his youthful glory.
All existents are perfectly reflected as objects of knowledge
In the great mirror of his profound and pure gnosis.

The senses of sight, hearing, recollection, and touch
Continually pour wish-fulfilling nectar into my speech.
O limpid Sarasvati, queen of the adamantine song,
Please play in the energy center at my heart.

I clasp my hands in the mudra of unbreakable faith
Before Manjushri and Sarasvati, chanting resonant prayers.
Effortlessly, your amazing, great compassion
Gives the gift of supreme wisdom and confidence.

If protected by the blissful kindness of the wisdom gods,
The sweet music of harmonious elucidation
Comes even from the speech of ignorant fools.
May I have the ability to hear this music played.

The subject of the text is profound and extensive:
Virtue, wealth and power, liberation, and love.
To illustrate these four classes of good qualities,
This text is written in accordance with dramatic works.

The words themselves are a poetic treasury
Magnificently arranged, like a garland of pearls.
The tale is the pendant on this necklace
For those who practice the language arts.

1

In which the stage is set for the birth of the prince and the unfolding of the tale

I N A TIME WHICH CAME AND WENT A LONG TIME AGO, in a land north of the mountain ranges of noble India, there was a realm called Joyous Groves. Its capital city, Open Lotus, was so radiant it seemed adorned by garlands of heavenly stars. Filled with people and wealth, the city was as auspiciously bright as the full moon—the king of constellations in the center of the celestial firmament.

The lofty and spacious palace of Joyous Groves' ruler was just like the castle of the immortals' king. Glittering light reflected from the pure beaten gold of its roofs and balconies illuminated the sky. Small bells dangling from fluttering banners and pennants created tuneful music. The palace was an ornament of the noble Earth goddess which you could gaze at insatiably.

Inviting pleasure gardens surrounded the palace. The ornamental trees, vines, and creepers were as cleverly landscaped as those in the gardens of the gods. The sweet music of the countryside's songbirds sounded without cease. In verdant, open meadows, the color of the outstretched wings of a parrot, there were wildflowers so exquisite it was as if they had been deliberately arranged. Young men and women adorned by the diverting qualities of love played in pools, lakes, and ponds filled with pure, refreshing water. The fame of this country, renowned as "Gem of the World," spread far and wide.

The ruler of this kingdom was Suryamati, a king graced by the lovely scent of the flowers of well-deserved fame. He inspired great fear in his enemies and ruled his rich land in accordance with the Buddhist religious Dharma. Like a wish-granting tree, he gave whatever was needed to ease the suffering of the poor.

The king had ten ministers to carry out his affairs. Four ministers had a wealth of wisdom. They were known as Jneyavan, Vidyeshvara, Atulyamati, and Parambhasvaramati. Four others—Virendra, Abhaya-balahanta, Laksaikadvitiya, and Abhayavrati—were intrepid in all fields requiring strength. Two other men, Chetadasa and Padmankura, assumed lofty and powerful positions although they were less intelligent and brave. The vast number of other courtiers could not be gauged.

> A multitude acclaimed Joyous Groves,
> Praising it hundreds of times
> As second only to the immortals' realm.

> Within its boundaries was the city Open Lotus,
> Rising from the womb of Mother Earth
> Like the capital of the wealthy serpent king.

> In this kingdom celebrated widely for its splendor
> As "Gem of the World" was a marvelous castle.
> Its jeweled bricks piled up higher and higher,
> Rivaling the palace of the Lord of the Three Times.

> There dwelt King Suryamati, a true Lord of Men.
> Like the sun, his glorious radiance
> Could outshine the heavens, earth, and underworld.
> His host of merits were incalculable,
> As were the servants and ministers who made up his court.
> Neither Indra nor Vishnu surrounded by his retinue
> Could rival this monarch in any way.

> The ruler of this land had a precious queen.
> Kundaladhara was born of a royal line;
> She lacked any faults common to womankind
> And was ornamented by all the feminine virtues.
> She was a worthy queen for a monarch of the universe.

Kundaladhara, the royal queen of King Suryamati, was beautiful and graceful. But for a long, long time this woman who was like a dryad of the flower gardens bore no child to continue the royal line. The king and his ministers became extremely distraught. Finally, King Suryamati summoned all his ministers to the royal council and delivered this command:

> This marvelous kingdom famed as "Gem of the World,"
> The crown ornament of the lovely goddess Earth,
> Has been well protected by us. To further our happiness,
> There must be a line of succession.

> If not, there will be no difference between myself
> And a merchant extracting jewels from the ocean depths
> In a boat without an arsenal of defensive weapons.

> I pray that through your counsel we find
> A means to extend my line like a garland of lovely pearls
> To adorn and protect this excellent land
> Possessing the four classes of good qualities.

In response the wise ministers instructed the king:

"For a person to have a male heir, six conditions must be met: first, the parents must have accumulated the karma for having a son; second, a being must have acquired the karma for taking these parents; third, the mother-to-be must be in the right stage of her menstrual cycle; fourth, the parents must come together in sexual desire; fifth, at that time the being with the appropriate karma must be between rebirths and in the vicinity; sixth, while watching the couple engaged in intercourse, the intermediate-state being must feel sexual desire for the woman and angry jealousy toward the man. In addition, it would help to make generous religious offerings without any avarice."

Then the heroic ministers advised the king:

"In order to make your hope for descendants fruitful, you should take a second queen. By either diplomacy or force of arms, take another king's queen. Failing that, any other lovely girl would do."

At this juncture, the wise minister Parambhasvaramati slowly raised his right hand. Pointing at a cuckoo soaring above, he said to the king and his court:

> Proud ministers of intelligence and strength
> Have captured the ear of King Suryamati.
> Although you may follow those words of counsel,
> I doubt the hoped-for result will actually occur.

You have the power impetuously to seize for enjoyment
Other men's wives, wealth, and possessions.
But afterward, would not Queen Kundaladhara,
Chained by her love for you,
Be tormented by a burden of painful despair?

Therefore, first by means of charity and worship
Engage in the proper conduct of pure virtue.
Those deeds joined with concentrated prayers
Will definitely accomplish whatever you desire.

Our unstoppable wishes will raise
The force of the inexhaustible karmic winds
To scatter the obstructing clouds.
May all you worthy ministers heed this counsel!

The king and all his ministers unanimously agreed to follow this advice. They undertook preparations for making unstinting offerings to please others. They planned to honor respectfully monks, brahmins, renunciates, solitary meditators, and all those who had abandoned non-virtue. They intended to supplicate all the gods of the realm, the city, the mountains, crossroads, ponds, rivers, and so forth. To satisfy beggars, they decided to give them whatever they needed or desired.

Then King Suryamati thought, "The positive results that come from going for refuge to those worthy of it are difficult to calculate." He knew that through the kindness of the Buddha, his teachings, the Dharma, and his followers, the Sangha, his wish could be fulfilled. So he clasped his hands like a lotus bud on top of his head and in a vibrant voice said:

O protectors worthy of being a refuge!
May you be the sun rising in the sky
Of my profound and vast merits.
May your shining rays of good fortune cause
A marvelous new bloom, a lineage-bearing descendant,
To flower in the center of Kundaladhara's womb.

When you do this, please show us amazing omens.
May goddesses and all those who perform in the sky
Cause a melodious rain of auspicious flowers to fall.
May fierce, wrathful deities clear away all obstacles.
O please use your unwavering strength to accomplish this deed!

After this speech, as if he were turning a great wheel, the king ordered the offering ceremonies to commence. Not long afterward, Queen Kundaladhara came to be with child. Just at the start of the tenth month of her term, when all the stages of fetal development were complete, her child was born. Like the first lovely bloom of the Chilpaka flower, he was born with much good fortune. Just as a drizzling rain languorously causes a lotus to open, all the wishes of the king and his ministers blossomed in him.

Immediately after his birth, he was strong, alert, and able to remember his former lives, and he had every sign indicating intelligence, power, and beauty. Nothing could compare with the sight of him. Truly, a child with a marvelous amount of merit had been born.

For seven days there were great celebrations of his birth. The seers and brahmins were so astounded by the child that they praised him as having no peer in the world. Therefore, they pealed the bells to announce Kumaradvitiya, "Incomparable Prince," as his name.

The waves of meritorious actions of those
Accustomed to virtue in former lives
Accomplish any desired goal effortlessly,
Spontaneously, and without difficulty.

No one can dispute the certitude and unmistaken order
Of the dependent arising of cause and effect.
In particular, pearly white results
Come from countless good-hearted deeds.

Thus, the ruler and his ministers attained the culmination
Of that wisely advised course of action.
A descendant, like the cooling rays of the moon,
Allayed the searing misery of their pain.

The prince surpassed all ordinary mortals:
He had every good quality in abundance.
His great intelligence, merit, and fame spread
Like blissful music through heaven, earth, and the netherworld.

Then, carefully sheltered by eight sorts of nurses (wet nurses, nurses to supervise his play, and so forth), the infant blossomed into the flower of childhood. Although the ministers were united in sincere friendship and respect for their ruler, their opinions regarding the way to nurture the growing prince were discordant. Each one related his own distinct wish. If you wonder what they were, well, I shall tell you.

The minister Jneyavan noisily cleared his throat to say:

> The glorious son of our king is
> More marvelous than the immortal gods.
> All of our hopes were brought to fruition
> By obtaining him as our virtuous lot.
>
> Now we should encourage him to strive for liberation
> So that his enlightened actions will lead
> Timorous beings out of this pit
> Of misery and pain which is cyclic existence.

The minister Vidyeshvara said with his palms clasped before him:

> If he still craves worldly pleasures after being born
> Into a royal lineage difficult to find in a hundred aeons,
> Greed, hatred, and ignorance will lead to all failings.
> Then, falling into perversity, he will take a low rebirth.
>
> But if from youth he sees the wondrous wealth of the world
> As a pit of intensely blazing fire, he will reject it.
> I pray that we encourage him to master
> Concentration and insight in a forest hermitage
> Devoid of all physical, verbal, and mental distractions.

The minister Atulyamati sonorously delivered the following petition:

> O Lord of Men, please consider!
> Why grasp at a kingdom if because of that desire
> The sufferings of greed, hatred, and ignorance arise?
> To enjoy continuously the nectar of supreme blissful wisdom,
> One must seek for the jewel of extensive instruction:
> The essence of that endeavor is comprehension of reality.
> That has benefit; worldly things are otherwise.
> Who would desire the playful bride of a dream?

Those three ministers realized it was unsuitable to have any confidence in samsara. They urged the council to teach the prince to rely

only on the holy Dharma. As they related their ideas, the minister
Parambhasvaramati, with a slightly dissatisfied mien, recalled their
solemn words. Twisting and twirling his mustache like a yak's tail, he
said:

Kye! King Suryamati, ponder a moment!
With all your counselors you are like
The thousand-eyed king of heaven in front of his retinue;
Like the full moon surrounded by the host of stars;
Like the fairy king beautified by his entourage.

The promises of the well-born
Never vary from their original intent.
They are inscriptions engraved in stone:
Such righteous honesty is the nobility's custom.

This prince who transcends the very gods
Was summoned as the object of our merit.
He is the result of our striving at many a trial.
Think! Shouldn't he increase the garland of this lineage?

To accomplish the essence of our wishes,
Kumaradvitiya must become our ruler.
His honored father, Suryamati, is aged.
He is close to his final sleep.

Then the populace of Gem of the World
Will have no lord. Protectorless, desperate anxiety
Will weigh heavily upon those pitiable folk.
If this is your noble plan impelled by love,
Your vow to benefit others gladly is quite degenerate!

Therefore, first the prince must place on his head
The crown of the realm's true father.
After he has protected the realm by propagating
A sprout on the pearled clinging vine of this lineage,
May he view this world of marvels
As a pit full of poisonous snakes!
Then in a peaceful forest hermitage may he endeavor
To attain the wisdom of enlightenment,
Thus acquiring the means to end others' misery.

The other ministers shifted uneasily in their seats. They did not dare to argue with what had just been said. The king and all his ministers came to an accord to follow the advice of Parambhasvaramati.

At the very same time that the prince was born, the elephants brought forth many young; the best of those came to be called Mighty Earth Guardian. The royal horses produced many colts; the most special was named Swift Eagle. The water buffaloes also calved; the most superior was called Lord of the Herd. Even many women of ministerial lineage gave birth; the best of their offspring later became famous as the hero Bhavakumara.

All the inhabitants of the kingdom were so happy that they applied the epithet "A Joy to Hear His Name" to Prince Kumaradvitiya.

2

In which the court searches for a suitable bride for Prince Kumaradvitiya

As Prince Kumaradvitiya grew up, his mastery of every science and art increased. By diligent attendance to his skillful tutors, his propensities from former lifetimes of studious discipline were refreshed. As a result, he developed a profound understanding of every sphere of knowledge without needing to study for very long. The subjects he mastered were the tantras of secret mantra, subtle rituals, the science of logic, the Vedas, symbolic language, philology, phonetics, etymology, poetics, and astronomy. He also studied the brahmanical schools of the Gamaka, the Grammarians following Patanjali, Vaisesika, Lokayata, and others.

Without the necessity of much instruction, his understanding and skill in an ocean of arts became vast. He spontaneously mastered the sixty-four arts: the thirty sorts of handicrafts, the eighteen types of music, the seven branches of singing, and the nine types of dancing. Even experts proud of their skill in archery or warlike feats of horsemanship could not vie with the prince. No one could equal his accomplishments in any arena. His excellent reputation adorned him as beautifully as an Utpala flower worn over the ear of a lovely woman.

Across the vast sky of stainless wisdom,
The celestial steeds of effort and action
Draw the sun of comprehension.
With its blazing light of discrimination,
The noblest wise men dispel the darkness of ignorance.

Through the prince's unified mastery of
Every conceivable worldly art,
A host of fierce but conquered foes
Offered him their crown jewels as a footstool.

There was not one praiseworthy
Religious or worldly skill he had not perfected.
His name consummately suited him: he had no peer
In this vast round of cyclic existence.

At a later date, the prince's father, King Suryamati, thought deeply about his son and was prompted to say to his ministers:

"O counselors, please listen! Kumaradvitiya, who was born as a result of our virtuous merit, has now grown into the flower of manhood. He has a penetrating understanding of every scientific field and has mastered every art. In all the world there is no one who can rival him. There is no disorderly brawling, no epidemic disease nor famine among the people under his dominion. His subjects enjoy a festival of wealth, prosperity, happiness, and good harvests. He has extracted the essential purpose from his sublime wealth by paying homage to worthy objects of refuge. He has extended a generous, impartial hand to the poor and destitute. Men brought to ruin by bad rulers flock to him like bees attracted to a lotus garden. Even the worldly gods extol his good fortune with noisy, good-humored clamor."

The king continued, "At this time a bower of six of the seven precious riches arches over this kingdom. First, we have a precious wheel to take the king and his armies a thousand leagues across the three worlds and four god realms in a single day. Second, we have a wish-fulfilling gem with many propitious qualities: like the autumn moon, it dispels the darkness of night and cools the scorching heat of the sun; exuding perfect liquid, it quenches the thirst of those journeying without water; there is no sickness for one hundred leagues around it; and so forth. Third is our elephant with perfectly proportioned limbs. He conquers all our foes as soon as we command, and in a single day he is able to circumnavigate the world three times. Fourth, we have a superb horse with a majestically shining coat, which also can compass the world three times in the cycle of a day. You ministers are the fifth wonder of the realm, for you understand whatever I desire without needing to be told. You have perfect judgment: you abandon whatever is not righteous and work to benefit the world. Sixth are our generals, so courageous that they do not even need their armies to aid them in conquering the enemy. Thus, our kingdom clearly has six of the priceless sorts of good fortune.

"So, my intelligent and courageous ministers, we lack only one thing. You must see that it is now time to consecrate a queen for the prince! We must search for a jewel among women: a girl whose body is perfumed with sandalwood, whose breath has the scent of an Utpala flower, whose transforming touch bestows warmth to those who feel cold and refreshes those who feel hot (a royal pleasure since no one other than a king may touch her), a girl who has features which are always pleasing, a superior young woman of an excellent lineage to match our own. So, O ministers, consult among yourselves. When you have completed a thorough search for such a young woman, report the results to me."

Then the ministers who bore the burden of fulfilling the commands of the king spied out entire provinces, humble abodes, imperial palaces, mountain villages, and fortified towns. Finally, south of Gem of the World, in the Jewel Field region, they found a large kingdom known as Radiant Array. The sovereigns of that realm, King Dyutimat and his queen, Chandraprabha, had only one daughter to continue their line. She was beautifully ornamented by all the lovely signs of womanhood: she had a figure quite pleasing to see, a blooming complexion, and perfect coloring; sandalwood anointed her body, and the scent of the Utpala hovered about her mouth. All men of passion were instantly captivated by her charms, for she was unrivaled even by the immortal goddesses who excel humankind. This youthful princess, named Manohari, was as radiantly lovely as the new moon.

The ministers exhaustively investigated every subtle detail of Manohari's nature. After carefully pondering their findings, they unanimously agreed that there could be no other girl so worthy of the crown prince. Manohari was the princess to be nominated as Prince Kumaradvitiya's bride.

However, because King Dyutimat had no male heir to protect his realm, he had been seduced into forming an alliance with King Chandramati and his handsome son, Devatisha. King Chandramati ruled his domain, Myriad Lights, from his palace in the great city of Flowering Estate. His castle was beautified by wealthy and fearless ministers who were wise in the ways of the world. Nevertheless, the king and his son dallied in bad company, and under the influence of their degenerate companions, they did many evil deeds. They did not believe that their nefarious actions would bear any fruit. Never supping on the taste of love and compassion, they murdered, raped, and imprisoned others. Although Devatisha so shamelessly committed such immoral acts, he and Manohari were betrothed.

After a time, King Suryamati's ministers heard about the treaty between those two kingdoms. Beset by scrupulous doubts, the ministers discussed at length whether that alliance should be an obstacle to their intentions. Impatient with the delay, the minister Laksaikadvitiya dauntlessly stated in a loud voice: "O friends! Nothing is ever accomplished by vacillating! Even a simple task like this one seems difficult if you have little strength of purpose. Now, because we have no covenant like the one between Chandramati and Dyutimat, we will have to do as follows to obtain Manohari. First of all, we should try smooth negotiations in the customary ways of the world. If that does not work, we should gain our objective by beguiling them with trickery. If that also does not bring our hope to fruition, we will wage war with our four fierce armies. We will expunge even the names Radiant Array and Myriad Lights from the face of the earth! Thus, we will make Manohari ours by force of arms."

All the ministers agreed with this wise advice. They gave an extensive account of their findings and decision to King Suryamati and his son. The delight of the king and prince increased during their recital, just as moonlight is magnified by reflecting on the ocean. They thanked and honored the ministers, commanding, "Do just as you have given counsel."

3

In which negotiations for the hand of Manohari fail

T HE MINISTER ATULYAMATI WAS ASSIGNED THE TASK of going to Radiant Array to ask for Manohari's hand in marriage. He was commissioned to present to King Dyutimat immeasurable quantities of jewels and other inconceivably valuable gifts. This bounty was a composite of all the wonders belonging to the gods of wealth. Atulyamati took up the command of the king as his burden and set out. He rode on horseback as far as it was possible to ride and then went forward by foot.

Finally, he reached the palace of King Dyutimat, where he heaped a virtual mountain of presents in front of the king. Kneeling down, he clasped his hands like a lotus bud and placed them on top of his head. Then the minister entreated King Dyutimat with these sublime phrases:

> Eh ma! An immortal fence of merit encircles
> A lineage like a wish-granting tree
> With a reputation like a magnificent open flower.
> The surrounding landscape is perfectly lovely:
> As if the delightful garden of the Lord of the Three Times
> Were transplanted to that fortunate place as an ornament.
>
> The great city Open Lotus shines like countless stars.
> Its central royal palace commands every direction.
> One cannot see the summit of the golden
> Ornamented roofs, balconies, and spires

Glittering with a blaze of light illuminating
All space, outshining the sun and moon.

In every corner and on every side,
Dangling from pennants, tassels, and decorative draperies,
Are sweetly chiming jeweled bells.
Their appearance is the essence of beauty.

The palace foundation is indestructible rock;
Its pinnacles rise above our world.
Even a fairy would tire trying to fly
To the smooth summit shaped like a cut gem.

All around are stands of splendid trees
Heavily laden with fruit and emerald leaves.
Exquisite birds perched on the boughs
Let forth the sweet songs of spring.
Their sweet song, like the tinkling of fairy cymbals,
Dampens the pride of Music herself.

In the center of the verdant meadows,
Are profusions of flowers in full bloom.
In this garden designed like Indra's palace,
Cool, pristine, pure, and clear waters
Form pools in which sensual men and women bathe
And sheldrakes sport on gentle waves.
This opulence humbles the pride
Of the gods of wealth with their vast holdings.

Refreshed under the shadow of their compassionate ruler,
The populace enjoys keen happiness.
These wise folk esteem their good fortune,
Placing their confidence only in him.
Suryamati, Lord of the Earth, is the
Lovely center of a retinue of countless
Superlatively wise and courageous ministers.

The son of this ruler has all the marks of high rebirth.
A god among men, born from a perfect womb,
He is handsome, wealthy, clever, and brave,
And he courageously overcomes his foes.

Prince Kumaradvitiya is a singular hero
At the peak of youth, a sapling in full blossom.

Now, to complete our realm's wealth of seven fortunes,
Only a superior queen is needed.
Thus, I have come for the Princess Manohari,
The child of your excellent family and line.
Gem of the World and this kingdom of yours
Should be united in a profound matrimonial alliance.
O Lord of Men, this is the only proper course of action.

The minister energetically proclaimed his suit at length in the lovely, persuasive tones of a cuckoo.

King Dyutimat pondered worriedly: "This matter will be very difficult to deal with. I have already made a royal proclamation that Manohari and Prince Devatisha of Myriad Lights will be wed to protect our two kingdoms as one. However, if I act contrary to the wishes of King Suryamati, I greatly fear that my realm will be brought to ruin. There is no one who can compare with King Suryamati and his ministers in their power, ability, and skill in subduing their enemies."

The king's shoulders slumped, and his face contorted. He changed from a youthful fruit tree into an old, cut, and dried-out stick. Then he had another thought: "Throughout the world, wise and intelligent nobility abhor deceit, pretension, lying, and ostentatious behavior. Their natural disposition is honest, and they do not break their promises. Those who turn away from such behavior take up the weapons of deceit to conquer the heavens, earth, and underworld. It is totally unsuitable to trust their words, for they lie, slander, and speak harshly to deviously burn out the hearts of their enemies. In addition, their nature is unstable, like fluff blown hither and thither by the wind.

"Therefore, I cannot reverse my earlier vow; I must clearly express my own situation without pretension. It is not right to leave the minister Atulyamati without a substantive reply."

So the king said:

Supreme among the ministers of the Earth Lord Suryamati,
You are a treasure of perfection and courage.
O Atulyamati, your song of the fame of your land
Fills the universe. It is right to be heard here.

Your sweet and charming speech is well received.
Your marvelous largesse fulfills all hopes and desires.
You have come desirous of friendship and accord,
For you wish to complete your fortunate opulence.

So, uninfluenced by crooked words bent like a bow,
Summon forth the continuum of your pure mind.
For a few minutes, reflect in your wise heart
On these honest words as straight as an arrow.

The brilliant light of King Suryamati's words
Shines down upon the lotus grove of my mind,
Making it instantly blossom. His incalculably kind gifts
Induce pure pleasure in my mind.

However, because this praiseworthy kingdom of mine
Lacked a royal heir to ensure its welfare,
My maiden daughter, Princess Manohari,
Was promised as the consecrated queen of Devatisha,
Crown prince of the lineage of Myriad Lights.
This done, our two realms are to be protected as one.

This vow is as unchangeable as if etched in diamond.
I have no power to unite your prayers with an act
Making Manohari belong to Gem of the World.
I am sorry, but the desire of your king
And ministers cannot come to be.

With these and other fine and charming words, King Dyutimat
explained the situation. The minister Atulyamati became extremely
angry. Three veins popped out on his brow; he clenched his fists
and said: "O Lord of Men, I question how you can direct words
like this to me! Lying words confuse the mind, do they not?
Therefore, I pray you, repeat once again whichever of your words
lack deceit!"

So the king replied:

First, please reflect and consider.
Only honest words have ever come from my lips,
Just as buzzing bees never leave a multipetaled lotus.
The custom of the truly noble is never otherwise.

Who would rely on the habit of low, common people?
Their speech flickers like lightning, never steadfast.
Again and again they speak without consideration,
In haste and without prior deliberation.

Is it proper to climb to the peak of the two
Inconceivable collections of merit resulting in enlightenment,
Or to fall into the abysmal chasm of nefarious deeds?
My prior speech was not deceitful.
There were no insincere words to confuse you.
I beseech you to accept what was said as the truth!

The minister's mind was suffused with powerful hatred, transforming
his face beyond a family resemblance. In a terrific, loud voice he said
the following words:

In the vast canopy of space,
The sun is an unequaled treasure of light.
It has no need to envelop a single realm,
For on its circuit its light pervades the entire world.
The sun simply is the lord of wherever he goes.

If you do not realize that below on earth
The lovely, luminous, shining colors of
A lotus grove are nurtured by the noble sun,
You will wonder if they are nourished by the moon!

You, Earth Lord, manage to act like a commoner
Without transgressing the manners of nobility!
Your speeches are crooked and fraudulent.
Dissatisfied, my mind transforms into a fierce weapon.

Prince Kumaradvitiya, who suits his name,
Now waits in the kingdom of Gem of the World.
His bravery, noble strength, and encompassing mind
Are characteristics without parallel in the world.

If you disregard him, he and his heroic ministers
Will take up an arsenal of weapons.
Their fierce attack will unbearably harm you.
Then will you not have regrets? Mark my words!

Not waiting to hear another word, Atulyamati flicked some dust off his clothes and sped back to Gem of the World.

Left in Radiant Array, King Dyutimat heard the echo of the minister's words again and again. The threats were thorns piercing his heart, causing it to ache. He thought:

"Kye ma! There is no way to countermand what must be experienced because of the force of karma created earlier. The nature of cyclic existence is our inability to obtain what we desire while unwanted suffering rains down upon us! Just like the moon entering an eclipse, the happiness and prosperity of the kingdom of Radiant Array have begun to diminish. But even the loser of a dispute must be able to bear up and do something. I will have to ask my daughter about this matter."

The king sat down next to Princess Manohari and Queen Chandraprabha and said:

> Kva ye! O daughter, know you well!
> This kingdom so worthy of respect
> Must be saved from ruin. To find a means
> To increase its glory like the waxing moon
> Must be the essence of this unified council.
>
> I have pledged to protect this land through
> Uniting it with a kingdom like a god realm.
> You have been tied in an irrevocable marriage pact
> To the lineage of King Chandramati of Myriad Lights:
> You are to wed Devatisha, a charming god,
> Intelligent, handsome in full youthful splendor, and
> A powerful master of the martial arts.
>
> However, quick as a shooting star,
> An envoy came bearing invaluable tribute.
> Gracefully setting out that assemblage of wealth,
> He stated his profound and vast purpose.
> You, he said, will complete their hopes,
> For you are worthy of the superior fate
> To be the queen touched by the flower of deeds
> Well made by Kumaradvitiya of Gem of the World.
>
> As soon as I stated honestly, without artifice,
> The matter of my former promises,
> The pleasantly smiling face of that minister

Changed, and fiery words blazed forth,
Scorching your father's mind like a piece of wood.
My intellect was transformed into a lump of coal.
Now in extreme, blank ignorance,
I cannot distinguish right from wrong.

O princess, you are known to have deep wisdom.
Discriminating skill is yours as well.
O daughter, with your perfect character and superior wisdom,
Please consider: tell me the proper course of action.

Manohari pondered carefully. She thought: "It is well known that the glitter of pure gold nuggets buried in the womb of the earth shines up into the sky. In just such a way the fame of Kumaradvitiya fills the world. My habitual actions in lives long ago created irreversible propensities to love him. Now, merely hearing the sound of his name makes me desire him greatly. O how wonderful it would be to be united with him as his lover! Although this totally exceptional thought comes unbidden to my mind, I cannot go against the commands already given by my father."

So, placing her ten fingers together like a flower petal at her heart, she said with a smile:

Father, your affection, glorious as ten thousand suns,
Sends forth peerless shining rays of love,
Causing my body to bloom like a multifold lotus.
Please look upon me with compassion and consider.

As a result flowing from former positive actions,
I have obtained a beautiful form and much wealth.
But this body is surely evil! It is linked to deeds
Preventing the happiness of my parents.

My understanding is that of a feebleminded woman.
I have not gone a step along the noble path.
I lack the power to obstruct any command
My loving father lets fall upon my faithful head.
I beg you to determine the propriety of
My respectful words about the nature of my thoughts.

Because you have no desire to lose your vision,
The irritant causing painful cataracts should be removed.

The basis of your dispute and quarrel with others
Is only my human rebirth of leisure and fortune.

Thus, I think the best course of action
Is for me to take up the essence of religious life.
I will abandon the fluctuating world.
I will make my life meaningful in a hermitage.
I will concentrate on tasks difficult to accomplish.

If I do not obtain your permission for this,
I continue to drown in the samsaric ocean's
Turbulent waves and troughs of sorrow.
Dearest father, consider well your last parental deed:
Choosing a husband for your flower-daughter.

The powerful and wealthy lord of Myriad Lights
Is a prince with the charm of the gods.
He is well endowed with intelligence and grace,
But I have heard he does many a black, evil deed.
A torrent of the world's curses fall upon him.
His mind is twisted by ignoble dishonor.
He acts vulgarly, neglecting the upright ways of dignity.

I am connected by profound virtuous propensities,
Thanks to love in many former lives,
To the man named Kumara, attractive as a fresh flower.
He is the sun letting forth myriad virtuous rays,
Never coming under the sway of sinful darkness.
It is his noble light, I believe,
Which causes every beautiful good deed to blossom.

He is the only object of my desire.
His figure so distinctly arises in my mind.
It remains there in an indelible fashion.

However, whatever you command I willingly will do:
I am unable to contradict my parent's words.
Those propensities from many former lives
Will remain fettered in my heart, tightly tied
By adamantine knots, which no one can destroy.
Between us there are unbreakable vows of love
Whose letters are etched deep into my heart.

The long rope of that recollection
Binds me from straying to another.
Thus, honored father, the fall of your commands
Upon my head is difficult to oppose.
But I have spoken without pretense about my nature.
True words have grown in the garden of Manohari's throat.

She decorously stated her feelings in the form of a song, singing as sweetly as the first birds of spring.

Then her father, King Dyutimat, thought: "When I consider these words of my noble daughter, I see that she is right. Without a doubt, one can obtain the essence of permanent happiness if one enters the holy path of religion from the first. Because she alone is the basis of my quarrel with other kings, she is willing to turn her back on her object of desire and engage in religious deeds so difficult that they are unseen for hundreds of aeons. In retrospect, I see that I should have discussed these negotiations with my daughter from the beginning. At this juncture, can I give Manohari permission to do what she desires? If she abandons her ardent love for all her close friends and relations to go to a forest hermitage, there would be nothing to quarrel over. But I wonder whether that would result in a state of unadulterated happiness for the subjects, ministers, and rulers of Radiant Array?

"If she is not to be a renunciate, then I must look at the alternatives. The northern kingdom of Myriad Lights has wealth and magnificence that humble the pride of the very gods of wealth. Although Prince Devatisha is charming and handsome, whatever he does is a wheel rolling down the road of impropriety. He continually engages in execrable actions that lack any goodness. Who could smile at such a one?

"Now, Manohari says she desires only the man known as Prince Kumaradvitiya, as a result of an unstoppable tendency to love him created during a series of prior lives. His realm enjoys great wealth because of his vast, purposeful virtues. Based on these facts, her claim is likely to be true.

"However, in the world it is well known that Earth Lords give their word but once. If I annul my promise to King Chandramati, everyone will say I am a sordid and lowly individual, a liar, and an example of fickle unreliability. It is better to die than to have the curses of the entire world fall upon me!"

4

In which two different kingdoms decide how they will win Manohari as the bride for their crown prince

K ING DYUTIMAT SENT A MESSENGER with a letter describing everything that had happened to King Chandramati, the ruler of
Myriad Lights. The document concluded:

In the world some rulers are always fickle.
They speak just what they think; carelessly
Spewing out words, they shamelessly prevaricate.
They act contrarily, as fitfully blown as cotton fluff.

Those of noble lineage think deeply before they act.
If they make a promise, whatever they vow
Is unchangeable as a diamond engraving.
They hold their word as dear as their life.
Such men are worthy of respect.

Mounted on a swift steed, the messenger traveled quickly to the
kingdom of Myriad Lights. When he arrived at the palace, he bent
down on one knee before the king and his council and presented the
letter to the king. As King Chandramati considered the contents of the
letter, he became quite angry. Because of his extreme displeasure, his
eyebrows arched in hatred while he gave orders to his court:

"O ministers! Listen to this account and learn what, by my vow, we
will do tomorrow morning.

"We have already presented the flowers of marital consecration to lovely Manohari, noble Dyutimat's daughter. We pledged to meld our two kingdoms and protect them as one after this pinnacle of his lineage became the noble queen of Devatisha. These true words are unalterable; it is as if they are engraved in diamond-hard rock.

"But some people are crude; they are inherently unable to know what is proper to do and what is proper to avoid! A ministerial envoy of Gem of the World tried to persuade Dyutimat with many astounding presents that Manohari should be made Kumaradvitiya's queen. He made firm demands supported by much logical rhetoric.

"King Dyutimat informed him of the matter of our former pact and vowed not to transgress his given word. However, this minister was blinded by anger. Unable to see the purity of Dyutimat, he put an end to all discourse with the blazing flames of lamentable harsh words. Then, as quickly as possible, he returned to Gem of the World. I am sure that they are now gathering up an army to kidnap Manohari!

"Therefore, you splendidly heroic ministers will be the leaders of my armies. Prepare the elephants, chariots, cavalry, and infantry for a fierce fourfold battle. Because Devatisha's prowess and bravery surpass all others', he will go first in battle. He will reduce the enemy to a mere name! The fruit of our hopes will then fall into our hands.

"However, if we do not secure the daughter of Dyutimat, you ministers will lose your lives! As for Devatisha, not only will he not inherit this kingdom but he will be just one among a line of beggars and dogs at the crossing of a narrow street!"

After these angry words were loftily proclaimed, the prince, ministers, and all the court were unable to say a word. They sat there as mesmerized as painters so absorbed in drawing a figure that they cannot be diverted. Then, after a short time, the wise minister Brahmadimat came out from the center of the rows of the court, sat down in front of the king in perfect meditation posture, and said:

Consider a moment, O Earth Lord Chandramati!
Your sight is obscured by clouds.
It is a lofty custom to analyze before you speak;
It is the nature of fools to act and afterward regret.

Therefore, first inspect the sequence of truth and falsity
In the events related in this report.
Has that singular goddess Manohari gone to Gem of the World?
No news of that comes to our ears.

We must contain ourselves to the content of this message.
Otherwise, as crows beset by uncertainty
In terror doubt their shadows are their own,
Our unscrutinized reflections will rise up as our enemies.

If a leader engages in unseemly, purposeless actions,
As if he were an actor in an insane play,
The populace will be burdened with torturous suffering.
Will we not come to regret that?

Since the king really did have enough intelligence to discriminate correct from wicked actions, these words mortified him. He decided that his minister's advice was valid. Still, he wondered whether Dyutimat's reason for writing to him was to tell the truth or to lie. Since he was unsure if it was just his anxious imagination that Manohari had come under another's sway, he sent envoys to King Dyutimat to ascertain if the words of the document were true.

Later King Chandramati came to hear that Manohari had had no mishap and was happy and carefree in her parents' home. The king and his ministers conferred from sunrise to sunrise. Finally, they all agreed on a single point: the brave and upright minister Uddhatamanas Mokshabhadra would lead an army of ten hundred men to Radiant Array. Their orders were to escort Manohari to Myriad Lights.

At the very same time the council in Myriad Lights occurred, the minister Atulyamati arrived back in Gem of the World. He sat down in front of the king and other ministers and clearly related what he had said to King Dyutimat, all that the king had said, and his own replies.

King Suryamati and Prince Kumaradvitiya did not think it would be difficult to obtain the princess, so they did not dwell upon the matter too much. The ministers, however, were different. A few hung their heads in regret and worried out loud: "I wonder if we didn't send enough of those imponderably precious and beautiful gifts to King Dyutimat. Perhaps we failed to satisfy him." One minister declared: "We know that King Chandramati of Myriad Lights is crafty and deceitful. Because we are masters of demonic magic, we can hoodwink Dyutimat by starting some slander between them." Yet another minister stated: "The sovereign Dyutimat is known to be a man of good character. He lives nobly and is cautious of the weapons of worldly curses. Thus, he refused to transgress his first spoken promise. That is proper and righteous!" The other ministers were displeased to hear these statements: a painful uneasiness welled up in their minds, rendering them unable to determine right from wrong.

They were all caught in a web of confusion about what would be the best course of action. Then, Laksaikadvitiya, a minister who used the crowns of all the heroes in the world for his footstool, and whose white banner of fame fluttered far and wide, addressed the Earth Lord Suryamati and all his ministers in clear, exalted tones:

O Lord of Men, shining bright as the sun and moon,
You are the earthly sky's beautiful ornament,
Surrounded by as many ministers as the starry constellations.
Among these men are the extremely wise:
Even the Lord Brahma is shamed by their able discrimination.
There are those whose imposing bravery is known
To be able to overthrow even Vishnu as a foe.

However, today the haughty words of the petty King Dyutimat
Have pierced your breasts like a sword.
Think! Why are you hanging your heads in confusion,
Unable to determine right from wrong?

At first we ministers all resolved as one
To avoid blaspheming King Dyutimat.
We delegated as envoy a high minister worthy of his name
To pile illimitable precious tribute before Dyutimat
And explain his reasons for coming in lovely words.

Although our minister observed the best worldly conventions,
Dyutimat did not satisfy our hopeful desire.
With artifice and duplicity he said
Manohari had been promised as the bride of Devatisha.

Those rash, impolite words infuriate me!
I, Laksaikadvitiya, am said to be fearless and brave.
It is difficult to live up to such a reputation
And make it more than mere words.

However, to repay the long years of my lord's kind support,
I would willingly sacrifice my life to accomplish his goals.
Assuredly, I will raze Radiant Array to ashes and dust.
Later, no one will even hear that formerly
There was a petty kingdom under the rule of Dyutimat!
Such a dance will be very easy to do.

The object of our quest, the maid Manohari,
Will be secured under our precious crown.
She will be consecrated as the prince's precious queen.
The banner of our fame will wave on the peak of the world.

If I am unable to bear the burden of this trifling task,
It is completely worthless for me to have been born a man.
My terrifying name will be an object of scornful laughter.
My own words will be akin to a mere echo.

Therefore, O king and ministers,
I beg you to bear in mind
My intentions made without any hesitancy.

By the end of his speech, Laksaikadvitiya was shouting in an incredibly loud voice. He was so displeased with the words of King Dyutimat informing them that Manohari was to be placed under another's control that he would be made happy only by destroying the kingdom of Radiant Array. When he said that, the other ministers of the court were unable to utter a word in rebuttal. Their faces fell, and they sighed long and loud.

Then the gloriously youthful Prince Kumaradvitiya smiled. He raised his right hand in the gesture which bestows blessings. His golden bracelets jingled, and he said:

"O commander of all brave heroes, as soon as you were born you displayed a dauntless and courageous mind. Now please consider.

"Your deep tones proclaiming your brave intention to destroy that other kingdom are themselves a sign of your valor. We are all men who abide by honorable customs: we are the paramount nobility who make the laws. If one of us should engage in fickle, capricious deeds, in this life and hereafter he would be cursed and compelled to suffer. Actions like that are of the base classes, done only by butchers and prostitutes. Therefore, you must see that even King Dyutimat is acting in accordance with the highest noble customs by stating his disinclination to contradict his first promise. So, O minister, this is not an occasion for hatred and anger. Be easy!

"Furthermore, recall the unanimous accord of our former council. First we said we would influence Dyutimat with smooth words and customary actions. Then, if that was unsuccessful, we would beguile him by deceptive action. Finally, if we still had not attained our goal, we would make Manohari ours by the great force of our arms. Is this not what we agreed?

"Therefore, at this juncture, we will send the hero Bhavakumara disguised as myself, with an escort of one hundred men, to Radiant Array. They will deceive Manohari and lure her away. Bhavakumara is exactly my age, and he has penetrating discernment about what should or should not be done.

"Manohari and myself are profoundly related through the karma of many past lives. Nonetheless, we cannot be sure that she will follow after Bhavakumara in disguise. If this stratagem does not bring her under our sway, then in accordance with what was stated by this heroic leader, we will engage in the works of war. Then he may have the sublime happiness of destroying our opponents."

These words greatly surprised the minister Laksaikadvitiya. He thought: "The prince is of so tender an age yet is unimaginably wise. He does not wish to counter the undertakings pledged at our first council, and he also considers as praiseworthy King Dyutimat's not damaging his avowed promise. His words are truly worthy of praise. We ministers are but ignorant fools." Then he said:

"O Lord of Men! It is just so. I greatly admire the purport of your speech. Without contradicting your orders, we will achieve our goal. My pride is humbled, and I prostrate myself before you."

5

In which Manohari is tricked into thinking she will meet Kumaradvitiya

THE HERO BHAVAKUMARA DRESSED IN BEAUTIFUL GARMENTS, provisioned himself well for the journey, and sent his entourage of a hundred men on ahead. The other ministers thought, "This youth is quite young, but he is a friend of wisdom." They bid him farewell saying, "With Chetadasa as your aide, do whatever must be done and avoid what you must to accomplish our purpose!"

The party traveled quickly and soon arrived at a spot near the capital of Radiant Array. They established themselves there in the guise of traveling merchants concerned with profitable trade.

Birds who inhabit a golden mountain eventually seem to be gold too. Similarly, because the hero Bhavakumara had continually engaged in virtuous actions by the side of Prince Kumaradvitiya, he had obtained some of the prince's good qualities. So, with subtle sagacity, he arrived at Radiant Array as if he were Prince Kumara himself and wrote this letter to Manohari:

> From the ocean of a stainless royal lineage
> Rises the fresh, beautiful full moon,
> Whose white light trickles down like nectar.
> As the moon, I have come to this mountain summit
> To befriend the night lily, a paragon of beauty.
> Manohari, in a smile of love, your petal teeth
> Should open into full, lovely bloom.
> When the moon and lily unite, they feel great joy;

I summon you to taste this supreme bliss.
Today is the very day of the perfect full moon.
After this we will be overcome by a dark time.
Then will not our karmic connection weaken?
Bearing the name Kumara, from the north I come,
In search of you, my lovely one.
This subtle proclivity comes from our former acts,
So will you not hasten to Gem of the World?

After he wrote this, he wondered what friend could be found to
deliver the letter. He went in search of an appropriate messenger;
merely half the distance to the cornerstone of the palace, he spied a
maiden on the road carrying water and singing a clear tune. He satisfied
her with some presents and instructed her to offer the letter directly to
the lotus fingertips of Manohari. The maiden accepted the task with a
happy smile and went off. Without any mishap, she placed the missive
in Manohari's hands. When Manohari absorbed its contents, a palpable
feeling of joy suffused her. She said to the water carrier:

O maid, you distribute to all
Pure, cool water to satisfy thirst.
From the tips of your fingers,
I have obtained a letter difficult to gauge.

Who acted so to place
This missive in your maiden hands?
Tell me from which direction,
City, and realm came he.

By what sweet name is he known?
What are the attributes of his form and family?
Describe to me all his actions and words.
Please speak clearly to dispel my confusion!

When questioned thus, the girl brought the palms of her hands
together to show her great respect for the princess. She said:

If one were to gather in one place
Everything lovely in the world—
The moon, fresh lotuses, and groves of lilies—
They all pale in comparison to Manohari.

If I were to speak falsely to you,
Would I not commit a foul sin?
So as an ornament for your ears,
Please take up this Utpala flower of truth.

As I carried with difficulty
My full water vessel to the palace,
A young man with a marvelous smile
Came up from an unknown direction.

He said, "Please help me to place
These tightly sealed lines
Into the hands of lovely Manohari."
I agreed and came hither.

Although I should have questioned him
About the location of his realm and lands,
His name, family line, and so forth,
I was so attracted to his great beauty
My hair stood up on end!
I was unable to ask sensible questions.

His virtues are completely unimaginable!
His qualities of youthful grace
Equal the essence of the immortals.
My mind was captivated at once
By the iron hook of his masterful methods.

Skillful as a robber or a thief,
He stole away my chaste fortitude.
A young man such as that
Is a sweet sight for tired eyes!"

When the maiden stated these words, joy and sorrow simultaneously
vied for the princess's heart. She thought, "Upon consideration, I cannot imagine that those wonderful qualities belong to anyone other than
Prince Kumaradvitiya. Her description accords so well with his renown.
In our past lives, we created the karma to love each other, and we
joined those deeds to profound prayers. Thus I am enmeshed in this
superlative love. When I think it is possible that his lotus feet have
brought him toward this kingdom, the intensity of my joy increases."

However, coming right after that thought was fear of the repercussions of disobeying her parents. Nevertheless, her mind focused on the prince without shifting to anything else for even a second.

Manohari was not able to find a way to send an answer to his letter that evening. She did not know what to do. Finally she concentrated on an image of the handsome prince which arose in her mind. Inspired, but with many sighs, she made an effort to compose some verses. Mistaking the hero Bhavakumara for Prince Kumaradvitiya, she lifted her voice in a harmonious song to answer the letter:

Because of prior accumulations of merit,
A nobly white, flawless pearl was conceived
In an expansive womb of mother-of-pearl.
The sole fruit of those matured virtues
Is a young man worthy to be this pure ornament.

Because of the force of actions in many lives,
We have vows of unshakable love between us.
This karma cannot be destroyed.
It is definite, marvelous, and beautiful.

However, the shining light of my hopes is dim.
I am a vassal of a dark, mighty power.
Exhausted by unbearable unhappiness,
My mind is tightly bound by great sorrow.

Your form, my love, continually arises in my mind.
In pain I pillow my cheeks on my hands.
I loosen my well-arranged, shiny hair
To fall free and cover my body.

I pass the time in heartrending tears
Accompanied by long, drawn-out sighs.
I have not obtained my parents' permission,
So I fear, but passionately wish, to see your face.

Alas! I have such a miserable fate. What shall I do?
With your compassionate wisdom, please help me form a plan.

She wrote this out, sealed it, and sent it off with the very same water carrier. The girl quickly ran to deliver the letter. Acknowledging receipt of Manohari's letter, Bhavakumara sent her this poem to spur her on:

> O maid of sixteen, perfect in every respect!
> This is the opportune time of the full moon.
> Its radiant light is beautifully alluring,
> Free from the jaws of overpowering darkness.
>
> The entire world is unimpededly flooded
> By marvelous pure light. Now is the time
> Enchanting lilies in full bloom and
> Groves of white lotuses with quivering pistils,
> Smiling in the intoxication of their honey,
> Should enjoy themselves freely, without hindrance.
>
> But if you are not inclined to oppose
> Your parents' essentially different intentions,
> What stratagem or plan can I have?
> You, Maid Manohari, must do as you will.
>
> I remembered our loving promises, deeds, and prayers,
> So I have endeavored to come in search of you.
> I have borne hundreds of risks,
> Traveling from my realm far away to the north.
>
> Insincere words claiming you are not free
> Render your missive pointless. If it is so,
> I need not continue to revere only you!
> There are as many lovely and attractive women
> As stars in the vast expanse of the sky.
>
> Therefore, do not doubt that without a long delay
> I shall depart for my castle in Gem of the World.
> Later, when in response to your malice a war begins,
> Do not speak of your regret and pain!

When Manohari read this harsh, scolding letter, she became even more unhappy than before. "Alas!" she thought, "it is so difficult to predict the outcome of any action. If I postpone doing what I want until I have my parents' permission, it seems I will lose the chance to be united with the loving companion whom I have desired so long. To accompany noble Kumara, I must contradict my parents' command. But then how can I repay them for nurturing me so kindly and well?

"If I come under the sway of the liege lord of Myriad Lights, I will be married to a man who engages primarily in sinful deeds. As a result, I will be yoked to unimaginable suffering in both this and my future lives. O anything would be easier than to be the wife of such a man! Even if I disregard my own misery and go to Myriad Lights, afterward the fiercely proud rulers of Gem of the World will reduce this kingdom of Radiant Array to a mere name. Both my parents would experience agonies difficult to endure.

"Although the king and ministers of Myriad Lights are very powerful, they shine like mere fireflies before the blazing sun of the men who rule Gem of the World. It would be hard to find anyone who could vie with or rival them. The most outstanding is Prince Kumaradvitiya: his fame wafts throughout the world like the fluttering white banner at the peak of worldly existence. He believes that good and bad deeds yield their respective results, so every one of his deeds is upright. He is called a religious king and noted for leading a purposeful life. In this life, I shall follow after him no matter if my actions appear bad or good."

So, breaking the chains of her doubts, she made a decision. She respectfully went before her parents and requested permission to go out to enjoy the pleasure gardens. Her voice was like the buzzing of a hive of bees intoxicated by their own honey as she said:

The amazing sweet song of the cuckoo
Invites the festive abundance of summer.
Fresh, pale blue clouds drift languidly in the sky,
And as if to compete, on the earth below,
Across the extensive and lush, verdant meadows,
The crowns of the trees and flowers gently undulate.
These excellent things give a nectar which cools
A mind tormented by the fires of misery.

The garden's many stands of trees
Are heavily laden with luscious fruits.
On the tips of the profusely flowering boughs,
Are birds whose sweet songs entice me.
In the garden's center, are pools with perfect water.
White bubbles laughingly gurgle
In amethyst waters, which cool all heat.

I beg you to permit me to go to that alluring place
To bathe, play, and refresh myself today.

Hidden in these words was Manohari's desire to meet Prince
Kumaradvitiya. But, without any suspicion, her father, King Dyutimat,
said with a beaming smile:

"Noble maiden, consider this well! If you wish to enjoy the wonderful
riches of summer, please do so. However, be aware that men always
follow after young maidens with doelike eyes to do them harm. You are
so lovely that as many noble lovers as swans at a lotus pond will pursue
you. You may become the basis of feuds and dissension, so it is not right
for you to go out carelessly. You must guard yourself as if you were a
wounded deer. As my offspring you are extremely dear to me, you are
the apple of my eye, and more precious than my own heart. Keep my
advice in mind. Be aware of what to do and what to avoid."

6

In which Manohari decides to run away from home to join Kumaradvitiya

OBTAINING HER FATHER'S concerned and loving permission made Manohari extremely happy. She and her maidservants began to prepare for their excursion to the pleasure gardens. Her hand-maidens carefully arranged the princess's jewels and garments. They placed a tiara of large sapphires and other immeasurably valuable gems upon her brow. Two multihued pendants dangling amidst strands of necklaces were beautifully draped at her throat. Clusters of blue Utpala flowers adorned her ears. Her upper body was graced with armlets, bracelets, and rings, all of the purest gold set with jewels. A wonderful golden belt with tiny, tinkling bells enhanced her slim, supple waist. The white silk of her blouse was delicately light and soft to the touch. When she moved, her skirts seemed to pulsate with the entire spectrum of rainbow lights. No one—not even the immortal goddesses Tilottama, Laksmi, Subhasini, or Gandharvavyati—could possibly rival her splendor.

As soon as she stepped outside the palace, she sent the water carrier with a message to the residence of the man she thought was Prince Kumaradvitiya. Then Manohari and her maidservants went to bathe in the pleasure gardens.

Bhavakumara, after receiving the note, dressed in luxurious clothes to disguise himself as Prince Kumaradvitiya. With a few men of his entourage, he slowly made his way to the pleasure gardens. There, through an opening in a dense thicket of trees and vines, he saw Manohari surrounded by her maidservants. Her beauty was matchless:

she was like the moon encircled by the constellations, or a strutting queen of swans amidst various other birds.

He watched her bathe and saw her shapely, firm breasts. Through the fluttering of her pretty blue undergarments he could see her well-shaped thighs. Her youthful white skin glowed like a desirable fresh flower. She was the very essence of all the lovely women in the world.

He was filled with wonder as he gazed at her. Despite his earnest efforts to control himself, he had no mastery over his body, and an intense desire to make love to her suffused him. He thought, "Eh ma! She is like an immortal goddess! It would be difficult to obtain even one of her handmaidens. Her exquisitely seductive beauty can be gazed at insatiably. Just to see a woman like this is a festival of good fortune—what need be said of having intercourse with her!

"Therefore," he promised himself, "I must capture this noble maiden, singular goddess that she is, to be the noble queen of Prince Kumaradvitiya. If that closest of relationships does not come to be, then Gem of the World will lack the essence of worldly happiness even though it has treasures which humble the pride of the northern gods of wealth.

"There is nothing that cannot be accomplished if there is a large enough expenditure of effort: with all my power I will endeavor to find a way to make the maid Manohari the queen of Prince Kumaradvitiya."

His body, in the throes of sensual desire, swayed like a vine on a mango tree in the breeze. So he paused, gained control over himself, and went toward the pool where the captivating maiden was bathing. By then, Manohari had risen from her bath and was in the process of redraping her invaluable jewels and clothes. Her smile emanated a sweet nectar as she arched her well-defined eyebrows, giving him a liquid, sideways glance. These lovely signs clearly indicated that she had completely mistaken him for Prince Kumaradvitiya. With her anklets and bracelets tinkling, she walked in the proud, swaying gait of a fierce royal elephant along the shore of the pond to meet her prince.

Without any apprehension, Bhavakumara spoke to her in a deep voice:

> Eh ma ma la! Today in the expanse of space,
> Is a drama performed by immortal gods and goddesses.
> Beautiful flowers mist down like rain,
> Ribbons of rainbows adorn the gods' raiment,

A snow white banner is hoisted aloft.
At twilight a canopy of fresh red-gold clouds is spread.
Good fortune, like the sun's rays, pervades every direction.
Varied types of music and countless songs are heard:
Flutists' fingers fly over their reed pipes,
Lutists cause their instruments to sing,
Drummers beat their drumsticks,
Cymbals and hand drums sound their song.
These are the auspicious signs displayed in the sky.

Today good fortune bedecks the earth below.
In marvelous stands of various trees
Sweetly singing birds fly and soar.
Flowers in full bloom carpet
Blue-green meadows, the color of a peacock's throat.
There are cool, clear, faultless ponds
Whose waters are like liquid sapphire.
Like a white crystal mirror, they reflect
The beauteous orb of your face.
Thanks to the profound force of earlier propensities,
We have been entwined in the bonds of love for a long time.
Now we have the wonderful fortune of enjoying these virtues.
We are united just as we had hoped!

He spoke these and other false words. Now, if a girl is of noble birth, she is skilled in eight sorts of aesthetic examination: she can analyze the qualities of mountains, trees, oceans and waters, garments, jewels, horses, cattle, and people. Manohari was just such a woman of good family, and so she clearly thought:

"When a youth of tender age sings such a profoundly elegant and harmonious song, the general public says he is worthy of praise. However, when the mere words 'Prince Kumaradvitiya' fall into my ears, my mind is totally engrossed by joy and sorrow vying for attention. Judging from the turbulent emotions I experience just hearing his name, I have thought about what a delight it would be to see his face. But now that I have the opportunity of actually meeting him, there is no feeling of unmistakable bliss as I had hoped. Whoever this is drawing near must be someone craftily disguised as the prince! I will use a gentle stratagem to sift truth from falsity and be sure."

So in a relaxed manner, she invited him to a wonderful pavilion on the lakeshore among the swaying flowers. There, to satiate him, she gave

him various remarkable dishes to eat and continually pressed him to
drink intoxicating liquors. When he became slightly drunk, the maiden
said with a smile:

> O fortunate youth!
> Intelligence, beauty, and a marvelous smile are yours.
> At a tender age you are a treasury of our ancestors' wisdom.
> Please listen to these words spoken for your ears.
>
> The pair of your faultless letters were
> Delivered by the water girl
> To the tips of the vines rooted in my shoulders.
> First I examined their meaning.
>
> "A superior son of the gods who has long desired you
> Has endeavored to approach the realm of Radiant Array."
> This was bliss for my eyes and music for my ears.
> While joy and sorrow vied in my heart,
> I sighed and wept continually over those letters.
> My copious tears streamed forth to greet you.
>
> I visualized meeting you
> As establishing a firm throne of bliss.
> So without obtaining my parents' permission,
> I pretended to go out to amuse myself in the park.
> I came hastily to this grove in order to see your smile.
>
> I have single-mindedly desired to make love to you
> For every part of the night and day,
> But now, when I see you, O youth,
> There is but a trifling increase in my joy.
>
> Just hearing the sound of the name
> "Kumaradvitiya" makes my hair stand on end.
> Fluctuating joy and sorrow
> Captivate my mind.
>
> Today I have the opportunity to meet someone,
> But because there is no increase in my bliss,
> I am certain you are not that best of princes.
> Thus, truthfully tell me who you are!

Otherwise, my fierce and powerful father,
His bloodthirsty ministers, and
His prisons like a terrifying hell
Will provide you with great misery!

When she spoke these taunting and elegantly satirical words, Bhavakumara realized she knew he was not Prince Kumaradvitiya. He analyzed the situation on its own merits:

"Obviously this maiden is interrogating me with reproaches and threats, hoping I will reveal my identity. There is no need to be in the least cowed by this. She penetrated my disguise either by relying on her superior intelligence or because of the spread of gossip by my own people. At any rate, however she came to know, it is clear that she is well aware that this is a sham. Although there has been an increasing series of lies and crooked words, this sort of behavior is not proper for me. There is no need to rely on further dissimulation; now is my opportunity to speak sincerely."

Thinking this way, he spoke without any pretension. "Kva ye! O maiden goddess, please listen well! My attempt to make you mistake me for the prince was not for the purpose of an improper lascivious deed. Let me explain how this was an expedient measure for a noble purpose.

"Noble lady, you and the wondrous prince named Kumaradvitiya prayed deeply for a long time so that you could meet. There is no doubt regarding that. However, we heard your father, Dyutimat, say that he had already promised you to Myriad Lights and would not be able to transgress his vow.

"Our fierce and relentless ministers, Laksaikadvitiya and the others, became extremely incensed when their plans were thwarted. Those ministers are like the ferocious Lords of the Dead: they enjoy combat and argumentation. Those heroic men proudly shouted in forceful voices: 'If it is not merely a rumor that we are to have no marriage alliance with Dyutimat, only the name of the kingdom of Radiant Array shall survive! We will make Manohari ours by force of arms.'

"Prince Kumaradvitiya's intentions were not in this line. He said that in our council we had first decided that the most expedient plan would be to confuse you, to lure you to Gem of the World.

"As for myself, placed in front of that most excellent prince, I am like the weak light of a firefly overpowered by the glare of the sun. I have no power to fulfill anyone's desires. Nevertheless, because the prince and I are contemporaries and I have the aptitude to utter at least some clever speeches, I was chosen to play the part of the noble prince. Despite the subtle connection of the karma and prayers between you and the prince from prior lives, it was not certain that I could bring you to Gem of the World. Nevertheless, it was our unanimous decision that I should try. I, who took this task as my burden, am the lowly minister known as Bhavakumara."

Then, taking the opportunity to express himself further, he said:

"Eh ma ho!
A mass of well-planted great virtues
Is an abundantly yielding field:
Such is the superb noble prince,
A powerful emperor of the universe.

Kumaradvitiya is his name.
As the sole ornament of the heavens, earth, and netherworld,
He is praised and renowned. He is the white umbrella
Cooling the public in his shade.

His radiantly penetrating discrimination
Is the faultless, clear, and full moon
Rising in the sky over the world.
It outshines all other arrogant men.

Many seductive, intelligent, wealthy, and
Beautiful women from all over the world
Have raised the banner of their wedding hopes
In front of this wonderful, powerful Lord of Men.

But the love who awakens earlier propensities,
The one struck by the flower of opportunity,
Is you, enchanting maiden.

According to your eloquent garlands of words,
The mere sound of his name gives you great joy.
If you follow my company of a hundred men,
Like the sky chariot which leads the sun,
We will endeavor to unite you in Open Lotus.

In the center of that great city,
Displayed like flower garlands on the earth,
Is a tall and spacious palace of jeweled bricks.
Its summit is so high it cannot be seen.

In this joy-inducing castle of Gem of the World
Is a lord who is a treasury of wealth, renown, and virtue.
Once seen, his glory cannot be disliked.
So, noble princess of the gods, come quickly
To that great place to view him with loving eyes."

When this was said,
Manohari's mental faculties were tightly tied
By the bonds of many doubts
And confusion about the proper way to act.
Finally there arose vast wisdom
Which clearly perceived reality.

"From beginningless time I have been tossed
On turbulent waves of birth, aging, sickness, and death.
Through the swells and troughs of the vast samsaric ocean,
I have never tasted true happiness.
In this existence devoid of the essence of joy,
I partake only the dregs of misery.

Thus, when I come here
Contrary to my parents' intentions,
My head is completely turned
By this sort of purposeless trickery.

Now, with gentle words I must explain
To this man Bhavakumara
For a time I will follow my own plan,
Returning to my parents' abode."

To that youth she gave
An incalculably priceless ring
Set with many a lovely gem.
Then she spoke these sweet words.

"Kye ma! My heart's sole desire
Has been to have the fortune to see
The face of Prince Kumaradvitiya.
Although your intentions are loving and sincere,
With intrigue and dissimulation
You have tried to deceive me.

If I were to follow you today,
My parents, court, and subjects
Would cast me out like spittle.
They would say, 'Manohari has gone!
Like a crazy woman she has accompanied
A minister of Gem of the World.'
The weapons of the world's curses
Will surely so destroy me.
Therefore, for now I shall return
To my parents in Radiant Array.

Later, when an auspicious time draws near,
In accordance with worldly convention,
May your king and his ministers compassionately
Come for me to accomplish the realization
Of our hopes and imperishable vows of love.
Look on me with love and consider this well."

In a low and deeply pained voice, she spoke clearly about her own character. When she finished, Bhavakumara returned her ring to her fingertips and said:

"The most famous Earth Lord of the world
Is the marvelous sovereign Kumaradvitiya.
He is a treasury of countless, inexpressible virtues.
The masses scatter flowers in his honor and praise.

His consecrated queen was to be only you.
Although you are tightly bound to him,
Under someone's influence or because woman's nature
Is cunning, you cry out, 'deceit!'
Refusing to see the value of the method.

If what you first recited to me
Were honest words lacking insincerity,
The highest form of love in this life
Can be yours today if you will it.

If you do not come quickly to Gem of the World,
Secretly without any of the cityfolk becoming aware,
Myriad Lights' countless armies will trample you like a reed.

Manohari, you will be carried off the way
A powerful eagle snags a poisonous snake.

Then will you not be sunk in a mire of regrets?
If deep in your heart you sincerely respect
Only Prince Kumaradvitiya, then come with me!

But if you do not wish to execute this plan,
We will not kill you. We shall not kidnap you.
We will not beg for you, nor steal you by force.
Since we will not obstruct your desire,
May you pray to be united in another life!"

When he let flow the ambrosia essence
Of the meaning of his spoken words,
The noble maiden Manohari
Once again considered carefully.

"The mirror of worldly actions
Reflects various pleasures and pains.
The realization of my hopes seemed dim
Because of the weak power of my virtues.

Although one may fall into an abyss of misery,
Even there the taste of happiness
Is definitely the result of the fruits of virtue.
But in Myriad Lights all the nonvirtuous actions
Revolve ceaselessly and easily like a wheel of sin.
They do not know about karma and its effects;
A thick cloud of ignorance covers the land.
If I wander there, surely I will fall
To the depths of the fearsome lower realms.

I must cut the bonds of my uncertainties and doubts.
In this life shall I attain the heights of virtue
Or penetrate the far limits of sin?
Either way, later, that karma must be experienced.
So, with no regrets I will go
Happily and quickly to Gem of the World."

7

In which Manohari regrets her decision too late

THEN MANOHARI PUT HER RESOLUTION INTO ACTION. She sent one of her maidservants to her parents. "Tell them tomorrow that I have been seized by the forces of Gem of the World and am their captive, borne away like a dust mote cast before the wind," she said.

Then she and four maidservants made preparations for travel. Manohari mounted a fine horse called Tornado. Bhavakumara was astride a horse named Fleet Hawk. The entourage of one hundred men and the maidservants also rode swift steeds. Only Chetadasa refused a good horse and chose a docile mount.

They sped off toward Gem of the World, riding all night, like wild animals just released from a trap. As the night was drawing to an end, a cool dawn breeze came up. Its chill touch reawakened and increased Manohari's anxiety and sorrow.

She thought: "The power of previously accumulated karma is strict: whatever causes have been created will come to fruition without any obstacle. All one's wishes to the contrary can never alter that. We are creatures of daylight, and it is dangerous and improper to range abroad at night. Yet here I am being led in that way!

"I have spat out like phlegm all the excellent things in my life: my affectionate, loving parents and relations, my happy realm, pleasant court, possessions, and ministers and subjects, who view their rulers with respect. How could I have thought to go to such a faraway, strange, and frightful place as Gem of the World?"

So she said to Bhavakumara:

"Kye ma! My loving, honorable father, Dyutimat,
Viewed me with only loving tenderness.
He gave me ambrosia to eat, nectar to drink,
And the chance to enjoy pleasant possessions:
Beautifully draping me in soft, heavenly garments,
And adorning me with ornaments
Priceless as the gems of the nagas and gods.

My eyes perceived a joyous festival.
My ears heard only pleasing speeches.
My mind was filled with the sweetness of virtue.
I was satisfied and made supremely happy.

Born from the wheel of her navel, my loving mother
Fostered me with her skillful behavior.
She sheltered me with boundless care, a love so strong
She could not bear to part with me for a moment.
The pith of that wish-granting tree was love for me.
I have deserted my mother, Chandraprabha!

In the kingdom known for its radiant prosperity and
Excellent array of wealth and power,
There are countless subjects and ministers
Viewing their rulers with heartfelt, guileless respect.
I have abandoned all their love and friendship.

Now I reside in places and go along a road
Whose course my eyes are unable to see.
I am in the company of strangers and
Have to endure many difficult tasks.
Saying you are a minister of the loving prince,
You bewildered me with pretense and cunning
To lead me unwillingly on a grievous route.

I have no wealth of psychic powers, but I know
The force of merits accumulated earlier
Resulted in my gorgeous, youthful allure.
An oyster which grasps a wondrous pearl
Is destroyed in the end. Just so am I!

Thoughts like this make me depressed and anguished.
Now I cannot even recall true happiness.

Since I am unable to bear my present suffering,
My mind is as unhinged as a crazy woman's.

You are matchlessly wise and strong,
You have the wisdom to discern propriety,
So, O youth, please earnestly consider this request.

When I remember my kind, loving parents,
Pain arises like a solid form,
A sickness bringing me close to death.
Then what fruits will your efforts to obtain me bear?
The best medicine to cure my anxiety
Is to grant my wish to return to my own land.

But only for a short time! You must help me
Find a way to experience the good fortune
To see with open eyes his radiant face.
The white light of the noble prince's smile
Will open a treasury of virtue before my eyes."

As she spoke, tears fell in a constant stream
From the lovely maiden's eyes.
The arrow of those pain-stricken words
Pierced the heart of Bhavakumara.

He noted the pretty maid's extreme disquiet
And her distressed mood.
The force of his compassion
Rendered him bashfully speechless.

Then as requested he carefully considered:
"We have exerted great effort to obtain Manohari.
Now we have her in our hands.
Yet, if we reverse our steps,
Our difficult labors will be in vain.

If you do not place a wish-fulfilling gem
On the pinnacle of your victory banner
But cast it carelessly in an unsuitable place,
What discerning man would not censure you?

As it is said, what one first vows
To undertake should never be abandoned."

Having fixed his purpose in his mind,
With soft and charming words
He spoke to the maiden:

"High in the sky of exalted royal birth,
The alluring, faultless moon is drawn in light:
Manohari, with your lovely, almond-shaped eyes,
You have arrived at the peak of the eastern mountains.

If once again you return to your home,
You will not come to this northern province later.
Even in your own eastern realm,
Will not many evil portents of degeneration arise?
I beseech you to tranquilize and calm your mind.
I am not a man who speaks deceitfully.

It is true this track is exhausting and discouraging.
But it leads to the felicitous palace of Gem of the World.
That inexhaustible treasure-house is extremely tall.
There you can gaze insatiably at the son of the gods.

His joyful and rapturous light pervades all directions,
Surpressing all darkness like the sun's bright rays,
Blazing with glittering magnificence.
His smiling face surpasses the beauty of the moon.
Incomparable wonder arises when he is seen.
The very instant he comes before your eyes,
You obtain totally satiating good fortune.

Therefore, set aside your unstable emotions.
Let us proceed happy and carefree."

With these and other encouraging words, her spirits were raised a bit, and they continued along the path.

The serving maid who had been left behind waited until after the first light of dawn to go to Manohari's parents' chamber. So at the very same time that Manohari and Bhavakumara conversed, she respectfully said to the king and queen:

"The single refuge of all our hopes, the delightful daughter of the gods whose wondrous beauty could be gazed at insatiably, she who was adorned with a wealth of virtues, the very heart of this land, is gone!

"Within the bounds of our realm came men deceitfully disguising themselves as traveling merchants. Their leader said he was

Bhavakumara, a minister of Gem of the World, accompanied by an entourage of one hundred men. As soon as our divine mistress finished her bath in the pleasure gardens, she was captured and taken away in a direction I could not discover. She was but a dust mote blown away by the force of the wind.

"Now I pray that this kingdom not wander onto the path of evil actions. Please do not engage in fighting or disputation."

Queen Chandraprabha deeply loved her daughter. As soon as she heard about her child's abduction, she fell into a dead faint. She lay senseless, like a willow sapling cut down at its root. Manohari's father, Dyutimat, was totally dumbfounded by the result of his allowing his daughter to go into the gardens. Not knowing what to do, he cradled his head in his hands.

Then the maidservant sprinkled the queen mother with sandalwood-scented water. Once revived from her faint, the queen wailed this earnest lament:

> Kye ma! I clearly see that the stringent force
> Of earlier deeds results in unstable, composite phenomena.
> It matters not if I give up this life of mine:
> What use is this body separated from its heart's love?
>
> For even an instant I cannot bear separation
> From my lovely daughter. My heart's delight
> Was spirited off by a demon in broad daylight.
> Not knowing the direction of their flight, we cannot follow.
>
> Thinking of this, a searing pain scorches my mind.
> O why is my heart not broken? Has it become stone?
> The good fortune of being with her in this life is lost.
> I am weighed down by the misery of bad karma!

As she recited this dirge, Manohari's honorable father, Dyutimat, was stricken with even deeper anguish. After thinking a short time he said:

> Kye ma! It is hard to block the fall onto one's head
> Of the results of karma, which must be experienced.
> The karmic wheel of all my actions
> Was made to roll along the path of righteousness,
> Yet it seems to have cycled to vile results.
> But my nature lacks any duplicity,

And I am untainted by any guile. Since this is true,
How could I come to such an abominable state?

Manohari, your face is as lovely as the moon!
It is hard to bear the pain of your abduction.
Because you are wise, extremely intelligent,
And know the correct and skillful way to act,
You captivated the heart of Kumaradvitiya.
Surely you were taken to become
His noble, consecrated queen. Thus, Radiant Array
Has been saved from ruin by your actions!

Although I said I could not renege my avowed promise
First made to the Earth Lord of Myriad Lights,
Who can censure an event which occurred
Suddenly, and out of my control?

Therefore, although this occurrence seems evil,
It definitely follows a moral path.
The force of karma, virtue and its result, is fixed,
They lack any ruse.
So dear Chandraprabha, do not grieve,
Be happy and carefree while accomplishing white virtues!

These smooth words slightly cheered even Manohari's devoted
mother, Chandraprabha.

8

In which Manohari is kidnapped by the army of the evil kingdom Myriad Lights

B Y THIS TIME, BHAVAKUMARA AND HIS ENTOURAGE, along with Manohari and her four maidservants, had passed far beyond the realm of Radiant Array. They had reached a place known as Endless Gulch, an extremely vast and flat desert. It was a plain so wide that the sun appeared to rise whole from the earth and to sink the same way. Upon their arrival, they saw the army of a thousand men led by Uddhatamanas Mokshabhadra advancing on them from not very far away. The hero Bhavakumara quickly realized that they must have been sent from Myriad Lights to claim Manohari. The hero Bhavakumara had Manohari and her maidservants don men's clothing, lower their faces, and join an unobtrusive group of servants. As the army drew nearer and nearer, he thought, "I will confuse them with cunning words."

Uddhatamanas Mokshabhadra came up quickly. He demanded information from the hero Bhavakumara:

"O youth, listen carefully! You and these not so few men who are mounted on horses, why do you come so quickly? Where is your homeland? Which direction are you going? Where are you coming from now? What is your reason for travel? You had better speak promptly and without any artifice. Tell me information that is worth my while to hear!"

Without the slightest cowardice, the hero Bhavakumara said:

Your army is like countless constellations
Transferred down to the earth from the sky.
As their commander, you appear like the jewel moon.

In answer to your questions,
I will speak honestly and guilelessly,
For I am beyond the lowly practice
Of engaging in crafty and inconstant lies.

We are mounted upon swift steeds
In order to avoid distress.
We are not many, nor are we very few;
Thus, we protect ourselves with only speed
Against the highwaymen and robbers of the road.

We travel quickly in order to arrive
Before the greatest of the Rulers of Men.
So to the land of Gem of the World
And the city of Open Lotus we go.

We come to this place from the lowly principality
Known as Radiant Array.
We came in search of a precious queen
For our prince, Kumaradvitiya.
We work on his behalf, the crown jewel
Of all the heroes of the world,
A treasury of virtues worthy of great praise.

The superb issue of the lineage of Dyutimat
Is a woman known as Manohari.
Her fame, like the sound of the immortals' deep drum,
Pervades all the directions of the universe.

Once we heard of her repute,
We came with much effort
As messengers to call upon the kingdom.
But that vile king called Dyutimat said:

"First of all, with Myriad Lights
I have a promise I cannot retract."
He proclaimed that promise three times.

Yet again we offered extensive tribute;
We assiduously persevered with earnest words.
Then, unable to withstand our pressure,
The woman came into our hands.

She does not accord with her fame!
An ugly, unlovely face was seen by me.
Her character is ill. She talks too much.
Her degrading behavior is not that of the nobility.
She has no respect for her venerable parents.
She tortures her servants, not protecting them with love.
Carelessly loosening her girdle, she sells her body.
That is the conduct of the woman who came to us!
The moment I saw her, all joy was gone,
Increasing disquiet filled my mind.

Prince Kumara gives joy to all who see him.
He is a magnificent ruler of the earth,
Unparalleled and unrivaled in the world.
Thus, a marvelous, astounding treasury of virtues
Should be offered to him as his consecrated queen.

A coarse woman skilled in vice,
Worthy of the lowest sorts, would be improper!
Although Manohari's fame spread like the wind,
She is unworthy of it. That ugly, cunning female
Should be cast away like grass clippings.

Now we come to this place
In search of a royal maiden;
She must be an extraordinarily pretty girl,
A faultless treasury of qualities worthy of praise,
Born into a lineage equal to that of the prince
And so worthy to become his queen.

May this news be sweet nectar for your ears!

As soon as he finished speaking, Bhavakumara led his followers away extremely quickly. Uddhatamanas Mokshabhadra and the others in his party agreed with one another for the most part. "Such a stripling youth would not dare lie to us," they thought. After some discussion, they concurred: "The daughter of Dyutimat is greatly renowned. Yet she cannot be as lovely as claimed; otherwise this minister of Gem of the World would surely have seized her for his ruler. We must carefully ascertain if her nature is as bad as the recitation we just heard. There will be no fruit of our labors if we act rashly, without careful deliberation."

Just when they had reached agreement, Chetadasa came slowly up. He had been left behind the others because of his inferior horse. Uddhatamanas Mokshabhadra unsheathed his sword and in a threatening manner interrogated him with the same questions he had asked before. Terror confounded Chetadasa. In a cowardly fashion, he tremblingly prostrated himself before Uddhatamanas Mokshabhadra and said:

"I am with those who preceded me; we are servants of Gem of the World. After the hero Bhavakumara and his forces obtained Manohari, the flower of King Dyutimat's line, in satisfaction they sped away. I am but a lowly minister named Chetadasa. I had the ill fortune to be ordered to mount this weak, miserable nag, and so I was left behind. Now, because I lack a protector and a refuge, if you so allow I shall place my faith in you. If I am permitted to become your follower, please shelter me with your kindness."

Chetadasa openly bared the others' secrets and all his own faults. Uddhatamanas Mokshabhadra, realizing he had been fooled by Bhavakumara, made this speech to his thousand warriors:

The fierce and fearsome Earth Lord of Myriad Lights
Spoke angry, incontrovertible words.
His strict commands sit upon our heads like a crown:
We must obtain the lovely-visaged
Manohari as a wife for Devatisha, our Lord of Men.

"If she has come under another's sway
You shall lose your lives," he said.
Do you not recall these fearsome words
Piercing our hearts like sharp thorns?
Thus, our army was mustered and sent out.

Now that we hear a minister of Gem of the World
Named Kumara and his entourage have seized
That paragon of beauty Manohari,
It is not right for us to remain calm!
Our fearless and strong forces must rise up
To completely vanquish our adversaries.

We must capture for ourselves that noble princess,
To fulfill the happiness of Devatisha.
If we are unable to accomplish this task,
My name, which means "fierce," lacks significance.
And this force of a thousand is just a bestial herd.

Therefore, each of you raise up your courageous skill!
Let us hoist the colors of our enemies'
Annihilation on the peak of the world!

Then he mounted his superb horse, Soaring Bright Eyes. Whipping him three times with his crop, he led the way. Like a meteor, he hastened in pursuit of Bhavakumara and Manohari.

When Bhavakumara glanced behind him, he saw a cloud of dust rising from the earth. Then he heard the sound of the horses' hooves beating the earth like a drum, and he knew that the army of Myriad Lights was giving chase. He became a bit anxious and said to the lovely maiden and her servants:

"O fair ones! My concatenation of ruses skillfully confused and deceived the forces of Myriad Lights. However, the nefarious Chetadasa, trailing behind us, must have given us away by speaking like the iniquitous character he is. Now the army of Myriad Lights, like a shooting star, is quickly coming upon us. It is not proper to leave them unchallenged; even though we have only a few men fit for combat, I will command our forces without any fear. Have no doubt that I will be courageous in the work of war! If necessary, I can endure being trampled into the dust and losing my life. While we engage in battle, Manohari, you with a few servants must undertake any means necessary to reach Gem of the World."

Once he gave them these orders, without any hesitation he went straight for the center of that army of a thousand men. He advanced the way an intrepid lion charges into the midst of a herd of powerful elephants.

"Is this the same deceiving youth come upon us again?" they said fearfully. To alleviate their doubt about his identity, Chetadasa said, "This man leaping like a bear into the midst of his enemies is the best warrior of Gem of the World. If you can overcome him, his comrades will be easy to destroy, for they are mere common city folk."

Then Uddhatamanas Mokshabhadra, imperiously brave and graceful, rode out on Soaring Bright Eyes. The bridge of his nose was wrinkled with anger. His eyebrows were raised in indignation. Brandishing his sword in the air, he shouted these loud words in intoxicated arrogance:

Kye! Youthful lad! We heard you are
A magnificent hero with your ancestors'
Impenetrably deep and constant wisdom,
And a body perfectly skilled in all the arts.

Yet you transgress the customs of nobility
By confusing others' minds with crafty lies.
Since in the end your words are irresolute,
It is shamefully foolish to defame yourself so.

The Earth Lord Chandramati
Rules over the kingdom Myriad Lights.
For his son Devatisha he made
A karmic connection for a superior queen.

Manohari accepted the invitation to be crowned.
Yet after that irrevocable promise had been made,
You came to deflect us from our intent.
You engaged in crooked deeds to divide us.

Show us if you have the confident pride of a hero!
I, who am of a lowly servant lineage
In the great court of Chandramati,
Call you to this battle demanding all a warrior's skills.
Your body and life shall be reduced to dust.
I shall totally annihilate you!
Let the battle begin!

Then Uddhatamanas Mokshabhadra lifted his sword to strike
Bhavakumara. But the hero didn't think a thing of it; not a hair on his
body stirred. He answered the minister's loud speech with a laugh:

Ha ha! From amazing depths my mirth erupts.
Confident of the strength of your thousand-man army,
You bluster courageously and brandish your
Sharp weapon to strike me, a feeble youth!

If you really are of a mind to engage in war,
Have no fear, I will compete with you!
You, the brilliant hero famed as "fierce,"
Today must act in accordance with your boasts.

Gem of the World has amassed all the universe's marvels.
In that great kingdom honored by the masses,
Is Suryamati, the all-conquering Earth Lord,
And his heir, the excellent Kumaradvitiya.

The white banner of his fame flutters so widely
The earth up to the horizons is his own.
His subjects are grateful to have the fortune
To be well protected by his kindness.

Below me is a fine mount, I wear armor,
And I am just able to hurl a hand weapon.
If you intend to vie with me in combat,
I will cut off the heads of all who can see!

If you take even one step backward,
I will chop your body into a hundred pieces
To scatter them in the ten directions.
This place will become the Death Lord's garden.

This is not an empty speech like an echo!
Later it will be clear whether this is true.
On the field of battle, a thousand foes will be destroyed
By my blazing magic wheel of weapons.
I shall slay all who come to challenge me.
I shall expose the hollowness of your boasts.

The cowardly who howl lamentations
Are objects of equanimity, if not pity.
Now if you have the confidence to compete,
Abandon your hesitation and come right here!

As he spoke, Bhavakumara's face became suffused with the flush of
hatred. Three veins popped out on his forehead while he twisted his
hands together. His horse pawed the ground violently. Then, without
any hesitation, he began to fight in the midst of that host of a thousand
men.

To reach those who hung far back, he stretched his bowstring back
to his ear and loosed great arrows. For those who came close in, he
whirled his sapphire sword like a lasso. It seemed that he wielded a veritable magic wheel of weapons. The entire army of Myriad Lights was
unable to bear his onslaught, just as the rising of the single orb of the
sun dims the shining light of a multitude of stars.

Some of the enemy, caring only for their own heads, covered their
faces with their hands and fled toward their homes. Others prostrated
themselves before Bhavakumara and begged, "If we are objects of your

pity, please bless us so that we may be without fear!" A few, quaking with cowardice and terror, did not know what to do at all; they stood dumbly on the path. Yet other men, wounded from head to toe, staggered about, their faces wet with blood and so deranged they could no longer distinguish friend from foe. Others bawled out curses in all directions: "That rotten King Chandramati could not tell good from bad. He acted rashly, and now we have to experience this suffering!"

Despite the vainglorious heroism and boasts of Uddhatamanas Mokshabhadra, he was mostly a coward at heart. He could not bear to come anywhere near the hero Bhavakumara. He retreated and remained a safe distance away.

Thus, the hero Bhavakumara joyfully entered the battle with great enthusiasm. The skirmish was clearly going his way. But just as it became clear that without much difficulty the remaining enemy forces would be completely vanquished, his sword shattered into fragments because of overuse. He was without a weapon. His horse was exhausted from the many fast charges. Even Bhavakumara himself, despite his youth, was quite fatigued. So he retreated to take a rest.

Shortly thereafter, he saw Chetadasa approaching his place of repose. Bhavakumara hoped that he would help him. "Please lend me your sword," he said. "The enemy forces are easy to rout. There is nothing to fear, I have them in the palm of my hand! But while I take a short rest, you must be careful and post sentries," he ordered.

Chetadasa's mind was caught in the grip of evil demons. "Now," he thought, "the enemy forces can overpower him!" So he said, "O Bhavakumara, please refresh your vigor. I will give you my sword later. But for now, as it is not safe to remain at leisure in the domain of the enemy, I shall carry the sword and be your sentry. Please rest for a time."

Then Chetadasa went to the place where Uddhatamanas Mokshabhadra and the remnants of his force of a thousand men had regrouped. He said: "Gentlemen, please listen! The hero Bhavakumara is without a weapon to strike his enemies. His mount is exhausted, and the youth himself is tired and fatigued. He is now taking a rest. So the time is right for you to gather up your strength and fight."

They answered him, "O minister, before when we tried to compete with that warrior, we came to this sorry state. We are in grief. We have had enough; all we want is to save our lives."

Chetadasa responded: "You are even weaker than women! Have you no limbs? Have you no strength of purpose? The time to enter into battle with that brave man is now; otherwise, later he will definitely destroy you. So gather up your forces now. I myself judge the time to be proper."

They decided he spoke truly, so they followed his advice to reengage their enemy.

Chetadasa quickly retraced his steps and said to Bhavakumara: "O youth, be at ease! I have returned from my reconnaissance: I have spied things out well. Be assured that Uddhatamanas Mokshabhadra and the few remaining men of his army have downcast faces. Their shoulders slump with grief and shame while they retreat to their homeland. Now you are free from any personal danger. I will protect you. Please relax comfortably tonight. Please inform your comrades in arms about this."

Everyone believed Chetadasa, because the diabolical shroud of his advice enveloped their minds. That evening, Bhavakumara and his fellow warriors let their horses out to graze. Without any hesitation, they all separated and retired.

During the last watch of the night, in the light just before the dawn, Uddhatamanas Mokshabhadra and his men approached, led by Chetadasa. They found the hero Bhavakumara incautiously resting without any suspicion. Many men animatedly seized his limbs. Like a lion cub overcome by a swarm of tiny ants, Bhavakumara was rendered powerless. His comrades scattered in all directions.

During this time Manohari found herself unable to bear the thought of abandoning Bhavakumara and happily proceeding alone to Gem of the World. She had no strength or skill to join the brawl on the battlefield. But from the exhaustion of her karma, she could not think of anything else to do. Lost in confusion, she continued her journey.

After capturing Bhavakumara, Uddhatamanas Mokshabhadra and his forces pursued her. Manohari was powerlessly borne away like a Champaka flower before a gale.

"All our wishes are fulfilled," said the men of Myriad Lights. They sent a messenger to King Chandramati to announce their success. And then with merriment and delight they swiftly directed their steps toward home.

> He was fearless and brave, heroic and fierce.
> He wore mighty armor and carried sharp weapons.
> A skilled master of the arts of war.
> He was able to conquer the enemy in any fight.
>
> It was his nature to be unrivaled
> By the skilled strength of other arrogant men.

Even the knees of Ravana, Lanka's ten-headed king,
Knocked together in terror of him.

That outfitted army of a thousand men was like
A herd of strong, powerful elephants.
They were destroyed: scattered like clouds in the sky
By the fearless singular lion among men.

This was the case. But the force of his karma
Was for the increase of black, nonwhite fruits.
It was impossible to prevent their occurrence.
Karma is definite. No one can get the better of it.

A lion cannot be oppressed
By harmful external factors,
But he can be injured by inner vermin.
Just so were the deceitful actions of evil Chetadasa.

For a time it seemed his plans were at an end.
He seemed to range onto a grievous path.
But when the moon is consumed by an eclipse,
It is always quickly released without a problem!

Manohari was pressed down by a heavy burden of grief and despair.
She thought: "Kye ma! This universe is a wheel of turbulent suffering.
Even the riches of the world are like a torrential river of blazing fire.
Not only is it definite that we are separated from occasions of happiness, but, blanketed by a thick film of ignorance, we are confused about
cause and effect and the nature of reality. Because of our possessive
attachment, we think painful things are pleasurable: our insatiable desire
tricks us into repeated rebirths.

"Thus, the only actions worth doing are those which bring samsara to an
end. But I have been doing the opposite. On the simplest level it is proper
to repay the kindness of one's parents: even in that regard I have acted
improperly! I should have obeyed the instructions of my loving, protective
parents. Yet I thought I could digress from their wishes and repay their kindness later. Now my hope to have the opportunity to be beside the youthful
religious king has withered like a lovely flower destroyed by frost.

"Because of the irreversible force of karma created in earlier lives, I
have the form of a lowly woman. No matter what I do, I am the basis
of bitter disputes. These quarrels over my body cause me and those I
love to lack all happiness and joy. Surely death is better than this!"

Her face was a vessel pouring rivers of tears that pooled in her lap.
She said:

> Kye ma! Cyclic existence is a play of illusion.
> Impermanent, unstable things lack any essence.
> We are born but to die. We collect only to consume.
> We meet but must part. That is reality.
>
> I had the good fortune to experience
> Living in the cool shade of my parents' love.
> But my present confusion is the result
> Of previously accumulated bad deeds.
>
> Worldly deeds shimmer like the moon's reflection on water.
> Desired things appear like the shadow of a cobra's hood.
>
> All existence is an ocean with billowing waves of suffering.
> The exhaustion of good karma is the loss of happiness.
> I pray to understand all this.
>
> May the righteous gods and anchorites
> Show me the clear path to liberation.
> May the results of my heartfelt prayers
> To these holy gurus come about just as I wish!
>
> This poor, lowly woman's body
> Is the basis for the misery of the lower realms.
> Thus, I am worthless—I will give up this life.
> Please bless me to obtain a religious form,
> So I may attain complete enlightenment in another life!

She seized a four-inch knife with a lovely turquoise handle that was
lying beside her. Her servants and captors had to physically restrain her
from stabbing herself.

Bhavakumara saw her actions and heard her unhappy words.
Although he was tightly bound with strong manacles, he fearlessly and
heroically spoke to her:

> Kva ye! Lovely Manohari!
> Is the marvelous flower of our hopes
> For which we strove for so long
> To be cut asunder by destructive hail?

Although I am an unintelligent servant,
My own strength reduced
The enemy forces to a mere name.
Now I am rendered powerless
As a result of the cunning deception
By evil Chetadasa, whom I asked for aid.

However, we do not lack a protector!
The Earth Lord, peerless in all the world,
Is a master of the ocean of skilled arts.
When he is aroused to wrath, even the Death Lord
Quivers in fear. So can other arrogant mortals
Ever chance to challenge him in the least?

The heroic, sagacious treasury of virtues,
Prince Kumaradvitiya, gives joy to all.
The banner of his sweet fame flutters
Over the heavens, earth, and netherworld.

In his marvelous presence,
I am but a lowly minister. But others,
Like fearsome Laksaikadvitiya and wise Parambhasvaramati,
Adorn him like Indra's entourage.

These countless heroes and warriors
Will not be able to bear our miserable state.
They will definitely take revenge!

The heavenly moon rules the heavens;
When eclipsed it quickly frees itself.
We can see this accords with our histories.

Therefore, O superb offspring of a noble line,
Why do you wish to end your precious life?
We are not like robbers, thieves, or brigands,
Who lack friends, refuge, or a leader.
These are not just words: please do not be downcast.

Manohari was a bit heartened by his words, but they caused
Uddhatamanas Mokshabhadra and his men some worry. "We have
heard for a long time about the king and ministers of Gem of the
World. They are famed as men who are masters of power and strength.

Bhavakumara is a mere immature youth, but we could barely compete with his mighty skill. What need is there to speak of the others! Therefore, in the future we must be cautious."

Chetadasa also overheard Bhavakumara. He decided, "Those words of Bhavakumara are definitely true. In the long run, who could ever manage to rival the power and strength of that king and his ministers? My mind was possessed by evil spirits that forced me to do terrible deeds."

He became quite anxious. Therefore, to regain Bhavakumara's good graces, he loosened his bonds a bit. Then he carefully prepared some tasty food and offered it to the hero and the other captives. Cheerfully he hung about them.

> In the world, an extremely intelligent enemy
> May still be worthy of praise.
> Friends and relations obscured by thick ignorance
> Are thin saplings with no cooling shade.
>
> The first action of a round of activities
> Should be analyzed and considered at the start.
> Otherwise you will be burned by fires of regret
> In the end, when it is too late to change things.
>
> Thus the stouthearted Bhavakumara
> Struck fear into the evil Chetadasa's heart
> By merely proclaiming in loud tones his pride
> In the magnificent heroism of another.

9

In which Manohari is married against her will

WHEN THE MESSENGER SENT AHEAD by Uddhatamanas Moksha-bhadra reached King Chandramati, he succinctly announced: "Manohari and her retinue are slowly making their way here. In a short time she will arrive in Myriad Lights!" This news was delectable nectar for the king and all his ministers; they realized that their hopes had been fulfilled.

They threw themselves into preparations for the customary bridal celebrations. In due course, extensive arrangements to receive Manohari were ordered.

Just before the travelers reached the city, men, women, and small children wearing enchanting ornaments and lovely clothes gathered at all the crossroads to greet them. The crowds appreciatively watched the charming songs and plays performed before them. Drawn together like swarms of bees in search of honey in a flower garden, countless men and women filled every inch of available space. They came to catch a glimpse of Manohari, because her beauty was reputed to be superior to that of all others. They buzzed with all sorts of captivating rumors:

> "Any man enjoying the realm of desire
> Is attached to the taste of sensual objects.
> In particular, who doesn't crave sexual fulfillment
> Arising from the touch of a nubile young woman?"

"This embodiment of every seductive allure
Can be gazed at insatiably.
She is unrivaled by any of the world's beautiful women.
There is nothing to dislike about the sight of her."

"Is she born from the seed of the gods of the air?
Perhaps she is an Earth goddess come here.
She is so astonishingly lovely that even
A woman of Brahma's imagination cannot compare."

So all the people of the city
Gossiped with one another.
In their minds' eyes they drew
Imaginary pictures of her glorious charm.

The lovely one herself felt extremely anxious
About not obtaining the fruit of her hopes.
However, a lovely but false smile
Was ambrosia for the adoring crowds.

Because of this supremely intelligent action,
Not a part of her internal thoughts
Was obvious outside. Who could have known
That action was a skillful strategy?

When they arrived at the palace, they found it beautifully decorated
with all sorts of ornamental canopies, banners, pennants, fringed silk
flags, and more. King Chandramati, his son, and Manohari sat down
upon precious, high, and expansive thrones. To their right and left
reclined the high ministers. In order to demonstrate their bravery,
Bhavakumara was insulted and forced to stand just inside the outer gate.

The hero felt extreme hatred in his heart. The king and his ministers
appeared as nothing more than dust to him. When those evil ones
flicked their fingers to mockingly strike him, he thought, "What sort of
punishment is this?" There was no obstacle to his ready bravery.

But, as do all intelligent people, he accomplished his deeds by
means of prior analysis. So again he carefully considered his situation: "No doubt I am courageous enough to dispute with them;
and it does not matter to me if I lose my life. But that would leave
great waves of work for others to finish later in order to benefit
the kingdom of Gem of the World. Thus, now I will rely on subtle

behavior, for to display my anger like a child would be ineffectual."

As soon as he thought that, he earnestly took up the astounding actions of the wise. He smiled and displayed a pleasing, respectful countenance.

> In the world, even Brahma cannot rival
> The wise man whose hatred blazes inside
> As fiercely as the fire at the aeon's end,
> But outside, a smile cool as ambrosia ripples forth.

> Those of weak intelligence are proud and arrogant.
> Even the slightest happiness or anger
> Can be seen in their fluctuating behavior.
> They have not even the merest hint of shame.

> Between the earth and sky the distance is great;
> The two shores of the ocean are leagues apart;
> Between wise men and fools the distance is immeasurable.
> Ordinary and superior actions are similarly divorced.

Then the extensive rituals of the bridal celebrations began. Their magnificence made the possessions of even the immortal Lord Indra look shabby in comparison. The rites were to go on for several days.

When the celebrations first began, the Earth Lord Chandramati, Devatisha, and Manohari were all thinking along completely different lines. The variance of their views was as follows.

As for the father:

> "Merely by seeing her lovely, moonlike face,
> The petals of my lily-mind flutter with joy.
> Eh ma! Even the lithe immortal goddesses
> Cannot rival this treasure of beauty's essence.

> We have fulfilled our hopes of enjoying
> The celebrations of obtaining the lot
> To have her as this realm's precious queen.
> But many come wishing to do harm
> To a land replete with magnificent wonders.

> In particular, based on desirable objects,
> The pain of greed, hatred, and ignorance arises.

For a long time we have heard words sharp as arrows
Because this lovely girl was the basis of dispute.
However, now, according to our plans,
We have obtained our goal. I am content."

The crown prince did not consider
An action's future consequences.
Concerned only with his present inclinations,
His thoughts of enjoying conjugal union
Were displayed like a visible thing.

He thought:

"Eh ma! Today I have the chance to have intercourse
With the amalgam of worldly beauty's essence.
There is no other feeling of joy like this.
Now I have the opportunity to make love
To a girl whose lovely face is a pleasure to view.

If you mix the essences of all worldly pleasures,
Then multiply it by a hundred thousand,
It could not compare to sex with her!
If it is my lot to enjoy her just once, then to die
From bliss, I would not have the slightest regret!"

Thinking thus, his mind filled with excessive joy.
He smiled broadly in delight.

As for noble Manohari, she thought:

"Kye ma! Samsara is a dance of illusion.
From beginningless time it circles like a waterwheel.
Not knowing its deceptive end,
We grasp for happiness and stability.
Even so am I. The impressions of prior dispositions
Were dormant in the depths of my heart.
By their power I firmly vowed to be the lover of
A righteous ruler, a youthful prince of the gods.

But thanks to bad karma and bad luck,
That hoped-for result has been perverted.

I have fallen into an undesirable, evil situation,
On a stage of imperishable iniquity.

However, the marvelous crown prince
Kumaradvitiya and his brave ministers
Are masters of superior power and strength.
They will extend an unfailing strong rope of compassion.
So, for a short time, in this kingdom
I can do nothing but partake of its nature.

Yet I am still young, an immature fresh flower
Which strong sunlight can harm.
I shall have to beguile them with deceptive words,
For I think it easier to die than to be
The lover of this sinful, odious prince. This I pledge."

Thus, the inner thoughts of each of them
Arose in completely different ways.

King Chandramati settled down onto his lofty, elevated throne with
these very pleasant thoughts in Manohari's praise. He cleared his throat,
and with a smile he said to her:

As a result of massive and powerful positive energy,
All the earth without a lack is under my control.
This excellent kingdom of Myriad Lights
Enjoys the marvelous festivities of a golden age.

You are the essence of all the world's beauty.
Obtaining you, O worthy lady,
Opens the door to an increase of prosperity,
As the waxing moon continually becomes whiter.

Manohari, you are famed throughout the world
As an enchanting maid who can be gazed at insatiably.
Your face is as gorgeous as the full moon:
From each tooth in your smile, white light streams forth.

Before you, every resolute man
Trembles and bows like a lily.

What can be said about salacious men such as myself?
As the essence fulfilling our hopes, know you are welcome.

Have you your loving parents' permission?
Was the long journey tiring or pleasant?
With a pretty smile please tell me about your travels.

Manohari knew she should sweetly answer his questions, but unbearable sorrow choked her throat. She hung her head, pretending to examine the lines of her hands, and said nothing. Just then Uddhatamanas Mokshabhadra got up from his seat. He went into the center of the large celebration stage and said in a highly elevated manner:

The jeweled crowns of countless rulers
Touch the lotus-cushion of your footstool.
Powerful Emperor of the Universe, Lord of Men,
You protect myself and others with compassion.
Please listen!

On cushioned seats in this wonderful setting,
We sit enjoying your amazing beneficence.
Here there are many inflated with wisdom and courage,
But only I could bear to lose my life
To accomplish the aims of our perfect lord.

Manohari is a perfect and beautiful queen.
Her face is like the new moon's light on an ocean.
She is a skilled speaker, able to compose
Sweet, harmonious speeches of profound meaning.
However, she hangs her head like a beggar woman
In the great presence of the Earth Lord and his son.

So today I will express from my throat
The nature of our situation. Please attend.

With stalwart efforts we triumphed over
The difficulties of the long road to the north.
Arriving near the kingdom of Radiant Array,
It seemed the mountains on every side
Had sunk down into the earth:
So extensive is the acrid plain called Endless Gulch.

There we saw the crafty minister of Gem of the World,
A master of the ghoulish demons' arts,
The one known as the hero Bhavakumara,
Now standing by the side of the outer gate.

He was in command of a hundred soldiers.
Deceitfully raising himself in haughty pride
Like the wind, he was carrying off
This lovely, lustrous Champaka bloom.

Then my forces and I gathered up our strength,
For we had your splendid orders as our task.
When fearsome weapons mixed in a heated battle
My thousand lowly comrades had but little might.

But like the Lord of Stars amid the constellations,
I was fearless; my ocean of skills was unbeatable.
I reduced them to a mere name!
Renowned Manohari is now our prince's bride.
This good fortune is thanks to my efforts alone.

Although no one else helped,
This one called Chetadasa, unable to vie with me,
Surrendered respectfully and did something a bit useful.
Thus, he is worthy of your protection.
My lord, it is as you wish:
These words are honest and devoid of deceit.

So sweet and euphonious were these words begging for favor that
King Chandramati and his son took them to be true. In joyful appreciation, they praised Uddhatamanas Mokshabhadra, made him prime minister of the realm, and granted him a large district as his personal fief-
dom. Chetadasa, too, was satisfied with many excellent presents and was
made an inner palace servant. As for those remaining from that army of
a thousand men: a few were executed; some had their arms, legs, fingers,
or toes chopped off; several were tortured; and all the rest were caused
to suffer incomprehensible misery.

Some people do not possess clairvoyance,
So they investigate the subtle details

Of every aspect of a cycling wave of actions
Before they begin. This is worthy of praise.
Who would be so foolish as to do every deed
Without any scruple or analysis,
Or to seize as completely true sweetly spoken,
Deceptive words as soon as they are heard?

That force of a thousand was greatly reduced in battle.
Those who remained to return home were blameless,
But the king did not question them.
Following another's crooked words,
He punished his own servants,
The rightful objects of his compassion.
From improper, sinful actions such as these
Come results which are difficult to bear.

Most of the other ministers praised the new prime minister among themselves: "This brave and courageous minister has ably demonstrated his extensive power on this occasion. He masterfully dominated our endeavors to obtain a perfect queen for Prince Devatisha. He forced the commander of the forces of Gem of the World, that boastful competitor, to follow behind him. After completely destroying the enemy forces, he has happily returned to Myriad Lights. It is difficult to express such forceful competency!" Hundreds of flowery praises were strewn about.

However, Brahmadhimat, and some other ministers who had superior intelligence, thought differently: "Here today Uddhatamanas Mokshabhadra was able to offer this superior maiden to our young prince's dominion. We have sought for Manohari for a long time, yet is it right to praise his deeds as good? The others are happy that the enemy forces were decimated and these ministers of Gem of the World were dragged along as prisoners. However, when one analyzes and considers this, it is not good at all.

"In the land know as Gem of the World, the king and his ministers are masters of power and strength. In the skilled arts of war, they do not trail behind anyone else. They are so proud of their superior heroism that they are bold enough to vie with the fearsome Lord of Death. They will not be able to bear actions which discredit them like this.

"As soon as they know of these events, they will surely make preparations for a fierce war. The four branches of their armies, unbearable to view, will be drawn up quickly. They will come to defeat us so completely that not even the name of Myriad Lights will ever be spoken again. Our minister's actions were the first step toward that end."

Feeling extremely worried, Brahmadhimat and the others rested their cheeks in their hands and painfully sighed long and loud. Seeing such behavior, the king realized that they were sorrowful.

"O Minister Brahmadhimat, you are exhibiting behavior indicative of unhappy thoughts. Tell me what is at fault."

"O god among men, please view me kindly! I have little strength and intelligence. Uddhatamanas Mokshabhadra and his forces performed their present duty well. But, in the long run, I wonder if we can bear to compete with the powerful king and ministers of Gem of the World. So joy and sorrow contend with each other in my thoughts."

Then the king snapped in reply: "Your intelligence is even less than a woman's! You are quibbling contrarily! You ignoramus! You do not know anything. Be quiet!"

The king's dislike of those words resulted in this sharp scolding of the superior and perfect minister Brahmadhimat. His lord's harsh, angry words were like swords piercing the minister's heart.

Throughout this time, the hero Bhavakumara had no seat; he was still standing outside the inner palace gates. He saw how Uddhatamanas Mokshabhadra fooled the king with deceitful lies. He also saw Chetadasa made an inner palace servant. He felt extreme hatred toward them both.

He promised himself, "Although I dearly wish to harm them all, I must disguise my thoughts. For a while I must take up the sole expedient means at my disposal. In the end I will destroy this king, his ministers, and particularly those two of his entourage."

So, with gentle and submissive behavior, he paid respectful homage to the king. He extolled him, lauded him, and in a cowering, servile manner prostrated himself completely before King Chandramati. Finally, holding his palms together the way a lotus closes in the evening, he put his hands to the crown of his head, and said:

> Eh ma ho!
> I bow to the best of the greatest Lord of Men:
> The master of power and wealth who controls
> The extent of the earth because of the power and
> Increase of his superior wisdom and merit.
>
> The Earth Lord named Chandramati
> Is an inexhaustible treasury,
> Your virtues are those of the moon:
> A source of the light of pure loving wisdom,

Gloriously radiating great beauty
Impartially upon all beings.
You are the night lily's refuge and friend.

These sweet praises are sung
At every point of the compass without exception.
Thus, it is no longer suitable for me
To be a lowly minister of Kumaradvitiya.

Even at the time of entering the battle,
I did not fight according to my abilities
Because of the awakening of former propensities
And my long-held, extremely respectful hope
To be close to you, O Lord of Men.

Although I lack any skill, fortitude,
Or expertise in the ocean of martial arts,
I am a master of mental machinations,
Accepting responsibility to accomplish my lord's purposes.

If I obtain the good fortune
To work as the lowliest of your servants,
Even if I am to be a mere shepherd,
This one named Chetadasa could not match me.
Let my ability and intelligence be your personal slaves.

Although the sun is high in the heavens,
It protectively shines on the lotus ponds below.
Similarly, you are above other rulers' crowns.
But I hope you will hurl your long lasso
Of compassion and great love around even me.
Please grant this wish to a lowly youth!

Uddhatamanas Mokshabhadra was pleased, because this speech did not contradict his own account. Therefore, he praised Bhavakumara as suitable to be a servant.

The other ministers concurred: "There is no doubt that, despite his extreme youth, this young man has the skill of a great master in harmoniously composing verses. As it is said, 'A wise minister is worth relying upon, even if he was your enemy in the past.' Thus, he is worthy to be your servant."

So Bhavakumara was installed as a retainer of Devatisha.

10

In which Manohari convinces her husband not to consummate their marriage

THEN THE RITUAL MARRIAGE CELEBRATION reached its conclusion. When the sun set into the western ocean and the moon and stars were shining as brightly as they could, Prince Devatisha was desirous of sexual union. He made his way to one of the palace chambers called the lovely suite, for its various comforts and beautiful features could not be matched even in the realm of the gods. There Devatisha and Manohari were to live together.

He made this pledge to Manohari, lusting for the bliss of satisfying his desire with her for the first time:

"The peak of the wish-granting tree of your lineage
Is an exquisite, youthful flower.
This heavy bloom is the best of enchanting women.
No sweet breeze other than I can make it flutter.

The tight strictures of karma draw you,
My good fortune, to the garden stage of Myriad Lights.
I am the brilliant Lord of the Day:
The unblemished glory of this glittering sun
Glows with passion to make love to only you.

You are the lovely, alluring night.
From the crevasse of the eastern mountains
Between your firm, round thighs,
My hand as the first dawn light

Will raise your soft, misty gown to your waist.
Then will you not enjoy the bliss of sexual embrace?"

He repeated again and again melodious words
Expressing the heart of his passion,
With an essence so very sweet
It was like the taste of honey.

Tormented by lust, his body shuddered
Like a vine in the breeze.
He came to the pretty maiden's bed,
Uttering those words of sexual arousal
To obtain the fruit of his desire.

Then lovely Manohari said in reply:

O enchanting god, protector of the earth, heavens, and below!
I have prayed for a long time to be with you.
The mere sight, sound, touch, or recollection
Of your wondrous ocean of virtues captivates my heart.

My mind is overjoyed and my hair stands on end
Thinking of the loving propensities of so many lives
Which culminate in our fortuitous meeting
In this wonderful, fortunate place.

It is natural for fierce, strong sunlight
To wilt an immature, fresh lotus bud.
Yet full sunlight is best for a developed flower.

Similarly, I am yet young, a juvenile of tender age.
At this time I will surely meet my death
If sexually involved with you, my marvelous prince.

Therefore, O prince, I beg you, do not abuse me now!
Wait until I have matured! At the age of sixteen,
I will be like a flower in full, open bloom.
Then it will be proper for you like a bee
To enter and blissfully partake of the honey of my embrace.

Consider this example well:
If a wealthy man uses up

All his possessions at one time
Will he not later always suffer like a pauper?

Yet another point to ponder:
Lower-class folk, like animals,
Meet and immediately enjoy sexual relations.
Nobility, like the sun and moon, proceed sedately and subtly.

When you reflect upon the matter like this,
How can we transgress the behavior of the worthy?
O Lord of Men, profound and vast treasury of wisdom,
I speak the truth, please consider this well!

Her extremely respectful manner and devious strategy confused him completely. She succeeded in disguising her age. He thought:

"When I examine Manohari's countenance, behavior, and words, there is no doubt that she cherishes the propensity to love me. If I take her for my pleasure before she is mature, it would be a crime. It might even kill her. Her examples truly illustrate reality: a lotus without fully opened petals will be scorched and wilted by fierce sunlight. Thus, I should not destroy my long-term happiness lusting for an instant of happiness right now. I must be strong for a while."

Thinking this, he emitted a long, drawn-out sigh and returned to his own bed. All night he was tortured by the sharp pain of lust. He did not sleep at all.

There are four types of sleepless persons: ascetics engaged in their austerities, people terrified of robbers and thieves, men whose minds are caught up in desire for a woman, and women who are bound by their love for a man. Here we have a case of the third.

The prince decided it would be unsuitable for him to ravish her before she was fully mature. So, from the very next day, even their residences were separate.

The maiden of sixteen, perfect in every respect,
Like a lovely moon, a paradigm of worldly beauty,
Dwelt in the lily of the Lord of Men's mind.
He longed for the bliss of sexual consummation.

But her artful actions and expressions
Were skillful and profoundly wise means to avoid him.
The prince was unable to perceive that
He was trapped in the cage of total confusion.

Turned away from his object of desire,
He lost his opportunity for sexual union.
Each watch of every night seemed as long as a year
As he experienced the suffering of unrequited arousal.

His young flesh wasted away.
His complexion waned and his hair fell out.
Even his lovely eyes fell into hollows.
He became exceedingly unpleasant to see!

Not long after that, as a result of the force of his jealousy of
Bhavakumara, Chetadasa thought, "I must definitely use some trick to
vanquish him."

So he went to the quarters of Devatisha and spoke very respectfully:
"O youthful god, please attend to me! Please hear these few words
which come directly from my heart. This man known as the hero
Bhavakumara is the best of the ministers of Gem of the World.
Because he is their master of strength and intellect, he could never
show proper esteem for King Chandramati and his son. It is like this
example: you can heat water until it boils away, but you can never
make it part of the fire itself. In a similar way, what need is there to
speak of relying upon this man as one of your ministers? It is more
suitable to kill him!"

Devatisha also was also jealous of Bhavakumara's youthful charm,
intelligence, and courage. Therefore, the force of these words struck his
mind.

"O minister, what you said is true! I will have it done just as you
suggest."

He went to inform his father of his intention. But the king did not
think that Chetadasa's analysis reflected the case at all. He replied:

"Young man, consider this well! If you kill a youth with profound
intelligence, will other wise men praise you as a hero? Has this young
man any chance to harm us now that he is without armed forces,
friends, or power? Therefore, you should understand what is stated in
our histories, 'It is sensible to rely upon your enemy if he has the insight
of a wise man.' So do not be jealous. Let him live in peace."

Although this was good advice, the prince did not enjoy hearing it.
His hatred prevented any obstruction to his murderous intentions. So
he bribed a few ministers to assassinate Bhavakumara. Contented with
their presents, the men made arrangements for the killing.

Manohari came to know about all that had occurred. She went to

Devatisha and prostrated herself before him. Courteously and reverently she supplicated him.

"Please see me, O Son of the Gods! Please do not do any evil actions which will ripen badly in this and other lives. Do not act under the influence of demonic jealousy. It doesn't matter if this man Bhavakumara is your friend or your enemy right now. Because he excels in the skills of the wise, if you protect him properly he will surely become the best of your ministers. On the other hand, if you kill a young man of such intelligence, the weapons of worldly curses will surely destroy you. O youthful god, I have no loving thought or desire for any man other than yourself. So without any deceit, abandoning all crooked words, I state these thoughts free from any artifice. Please consider them!"

Devatisha thought about what she had said. "It is absolutely impossible that Manohari would ever speak falsely to me. Chetadasa spoke improperly."

Heeding her words, he retracted his evil orders and made Bhavakumara his closest personal retainer.

11

In which Prince Kumaradvitiya decides to wage war to rescue Manohari

DURING THE TIME ALL THIS OCCURRED, the few survivors of the hundred men who had accompanied Bhavakumara slowly made their way toward the palace of Gem of the World. They were in a sorry state. They were without horses and weapons, so they came by foot, leaning on walking sticks because of wounds on every limb.

King Suryamati and his son observed them approaching from the palace battlements. As they came closer, the king and prince could see that the men either had been routed in a fight with the enemy or had been brought low by brigands. They were unsure of which, so with their ministers they went out to meet them. The king said:

"Kye! Those who live under my command should know what has happened to you. Please tell us how you came to such a pitiable state. Why are you so feeble? Why has your strength so diminished that you stagger, coursing unevenly like a raven that has lost its shoulder feathers? Why do you lack mounts and weapons?"

The exhausted servants prostrated themselves before the king, collapsing to the ground as if they were felled trees. The eldest among them, a man with hair shot through with white and a brow wrinkled like a well-cut carpet, folded his hands together and said in a low, almost inaudible voice:

O supreme lords who rule the world,
You are treasuries of immeasurable, perfect kindness;

Like mothers you lovingly protect your servants.
O father and son, kindly listen to me a moment.

The hero Bhavakumara and his companions
Were supreme warriors of the heaven, earth, and below.
But those fearless, courageous men in armor
Were pierced in the side by a thorn:
The evil deception of our comrade Chetadasa.

Together we bore the travails of the long journey.
When we arrived near the palace of that kingdom
So lovely to see called Radiant Array,
The hero Bhavakumara, a repository of knowledge
And a treasury of masterful wisdom,
Sent a love letter to Manohari indirectly,
Via the lotus palms of a maiden water carrier.

Manohari is adept at captivating firmly chaste men.
She is a seductive young woman:
With glancing, long-lidded, Utpala-petal eyes,
And cheeks blushing like red dawn on a full-moon face.
Her marvelous beauty surpasses even the goddesses'.

She accepted the missive and went with her maids
To the verdant groves of the pleasure gardens.
She pretended to go to playfully bathe
In the pools of perfect water,
Amidst the trees filled with sweetly singing birds.
Really she hastened to see your face, Prince Kumaradvitiya.

Bhavakumara put on superb clothes and jewels
To disguise himself as the prince.
But Manohari is like an experienced seafarer:
She discerned a minister or some intelligent man
But not the prince was approaching her.
Wondering, she melodiously questioned him.
Then Bhavakumara spoke the truth, no longer able to lie.

She came with us because of her love
For you who bear the name Kumara.
So we turned our mounts to quickly return here.

When we came to Endless Gulch, a desert plain
So vast the sky seems to touch the earth on all sides,
We saw from afar the approach of Uddhatamanas Mokshabhadra,
A minister of Myriad Lights boastful of his martial prowess.

With him was an army numbering ten hundred men.
The sharp points of their spears reached the sky.
Their fluttering, fringed banners furled far and wide.
White light glinted off their armor and weapons.
Their horses' hooves beat the earth like a drum.

Then Manohari and her maidservants
Disguised themselves by wearing men's clothes.
Relying on that and Bhavakumara's spoken ruses,
We fooled them and continued upon our way.

However, Chetadasa cannot tell friend from foe.
He bared his evil nature and betrayed us to them.
That army pursued us like a meteor.
As soon as we saw that, Bhavakumara said:

"Even if my body and life are trampled into the dust
Of the battlefield of our bellicose fight,
I can bear it. For today I can repay the kindness
Of our ruler, the best of princes, Kumaradvitiya,
Who has kindly protected me for so long."

The fearless youth then entered the fray.
He began to fight with marvelous courage and
Pride in his fierce, heroic powers.
In a short time he was near to subduing the enemy.

They shivered like poisonous snakes
In front of a terrifying, adamantine-beaked eagle.
Their ability to rival him was minimal:
The loud sound of their weeping and wailing
Filled the earth completely.

But yet again Chetadasa deceived that great hero.
His power lessened and our army's strength reduced,

We could contend no longer.
A burden of unwished for suffering pressed heavily
Upon Manohari: we saw her led away.

Kye hu! So many previously accumulated black,
Negative deeds came to fruition all at once.
Please consider this well in the depths of your hearts,
Do not cease to regard us with loving compassion!

King Chandramati and his forces are too weak to fight back;
They have struck their bare fists against a sword blade.
Without cowardice we should reduce them to a mere name!
This will be but trivial sport for the marvelous treasure,
The ocean of fearlessness and able prowess,
Prince Kumaradvitiya, and his ministers.

Since there is no doubt you can conquer our foe,
The noble maid Manohari, a paragon of beauty
Renowned far and wide, and heroic Lord Bhavakumara,
Do not lack a leader or a protector.
Please bring about a compassionate rescue
Of those two oppressed by a burden of sorrow.
This is our hope; may it have a good result.

From start to finish he spoke properly and truly. He told the entire tale in
clear words, in a manner untainted by trickery. The handsome faces of the
king and his ministers, like full moons, were usually a pleasure to see. But
now dark clouds of anger obscured those orbs. Their flashing smiles transformed into infuriated expressions, and harsh, incensed words were said.

The minister Virendra was the first to react. Without the slightest
hesitation, he laughed, slapped his right thigh, and said:

The vast pleasure gardens of the immortals' abode
Have in essence come to earth here.
This singular gem of all the world
Is a place which humbles all arrogant men.

Like the sun in the sky, our Lord of Men
Adroitly controls the earth to the horizons
Of this noble kingdom esteemed by the multitudes.

A lesser ruler, a lowly firefly,
Attempts to defy you.
That tricky, unseemly King Dyutimat
Has acted improperly and contentiously.
He is a field where poisonous plants grow.

Thus, first of all, let us destroy him.
Afterward, I will happily reduce
Myriad Lights to a mere name.
Please let me be the leader of our armies.
Let us quickly engage in ferocious warfare!

As he made this brave speech, the minister Abhayabalahanta thought:
"It is not necessary to destroy the kingdom of Radiant Array; they are
in the palm of our hand. It would be better to conquer Myriad Lights
first, because they are arrogant and powerful." As soon as Virendra finished speaking, he spoke his mind in a loud, forceful tone:

This lord of all ferocious heroes
Spoke honest words; their meaning is good to hear.
He said, "I have disgust for the evil king
Who acts contrary to the wishes
Of our high Earth Lords, the king and his son,
So first, let us destroy him."

Although this is perfectly true,
Our primary and most potent enemy
Is the Earth Lord known as Chandramati.
Let us prepare for a battle to annihilate him,
His crown prince, and all his ministers.

After we have reduced them to nothing but a name,
The weak and powerless King Dyutimat
Will be in the palm of our hand.
There is no point in fighting with him.
Now our fearless armies should go
Quickly to the realm of Myriad Lights.

The minister Abhayavrati thought, "It does not make the slightest bit of
difference which of those two kingdoms we conquer first. It will be as easy
to destroy them as it is for the rising sun to dispel the darkness of night. But
it is not right to leave Manohari and Bhavakumara in such a miserable state,

so I will exhort the king to make preparations for war with Myriad Lights."

Abhayavrati's eyebrows arched in indignation, causing his brow to wrinkle. He said:

> Kye! Lord of Men, please look upon me!
> Myriad Lights is powerful,
> But although it has countless ministers
> And subjects as many as the stars in the sky,
> They do not emit a strong, piercing light.
> They are weak, slumbering in the dark.
>
> Just as the sun's power outshines the stars,
> Our lord's fearless skill fiercely radiates,
> Conquering his dark enemies with a single light ray.
> The glorious sun among men who gives joy to all
> Is Prince Kumaradvitiya, brave and wise.
> Who could rival the powerful force of his merits?
>
> The bodies and minds of the rulers of Radiant Array
> Are as feeble and irresolute as a firefly's light.
> They will flicker out and capitulate to us,
> After we annihilate our primary, irredeemably evil enemy.
>
> A person who could rival our prince
> Does not exist anywhere in the world.
> Therefore, without hesitation
> I volunteer to lead our fourfold army.
> If we delay, will you not feel pity
> For lovely Manohari and the wise Bhavakumara?

The king and all the ministers except Laksaikadvitiya agreed to this proposal to quickly raise up an army to march on Myriad Lights. He, the bravest and wisest of all those courageous men, wanted to destroy both enemy kingdoms simultaneously.

His face changed color, his eyes opened wide, and he wrung his hands. Like an eagle with an irrepressible desire to fly off to destroy the realm of poisonous snakes, he said in an imperious, angry voice:

> O Lords of Men, you make use of the wondrous earth
> As the heirs of powerful emperors of the universe!
> You destroy evil enemies like the Lord of Death,
> And you lovingly protect your subjects with peace.

Kingly father and son, verily the sun and moon,
To you I speak sincere words worthy to be heard.

In the past I never acted dishonorably,
Enjoying besting our enemies.
However, while we were living peaceably
This cursed pair of foes
Arose to try to vie with us.
These insatiable men may succeed for a time,
But in the end they will be ruined.

I can no longer bear their infringements.
Our rivals are fools who beat their heads
Against an unbreakable adamantine mountain.
I can face them alone! What need be said about an army!

So there is no need at all
For you to stir from your lion throne,
O youthful god, the soul of all living creatures,
And the one who sustains our well-being.

Send me to do the fierce work of war.
I will raze to a heap of rubble
Flowering Estate, the capital of Myriad Lights,
Sparing the Earth Lord Chandramati and his heir, Devatisha,
Only in order to make them our slaves!

With immeasurable love and compassion,
You viewed even evil Chetadasa with equanimity.
Now I will chop his heart into bits to eat!
I will suffer to drink a mouthful of his warm blood!

Sweet songs in praise of Manohari pervade the universe.
Her lovely form has no rival in the world.
This noble lady we have sought so long
Will be crowned as our superior queen.

I shall attack them in the hope of rescuing
The one renowned as the hero Bhavakumara.
Although he is young, he is fearless,
A superb warrior, and wise as an elder.

If I cannot accomplish these slight tasks,
What else could I do to repay the kindness
Of the lord who protected me for so long?
How can I be proud of my ability to fight the enemy
If I cannot fulfill the wishes of my clansmen?

The deceitful and crafty King Dyutimat
Is a mere adjunct to our real,
Arrogant, and contentious foe.
But he and his subjects will be destroyed.

This work will not be difficult in the least.
I will take on these despicable enemies simultaneously.
I have the confidence to vanquish them.
Later it will be clear my harsh words are true;
You will know it by my deeds.

If one can do battle without regard for life or limb,
Conquering a million foes becomes a mere game;
Even a fierce enemy warrior will be an object of pity,
One can beguile masters of trickery,
And take the wealth of the foe as your ornament.

Not a hair of a regal lion ruffles
In the face of a herd of innumerable elephants.
Just so, a man who has mastered all varieties of heroism
Does not fear a field swarming with the enemy.
He destroys them all simultaneously, without distinction.

So, O Lord of Men, please remain here happily.
Give me the chance to do this task!

When this minister spoke of his brave intentions, King Suryamati smiled broadly. His minister's words pleased and delighted him.

"O flawless best of warriors, it is true, it is true. It shall be done just as you have said."

Prince Kumaradvitiya thought, "Because Laksaikadvitiya is a superb warrior, his words are not mere idle bluster. I have no doubt he could accomplish his aims.

"However, if we achieve our goal of making Manohari my wife, the rulers of Radiant Array become my relations by marriage. Thus, it would be unsuitable to destroy them. These ministers will not like to hear the situation explained like this. I shall have to chose my words skillfully to convince them we should not harm Radiant Array."

So, with a smiling countenance, he spoke to his father, Suryamati, and the assembled ministers:

Each courageous minister has enunciated his own wish.
If undertaken, those tasks would easily be done.
Yet I have carefully analyzed and impartially considered,
Honorable father and advisers, please listen to my words.

Myriad Lights, with its proficient and valiant ministers,
Is our main foe; we must conquer them first.
There is no point in vanquishing powerless
Radiant Array, the mere basis of our dispute.

When a forest fire is ignited by a small lamp flame,
Is it any use to douse the lamp
Saying, "This flame started it all,"
Without first quelling the blazing forest?

Therefore, we should first conquer
The unseemly powerful forces of Myriad Lights.
Then Radiant Array will naturally become ours,
Even if their pathetic forces have the conceit to fight.

I too am exceedingly pleased to engage in battle.
I go to war like a king of swans
Eagerly strives to dive into a lake.

From my youth I assiduously practiced the martial arts
And perfected the skills used by wise men.
What is the use of all that training
If the result is no help in subduing our foes?

Some men harass their retainers in court.
And at home, in front of their womenfolk,
They loudly proclaim their heroic deeds,
Proudly boasting of their fearless behavior.

Yet when the time of battle
With the enemy draws nigh,

They cower in fear.
Such men are despicable!

Thus, if I do not go to battle
And remain here at home,
The censure of the world shall destroy me:
What difference will there be between me and a girl?

Therefore, O parent, please give me your
Permission to go to war!

If I kill many men of Myriad Lights in battle,
It would be a heavy sin.
However, that will not be necessary.
They will surrender when they see a few of my skills.

Nubile Manohari and I are profoundly joined
By unobliteratable deeds and prayers
Held dear to our hearts for a long time.
I must arrange for her shining white happiness.

Bhavakumara must be freed from
His heavy burden of sorrows.
I shall quickly go as the leader of our forces
In order to complete the fruition of our hopes.

After he made this announcement, he left the council to prepare his
mighty adamantine helmet and armored corselet. He readied his
weapons to subdue the enemy, and he gave orders to his subjects for the
quick departure of the four branches of the army. The heroic and
courageous ministers also arranged for war.

12

In which the preparations for war are described

WHEN THE GREAT ARMY WAS READY TO MARCH, you could hardly bear to look at it. The elephants were as immense as mountains; the horses were as large as elephants; the chariots were as enormous as palaces; and the foot soldiers were as tall as plantain trees.

"The prince had brave and heroic tendencies from the moment of his birth. There is no doubt about it even now; his words and actions clearly show he is quite happy to go off to war. Yet he is very young, a flower which has just bloomed. Surely he will be killed: it is absolutely wrong for me to let him go." Thus thought King Suryamati, so he spoke these loving words:

O child, you hold the wisdom of our ancestors,
Masterfully knowing the proper thing to do.
No one can come close to your vast skill.
O seed of this race, listen to your father's words.

We have many courageous and able ministers
And an army with four divisions
To engage in battle to destroy our foes.
Their fierce deeds will annihilate
The enemy host easily and instantaneously.

Because they could never
Be conquered by an enemy power,

There is no need for you to lead the army,
Without regard for your body and life.

Therefore, it is not right for you to engage in war.
Please remain happy and at ease here.

After he spoke, the prince entreated him:

"Great in both years and wisdom,
Honorable father, Suryamati,
I beg you to consider:

Is it right to hoist a victory banner
Lacking a precious crown ornament?
Similarly, if an army has no leader,
What enemy would fear it in battle?

Since this task is not difficult in the least,
It is certainly right to give me permission
To go with the force of a king of eagles
Amidst the deep and vast ocean of our armies."

Although this was bravely and loudly said,
King Suryamati was unbearably pained.
"It is unsuitable for the prince to go,"
He thought yet again, and he said:

"Only a father can properly exhort his son,
For he alone knows the correct path.
There is no necessity for you to go to war
As the single leader of our armies.
O prince, you shall remain in your parents' home.

We have many brave and heroic ministers,
Masters of Brahma's wisdom and Vishnu's skill.
The jewel among them, the minister Laksaikadvitiya,
Has been appointed our troops' commander."

Although he heard the calm, loving words
Of a father who could not bear to part,
His desire to go was too difficult to resist:
It was a torrential river bearing him along.

He respectfully bowed to his father
And again clearly spoke of his character.

"O holder of the ornament of great learning,
Please consider the purport of my entreaty.
On top of a conqueror's victory banner,
One should put a precious wish-fulfilling gem.
If you place a lesser ornament there,
Can it rain forth what is needed and desired?

Similarly, what wise man would be fooled
If a servant is called 'king,'
And appointed to lead the realm's army?
So how can we accomplish our desires this way?

If you begin a task without consideration,
You fall into a chasm of unpleasant anxiety
And cannot follow a proper course of action.
So, O father, consider this matter well.

Although you are moved by kindness for me,
It is time for me to earn my reputation.
Who will believe your exalted praise of me
When you wish me to remain at home?

I do not lack ability to contend with the enemy.
So how can I say that I am rightly your son
If I cannot subdue the barbarian enemy hosts
Who angrily act to disturb our peace?

If a son befriends his father's enemy,
The son himself is verily a foe.
Then he will become an object of scorn
Even if he was known to be skilled and wise.

That improper course I will not follow.
My enthusiastic intentions cannot be ignored,
So this task at hand is what I will undertake.
If the sound of a victory drum beat in triumph
Over the enemy ringing from the peak of the world
Pleases you, my father, you should have no worries!"

A superlative warrior goes to battle as happily as we go to visit our friends and relations. King Suryamati knew that such an attitude cannot be obstructed. So when he heard Prince Kumaradvitiya's words he thought:

"I am totally without an answer to my son. His desire to go to war is irreversible. He has wisdom far beyond the comprehension of ordinary beings and superior mastery of the martial arts. The enemy will be unable to oppress him. I must accede to his desires. I can find no means to do otherwise." So he said:

> O son, as soon as you were conceived
> In Kundaladhara's womb, auspicious signs
> In the heavens, earth, and intervening space
> Made us rejoice in our good fortune.

> At your birth we saw your propensity
> For heroism and bravery. Nurtured,
> You soon mastered all the sciences,
> Intuiting every object of knowledge.

> Naturally, without any need for practice,
> You became skilled in every art.
> Now you are Brahma's equal in the world,
> I cannot oppose you. I grant your wish.

> However, I have heard it said,
> A lion vain of his fearlessness
> May be tricked and conquered by a clever rabbit.
> So, even if you have powerful courage,
> You need profound wisdom.

> If you enter into battle bravely conceited
> Without making your mind clever and adroit,
> You may jump like a bear into the proud enemy host,
> But such heroics will forfeit your life!

> Ready yourself well to avoid later distress.
> Be confident that you can rely
> On adamantine armor to protect your life,
> Your weapons, mounts, and so forth
> Needed to destroy the enemy legions.

Some foes come down from the sky like meteors.
Others like worms emerge from the womb of the earth.
There is no knowing from where a crafty foe may come,
So at all times, unceasingly, use army sentinels.

Once you have entered into the battle,
If you reverse your intent, and lead a retreat,
You will be cursed by all the beings
Living in all the world.

When victor and vanquished seem indistinguishable
Because countless heaps of corpses stain the ground
Red with blood like the Death Lord's realm,
Be brave and pitilessly kill the foe.

After you conquer the enemy leaders,
Even if many contentious foes remain,
They will be weak and easy to subdue.
It is a heavy sin to kill them all then.

When cowards unable to vie with you
Come to surrender, do not be angry.
Do not say, "You are my enemy!"
For they come to accept you as their leader.

In general, do not kill with enmity
Any person who comes to the battle.
For in the end, whatever you do,
The weak foes are in the palm of your hand.

However, evil men with minds like sword blades
May seem to be pacified and contained.
But in the end, they will show their ferocious nature.
Therefore, kill them or train them soothingly.

Men like the nefarious Chetadasa
Deceive their relations in hope of new friends.
They may do some deeds to benefit you,
Yet they should not be relied upon or trusted.

Reward the heroic wise men of your forces
Who display courage in their efforts

To vanquish the enemy hordes.
Then, others will become increasingly brave.

Only verbally exhort weaker men
Who are timorous and fear to see the foe.
Punishment will yield the dreadful result
Of defection to the enemy to divulge our secrets.

O noble son, leader of the fearless host,
Go before all our heroic ministers
To endeavor to fill the entire universe with
The sweet repute of our foe's annihilation.

I have no claim to wisdom or bravery,
But age grants me knowledge of the ways of the world.
Rely upon what I have instructed
And you will know what to do and avoid.
May you attain the fruit of all your hopes!

King Suryamati properly instructed his son on how to engage
in battle when he realized he could not block his going to war.
The prince and the ministers joyfully and respectfully saluted the
king.

When Queen Kundaladhara heard the chant "The prince is to head
the army!" she became quite distraught. She went to him and spoke of
her great love that could not bear the pain of his departure from his
place of origin:

I am a mother who loves her son.
Never have I spoken to you improperly.
Thus, now you must listen to my frail uttering
Of a lament about a torture difficult to endure.

The seven-horse chariot of the sun goes
To all four continents, not just one.
It alone can fill space with a glorious light,
Awakening all beings from dark nescience.

The eagle, lord of the sky, does not stay in his nest.
He goes to the ocean's far shore
To combat the race of poisonous snakes.
Because he has no entourage, perforce he must go alone.

Our ministers and powerful army
Have the courageous ability to conquer
The innumerable enemy hosts alone.
There is absolutely no reason for you to go!

How can you bear to go to war and leave
Your loving, protective father and frail mother?

She spoke hoping to stop the prince's departure by the force of her love. The prince replied:

O mother, you gave my body life,
Nourished me daily with sweet nectar,
And watched over me with boundless love.
Please listen, O treasury of compassionate kindness!

If it is right for the sun to go to four continents
To raise all beings from the sleep of ignorance,
I should increase the glory, not work to the detriment,
Of this kingdom of Gem of the World.

The diamond-beaked eagle goes with no companions
To the ocean's far shore to conquer the poisonous snakes.
I go with a courageous army: so what difficulty
Can there be for us to reduce them to a mere name?

The four divisions of our fearless armies
Are so large they completely cover the earth.
Yet if I do not go in the forefront,
The army will be a body without a soul.
Then what could it possibly do?

It is right to endeavor to protect one's life
And to find no difficulty in possibly casting it away.
Though my parents have kindly protected me,
I will go far away to battle the enemy.
But once I have achieved my goal of terrorizing the foe,
You shall have the chance to see me soon again.

These mollifying words greatly pained the mind of the queen mother, Kundaladhara. Her tears fell in continuous pearly drops. Unable to bear the pain of separation, she grieved in an almost inaudible voice:

"O youth, you are confident of your powerful skills,
Yet are you sure you will not be killed in battle?
What purpose is there in going to war saying,
'I shall work for the realm not caring for my life'?
What is the point of drawing wonderful figures
In front of wise but completely blind men?

O son, if you do not joyfully heed
The instructions of your loving mother,
Who will be left to adequately protect
Our kingdom, which is like a wish-fulfilling tree
Bowing under a foliage of marvelous wealth
And the fruit of generous charity?

Without you, your mother cannot live.
Please pray that we will have the lot
To be joined together in other lives.
Do you not sorrow that in this life
Our karma to be together has ended today?"

The queen mother was so afflicted with anguish
At the prospect of separation from her adored son,
Her mind became deranged.
Both her eyes streamed with tears.
Her swollen cheeks rested in her hands.

Prince Kumaradvitiya stared fixedly.
Mesmerized by his mother's agony,
He did not move for a long time.

Then, once again he thought,
"It is better not to begin a task;
For to start and then retreat is child's play.
How can a warrior stay at his mother's side
When he has readied himself for battle?
I shall return here quickly,
Untouched by the slightest mishap."

Once again he said to his mother:
"Eh ma! O treasury of immeasurable love.
Honorable mother, please listen to the truth.

I am not going to fight the enemy
Without purpose or without reason.
If we carelessly shrink away from contending
With evil-natured men who cannot bear to see
Any of our work accomplished,
Surely strife will come to this kingdom too.

Our proverbs say: a tiny spark
Ignites a blazing inferno, killing all.
Just so, now our insolent enemy hordes
Lack strength and will be easy to subdue.

These are not just words:
Later you will see the truth in them!
Without the least hindrance or harm,
I will soon return to Gem of the World
To partake of the nectar of my parents' smiles.
So please calm your suffering mind."

He prostrated himself before his mother after he spoke these words
to calm her. His speech was as sweet as the taste of honey. Queen
Mother Kundaladhara gazed at the prince's face with eyes wet with
tears. Finally, she returned to her own residence with an unhappy heart.

13

In which the fearsome army departs on its mission

T HE READY ARMY WAS SO FEARSOME it humbled even the ferocious
hosts of the Lord of Death. It was so large that when it mustered it
filled the space around the castle as if all the stars in the sky had
come down to earth. The light glinting off the men's weapons banished
all darkness, rivaling the brilliance of the sun. The passage of the horses,
elephants, and chariots shook the earth, raising great clouds of dust that
obscured the sky. Lances, spears, swords, and other weapons were held
aloft. The sound of their rattling was like the bellowing of dragons and
the crashing of thunderbolts. So many banners and flags fluttered from
long lances that even the sun and moon were cast into shadow.

Hatred for the enemy intoxicated the hearts of the warriors. Their faces
flushed red, and wrinkles of anger gathered on their brows. They acted as if
they were going to defend the land of men from attack by the ten-headed
demon king of Lanka. The roar of their fiercely heroic battle cries—"Kill!"
"Fight!" and "Ki so!"—seemed to rend the empty space of the heavens.

When everyone was ready, Prince Kumaradvitiya went to the well-
stocked castle armory to take up his helmet and corselet to protect his
body and as many weapons as he would need to destroy the enemy. His
comrades could hardly bear to see the light that blazed forth from his
weapons. Then the prince came out of the palace joyfully confident of
his ability to conquer the enemy. He was like a fearless lion baring sharp
fangs, waving sharp-clawed paws, dancing his mane, and roaring
unabashedly before charging to the center of an innumerable herd of
elephants.

Surrounded by all his powerful and courageous ministers—Virendra, Abhayabalahanta, Laksaikadvitiya, Abhayavrati, and so forth—the prince mounted his charger, Swift Eagle, who was outfitted with a lovely saddle and bridle. He rode to the head of the four-division army. Then this great host, which was difficult to view, was fit to go to Myriad Lights.

> He was like Indra mounted on his elephant Arawan
> With his generals and army of the gods
> Coming forth from their abode on Mount Meru
> To conquer the demons in battle.

> The Lord of Men was young but brave.
> Surrounded by his heroic armed men,
> Whose eyebrows arched with anger,
> He went to subdue the enemy.

> Their weapons blazed with light.
> The horses' hooves raised dust, hiding the sky.
> When the Death Lord's hosts heard
> The confident song of those fearsome heroes,
> They quaked and dropped their weapons!

The wise ministers, Parambhasvaramati and the others, escorted the army for a few leagues. Then they respectfully saluted the prince. With folded hands, Parambhasvaramati said:

> Eh ma ho! Skillful son of the king!
> Wondrous youth who can be marveled at insatiably!
> You have perfected an ocean of martial arts.
> You are the lion among men who destroys the lowly.
> You are a master of able prowess.

> Although the enemy forces cannot defeat you,
> Your parents, we ministers, and all your subjects
> Have a heavy burden of sorrow difficult to bear:
> For you, at a particularly young and tender age,
> Are the king who will lead all our armies
> Going off to conquer our enemies.

> We beseech you, do not be overanxious to destroy them.
> The foes are many, brave, and skilled men.

Heed the methods we have taught to bring them to ruin.
With your bravery and encompassing wisdom,
Go to reduce the enemy to a mere name.
May the white light of your full-moon face
Soon shine down again upon us night lilies.

After his speech, one of the ministers burst out in utter amazement: "For a youth of such a young age bravely to go off to fight the enemy is beyond the bounds of thought!" A few men were agitated and in trepidation found nothing to say. Yet another worried aloud, "This pure youth will surely tire from the difficulties of the arduous road. Then, during the dangers of battle, his ministers and servants will be far away. What sorts of things shall befall him?" All of them suffered the unbearable pain of parting, and tears wet their faces.

When Prince Kumaradvitiya saw his courtiers, he soothingly spoke:

From the earliest time of my youth,
Wish-fulfilling knowledge came to me easily.
Because I am fearless, skilled, and learned,
Listen to the sound of the music of my advice.

For a long time I have had a warrior's ability
To subdue the enemy completely.
No other confident hero in the world
Has my experience in all the martial arts.

It is said that many ants can conquer
A lion vain of his solitary bravado.
I shall not be like that!
I go with peerless companions.

A fearless army of thousands:
Elephants white as clouds and large as mountains,
Horses the size of elephants,
Chariots spacious as palaces,
And infantry tall as plantain trees
Cover every inch of the earth.
Their assorted weapons glitter in the sky.
The shine of indestructible armor banishes darkness.
The heroes loudly shout their battle cry.

Therefore, no adversity shall touch me.
My face, shining bright with light
Like a wonderful full moon on a cloudless night,
Will soon rise again in the sky over this realm.

O wise ministers, who view your ruler with loving respect,
Please listen contentedly
To my sincere, compassionate words of advice.

Good men and bad men are different:
As far apart as heaven and earth.
The end results of their deeds are opposites.
Do not mix black and white actions!

Although some men, intoxicated by evil,
Display themselves beautifully before the king,
Those men who strut like proud peacocks
Are objects of scorn. Do not behave like them.

A man may not know how to honor the king
With well-composed, elegant speeches,
But if he accomplishes his ruler's will
Purely, without deceit, he is worthy of praise.

Some men will speak respectfully to you,
Praising your virtues despite your faults,
But behind your back they slander and curse you.
Cast away such ill-bred, dissimulating behavior.

Although you accomplish with great effort
The commands of your kindly, protective ruler,
Do not be arrogantly proud! Peacefully,
Calmly engage in the superior customs of the nobility.

If a subject honors his sovereign Earth Lord
During times of prosperity, but during adversity
Disrespectfully flies away like a mountain bird,
He is absolutely despicable. Refrain from such deeds.

If you unwaveringly work to accomplish the king's commands,
Always acting according to our ancient customs,

Despite the extremes of prosperity or adversity,
Then you are acting like a superior being, worthy of trust.

Who would behave like a disreputable fool,
Irreverently disclosing state secrets,
Evilly cursing the king while praising himself,
Running away from work but showing up for the feast?

To gain others' trust, do not waste their wealth;
Increase it like a pond during the rains.
Moreover, a superior minister perfects
The methods of extremely pure, virtuous deeds.

Sinful companions encourage you to act
Improperly and to engage in rash deeds.
The advice of evil men blocks the right path.
Endeavor to turn away from such people.

Do not continually chatter senselessly,
But do not refuse to reply to a question.
When it is suitable, clear your throat
And explain matters clearly. That is honorable.

Always urge yourself to follow
The pure deeds of the nobility.
Always be extremely cautious of a man
Infamous for his sins and worldly ways.

Thus, O ministers, like bees in search of honey,
Bear these things continually in mind:
Take up whatever is worthy of praise,
Cutting away the roots of disgraceful behavior.

When he finished speaking, they saluted him: "O Lord of Men, we will do as you say! The advice you have offered us is good. Your father never exhorted us so. Nor did your mother ever instruct us like this. Now we have heard such advice and profited."

Then Prince Kumaradvitiya and his army set forth on the road. Their passage seemed to shake the very earth girdled by the oceans. They went joyously as kings of swans diving into a large lake. The ministers respectfully gazed after them for a long time.

14

In which Manohari despairs

DURING THE PREPARATIONS FOR WAR in Gem of the World, Manohari languished in Myriad Lights; it seemed to her that a very long time had elapsed since her arrival. She thought: "My kind parents have not sent even a short message to me. Surely if Prince Kumaradvitiya loved me, he would be on his way here by now; but I have not heard any hint of that. Could all of them have cast away their love for me?" She sighed continuously.

Her mind was agitated by despair. Her body was also afflicted by sorrow: misery dulled her bright eyes and tangled her long hair. She became so weak and thin her bracelets could slide all the way to her shoulders. Her face, which had been like the full moon, had hollows and was pale, thin, and lean.

One day, in an extremely depressed state of mind, she went with her maidservants to the palisade walk around the golden dome on the rooftop of her residence. There she indolently paced to and fro, listlessly staring at the view. In the direction of Radiant Array, the sky was a stainless clear blue, as glowing and lovely as a sapphire. Masses of fresh white cumulus clouds, like white crystal stupas, languidly floated by. This sight reminded her of her parents. Her heart ached unbearably. She spoke these words of tortured grief:

> In the clear, sapphire blue eastern skies,
> Are clouds like stainless crystal stupas.
> Why do the movements of those amazing shapes
> Remind me so clearly of my loving parents?

I can see from here that below those clouds
Must lie the kingdom of Radiant Array.
I am separated from the place of my origin.
It is but a figure in my mind.

I was unable to follow the commands of
My boundlessly compassionate father, Dyutimat.
I am tortured unbearably by regret,
But I can do nothing but confess my faults.

O loving mother, named after the moon's light,
I should never have parted you from my lily-mind.
How could I have left you to wander to this dark place?
Please see how my karma ripens so unpleasantly.

Then, with slow steps, she walked toward the southern part of the
wide roof terrace. From the south, a pair of wild red ducks soared up
into the sky, emitting clear calls. As soon as she saw them, she thought,
"Those birds must have come from Gem of the World." She further
thought, "This couple makes me suffer anew, for I lack such a loving
husband." Her grief nearly drove her insane. Her face was covered with
tears as she hoarsely wept:

From the vast space of the southern skies,
Come a lovely mated pair of birds,
Who let forth many sweet cries from
The throats of their red-gold bodies.

Do they come from the realm ruling every direction,
The land known as Joyous Groves?
Its heart is the palace in the city Open Lotus,
Esteemed by the multitudes as "Gem of the World."

Is it not tragic that I have not met
The man it should be my lot to wed?
Crown Prince Kumaradvitiya protects the world
In the shade of the white umbrella of his fame.

I transgressed the intentions of my loving parents,
For an image of the youthful prince's form
Arose without cease in the lake of my mind.
So now I have fallen into this deep defile of evil deeds.

Kye ma! I am drained by unbearable sorrow;
I am friendless and all alone.
I am cursed with the ill fortune to be weaker
Than even those simpleminded birds.

I have lost the opportunity to be united
With marvelous Prince Kumaradvitiya in this life.
In some other life may I have the good fortune
To enjoy the bliss of intercourse with him.

As she spoke, the even palisade walk seemed to become a precipice.
In an instant, she tumbled to the floor. Her maidservants were alarmed
and perplexed. They sprinkled her with cool water scented with sandalwood. Revived from her faint by their aid, she again began to
think:

"The wonderful Prince Kumaradvitiya never loosened the tight
noose of love binding us. If his love had been weak, there would have
been no reason for him to have exerted so much effort to obtain me.
Even if now he no longer cares for me, it is utterly impossible that he
could cease to love his intelligent, eloquent minister—a skillful man
who without any hesitation took up as his burden the commands of his
brave lord."

Then another new idea came to her: "I must pray in front of the
statue of the Buddha Munindra given to me by my father as part of my
religious heritage. It has the power to prophesy what is best to do and
to avoid." Manohari had brought only this devotional object with her
on her travels.

So she went down to her rooms and sent her maids away. She
erected a high throne encrusted with many valuable gems for the special statue of the transcendental Buddha. She set out masses of real and
imaginary offerings. The maiden's eyes were red veined and swollen
from weeping, her complexion had deteriorated, and her emaciated
body shuddered miserably, like a thin Tsuta vine in the wind, but she
bowed to the statue hundreds of times. Then, with her hands clasped at
her heart and her knees firmly planted on the floor, she uttered this
prayer:

I bow to the supreme teacher, Lord of the Three Worlds,
Whose enlightened body blazes more brilliantly
Than the light of a thousand suns revolving
Around a mountain of pure refined gold dust.

I prostrate myself before you, an incomparable guide.
In former aeons you attained consummate wisdom,
Stainless good deeds, and miraculous powers.
Your religious practice is fearless in every way,
Triumphing over delusions, death, demons, and aggregates.

I supplicate the one with matchless wisdom:
With mystic power you took seven steps covering
The three realms as soon as you were born.
You are the peerless treasure of the universe.

O lord, you have compassionate power
To accomplish easily whatever is requested.
I place my trust and reliance in only you.
So please send forth your blessings.

The effects of former black, nonwhite deeds
Have now come to fruition upon this suffering maid.
I have cast off my loving parents, who gave me life,
In hopeful desire for marvelous Prince Kumara.

Despite my faith in that lord like the sun,
I am blanketed by a fog of dark misery.
Poor me! I do not want to be in this kingdom.
The maturation of evil deeds is a heavy burden to bear.

Although I have made many heartfelt prayers
For the prince who has great love for me
To come here quickly as an emperor of the universe,
We have remained apart for a very long time.

Perhaps my love no longer cares for me
Because I have strayed onto an erroneous path.
Then, I should give up all hope for now
And wish to be with him in another life.

Please instruct me what is best to do;
Remove my doubts about his love for me.

As she prayed with concentration from the depths of her heart, the
statue smiled. Light streamed forth from his lips, illuminating the whole

room. The Buddha Munindra granted her wish: "You shall soon achieve your goal." She lauded the sage's words. Finally carefree, she happily rejoiced.

> The meaning of the harmonious words
> Spoken by the Buddha statue
> Were like the taste of sweet nectar.

> Hearing she would soon have what she wished,
> Her mind was freed from the tortured
> Pain of her hundreds of sorrows.

> Although she tried to conceal her
> Radiant smiles and heartfelt laughter,
> Her blissful happiness was clear to see.

So Devatisha once again was entrapped in doubt. With a smile he said to Manohari:

"O lovely one, please heed me. Before, your eyes were swollen because you wept streams of tears. Your mind was tortured by undesirable sorrows. But now you are extremely joyful; you laugh from the heart, and your smile illuminates every direction. Without any pretension, please explain to me truly why your behavior has totally changed."

Maid Manohari replied: "O youthful god, please see me! Because you have wonderful wisdom, discernment, and subtle analytical powers, you will understand the change in the nature of my behavior.

"Up until this time, the cause of my misery, O prince, was that you had to remain alone because I was not mature enough to unite with you in marital bliss. Also during this time, I wondered how we could compete with the armies of Gem of the World, because our ministers are not very wise or brave. Because of fear and ignorance, tears covered my face.

"Now, as to my present smiles and joyful demeanor, O seductive prince with godlike beauty, not long from now we shall unite. Soon we will surely experience the great bliss of sexual union! In addition, the wise lord of warriors, the hero Bhavakumara, is under our command. Even though the armies of Gem of the World are great, no one can rival Bhavakumara's superior intelligence and courage. So I thought: 'Why not rely on him?' Now I remain without a care in the world."

It is said that clever, pretty girls can lead men along the path of fools.

Devatisha was completely deceived by her words, spoken in such an artless and respectful manner.

"Eh ma! I find that ravishing Manohari has never loosened the bonds of her love for me. Also, Bhavakumara really is suitable to rely upon." Thinking this way, he too became happy and joyful.

Then Manohari spoke in extreme secrecy to the hero Bhavakumara: "I prayed with great concentration to the statue of our refuge, lord, and friend, the Buddha Munindra. He prophesied, 'You shall soon achieve your goal.' This liberating omen leaves me no doubt that Prince Kumaradvitiya will come soon with his great and fearsome armies. Since you are a master of wisdom and strength, you should pursue a scheme to harm our enemy while seeming to help them."

He happily agreed to her exhortation. He thought, "Yes, now is the time!" And he considered how to harm his enemies. "First of all, somehow or other, I will bring to ruin malevolent Chetadasa. He should be uprooted like a field of poisonous plants."

15

In which the kingdom of Myriad Lights is destroyed from within

ONE DAY KING CHANDRAMATI AND HIS COURTIERS went to the palace gardens to inspect the royal elephants, horses, buffalos, and other animals. The hero Bhavakumara went with them as far as the garden, but he did not go into the fenced stable area. This was part of his mischievous plan.

When the king and his ministers finished scrutinizing the grounds, they returned to their residences in the palace. That night, when Chetadasa was deep in sleep, Bhavakumara crept stealthily into his quarters, took his sword, and slipped out. He then went to the elephant stable and clambered onto the roof. He found the spot directly over the head of the king's favorite elephant, Powerful White Cloud. He made a hole in the roof and tied Chetadasa's sword to a long stick. He grievously wounded the tethered elephant; brains and blood splattered all over, and finally the beast died.

Bhavakumara repaired the hole in the roof so that his tampering could not be seen. Then he went back to the palace. He put the bloody sword back into its scabbard and replaced it in Chetadasa's room.

The next day at dawn, the elephant mahouts saw the slaughtered elephant. With fear and trepidation, they went the king. In low and terrified voices, they said:

> Kye ma! O Earth Lord, kye!
> It is hard to tell you what happened!
> The lotus garden of our merits
> Has been destroyed by unwanted frost.

In the middle of the dark night,
The incomparable king of elephants
Your best mount, Powerful White Cloud,
Was sorely wounded on the head.

Masses of blood and brains spewed out,
Splattering in drops all over the ground.
Anyone can see that the elephant was slaughtered.

We elephant mahouts were never negligent,
Nor did we do this evil deed.
This was not done by a fearsome lion.
Some vicious and intelligent man
Did this in order to harm you.

That man should be found and tried.
The man who countered the king's designs
Should be punished by the king's laws,
Which are as heavy as gold-ringed Mount Meru.

Timidly trembling, they supplicated their ruler. The king became incredibly angry. The proud flesh of his face was pinched with fury; his upper lip curled, and he spoke forcefully to his ministers:

O knaves! Know you well!
I have heard that my best mount
The peerless, precious elephant,
The wonderful Powerful White Cloud,
Has been slaughtered with a weapon.

Whoever did this foul deed
Will soon see the Death Lord's garden!
Consult, O fierce ministers.
Discover and tell me who did this!

The ministers said: "This disaster must have been brought about by the enemy retainers among us. Only about Bhavakumara and Chetadasa do we have any doubts."

So the two men were taken to the temple of the fierce protector deities for interrogation. There they were to take an oath. The hero Bhavakumara swore: "I absolutely never struck the king's elephant with my sword. Nor have I ever crossed the threshold of the elephant stable."

Because Chetadasa had gone into the elephant pen the day before along with the king and his party, he could not make the same vow. "I did no wrong deed which killed the elephant Powerful White Cloud. I am unable to speak falsehoods, so I cannot say I have never been into the elephant stable." The ministers considered Chetadasa's statement to have less force.

Then King Chandramati again commanded, "Find the villain!" To investigate further, the ministers went to the residences of Bhavakumara and Chetadasa to see if any clothes or objects were stained with blood. In their thorough search, they found Chetadasa's bloody and brain-smeared sword in its scabbard.

"It is obvious you committed this crime!" they said.

Terrified by their fierce abuse, Chetadasa wailed and wept: "I did not do it! Somebody else did this to implicate me!"

However, they did not listen to him, for they had found a culprit. When informed, the king ordered in a violent fury, "Put that evildoer to death immediately!"

Bhavakumara intervened with a request: "O Lord of Men! You are a treasury of wisdom. In your great compassion, you trusted this man, made him your servant, and protected him with kindness. Yet in return he abused you with wicked actions. Please grant me leave that I alone may undertake to kill him."

The king granted his plea. "Yes, it is so. You may do just as you wish."

> The varied sorts of actions in the world
> Always appear later in the mirror of experience.
> The karma of men is amazingly straightforward:
> The laws of cause and effect are true, without deceit.
> So Chetadasa soon had to experience the ripe
> Fruit of his innumerable nefarious deeds.

> That uncivilized man named Chetadasa
> Cast away all propriety and shame.
> So executioners, like the Death Lord's minions,
> Holding black nooses in their hands,
> Tightly bound his neck and limbs.
> Naked and crying loudly, he was led
> Through all the streets of the city
> To the execution ground, stained red with blood.

There Chetadasa's limbs were stretched out and tied to crossed boards. The hero Bhavakumara held up a sharp sword that emitted an amazing reddish light. While he prepared to put out Chetadasa's eyes, he said:

Evil one, you did not wish to look
At the face of Prince Kumaradvitiya.
His compassionate eyes view friend and foe alike.
Now look at the face of Uddhatamanas Mokshabhadra!

After he plucked out Chetadasa's eyes, Bhavakumara said:

When he spoke in a rough or harsh manner,
His intention never varied from pacifying love.
If you intend to counter the commands of Prince Kumara,
Supplicate your preferred leader and protector now!

When he had said this, he cut out Chetadasa's tongue at its root.

When I was in danger, your hands held a sword.
Stubbornly you refused to lend it to me.
Do you think you can hold on to a weapon
Today as I carve you into small bits?

With those words, Bhavakumara cut off every one of his fingers.

You did not want to ride a superior mount,
Which could travel continuously without tiring.
Then, criminal, you defected to the enemy.
If he is your protector, go to him directly!

Then he cut off Chetadasa's legs at the hip.

You were never satisfied with
The Earth Lord whom to see gives joy,
Our kingdom, friends, or amazing wealth.
Now, you odious being, be satisfied!

Saying this, he plucked out Chetadasa's heart, sliced his skin into ribbons, and chopped his body into small pieces.

Chetadasa's evil deeds had festered in Bhavakumara's heart. But
through cunning, Bhavakumara reduced his enemy to a mere
name.

"That hero is proficient in the ways of the brave and wise. He is a
master of killing the indecent according to the letter of the law." So did
the others praise him.

At a later date, Devatisha offered the hero Bhavakumara many marvelous presents to satisfy him. Devatisha then spoke these words from his heart:

> Do the power and assets of Gem of the World,
> Centered on the garden city Open Lotus,
> Compare with those of Myriad Lights?
> Or are they less well off than we?
>
> The man famed as Kumaradvitiya
> Is said to be a paramount warrior
> That no one in all the world can rival.
> Are these rumors of his deeds,
> Fluttering far and wide as a banner, true?
>
> As for the wise and brave ministers
> Who directly serve him, what are they like?
> O Bhavakumara, you are worthy of my trust,
> A superlative warrior loyal to your ruler.
> Please speak secretly and truly to me
> To cut through my web of doubts.

"Now this is the opportunity I have been waiting for!" thought Bhavakumara. So with a smile and every sign of respect, he bowed deeply. Then, clasping his hands together at his crown, he reverently spoke to the prince:

"O son of the king, please heed me well. A dutiful child never speaks falsehoods to his kind mother. I am like an only son before you, my kind ruler. If I spoke falsely, I would harm only myself. Therefore, I offer these honest tidings for you to hear.

"The power, wealth, and resources of Gem of the World are a little bit inferior to those of this kingdom. They have nothing that is better.

"Prince Kumaradvitiya has a calm and peaceful nature. He has an extensive understanding of every field of knowledge, but that is about all. The reason he is famous for his martial deeds is that when he enters the battlefield he wears a special helmet and corselet. His sturdy armor is indestructible, for it is made from a special formula of molten iron. Anyone wearing a helmet and corselet like that cannot be injured by his enemies' weapons. It is because of the power of this armor that the sweet music of the prince's fame spreads far and wide. But other than this, he has no courage to mark him a leader of fearless heroes.

"The best of their wise ministers was that Chetadasa! I tell you honestly, I am known to be the best of their brave ministers. There is no one else skilled at anything.

"Even if a king is a master of brave deeds, if he has a helmet and corselet made from iron of this special formula, he becomes even greater, just as the moon's white light increases the natural shine of the snows of Mount Kailash."

The prince replied, "O hero Bhavakumara, you are wise. It is just as you have said. The mighty armor you describe is superior to any other. We do not have anything like that here, so please tell me how to have it made."

"The realm of Myriad Lights is such a powerful empire, there will be no difficulty in manufacturing such armor. This is how to do it. From every family in the realm gather as many sharp pieces of good-quality iron as a man can carry on his back. Smelt that until you have its essence and temper it to the thickness of a finger width. Make the helmet and corselet out of this extract. When you put on that adamantine armor, no kind of weapon can injure you.

"However, making this armor will cause tremendous hardship for the public. The people will lose their respect for their lords. Will you not be the focus of their infamous criticism? Therefore, it is my heartfelt, honest opinion that this difficult labor should be left undone."

In answer the prince said: "There is no problem here! It is the rightful nature of kings to levy taxes on their subjects. Thus, there will be no cause for infamous slander."

Devatisha became as happy as a peacock touched by the first fine drizzle of the rainy season. He went to the residence of his father, King Chandramati, put his hands together, and bowed. He said:

"O honorable father, please listen. The kings of two realms are preparing for a fight. This dispute is founded on an agitated inability to bear a rival and craving for the other's wealth, particularly the lovely maid Manohari. As part of our arrangements for war, I beg you give me leave to make our leader an invincible helmet and corselet from a special formula of iron."

The king said: "Whose profound idea was this?"

"I heard it from the mouth of Bhavakumara."

"Well, young man, did I not tell you right from the start, when you wanted to kill him, that he was a wise retainer worthy of our trust? It is a good idea. But how can we make armor like this?"

So the prince described how they must collect as much iron as a man could carry from every family in the realm.

The populace could not offer up that much iron from their household stores. To meet the demands of the iron tax, they were forced to part with all their weapons, even down to the minuscule amounts of iron in spear tips and arrowheads.

Then the palace forgers had to obtain enough coal to smelt all the iron. The common people wondered how they could provide enough fuel to produce an extract the width of a finger from all those bundles of iron. Then, although evil mumbling about the king was heard on all sides, out of fear of the law, the populace made charcoal from all their wood. Even their staircases had to be burnt! The disgruntled people gathered in front of the palace saying, "We offer our tribute."

During this time, Bhavakumara contemplatively gazed at the castle of Myriad Lights. It was the mightiest and tallest fort of the kingdom. It had catapults and other projectile weapons, castellated battlements and window slits. The cornerstone of this fortress was a pair of square and oblong-shaped, smoke-colored boulders.

"I see how I will destroy this edifice!" he thought. So he said to the king: "To temper and form this unique molten iron, we will need special tools. Ordinary ones made of iron will not do. I have thought about what was done when this armor was made for Prince Kumaradvitiya. The equipment was stone: diamond-hard boulders the color of smoke. There was a square one and a pestle-shaped one. The square one was used as a bed underneath, and the other was used as a hammer."

"Well then, we must quickly find marvelous stones like those. If they do not come into our possession, we will not be able to finish our task," said the king, and he sounded the bell to call his servants.

All the men, women, and children of the city were sent out to search for the right type of stone. However, they found nothing. When they were tired and weary, no one noticed Bhavakumara give a hint to a young child. The youngster listened and considered what he heard. He realized the boulders which were the foundation of the mighty fortress were precisely the ones needed. He went and told the king.

The king thought, "These words are music for my ears! The force of my virtuous merit must have impelled this child to perceive the solution to our problem." Then he said to his ministers, "You tried very hard, but there was no fruit to your labors. My virtuous merit caused this child to appear and inform me of the location of the required rocks. Now, dismantle this mighty fortress in order to take out those two wonderful stones!"

When he ordered that this be done, the hero Bhavakumara said, "To do that is not right!" He was wise and skillful and so deceived the king and prince by saying:

Bad characters who act craftily
Entrap others' minds in deception.
Because I know this is ignoble,
I always speak the truth.

Although it is extremely important
To make an invincible helmet and corselet
So you will be able to contend with
Prince Kumaradvitiya of Gem of the World,
I pray you do not demolish this marvelous fortress.

If you do, some of your ministers
Will make me an object of censorious abuse.
Those ministers have vicious minds.
Unbearably jealous of another's wealth,
They will criticize both you Lords of Men.

"If it enables us to manufacture armor that will protect us from fear of our enemies, I will order strong men to destroy and then rebuild the fortress. There is no problem in doing that," the king answered.

So preparations were begun to remove the boulders. Just when they were ready to start demolishing the castle, some ministers who had been dear to the king could not bear it any longer. With faultless motivation they went to him. Brahmadhimat as their spokesman pleaded with him:

"O god-king, please see us! Our intelligence is weak, we have no courage, and we lack the power of wise discrimination. So in all we have little to say. Nevertheless, consider this small matter which comes from our hearts.

"Your former ministers were wise and of mature age. They viewed your majesty with the utmost respect. Yet you have cast off those men like a change of old clothes for a new minister who is unsuitable to rely upon. You clearly have come under the influence of a malevolently intelligent man who is conceited and jealous.

"You have been influenced to torture your people, who are as worthy of love as your relatives, by pressing them like sesame seeds in an oil press. First you ordered, 'Make the king's armor!' so even our weapons were confiscated. Then as fuel to melt our weapons down, all our staircases, doors, and so forth were burnt in a forge. Now we have heard that to get some boulders, you have ordered the destruction of a fortress which could not be invaded by any enemy. Please tell us who has advised you to follow such an unseemly course of conduct."

Ignorance completely fogged the king's mind. Although they spoke properly, he misunderstood. He mistakenly assumed that jealousy among the ministers prompted their words. He was like an old owl resting on a rock, proud of the fact that he has eaten enough fish to fill his stomach, priggishly ignoring otters who catch fresh fish and place them all around him as offerings. In just such a way, the ministers found disfavor in the king's eyes.

The fingers of the king's right hand curled like a lion's claws upon his right thigh. His eyebrows arched in anger. He sat up proudly and arrogantly crooked his head to look down upon them and say:

"Your intelligence is as small as the eye of a needle! Do not speak vain words arising from jealousy toward one another. Mighty armor which cannot be damaged by enemy weapons is extremely useful. Although it may seem wrong to dismantle the castle and oppress the populace, both can be restored to a better condition later. Do not be jealous because this good counsel was given by the hero Bhavakumara."

Dismay and befuddlement robbed the other ministers of further speech. Their shoulders slumped and their faces fell. They lost all their self-confidence and were totally miserable. Then, once again, the minister Brahmadhimat spoke up honestly:

> O Earth Lord, your heart is the pure moon,
> An amphora filled with the nectar of wisdom,
> A wealth of faultless light worthy of praise.

> You are caught in the jaws of nefarious darkness.
> Now uncommonly beneficial advice
> Offered honestly wanes like the moon.
> Murky faults increase while virtue dwindles.

> Deceitful words have poisoned your heart.
> I pray that you have no regrets or anguish
> When you see the end of this improper course.

The king was not pleased with that speech, so he answered:

> The excellent character of the Buddha
> Is outside the bounds of a demon's thought.
> The deeds of the wise are unbearable
> To ministers with inferior intelligence.

This is logical, so I will not stray
From the advice of the wise.
I never rely upon a counsellor's lying words.
So why do you importune me so often?

The king sharply rebuked his loyal minister. After upbraiding him for many faults, he demoted him to a common manservant. Like Brahmadhimat, the other ministers had pure natures; they had guilelessly spoken the truth and lacked deceit. But the king disposed of them as if they were scraps of leftover food.

The hero Bhavakumara always spoke sweetly and never gave the king any bad news. So his words were like music to the king's ears. The king glorified everything the hero said and granted his every request. Bhavakumara was skilled in verbally accomplishing his aims. Whenever he spoke, he hoaxed them. He only seemed to work for them; everything he accomplished was to their detriment.

The essence of helpful advice is nectar
To pour into the precious vessel of the ear.
All the fierce heat of sinful activities
Can be cooled by honest exhortation.

However, unable to discern right from wrong,
The Ruler of Men was led astray by another.
Shown the entry to the right path many times,
He feared seeing it as if it were a deep chasm.

The hero strung his crooked bow of destructive intent
And let fly the arrows of his devious words.
These struck pleasure in the heart of the Earth Lord.
He did not feel the least disquiet or pain.

In this world, helpful instructions
Are as rare as stars in the daytime.
But rarer yet are those who listen
To such proper exhortations!

Attend to unpleasant-sounding beneficial advice.
Disregard the sweet sounds of bad counsel.
Why throw away nectar held in a serviceable cup,
Just to drink poison from a golden vessel?

Then, using the charcoal, they began to melt down the iron collected as taxes. Others endeavored to destroy the mighty fortress; slowly they began to wrest out the two stones. Then Bhavakumara thought: "Now, for the most part my hopes are complete! The populace has no weapons or much of anything else. The most mighty of their forts will soon be reduced to a pile of rubble and dust. Now is the time for me to fly away like a mountain bird."

Devatisha's best horse was called Wind Wings. During the night, Bhavakumara stole him and fled toward Gem of the World like a bird freed from a snare. He vowed he would never return to Myriad Lights.

16

In which the kingdom of Myriad Lights must prepare for war

THE NEXT MORNING THE STABLEHANDS NOTICED that the magnificent horse Wind Wings had run off during the night. Trembling anxiously, they went to tell the king.

The ministers said: "Bhavakumara must be brought before our eyes. Otherwise how can we say he has not deceived us?" They searched for him everywhere but could not find him. Everyone was greatly disturbed; the king, his son, and the ministers blamed one another. Their clamorous cries of "It's your fault!" mounted into a cacophony of gibberish like *di ri ri*.

King Chandramati's mind was oppressed by a heavy burden of sorrow. But as if he was not worried at all, he lightly prevaricated:

"O leaders of my realm, are there not as many varieties of worldly happiness and sorrow as colors in a painting? Similarly, some birds live on the earth below while others soar high up into the sky. In like fashion, on some occasions we have had the best of all that is magnificent, but during degenerate times unwanted circumstances befall us. This is the nature of things, so why be fainthearted? Do not be in the least upset. Some of you brave ministers should go with your entourage and bring that deceitful trickster back into our hands. He is unfit to live."

When the king gave his command, most of his ministers and servants thought as one. They said in unison, "O king! You blundered onto a foolish path and had us complete some asinine tasks. O why did you follow that wicked man?"

They had lost all respect for their ruler. They ignored his commands as if he were a tree which offered no cooling shade. His words blew past their ears like the wind. Right in the king's presence, evil muttering and secretive whispers were to be heard.

Despite the fact that the minister Brahmadhimat had been chastised for many trumped-up faults and had been reduced to a common manservant, he was still of a noble, pure lineage. Such an individual does not let little personal setbacks or pleasures unbalance him. The king's clearly deteriorating situation was unbearable to his unswerving loyalty. He spoke to the ministers and subjects:

> If a jeweled crown falls onto the ground,
> You pick it up and put it back on your head.
> How can it be right to abandon our Lord of Men
> Saying, "He has fallen into a base state now."

> Our Earth Lord, intoxicated by lies,
> Entered an iniquitous path leading to beggary.
> But worldly curses shall surely destroy you
> If you do not repay him for his protection respectfully.

> Even if we are unable to destroy
> Brilliant and fearless Bhavakumara,
> We should vow to make an effort to try
> To fulfill the orders of our Lord of Men.

The minister Brahmadhimat was aged and good-natured. He loved all the subjects of the realm as if they were his own family. In front of the king, he respectfully praised the populace. Outside the palace, he told the people the king's laws were forthright and praised his loving protection of the people. Since he was skilled in the methods of arbitration, everyone listened to his words.

The minister Pravadivadhaka and a hundred companions went off in pursuit of Bhavakumara. But because their spirits were depressed, they procrastinated and proceeded indolently. By the time they reached the base of the mountain called Eagle's Despair—a mountain so tall its peak seemed to touch the sky and then go even higher—the hero Bhavakumara had already attained its summit.

Bhavakumara turned around and gazed in the direction he had come. A smoky haze covered all of Myriad Lights; it was impossible to distinguish details. He saw his pursuers climbing the mountain with great difficulty, as if they were in a daze.

Then he looked in the other direction. In a wide, verdant park at the base of a nearby peak, he could clearly see a large army. The sparkling light reflecting from their weapons was like all the stars come down to earth. He had no doubt that these were the battle-ready forces of Gem of the World. His satisfaction was so strong it seemed like a corporeal thing. He smiled broadly and, although he was completely alone, suddenly burst into song:

> Ah la la! O what a jubilant feeling!
> This is the result of powerful merit.
> Prince Kumara gives joy to all; no one can combat him.
> When his army of courageous warriors arrives,
> Myriad Lights will be reduced to a mere name.
>
> Ah la la! O what a jubilant feeling!
> In this valley I see the four-division army.
> I know that behind me is the enemy's realm.
> They are in our hands! We will be victorious.
> So Chandramati is now an object of my pity!
>
> Ah la la! O what a jubilant feeling!
> Now to whom will Devatisha go for refuge?
> My leader, fearsome as the Death Lord,
> His ministers, masters of warriors' brave deeds,
> And a ferocious army are about to overpower the enemy.

Then he proceeded down the far slope of the mountain Eagle's Despair. Finally, when he reached the meadowlands of the park below, Pravadivadhaka and his companions reached the summit. Every single eye carefully spied into the far distance. On the steep slope of a far-off valley, they saw a herd of excellent horses grazing. Then, when they looked more attentively nearby, they saw the army below them, gloriously glittering like the blazing sun. The soldiers were uncountable. From the army's center, you could not see its bounds, for it rippled outward like the waves of the great ocean. It covered the earth without a gap on all sides.

"This is definitely the army of Gem of the World come to engage us in an unending battle." This realization made them sigh long and loud. Just as they were about to flee homeward, Pravadivadhaka thought:

"If we fly back to our own land like birds freed from a snare, men will spit when they say our names. We will be reduced in stature because we were unable to bear even a glimpse of an enemy like this. We should muster whatever force and skills we have. Just this once we should act without any timidity."

So he spoke to his companions:

> I can see innumerable players for battle
> Filling the vast, spacious valley below.
> As the sun overwhelms a firefly's glow
> They come to burn away even the name Myriad Lights.
>
> However, if we return to our own land
> Terrified by just the sight of the enemy,
> Everyone will say, "You are like trembling women
> Who are unable to do battle even once!"
>
> Thus, although their weapons may chop
> My weak body into a thousand pieces,
> Without a single regret I will challenge them.
> Let us play on the stage of battle!

With these words, he remounted his charger, Thunder Cloud. Without a qualm he whipped the horse to dash down into the midst of the enemy. He was as zealous as a bull elephant in rut smelling a female. But his companions seized him and held him fast. Pravadivadhaka could not resist them. One of his men, an old fellow whose brow was wrinkled like a well-cut carpet, spoke out:

> You have the pride of a superb warrior,
> So please listen to these words of advice.
>
> We cannot bear to view the uncountable numbers
> Of the foe's army, which shines like the sun.
> In front of the brilliant blaze of their power,
> We have the humble, weak light of a glowworm.
>
> If we worms have the conceit to vie with them,
> Our weaknesses will be bared and clear to see.
> What wise man would believe we were fighters?
> Would we not be more like moths drawn
> To battle a candle flame to the death?

Therefore, we should retreat now
To warn our lord, ministers, and populace.
Then, with the confidence of preparedness,
We will go to engage in fierce combat.

Pravadivadhaka's demeanor was implacable: he was not happy to hear
those words. However, since all the other men were of one mind, his
resolve to enter into battle weakened. They all returned to Myriad Lights.

While they were on the summit, the hero Bhavakumara quickly sped
farther and farther away as happily as a king of swans enters a great lake.
He arrived in front of Prince Kumaradvitiya encircled by his vast
entourage without further mishap. The heart of every man there over-
flowed with joy: they greeted him the way a mother welcomes a son
just freed from the jaws of a deathly illness. The prince smiled with
pleasure. He said, "Welcome, Bhavakumara! Are you well, or did you
suffer poor health? Are you not tired and fatigued? Now you have
reached a place of happiness!"

Bhavakumara saluted him and said:

Eh ma ho! Unparalleled son of the king!
Eh ma ho! Treasury of magnificent qualities!
Eh ma ho! Lord who is able and powerful!
Eh ma ho! All-powerful conqueror!

I, Bhavakumara, am the result of your care
And loving compassion throughout many lives.
Therefore, with concentrated effort,
I undertook many tasks to accomplish your aims.

But until now despicable Chetadasa's evil mind
Blazed like the fire at the end of time,
Outshining the sunshine of my powers,
Leaving me eclipsed in unpleasant darkness.

This situation was an iron thorn in my heart.
I could not bear it, so with trickery I killed him.
Chetadasa was like a field growing poisonous plants,
Ignorant of cause and effect and lacking all shame.

I found opportunities to harm the enemy
By devising clever and profound deceptions.

To make adamantine armor from special iron,
I had them order their weapons melted down.
Their best fortress, a mighty bastion of weapons,
Is now a heap of rubble and dust.
I also slaughtered their lord's superb mount,
The priceless elephant Powerful White Cloud.

O prince, now like the cool, crystal moon,
You quickly rise in the sky over this place.
But in your long absence while you journeyed here,
Manohari thought of no man but you.
She was oppressed by a multitude of painful sorrows;
Her food was misery and her drink was tears.
Because of this, only a breath of her life remained.

I too nearly died, trampled in the dust,
But I found the means to survive.
For it is my lot to be of the army
Drawing forth the chariot of the sun.

So, without pretension or hypocrisy, he told them what had actually happened. The prince and his entourage were completely amazed. Then Prince Kumaradvitiya said with a smile:

As soon as you were born,
Your qualities were worthy of praise.
You mastered every aspect of the martial arts
By the time you had grown to sixteen.

To accomplish the goals of your ruler,
You endured many tiring trials.
But the law of cause and effect is not deceptive,
Its truth is obvious: for now without injury
You are here, a man freed from the jaws of death.

To call you Young Hero of the Universe
Is no mistake; you accord with your name.
You are a wise, completely full moon,
Rising up into the cloudless sky.
My mind, a night-blooming lily,
Rejoices in this opportunity to meet you.

There is no work for an able warrior
Other than to destroy the enemy.
So may you be filled with joy
And not shrink before the play of battle.
Let us bravely sally forth right now.

With these words and the exchange of other joyful news, the great
army set forth once again.

Pravadivadhaka and his entourage had darted away like deer fleeing a
beast of prey. Finally they arrived at the residence of the king and his
ministers. With his head bent down like a lotus closing at the end of the
day, Pravadivadhaka said:

Kye ma! Can you see the inexhaustible results
Of your many black deeds are coming to fruition?
Soon you will die, for that is the end
Of having engaged in grievously regrettable deeds!

Some days after we left here, we reached
Eagle's Despair, a mountain so very tall
Even birds have difficulty flying over it.
When we ascended its summit, which touched the sky,
The hero Bhavakumara had reached the valley beyond.
His passage had vied with a bird's flight.

Searching every direction once more, we saw
On the verdant meadows of an adjacent peak
The four-division army of our evil foe,
A force so vast that like an ocean
We could not see its bounds.

If I lacked ability to fight just then,
I felt life would be no different from death.
So I firmly vowed to enter into battle,
Even if my life were to be trampled into dust.

The sentiments of the others were different.
I could not change the way they thought.
Like an iron hook controls an elephant,
The coercion of my hundred comrades
Compelled me to return against my will.

Quickly advancing into our kingdom's bounds
Is a force vowing to destroy us definitively.
This enemy is like a thorn in your eye,
So put on your new specially made armor
If you believe it will protect you!

If Bhavakumara is your wisest brave minister,
Appoint him general of the army!
Without jealousy we shall follow him to war.
The time has come to show whether the confident,
Brave men of our forces can conquer the enemy!

Candid advice as nourishing as ambrosia
Was faithfully offered to you again and again.
Arrogantly you threw it away as if it were
Salt water unable to quench your thirst
And cast out the waiter serving the truth.

You drank the poison water of knavish words
Pouring from the vessel of a liar's throat
As if it were delicious, reviving nectar.
Now do you see the results of partaking of that?

Hearing these and other harsh words made King Chandramati and
his son think:

"It is highly improper for our own ministers to scold us critically! Yet
when we look at it this way, we acted precipitously and caused others to
do so too. We were happy to accomplish a few ephemeral goals. We
greatly regret that we did not consider the effects of our actions. What
our minister said is true."

They found nothing to say. They were mortified. Their shoulders
slumped, their faces fell, and their minds were agitated. The other ministers stared at one another, unable to utter a word. Then the prime
minister, Viradhiman, became intensely angry. In fury his brow creased
and his eyes opened wide, completely transforming his face. Then he
said:

When in power, haughty men arrogantly boast.
When they lose, they cannot even sigh.
O Earth Lords, father and son, with your ministers
Please consider my words for a moment.

In general samsara is like a cunning harlot:
Her embrace tricks men out of their happiness.
Because they lack a clear view of the future,
Men act without deliberation, always coming to grief.

While we searched for a suitable queen
To join to our powerful kingdom,
We did not consider the results of our actions.
We beat our fists upon a sharp razor's edge.
Now those past hasty deeds' outcome is clear.

Once you produce an irreversible
Course of events leading to war,
There is no benefit in wailing
Or muttering your regrets and sorrow.

If we are but the least bit happy,
Our proud words fill the world.
When our lot degenerates slightly,
We're impotent, unable even to sigh.

Former actions, good ones and bad,
Do not bear fruit just anywhere.
They definitely ripen upon ourselves.
Even prayer rarely prevents that harvest.

The results of our former actions
Are definite; we should respect their force.
Without doubt Devatisha and his heroic ministers
Should join the four-division army of this land
And comport themselves properly for war.

The others judged his words to be as worthy of taste as sweet honey.
They sent messengers to every marketplace in the kingdom to order all
the men to form an army of four divisions immediately.

But some of the people could be heard to say: "Kye ma! The king's
command is not a noble one! It is carelessly given without thought.
We have no means to fight; we had to give our tools and weapons
down to the last arrowhead to make a suit of armor to protect the
young prince. Right after that, even the doors and staircases of our
houses were taken in a charcoal tax. Since then, every day it has been

hard to find enough food to eat. It is not going to be easy to fight a war!"

They whispered censoriously and cast evil eyes upon the messengers. So the wise ministers requested and received permission to bribe the populace with lovely presents from the vast treasure stores of the palace. The brave ministers firmly warned the masses, "If you people counter the commands of the king, you will be punished by his terrible laws." So the men were forced to join the army.

Despite this threat, all the soldiers thought: "We have undergone much hardship laboring for this king. We have already endured great sorrow, and now we must go to war. From now on, we will do nothing; everything will be a sham. When we are ordered to take up arms and mix in battle, we will only pretend to obey."

17

In which the prince of Myriad Lights undermines his own battle preparations

NOT LONG AFTERWARD, the great army of Gem of the World inexorably approached, like the strong current of a deep river. The army halted in the valley below the capital city. This is what was said about them:

Eh ma ma la! This fearless army
Is like Indra's innumerable legions
Going to conquer the demons in battle:
Its ferocity and power are overwhelming.

The chargers go quickly and never tire.
The elephants seize weapons in their trunks.
The sturdy chariots have magic arsenals.
Countless fierce and stalwart warriors'
Brows wrinkle in ferocious anger
As they let forth a great shout, "Ha ha!"

They brandish swords, spears, battle-axes,
Maces, iron hooks, crossbows, and more.
As they advance, the earth trembles with fear.
Dust rising from their march fills the sky.
Birds flying above can find no space to land.
The demeanor of the warriors going to battle
Makes the Death Lord's minions recoil in dread.
Such forces now crowd all of Myriad Lights!

When the men of Myriad Lights saw this military force, they did not dare to come out beyond the iron paling surrounding the fortress. They were like marmots content to stay in their burrows. So for a time a calm ensued.

During this lull Manohari thought: "Now that such an army has arrived, I must employ a stratagem to have our enemy conquered quickly." So with a respectful attitude, she went before Devatisha and his ministers. There she said:

> O wise ruler and ministers,
> Please consider my words.
> Bound by anxiety, I pondered
> How to achieve this kingdom's goals.
>
> The vile enemy forces approach!
> Their encampment fills all space.
> I think they will lay siege to us
> Like eagles waiting to strike a cobra.
>
> We are like birds trapped in a cranny
> Or deer encircled by nets and snares.
> We have enough food and water for now,
> But later our stores will be consumed.
>
> So while our adversary's forces
> Are weak and tired from their journey,
> I think it is time to begin the war,
> As a fearless king of noble lions
> Bounds into a large herd of elephants.
>
> These words come straight from my heart.
> They are without artifice or fault.
> Please examine their propriety.

Manohari spoke in a pained and frail manner. Devatisha and his ministers could not dislike those smooth words; they had no doubts. "Her advice is wise and worthy of trust," they said, and they became pleasantly excited.

Then the best warriors of the kingdom—the ministers Uddhatamanas Mokshabhadra, Pravadivadhaka, and Sattvavati—ordered up the army. Just as they were about to pass out beyond the iron fence surrounding the castle, Prince Devatisha came up bedecked with armor and weapons. Although he knew nothing of the works of war, he was conceited about his prowess. So he spoke to the generals of his army:

"O battle chiefs, attend well! The mighty armor, sharp weapons, and good horses of the enemy before us will be our booty and treasure! Our adversaries have the bearing of women; what can they possibly do? They will be easy to conquer, for they are like fools beating their heads upon a diamond-hard rock or moths doing battle with a candle flame! If you are resolute and brave, they will be reduced to a mere name. But as we demolish them, we must remain aware: for when in danger of its life, even a fox can fight like a lion. If I see anyone with cowardly actions running in retreat, I myself will kill him!"

Most of the ministers smiled deep inside and said nothing about the faults or attributes of his inconsiderate speech. However, the minister Sattvavati always unsuspiciously spoke the truth. He wrinkled up his nose, snorted loudly, and said:

"O Lord of Men, please consider! It is easy to make speeches about going into battle, but the actual work of war is not quite so simple. From the time you were drinking your mother's milk until now, I have been perfecting the various martial arts. Now, after all my training, are your orders to any purpose?

"You are a master of all the movements to be done amid silken bedclothes. You enjoyed young women, philandered and fornicated. You satiated yourself with nectars having a hundred tastes. You passed your time with the false praises of the court.

"But you know absolutely nothing about fighting a war. So please be silent! It will be as difficult for us to contend with the army of Gem of the World as it would be to reverse the current of a great river! Now, O Lord of Men, if you have any powerful abilities at all, this is your chance to use them."

The prince found these words unbearable; they were like iron arrows piercing his heart. He lost his temper. Angrily wringing his hands together, he said:

"If this peon sees the present moment as an opportunity to scold me, how can he command an army? Execute this pernicious man who has evil designs toward me!" The prince ordered the executioners, whose arms were so red with blood they looked like branches of coral. At this point the other ministers interceded. They pleaded three times:

"These words were uttered honestly by a man who holds our ruler dear to his heart. Please release him from this fearsome indictment!"

The prince naturally inclined to unseemly behavior. He believed

propriety was indecent and saw evil deeds as proper. So, although the
minister Sattvavati had committed no crime, he was put to death.

> Kye hu! Samsara is like a lightning storm:
> The flashes are obviously impermanent,
> Yet we hold things to be everlasting and real.
> This is the chain binding us to life after life.
>
> Our actions authoritatively condition our future.
> Even the powers of a Buddha have difficulty
> Blocking the fruition of a former evil deed,
> So what relief is there for others?
>
> The prince's powerful immoral deeds
> Were not on a path followed by nobility.
> Without any pity, he immorally
> Killed a friend offering good advice.

None of the men liked this. "The first thing he does in our battle
with the enemy is to use our weapons to afflict one of us! He murdered
a brave and honest man who dearly loved his country," they thought
and lay down listlessly, like dried-out reeds. Their minds were filled with
anxiety.

18

In which a tremendous battle is fought to no conclusive end

ONCE AGAIN THE ARMY OF MYRIAD LIGHTS was ordered to march. They regrouped not far from the forces of Gem of the World. Then the minister Viradhiman said loudly:

Men! Listen to my fearless words!
Be like a strong, iron-beaked eagle
Courageously flying to the ocean battle
To decimate the bodies of the enemy snakes.

Be not like a man who sits safely at home
On soft cushions boasting of his bravery
And spitefully undermining the rest of the court;
But when an adversary merely slanders him,
In fear his limbs tremble like cotton fluff
And his eyes are rigidly fixed in terror.

The battleground will be wet with blood.
Piles of corpses will be scattered about.
Pitiful, but no object of mercy is there!
Take as a trophy the hands of your victims.

If I see someone giving up the fight,
Surrendering with a smile, genuflecting,
Sweetly praising the foe and making a bow,
I promise you, I will kill him myself!

In this vast round of samsaric existence,
Daily, monthly, and yearly swirling like a dance,
Enemies become friends, and friends become foes.
It is unsuitable to have any faith in this world.

With the power of truth lacking dissimulation,
Each of us should engrave our duty in his heart.
Whether your call is to be peaceful or violent,
Be diligent in your effort to accomplish it.

The other ministers let forth a deep roar of self-confidence. They gathered themselves up and began to hurl their weapons into the enemy camp.

Then the four divisions of Gem of the World prepared for battle. Prince Kumaradvitiya put on his mighty armor and bedecked himself with weapons to conquer his foes. He mounted his war elephant, Mighty Earth Guardian. This elephant, wearing a gold chain-mail chamfron over its face, was like a living, moving Mount Kailash.

The generals put on their armor and mounted chargers as fleet as the wind. Everyone grasped a plethora of sharp weapons. The wrinkles of rage on the warriors' brows made their faces quite fearsome. The glitter of hatred in their red, wide-open eyes outshone the light of the sun.

Innumerable men yelled, "Beat them!" and "Kill them!" so loudly the din seemed to rend the sky. The buglers sounded the battle call. The beating of the war drums was like a thousand dragons roaring. Like wolves passionately eager to devour their prey, the army of Gem of the World raced toward their foe. Then, with a feverish brandishing of weapons, the two sides clashed.

The brawl between the strong, mountainous elephants raised up a dust cloud so thick you could hardly breathe. The loud noise of the chariots grinding the enemy to a powder beneath their wheels filled all space. The foot soldiers, emulating the host of the Lord of Death, loosed a swirling storm of arrows and missiles.

At the start of the battle, the minister Laksaikadvitiya experienced great happiness. He went into battle as an eagle joyfully flies to the sea, saying:

This vast battlefield is a stage
Where two groups of warriors gather.
It is impossible to tell them apart
By their mighty armor blazing with light,
Or by their weapons as sharp as razors,

Or by the swift mounts below them.
But, if you examine their intelligence,
Some are as high as the vast sky above
While others are as low as the earth!

I earned in my youth the sweet epithet
A Man Worth a Thousand Other Comrades.
But now the noose of old age binds me tight:
My mind is caught in a web of senility,
My power and skill have diminished,
My courageous strength has weakened too.

Many times in the past, fearless armies
Gathered for war with faces contorted with anger,
But when they heard I was prepared for battle,
They became unable to pursue the confrontation.
I totally severed their cunning train of thought
So that even the term *enemy* was not heard.

Marvelous Kumaradvitiya gives joy to all.
His steadfast heart is vast and encompassing.
Because his inner nature is like cool nectar,
He is the protector and refuge for all beings.

But outside, his ferocity destroys the unworthy.
He is the best of all the world's warriors,
Excelling in all the martial arts.
His fearless speech is the laugh of a hero.

Now you make me laugh!
You mass here like a herd of cows
To counter that lion among warriors.
As soon as you enter the fray, you'll retreat!
Your bodies will be corpses without souls!
But if you have any courage, then come,
Today we will see who is particularly brave!

Even if the enemy filled the universe,
I would be without fear or hesitation.
When I hear a report of an enemy army,
I abandon misgiving and advance.

He brandished his sword aloft so it seemed to create a circle of blazing fire. Then, like a meteor, he crashed into the middle of the enemy host.

Similarly, the hero Bhavakumara, the ministers Abhayabalahanta, Virendra, Abhayavrati, and the others arched their eyebrows in hatred of the enemy and said:

> Experts are tested before other masters.
> Heroes are distinguished from cowards in war.
> Cowards are a thorn in other men's sides,
> At home demanding food and drink from women,
> They boast and brag of their courage.
>
> But when the base man goes into battle,
> He rolls his eyes in fear and runs away
> Like a young deer freed from a trap.
> When people see someone act so shamefully,
> They spit in his face rather than on the ground.
>
> Even if our contentious foes
> Cut our bodies into a million pieces,
> We are heroes who never lose heart;
> It makes sense to call us warriors.
> Let us advance like soaring eagles!

They picked up a variety of weapons—swords, pikes, battle-axes, iron hooks, lassos, and so forth—and rushed far ahead of their own army to fight. It was like this:

> Amidst this clash of weapons,
> Many men came to their ruin.
> The terrified cowards' loud, howling
> Laments stirred the ocean!
>
> Horses, elephants, and chariots
> Skirmished in this battle with the foe.
> Underneath, the earth shivered pathetically.
>
> The adversary fell under
> The hail of sharp arrows.
> Their crowns, mounts, and armor
> Were muddied in the bloody dirt.

Their throats were bound with ropes;
Their necks were caught by hooks.
So, like beasts of burden or dogs,
They were forced to follow behind.

The ground was red with blood,
Like the garden of the Death Lord.
Heads, arms, and legs lay everywhere;
The corpses were so thickly strewn
It was hard to pick a way through them.

The warriors rolled their armor
Up to their shoulders; their hands
Flourished weapons covered with skin and blood.
Baring their teeth, they fearlessly laughed,
"Ha ha!" shattering the hearts of the weak.

The actions of the furious army
Stirred up the dust of the earth
So that it blocked the light of the sun:
A fearsome darkness pervaded the land.

The cringing foes fled
Even from the sight of their friends.
They confused their antagonists
With friends and bowed their heads.

Kye ma! Our experiences accord with our deeds,
So the foe was unceasingly attacked.
For many it seemed that the burning ground
Of hell had manifested there on earth.

Composite things are impermanent, they are easily destroyed. Like
water bubbles, they dissolve after a while. People's actions, particularly
bad deeds, irrevocably lead to specific results. The stains left by these
actions are hard to purify. Because the nature of samsara is suffering,
these men came to die.

Although an incalculable number of men were killed, the forces of
Gem of the World found no opportunity to harm the enemy generals.
The intelligent and heroic ministers of Myriad Lights were experts in
all the arts of war. Like eagles they knew how to dash out the brains of

their prey. Like owls they knew how to come and go without anyone being aware. Like phantoms they could come up suddenly out of the earth or down from the mountain slopes. Their tread was as unstoppable as that of an intoxicated elephant. So, at the end of the day, all the fighters retreated and went to their camps.

19

In which Prince Kumaradvitiya vanquishes the enemy forces

THE NEXT DAY, AS LAKSAIKADVITIYA AND THE OTHERS again prepared for battle, Prince Kumaradvitiya thought: "I must make an even greater effort to subdue our enemy." The prince's attendants hoisted silken victory banners over his magnificent chariot and spread heavenly fabric upon its seat. Seemingly drawn by a thousand horses, it was brought before the prince. He mounted and ordered it forth into the enemy host.

The enemy army melted away before the power and glory of Prince Kumaradvitiya. Then he ordered his chariot to pause before the brave enemy ministers. His smile shone forth as he addressed them:

"Kva ye! O adversaries! You have entered into an improper course of action. If you are prepared to vie with us, then try to best me—for I am Kumaradvitiya, the basis of this enmity."

The enemy generals wondered: "Is he really the prince? He looks so splendid, he probably is the man who is the primary source of this war."

So with all the strength and skill at their disposal, they tried to hew, chop, and strike him with their weapons. But they were unable to harm him at all.

"Is he a man or an illusion?" they doubted aloud. In reply the youthful prince said: "If you vain men think you can rival me, try to do something like this!"

The prince strung his golden-colored bow and let fly a great iron arrow. His target was a small rock on top of a cairn a long distance away. The arrow shattered the stone as if it were dried mud.

The ministers could not believe what they saw. Once again they speculated: "Is he an apparition?" So again the prince spoke: "If you doubt that, have you the skill to do this?"

Then, with one hand, he hoisted up in the air a powerful elephant that walked near him. "Are we hallucinating?" they puzzled. In response the prince said:

> Ah ho! My amazing practice
> Of the martial arts is real!
> But it appears to your eyes
> As a chimera or delusion.
>
> I am the champion of the world.
> I kill my malevolent enemies
> Without relying on others' power.
>
> Sundering a body and soul is easy,
> But it is a sin that is heavy to bear.
> It is vain to try to vie with me.
> I will demonstrate your error right here!

The prince put one finger under Viradhiman's belt, swung him around in the air three times, then pounded him on the ground. He did this in turn to each of them. They all fainted, falling over as if dead drunk.

By now Myriad Lights was close to defeat. Devatisha did not avoid any sin; he did every misdeed possible. Just like an elephant in battle, he harmed others without compunction, totally ignoring the law of cause and effect. He blamed his own people when they were too weak to vanquish the mighty enemy. When his army retreated, he had many men put to death. Finally, as a result of his evil actions, even his friends seemed to him to be foes. Multitudes of his men were made to suffer.

The remainder of his army lacked the will to continue the fight. They fled in every direction with whatever strength they could muster. Some of them jumped into the rivers and drowned. Other men leapt down into deep, rocky defiles and died. A few perished from hunger and thirst. Yet others were so exhausted they could not breathe any longer. Each man experienced suffering in accordance with his karma.

When his army was routed, Devatisha did not have the fortitude even to lift his weapons. A coward to the core, whipping his horse he raced back toward the palace just as darkness flees before the dawn.

The men of Gem of the World understood the meaning of that sight! Laksaikadvitiya mounted his charger Tornado and pursued Prince

Devatisha. He held a noose in one hand and a weapon in the other. Just as he was about to catch him, he let forth a laugh and said in a deep and frightening voice:

> Kva ye! Listen here, you terrified coward!
> Peerless Kumaradvitiya gives joy to all.
> Every man bows his head before him,
> A warrior controlling the three worlds.
>
> Manohari's fate was to follow him.
> Think, malefactor! For carnal pleasure
> Did you not impose yourself on that beauty?
> An earthbound man may desire the moon,
> But should he dare reach up to the heavens?
>
> You were not content to enjoy
> Your wealth superior to the gods'.
> Finding others' affluence unbearable,
> Drunk on delusion, you acted indecently.
>
> As a result, now like a deer freed from a trap,
> In terror you scamper toward the safety of home.
> How can you show your face to that pretty maid?
> What will you tell your loving friends and family?
> To whom will your poor subjects turn in hope?
>
> Who could rival our fearless army?
> Like the Death Lord, Laksaikadvitiya am I!
> Have you heard of any enemy of mine going free?
> Know you well, today is your last day to live.
> Here and now you will see your next life begin!

Then Laksaikadvitiya pushed his chain mail up to his shoulders. He bent back his stiff bow, aimed at Devatisha's shiny white helmet, and let loose an arrow. The force of the sharp arrowhead shattered the helmet and pieces of its crown ornament, decorated with Devatisha's personal deity, scattered far and wide. Devatisha's mind reeled from the force of the blow. He fell from his horse like a bird whose wings have been singed.

"This is it; now is the time for my next life to start," he thought in terror. Cowering like a pigeon before a hawk, he bowed obsequiously to Laksaikadvitiya and said:

O great hero!
You are mistaken! Please be tolerant!
Like a butterfly driven before the wind,
I had no recourse but to act impiously.

Men stupefied by liquor dance insanely,
Unable to tell a right move from wrong.
Some of them, despite their open eyes,
Step over the edge of steep cliffs.

My mind was in the clutches of an evil demon.
The results of my evil deeds have come about.
So am I not an object of a warrior's pity?

Please be merciful! Grant me the fortune
To see the face of Prince Kumaradvitiya
And experience that medicine for sore eyes.

He evaded execution as a result of his pleading. But he was not free;
Laksaikadvitiya tightly bound all his limbs and dragged the prince
behind him. Finally they neared the spot where Kumaradvitiya stood
after his skirmish with the enemy ministers.

Just before they reached him, the four brave ministers of Myriad
Lights revived from their faint. They all thought in the same way:
"Prince Kumaradvitiya surpasses ordinary men. Just look at his skill in
creating illusions. There is no doubt that he is a leader and protector of
worldly beings. We too should turn to him for refuge."

They respectfully bowed to the youth's lotus feet and went off to one
side and sat down. Just then they saw Devatisha bound and being led along
behind Laksaikadvitiya. They were not pleased; stirred by anger, they said:

The Earth Lord protecting this land,
Chandramati, has a pure exalted lineage.
His heir is the young man Devatisha.
Out of ignorance and lack of pity
You have tied his limbs with black rope.
Can this be borne? Is this heroic?

A crow pretends to soar like an eagle
When he spies the corpse of a snake.
Cowards only display their bravery
Before one who has fallen low.

We could not vie with Kumaradvitiya,
A prince surpassing all ordinary men,
A treasury of love, peace, and fortitude,
So we bowed to his perfect ocean of skills.

But we have not lost the courage to fight
Unreservedly a retainer equal to ourselves.
If you do not free the limbs of the royal youth,
Your life will be our target! Let us battle!

They unsheathed their swords and displayed the fierce behavior of men ready to strike. Laksaikadvitiya was naturally ferocious. He did not think a thing of their threats and said with a sneer:

Listen here, you fainthearted servants!
Although you proudly boast of your fame
As warriors in accord with your names,
Those words are empty! Mere echoes!

Sitting on comfortable cushions,
Fiercely you try to intimidate me
So I will spare the young Lord of Men.
But if you are so courageous and bold,
Why did you not fight me in the battle?

Knaves! You praise the noble line of your king,
But who are you reverently gazing at now?
Your words and deeds are a contradiction.
What intelligent witness would believe you?

Although highborn, this prince is evil.
I trample this iniquitous man like grass!
A ruler of a kingdom now is my slave.
His good looks make him weak as a woman.
He had massive wealth, but now it is mine!

If you cannot bear to see him in bondage,
What will you feel when I grind him into dust?
Will all of you lowly ministers together
Have the power to fight my solo advance?
If you enjoy practicing the martial arts,
Get ready and come here now!

Through fierce battle we shall see
The nature of cowards and heroes.
Who relies on the sound of empty words?
Today you will find mine to be true.

Laksaikadvitiya wondered: "If they speak so bravely because they cannot bear to see Devatisha in bondage, let's see what happens if I take his life."

So he drew his sword from its scabbard and immediately went to strike him down. Prince Kumaradvitiya quickly spoke to avert this unseemly deed. He chose his words carefully, to smooth over the grudges between the ministers:

O ministers! Attend!
Take my true words to heart.

What is the difference between man and beast
If men cannot tell good actions from bad?
It is right for warriors to fight in battle,
But it is foolish to kill one another
Now that the victor has been determined.

When the blazing sun rises,
Outshining the glow of the moon,
The stars are subdued and shed no light.
Now you are misguided, like stars
Endeavoring to shine in the day.

The enemy's power has been consumed
Now as fuel for my blazing fire.
They are burnt and cannot rival us.
It would be infamous to cut off
The head of a man come to surrender.

This fighting is fruitless.
Please give up contentious behavior.
Live in peace!

This uncommonly noble speech was for the benefit of his listeners. The ministers found they could not disobey the prince's command. Each man sat down composedly upon his own seat.

Soon after this, the hero Bhavakumara approached and saw Uddhatamanas Mokshabhadra. This caused him to recollect his former state of degradation and revived his desire to destroy him. He saluted Prince Kumaradvitiya and, without disguising his inclination in the least, said:

"O Lord of Men, long may you rule! I rejoice in your loving and compassionate nature. You strive for all beings' immediate and long-term benefit.

"Nevertheless, some men have the nature of hateful crocodiles. They are drunk on greed, hatred, ignorance, and pride. They are so jealous they cannot bear it if others possess any wealth, nor can they suffer the thought of a rival. They can leave no land unclaimed; all the greater and lesser kingdoms in the world must be under their umbrella of control.

"This prince and his ministers are men like this; they are always discontented and will try to best us again someday. It would not be good to let them go free without harm! In common custom we leave scraps of food alone, but to leave your enemies at large is not right!

"In particular, this man known as Uddhatamanas Mokshabhadra is cunning and deceitful. He is totally dishonest and boasts of his heroism. With all his ability, he will always endeavor to subvert the aims of Gem of the World. Let today be the day of judgment for this minister. Let us fight in single-hand combat. First we will contend bare-handed, then we will test our skills with an arsenal of weapons. Finally, we will fight to the death! I have absolutely no doubt who will win. Please grant this request."

Bhavakumara could not bear to leave Uddhatamanas Mokshabhadra in peace. He harshly advised the prince to give him permission to kill his enemy. The youthful Prince Kumara never slavishly adhered to advice; he carefully analyzed what would occur upon a deed's completion. He understood Bhavakumara's motivation, but he examined the situation properly and replied:

"O hero Bhavakumara, understand these three points well: First, your wish to combat the evil one who caused your earlier importunities is straightforward. Second, you are stouthearted in pursuit of your ruler's aims; your willingness to persecute my opponents is worthy of praise. This is certainly no matter for reproof! Third, this prince and his ministers were unable to rival me and humbly come to surrender. They would be easy to destroy now, but in a later life that black action would cause you to bear a heavy burden of misery. There is no need to kill them; they should be objects of our pity. Let them go in peace. Furthermore, please listen to this:

Believing situational friends, strangers, and foes
Are unchangeable binds us to cyclic existence.
In life after life we guard against our foes,
But new ones arise, turning like a waterwheel.

The malevolent, depraved minds of these men
Did not take form just during this life.
They are the fruit of the seeds of black deeds
Planted with negative energy in former lives.

You may destroy those you label foes today.
But every being wants the best for himself;
They truculently contend, filling all space.
How could you ever vanquish all of them?

If you treat your enemy as a friend,
The results of that virtue will ripen,
Shedding the white light of love and concern.
Others' dark intent can never engulf you.

If we turn away from virtuous acts,
Carelessly doing unrighteous deeds,
In another life we will surely be devastated
By the inexhaustible tortures of the hells.

Annihilate your greed, hatred, and ignorance
And always engage in righteous deeds,
Desiring to lead others to enlightenment.
Do not stray from these lovingly uttered words.

The prince's speech elucidated some points in the Buddhist Dharma. Although the ministers were not very interested in religion, they were wise about the ways of the world. So they understood the prince's reference to the rigid law of cause and effect and praised his advice. Devatisha was freed from his bonds, and the brave ministers were left in peace.

20

In which the king of Myriad Lights is forced to surrender

KING CHANDRAMATI, HIS WISE MINISTERS, MANOHARI, and many others had been watching the battle from the rooftop of the palace. They soon saw that Myriad Lights could not contend with the glorious power of Gem of the World. The army of Myriad Lights scattered like black clouds before a strong wind.

They saw many men being killed. Watching Devatisha flee pursued by hordes of the enemy was like seeing an owl chased by crows. Even common foot soldiers hunted him as crow fledglings attack a senile owl venturing out of his nest during the day.

Tears ran down the face of the king as he pondered this wretched state of affairs. His hair stood up on end in terror. He could barely stutter these words:

Kye ma! Kye hu! O conclave of ministers!
Do you not see how a debased, ignorant king
And others dear to me experience misery?
My earlier deeds of little merit are bearing
Various unpleasant fruits on the field of life.

In general, a moth leaps to death
In a fierce and powerful flame,
Blown by the force of its bad karma.
What evil spirit was in my poor heart before?

Since I lacked contentment despite my vast wealth,
Unbearable jealousy poisoned my deeds.
The result of my hasty, ill-considered actions
Is the approach of enemy armies unbearable to view.

This verdant meadow is wet with spilled blood,
Transformed into the Death Lord's garden.
Even the blue midday sky reflects this;
It is as reddened as sunset's ruby clouds.

Like bees swarming over a lotus grove,
Flocks of vultures come to feed
On the piles of hacked-up corpses
Of the unfortunate men slaughtered here.

Blinded, some men trip upon level ground.
Others with leg wounds walk like cripples.
A few escape, leaving crooked trails
As blood streams from their pierced flesh.

The badly injured roll in agony on the ground;
Like logs they cannot rise on severed limbs.
Some men blinded by fear and danger
Run up to the enemy without suspicion.

Hunger and thirst confuse the uninjured;
They stagger, not knowing what to do.
A few tremble like reeds in the wind,
Leaning upon their cudgels like old men.

No one at all can contend with the foe:
Some men surrender with bows and salutes,
Others retreat with clamorous wails.
Their laments seem to shake the realm.

The superb enemy warriors are uncountable.
They wear unyielding armor and triumph
Over my forces with a plethora of weapons:
Sharp swords sever heads from necks,
Battle-axes cleave limbs to the bone,
Long ropes and iron hooks drag men down.

Everyone is drenched in streams of blood.
Just the noise of their elephant charges
Violently churns our forces like butter.
The dust kicked up by their horses' hooves
Clouds so thickly it obscures the heavens.
The fainthearted find it unbearable.

Their victory banner waves atop the mountain peak.
The unceasing pounding of their victory drum
Breaks my heart. There is no cure
To ease the pain of the agony of war.

The minister Brahmadhimat offered this nectar to cool the king's suffering with no thought for himself:

O Earth Lord!
Your wisdom is vast as the moon.
Please listen to these few honest words.

Daily you enact encompassing laws,
Wisely administering a powerful land.
Do not worry too much over one setback,
That is the manner of weak fools.

The stage of cyclic existence displays
An ever-changing, insubstantial dance
Of happiness, sorrow, wealth, and poverty.
What wise man believes them to be permanent?

A wealthy man may become destitute one day.
Wealth doesn't last; if it were permanent,
All the universe couldn't store our treasures.
Paupers' virtues can make them wealthy;
Absolute poverty is impossible for long,
For no beggar can live on nothing at all.

So you see, every situation in the world
Is impermanent, a composite phenomena.
Do not expect anything to endure forever;
Clutching appearances as real is true bondage.

Your present joys and sorrows
Arise from the power of former deeds
Interwoven like a patterned brocade.
Knowing this will free you from misery.

Today we cannot vie with our foes.
But when noble men engage in warfare,
If their foes submit with discipline,
The victor treats them fairly.

We should decorate the castle ramparts
With banners, pennants, and silk tapestries.
Let lovely music fill the air to welcome
The best of princes to Myriad Lights.

If we skillfully behave like this,
The prince will surely care for us,
Because he follows noble custom.
So please consider this positively.

This reasonable and wise speech suited the king's mind. He vowed to do exactly what had been suggested.

Just then Manohari realized her hopes were about to be fulfilled: "I will soon be able to make love with Prince Kumaradvitiya!" Sensual arousal made her happy deep in her heart. But when she gazed down at the field of battle, she saw numberless men who had lost their lives. She saw the vestiges of the army, who, although alive, were enduring extreme misery. She became very depressed: "Kye ma! These men are experiencing utter ruin and unimaginable suffering only because of me!"

Filled with heartrending pity, she looked in every direction. She tore off all her jewelry as if they were but trinkets to trade and piled it up as offerings to the Buddhas and bodhisattvas. She even sent forth clouds of imaginary offerings, as had the famous Bodhisattva Samantabhadra. Then she made prostrations and concentrated prayers in a hoarse voice:

I bow to the Buddhas and bodhisattvas,
Lords who gaze with unfailingly loving eyes
Upon those in distress throughout the day and night.
Please attend to me from your heavenly spheres.

The deep, boundless ocean of cyclic existence
Is churned by unceasing waves of karma and delusion;
We are drowning, trapped in a crocodile's jaws.
Please save us from this unbearable misery.

Greed, ignorance, hatred, and jealousy
Motivated this dispute between us.
Combat filled this vast valley with blood;
Corpses piled high make roads impassable.

Although some men remain alive,
In human form they suffer the tortures of hell.
These men came to ruin because of me, a lowly maid.
Excruciating pain is breaking my hard heart.

I supplicate the compassionate Buddhas,
The only source of hope, refuge, and protection.
Please free all beings burdened by sorrow
From fear of rebirth in the lower realms
And grant us the marvels of liberation!

21

In which Manohari and Prince Kumaradvitiya meet during the armistice ceremonies

THEN, FOLLOWING BRAHMADHIMAT'S ADVICE, the people of Myriad Lights decorated every part of the palace with victory banners, pennants, and so forth. Various types of musical instruments were readied: trumpets to blow, cymbals to tinkle, and drums to beat. From the upper floors of the residences, they dangled various exquisite ornaments. And finally they erected a high, jewel-encrusted throne. Their preparation for the welcoming celebration could not be rivaled even by the amazing wealth offered by the immortals to their king. Once they were completely ready, Brahmadhimat was sent as an envoy to invite Prince Kumaradvitiya to the palace.

Carrying smoking bundles of incense, he quickly went to where the youthful prince was taking his ease. He prostrated himself respectfully and courteously before the prince. Then, quivering with hopeful expectation, he knelt down, put his hands together, and said:

> A perfect moon, a marvelous, youthful prince,
> Emitting the cool nectar of happiness,
> Arose from churning the ocean of virtue.
> O Lord of Men, please listen a moment.

> We heard that many lands were sheltered
> By your fame, a canopy arched over the world.
> But we acted wrongly, influenced by prior evil deeds.
> Today I am contrite and confess our impropriety.

We deeply regret acting under demonic possession,
Trying to block the noble sun with our hands.

You are a nobleman and a true refuge,
Protecting others with love and firm compassion.
I come to be the seven horses of your chariot,
O Lord of Men, for you are the beneficent sun.
I invite you to the castle of Myriad Lights
To radiate bliss from its vast environs.

We all are in accord with this request.
So, O well-favored prince, please come
Without delay as an emperor of a universe!

After the minister spoke these smooth words of invitation, Prince
Kumara said with a smile:

"O retainer, listen well! An emperor of the universe travels high in
the sky on his golden wheel. Every ruler in the world, on land and in
the heavens, has said to him, 'Welcome, O god! We are at your command!' So isn't it redundant for men of a petty kingdom already under
his control to say, 'We will be your servants and make offerings to you'?

"Similarly, I have taken under my control even the tiniest dust motes
of this land. I rightfully claim all the marvelous possessions of Myriad
Lights, so what need is there to speak of it?"

"O god, you are right! But, consider this. Buddhas comprehend all
phenomena and lack any greed. They hold a clod of dirt to be as valuable
as a lump of gold; they make no distinction between vast offerings that fill
the sky and those fitting in the palm of one's hand. Yet if you sincerely
offer a mouthful of food or a handful of sand, the Buddhas are pleased,
because it increases your store of virtuous merit. In just this way, O noble
prince, because of your concern for us, you should grant our request."

Prince Kumara enjoyed this artful logic. "It is so, O minister. I will do
as you ask."

He mounted the throne of his chariot and approached the palace of
Myriad Lights surrounded by his vast entourage. As he passed through
the city's crossroads, men, women, and children gathered as suddenly as
thick rain clouds in the sky. They stared at the prince in wide-eyed
amazement and said to one another:

Both the sun and the moon dispel darkness,
Yet their light is very dissimilar.

The nature of the qualities of men
Obviously differs far more than that!

Our prince is reputed to be lovelier than the gods.
It was said no one could dislike his charms.
But the blazing bright glory of this prince
Outshines him like the sun beside a firefly.

The stern manner of this host of warriors
Is as frightening to see as the messengers of Death.
To try to vie with them was insanely improper.
We were ignorant or possessed by a demon.

A nobleman lovingly protects his court and friends.
A tormenting wraith cruelly squeezes his people.
It is pleasurable to see an honorable noble.
Thanks to good fortune, we now have this succor.
Relying on him will make our lives meaningful.

With many more praises, the prince was ushered into the lovely palace, which had been made even more beautiful by their amazing preparations. The sovereign of all the earth, King Kumaradvitiya, sat down upon the proffered jeweled throne. His actions and manner were dispassionate: like the king of elephants he had no arrogance. His good qualities amazed everyone. His glory blazed forth, glittering like a golden mountain as the sun revolves around it. Surrounded by his ministers, he seemed enveloped by the light of a thousand suns. Together they could be described as a lordly bull encircled by a herd of cattle; or the moon in the midst of garlanded constellations; or Indra surrounded by the gods of the heavens; or Brahma in the center of his pure land.

Replete with joy, the populace began to make superb offerings. The gifts were like the wealth of the gods of affluence during the opulence of summer.

At this time every possible taste of happiness and joy suffused Manohari. She rejoiced far more than a trader realizing a great profit, more than a farmer reaping a bountiful harvest, more than a warrior victorious in battle, and more than a sick person cured of an illness.

Her maidservants prepared her priceless clothes and ornaments. Emeralds, sapphires, rubies, pearls, coral, and opals were braided into her shiny black hair. Half her hair was left loose to her waist and half beautifully knotted at the nape of her neck. Across her forehead dangled strands of pretty multicolored gems. Scrimshaw carved pearls separated each jewel shaped like a flower bud. Her eyebrows were arched and finely drawn to attract men like a swarm of bees. Her thick eyelashes fluttered over her half-closed eyes, the shape of a lotus petal. Through these oval lids came liquid, sidelong glances. Her nose was nicely shaped; a bit high, and as straight as a reliquary to which men bow down. Her cheeks were the color of the rising sun because of the flush of sexual desire. Her captivating lips, the color of hibiscus, opened in a smile through which you could see her even, pearly white teeth. From her ears, shaped like a cluster of gardenias, hung gold earrings inset with turquoise and pearls. The dimensions of her throat were pleasingly moderate and draped with necklaces of priceless jewels twisted together like a conch shell. Pendants dangled beautifully from these strands of diamonds, coral, sapphires, and topaz to ornament her throat. On the smooth, supple flesh of her arms were bracelets of purest gold and silver inlaid with gems. On the joints of her fingers were many lovely rings. A filmy linen blouse was attractively draped over her seductive upper body. Through it you could see the protrusions of her high and firm breasts. Below her slim waist, at the curve of her hips, she wore a girdle woven of the best gold and precious gems. This was nicely trimmed with tiny bells, which gave forth a pleasant tinkling sound. She wore an elegant petticoat draped to show off the shape of her round, white thighs. She had slender and pretty ankles, and feet as lovely as white alabaster. As she walked off like a queen of swans, her foot ornaments jingled sweetly.

The sight of her made libidinous men drunk with cupidity and pained by the pangs of lust. When she arrived at the part of the palace where the prince and his ministers were sitting, every man there without exception thought:

"Eh ma! The essence of everything lovely in the world is gathered here in one. Her body and form are charming. She is innocent yet possesses all the arts of giving pleasure. She is like a nymph among the flowers of a forest grove. She is the most incredibly beautiful woman in existence. She could steal the presence of mind of ascetics who have abandoned all desire and craving for anything in the worldly plane. If she can do that to them, what can we say about what she does to those of us who have been under the power of licentiousness from beginningless time!"

They murmured among themselves. They were as mesmerized by

the orb of her face as if they were drawing its lines. They were completely bound by the long ropes of prurient desire for carnal enjoyment.

> The lovely visaged maiden
> Coyly lowered her face,
> But a glance from the corner of her eye
> Was directed at wonderful Prince Kumara.

> When her discerning eyes picked out
> The moon among the stars, the whitest lotus on a pond,
> She was ensnared by his handsome allure
> Like a doe caught in a trap.

> As soon as that beautiful maiden
> Came into the prince's line of vision,
> He trembled in the winds of desire,
> Though he pretended to be firm.

> He thought, "This is unbelievable.
> A lovely form appears before my eyes.
> The fingers of skilled artisans
> Could not have fashioned her so well!"

> She should be put on a jeweled throne;
> So men can bow and make offerings to her.
> Her qualities surpass those of humankind.
> He lusted for the bliss of sexual consummation.

> At this time, the seductive damsel
> Glanced at him very sensuously
> And sang this freshly composed song
> With a multitude of melodious sounds:

> "Eh ma ho!
> Today in the all-encompassing heavens,
> Immortal gods and goddesses dance
> And sing many a sweet melody.
> Their auspicious songs fill the universe.

> The sky is filled with propitious signs:
> Luminous rainbows festoon the heavens;

The thousand-rayed sun is at its zenith;
Pretty clouds are a lovely white canopy.

The five lovely sense goddesses
Dance beautifully and sing sweetly
To pay homage in a way never done before:
Lovely Form displays a stainless mirror.
Sound plucks a thousand-stringed lute.
Magnificent Scent wafts forth a perfumed mist.
Taste satisfies everyone with ambrosia.
Touch adorns all with soft, godly raiment.

Flowers float down in a refreshing drizzle.
Various sorts of music are played all around.
The pleasant melodies of the songs and dances
Draw the figure of happiness in everyone's heart.

The castle of Myriad Lights is the center
Of the opulence of the vast earth's bounty.
To see the palace made of jeweled bricks
Is now a source of my joy.

Here is the prince who is the fruition
Of my prayers and deeds of so very long.
Merely to hear the name Kumaradvitiya
Pleases my mind as never before.

Craving the piquant experience of connubial love,
I lacked the good fortune to see your face.
But that enervating sorrow is over today!
My bliss glitters like a thousand suns
Revolving around a precious golden mountain.

The joy of being crowned emperor of the universe
Is only a fraction of my pleasure here today.
Hearing your speech is a fount of ecstasy
Unequaled by Brahma's song or a dragon's bellow.

From the propensities of our unbreakable love
Placed deep in my heart, I concentrated and prayed
To end my long separation from your loving eyes.
Today my wishes are fulfilled just as I hoped.

I cast away affluence, friends, and retinue,
Wishing to see your face and touch your feet.
But the flower of my desire was blighted by frost.
Now my dark sorrow is pervaded by joyful light;
I have the good fortune to see your face today."

Prince Kumara listened with great concentration to these and other sweet words of supplication. He listened the way a swan on the bank of a lotus pond arches his neck to attend respectfully to the rushing sound of a waterfall. The prince experienced the taste of joy; nonetheless he desired to test the true sentiments of the maid Manohari:

Nubile maiden, all women are dishonest!
You let fall a rain of sweet elocution.
Yet the moonlike image of your thoughts
Is obscured by clouds of chicanery.
Is it not right to label you hypocrites?

Usually if common folk see degradation,
They fly away like mountain birds.
But they cluster around something marvelous,
Though you beat them off like dogs.

Similarly, O temptress, for a long time
Your first lover, Devatisha, satisfied you.
But now that he is ruined, you bow to me;
Is it right to cast him out like spittle?

Curtail your expression of deceitful words.
With good nature serve your former husband!

Manohari thought to herself: "For a very long time I have subsisted on the food of sorrow and have drunk only tears. Not for a minute have I wished for anything other than to be with this youthful prince. But he seems to be bound in a web of evil doubts about my virtue. He is as suspicious of his own shadow as a crow. So I will tell him the truth again." Then she spoke:

O Earth Lord, your pure crystal mind
Is obscured by the stains of base doubts.

You admonish me with ill-considered words.
But I am reputable, not a basis for aspersion.

You exaggerate, saying women are deceitful.
It is not right to slander all so!
One discerns the quality of women
By their deeds; it is the same for men.

On no occasion did I ever think
Of a man other than you, my lord.
Although you pile bundles of green grass
Before a beast of prey, will he enjoy it?

That prince was inflamed with passion,
Drunk with lust, he trembled like a reed.
Although he strove to gain me as a lover,
I held him off with skillful, confusing words.

He never had me as a passionate mistress!
I smiled and spoke calm pleasantries,
Which like the white light of the moon
Cooled the heat of lust in his heart.

I made myself lovely for others to see,
But I never sent improper signals:
No man was a target at which I shot
Glances desirous of sexual play.

I am as young and lovely as a fresh flower;
My voluptuous form entraps men's minds.
Although they burn with the fire of desire,
I have never satisfied their thirst.

I am of a noble and honorable lineage.
I have matured to an intelligent age.
I have never had occasion to act deceitfully
And confuse your mind with crooked words.

You have been my mind's sole support,
The object of my eyes and my pillow for sleep.
I planted the banner of my hopes in this,
Yet you wound my mind with this untrue speech.

Woe is me! I thought of no one but you
During the long time before you arrived.
Time did not pass; each day seemed a year.
In distress I spent the long days lamenting,
And now you cast me out of your net of love!

I gazed with eyes swollen with tears
From the topmost roof of the palace
As a pair of birds from Gem of the World
Came joyfully soaring, united by love.

This natural occurrence in the sky
Made me wonder if I could accompany you so.
My doubts caused me unbearable sorrow.
I fainted and fell like a hewn tree.

My servants revived me with water and fans,
But I miserably wept unceasing tears.
I wailed without intelligible words,
Like a wild, wounded creature without succor.

I lost desire to eat; my flesh wasted away.
Sorrow dulled my bright complexion and eyes.
To assuage others' doubts, I smiled brightly,
But streams of tears trickled over my face.

Because of the power of negative energy,
My voluptuous sixteen-year-old form,
Filled with the essence of beauty,
Became as thin as a new sickle moon.

Then, O prince, your form's amazing image
Arose clearly in the mirror of my mind.
Clutching that thought, I chanted
Your name repeatedly in my throat.

Someone addicted to his own pleasure
Cannot see another's suffering nature.
Just so is your scolding of me.
This is slander, not noble behavior.

A massive dark cloud of doubts
Prevents your moonlike mind from shining:
It has lost the power to emanate streams
Of the white light of happy thoughts.

Although my nature is straight as an arrow,
You call me a knave crooked as a bent bow.
Do not upright people shun such calumny
And regret such a heavy sin of speech?

So, with the weapon of deep analysis,
You should chop through the cords of doubt
Tightly binding your mind in many layers.
Protect me always with your far-seeing eyes.

In the garden of the gods, my virtuous merit
Has grown into a tree with flowing branches,
Heavy with the ripe fruit of my hopes.
Today I have the chance to pick and enjoy them.

The cumulative effect of earlier black deeds
Was a thick, dark cloud of enveloping misery.
The blazing light of your compassionate heart
Auspiciously burns away the clouds like the sun.

When I see you here at our first meeting,
My mind is captivated, my eyes held fast.
Although we are yet unacquainted, you are my only love
Thanks to the force of former prayers and deeds.
O please love me well!

Prince Kumaradvitiya's mind did not wander; he listened attentively to her sweet words. For him they were as delicious as the taste of honey. As she spoke, he gazed at the fair maiden's seductive form. Her throat palpitated like a blooming lotus in a breeze. Her supplication was like the song of a flock of swans playing in a lotus pond.

Joy suffused him, and he thought: "Ah ho! If you gathered all the lovely qualities of a thousand goddesses into one, it still could not compare with her! She is the essence of feminine beauty and propriety. She is skilled in the arts of love and has all the auspicious signs of a precious woman: she is a joy to see, the sweet scent of sandalwood wafts from her body and mouth, to touch her gives sublime happiness, and so forth. Not a single fault can be found with her.

"I have found this creature in the world of men thanks to the lot created by my virtues. And well found she is!"

He felt a bit ashamed of his earlier scolding to test her. So he said:

> You did not arise from Brahma's primeval womb,
> Nor were you born in the lineage of Indra.
> Although you were not born a fairy of love,
> You are superior to all the nymphs and goddesses.
>
> The universe lacks an example
> To illustrate beauty like yours.
> The moon is the paradigm of loveliness,
> But it is eclipsed by the rays of the sun.
>
> You are a tendril of a wish-granting tree;
> Your form is the flower that decorates it.
> Your behavior is a bloom of auspiciousness.
> Its sweet scent, your reputation, wafts forth.
>
> A woman like you is a mere rumor
> In the heavens and god realms:
> Never before has one like you
> Existed in the world of men.
>
> Virtuous merit accumulated over many aeons
> Resulted in my being an emperor of the universe.
> Such a ruler has seven precious assets;
> You are the best, you will be my queen.
>
> On your seductive form undulating like a lotus
> Are luscious breasts as desirable as honey.
> Your face, like the orb of the waxing moon,
> Is beautified by your wide, doelike eyes.
>
> Lovelier than the evening clouds
> Are your ruddy cheeks and gleaming smile.
> On your shiny, black, well-dressed hair

Are crown-jewel ornaments glittering with light.
Your smiling lips emit a fresh, sweet smell;
Their color and shape humble a pomegranate's pride.

Your throat and marvelous, slim waist
Are perfect for the play of embrace.
Beautified by strands of glittering gems,
You are a purifying vision for ailing eyes.

For aeons I treasured you deep in my heart;
You were never loosened from my love's hold.
But I wondered if the pure good of your nature
Was tarnished by adverse circumstances.
So I spoke castigating words to test you.
I know they are contrary to the truth!

Because of the profound links of our karma,
My love for you never slackened.
So I clearly vowed to come here
To this kingdom in order to obtain you.

Then my parents, subjects, and court
Tried to obstruct me, crying many tears.
With pained hearts they wailed aloud,
But they could not dissuade me from pursuing you.

Steadfastly I came to this realm thinking
I would subdue them with pacific means.
However, men's karma is irreversible:
Despite my hope, they were reduced to dust.
This heavy sin will cause me to be reborn
In cyclic existence and endure much sorrow.
Yet my resolve to obtain you never weakened.

O lovely maid, previously your fresh visage
Was blighted by the tormenting touch of winter.
Now you may enjoy the happy festival
Of the auspicious opulence of summer.

O slender maid, you are a fresh white lotus
Arising from the stainless lake of a good lineage

Temporarily wilted by unfortunate clouds;
Now you are nourished by your lover, the sun.

O youthful maid, grown on the fertile field
Of good deeds our hopes were ready to harvest.
Although a cutting hail tried to destroy it,
My skill dispelled those threatening clouds.

O nubile maid, you experienced misery
As evil hunters spread traps everywhere
To capture you, a lovely doe.
But now you are freed from the snares of sorrow.

O delicate maid, the moon of pure thoughts
Rises unobstructed in the sky of proper actions.
For a time, thick, importunate clouds darkened it,
But now, free from clouds, its light shines forth.

O doe-eyed maid, the moon rises in the sky;
The night lily remains far away on earth.
But they hope to enjoy sensual bliss together
Thanks to pure white deeds and prayers.

O seductive maid, men wishing to enjoy
Your sensual body tried to thwart your hopes.
But now, free from their sway,
You have the chance to be with whom you wish.

So he spoke these and other joyful words, expressing the essence of
his desire. Then he offered her a place upon a silk-covered throne. Once
again, the young maiden respectfully and politely bowed to Prince
Kumaradvitiya with her body, speech, and mind. She sang this versified
song expressing her strong love for him:

O lamp of the world, an eminent orb
Beautified by a thousand beneficial rays.
May your pure light nourish this white lotus
Free from muck yet growing from the swamps.

O glowing white and perfect moon,
Vast treasure of love and compassion,

Please cause this night lily to open
Its white petals of pure thoughts.

As summer thunder you reveal lovers' secrets
High in the layers of adoring clouds.
Please grant this peahen great bliss
As your sound reaches the ground below.

Firmly rooted by impartial compassion,
Your love is a tree with spreading branches.
There sits a cuckoo singing of true joy.
Please let me fill the universe with this song.

O Lord of Men, the force of our love
In other lives resulted in my propensity
Ardently to wish to love only you.
Please never waver in your care of me.

In response to her words, the prince smiled and set forth this garland
of words sweet to hear:

Joy, sorrow, wealth, and poverty
Flash like lightning in cyclic existence.
We know they are impermanent and faulty,
But it is difficult to stop delusion and desire.

Therefore, the essential point of religion
Is to act honestly and without ignorance
About the functioning of cause and effect.
A man who supports himself so is a noble.

Noble maiden, we have the results
Arising from our earlier proclivities.
I have wished in my heart to unite with you
As closely as the moon and its light.

In the world some men have strong jealousy;
They cannot bear to see others' good fortune.
So these men attempted to divide us.
But my love for you is unbreakable,
As firm and unmoving as a diamond mountain.

The winds of divisiveness and slander
Shall never shake it in the slightest.

Because of the residues of some black actions,
You had to suffer some incessant sorrows.
But now the fruits of virtuous merit
Are ripening like flawless white pearls.

Therefore, please hold in mind
These words of my profound love,
Springing from my honest heart.
Let us enjoy the play of our love.

Manohari's mind was freed from the bondage of doubt when she heard this clear song. A bliss that she had never before experienced suffused her. "It is as I had hoped for so long. I have not fallen from the net of this prince's love," she thought. She was in a carefree state of mind.

22

In which the terms of peace are laid out

THEN KING CHANDRAMATI, his royal heir, Devatisha, and their ministers approached the victorious prince. They bowed and touched the crowns of their heads to the jeweled footstool in front of his throne. After this they sat down on one side.

The noble prince had a peaceful and compassionate nature. For many, many lifetimes he had been attempting to reach enlightenment solely in order to benefit other living creatures. Thus, he had completely dispelled the darkness of hatred from his mind: the white light of his compassion invariably shone forth. Yet, at this point, he decided to test them for a while. So he loudly sang this song:

> Men who live with me in peace
> Never have occasion to feel my anger.
> But I do not exercise my compassion
> Toward those who pugnaciously fight me.
>
> Thus, there are two possibilities:
> To kill you or to let you live in peace.
> To clarify doubt as to which it will be,
> Please respond honestly to these questions.
>
> The ministerial council of Gem of the World,
> A kingdom never varying from the noble path,

All agreed that the enchanting maiden
Of Dyutimat's lineage, Manohari,
Was a rope binding the deer of my mind.
So we were to be ritually united in marriage.

We made great efforts to fulfill this plan.
But when we were about to obtain her,
An unseemly hindering wind scattered
Our good work like clouds in the sky.

So later our armies that cover the earth
Raised their fearsome arsenal of weapons.
Tell me clearly who caused this situation
Through having the foolish vanity to thwart me.

In general, elephants do an insane dance,
Heedlessly treading toward a confrontation
With their enemy, a fearless king of lions.
However, those fools are committing suicide.

When the evil-natured lack any other option,
They bow their heads and surrender.
That is the sign of an ignorant fool.
What intelligent man would be pleased by it?

You raised the most powerful army you could
To battle us fiercely and heroically.
Yet you never found a chance to harm me.
You were but fuel for my blazing fire.

Now you try to beguile me with welcoming,
Peaceful words, sweet music, and celebration.
I already control even the dust motes
Of this vast land of Myriad Lights,
So is it not pointless to request
"Please grace this land with your presence"?

You were not satisfied to enjoy
Your own plentiful treasure of marvels.
Do you see now the results of evil deeds
Motivated by coveting others' wealth?

It is the mark of a fool to be tortured
By painful regret after completing an action
Destructive as the dance of a zombie
Done without any consideration beforehand.

Therefore, you will have to experience
The effects of your despicable deeds.
You shall see the void nature of the mind
When your contaminated bodies are reduced to dust!

This sharp denunciation deeply pained the men of Myriad Lights. However, the prince's intention was to tell them subtly that his powers had been exerted only to obtain Manohari. He had no anger toward those who came to surrender. Nevertheless, they were all frightened and dismayed by the prince's criticism. So they thought:

"We thought this prince followed all noble customs and so, assured of his compassion, we respectfully surrendered. Yet our hopes are dashed. We misjudged the prince, he is like other men; his inner thoughts vary greatly from his words. It is so hard to penetrate the depths of a man's intentions! This prince lured us like fish. He disguised his sharp hook with a desirable mouthful of food. Now he has caught us for slaughter."

Distress paralyzed most of the men of Myriad Lights; immobilized like cuckoos in winter, they stared without winking and could not utter a sound. Only the minister Brahmadhimat thought with his penetrating mind:

"This prince has totally discomfited us with biting calumny. The end result seems to be that we are close to losing our lives. He seems not to have the slightest regret about this! I cannot bear to sit in silence. I must honestly express our true nature."

So he straightened his shoulders and said:

I bow to you, a master of bodhisattvas' deeds.
Your beautiful body blazes with glory.
Your pure speech is music for the ears.
Your mind is naturally compassionate.

Kye! O sovereign of the earth!
To see you is a fount of joy.
We hear you praised throughout the world.
Recollecting you induces great happiness.
Your touch pacifies all sorrow.

We repent and regret! Because of karma
We wandered in the dark land of ignorance,
Ascending the rocky peaks of greed and hatred.
Drunk with pride, we demonically wielded weapons.

O prince worthy of refuge,
I confess and concede we tried to best you.
Like owls we are unable to bear sunlight,
But nonchalantly we went out in the day.
Now other birds have found us and will do us in.

Nevertheless, the nature of the nobility
Is always to speak with honesty,
Never occasioning the slightest shame.
Kye! Consider this minor matter for a moment.

First, this lovely new moon
Arising from the ocean of Dyutimat's line
Was promised as a bride to Devatisha:
Our two realms we vowed to protect as one.

Afterward, we could not bear to hear
Of the incursions of Gem of the World.
We sent our forces to escort her here,
Not intending to rob you of your true love.

Later, your titanic, fearsome army
Came and filled this entire land.
Thus provoked we came out to fight,
Thinking to vie with men of similar strength.

In particular we did not know
About your extraordinary qualities,
A prince who surpasses ordinary men
And tames all beings with magic displays.

We were not the first to attack!
But the decision to do battle,
Whether good or totally evil,
Was something determined by me alone.

Now with fervent trust we come
To no other ruler but you for refuge.
If you cast us out of your compassion,
Without regret we will endure our karma.

However, if you are a superior nobleman,
Never varying from peaceful compassion,
And a lord and guide of all beings,
Is it not right to care for us too?

O sovereign of men, Prince Kumaradvitiya,
Please attend to these words of Brahmadhimat.
They are untainted by craftiness and deceit.
I beg of you, please view us with love.

Prince Kumaradvitiya had the ability to discern truth from false-
hood. So he found no reason for displeasure in Brahmadhimat's honest
words. He smiled broadly and said:

"O king and ministers, listen well. My words were disingenuous; I
was testing your nature. If I had meant what I said, in battle I would
have destroyed your forces, killed you, and reduced your kingdom to a
mere name. That would have been so easy to do, I could have done it
with one hand! Now that I have come into your house, what need is
there to boast? I make no distinction between my friends and former
enemies; so cast off your bonds of doubt and suffering! I give you leave
to live; be joyful and carefree."

Prince Kumaradvitiya anointed both King Chandramati and
Devatisha and placed them on the thrones of small principalities worthy
of them. He did not differentiate between his former and new ministers; he had them abide as loving elder and younger brothers.

Thus, all went according to the nature of things: whatever actions had
been done ripened into their accordant results. The Earth Lord
Chandramati and his son bent their heads before Prince Kumaradvitiya
with great deference. They bowed so low the prince could see only their
jeweled crowns. The ministers of Myriad Lights respected the prince more
than they had their former ruler. They held him dear to their hearts, gave
him good advice, and tirelessly took up his commands as their burden.

Fools infuriated by the slightest contradiction
Are agitated and rampage like wild elephants.

No one respects people who harshly slander others;
They are seen as crooked saplings offering no shade.

The wise kindly protect their enemies as friends,
Satisfying their desire for food, wealth, and so on.
They speak nicely, so we are pleased to rely upon them.
Like devoted children, we happily do their bidding.

From beginningless time we have been lost,
Wandering in cyclic existence without a guide.
Our friends become our hated enemies after a time.
The foes who destroy our property and lives
Transform into cherished friends we lovingly protect.
Sometimes strangers become vicious and murder us;
Other times they become our dearly beloved children.
Samsara is misery, unworthy of the least trust.
Not recognizing it, we are deceived into desire.

The noble prince had developed equanimity:
He had neither love nor hatred in his heart.
Satisfying all beings with the taste of joy
Creates virtuous merit beyond measure.

Whatever seeds of virtue or sin
Are planted in the field of our lives
Ripen into their accordant fruit.
None can dispute this: it is seen in the world.

The loving eyes of that Lord of Men
Relieved misery like the moon's cool light.
Every being with any intelligence vowed
To respect him with body, speech, and mind.

The virtuous merit created in abundance
By the righteous, discerning Earth Lord
And his respectful ministers and people
Led to everyone's obtaining worldly plenty.

23

In which Prince Kumaradvitiya and Manohari are married

THE BRIDAL CELEBRATIONS FOR PRINCE KUMARADVITIYA and
Manohari went on for seven days. The vast outlay of provisions par-
taken during the marriage party seemed to arise from the essence
of the wealth of the immortal gods. The guests enjoyed beer, honeyed
wine, liquor, and intoxicants of many sorts. Young men, maidens, and all
the rest became inebriated and lusted for the great bliss of sexual contact.

Arising from an ocean of the essence
Of marvels that can be enjoyed insatiably,
Festive clouds filled all space, delighting
The mind by drizzling the nectar of wealth.

Everywhere in beautifully decorated rooms
People imbibing quantities of honeyed wine
Danced and sang absorbed in desire
For an ever fresh wealth of sensual pleasure.

Seductive young women and handsome men
Gracefully engaged in courtship dances.
They so beautified the wedding ceremony
Even heavenly courtesans were put to shame.

Joyous marriage rituals like this
Went on for a garland of seven days.
Following noble customs, the new couple

Were unable to shed the clothes of modesty,
Nor could they find the chance to unite.

Until the festivities ended on the eighth day,
The prince pretended to be firmly chaste;
But the wind of lust from lifetimes of experience
Blew, and he quivered like a tender vine.

He thought, "The quintessence of sensory pleasure
Is the touch engendering sexual bliss.
Without that there is no point at all
To this joyful celebration of food and drink."

Each day of the weeklong marriage feast
Seemed to the prince to be a full year.
Every moment of the last day was endless,
Seeming to go on for a hundred hours.

Finally the profoundly wise
Sun god, the lord of the day,
Slowly sank in the western skies
To fulfill the lovers' wishes.

Over the high crest of the eastern peaks,
The crystal orb of the moon majestically rose,
Shedding lovely light as if to rival
The beauty of the goddess Manohari.

Then, on a sweetly scented lotus pond,
A cluster of fresh maiden night lilies
Unfurled their petals in desire,
Shaking their pistils in a smile of love.

The red–clothed goddess of sunset,
Wantonly lusting for her lover the moon,
Threw her modest garb across the sky,
Awaiting the taste of sexual bliss.

The seductively youthful sky goddess,
Ready to consummate the festival of love,
Draped herself in necklaces of stars
And put on her enchanting moon earring.

When night's full beauty shone forth,
The couple who for so long had dreamed
Only about a fete of bliss with each other,
Joyfully went together to a private residence.

They cast off all their delightful ornaments
And heavenly raiment soft to the touch.
Their naked bodies were beautiful,
Adorned by the clothes of former chastity.

Their shining eyes delighted in each other.
They insatiably gazed with desirous eyes
At the marvels of their amazing bodies,
Seductively free from obscuring clothes.

Soft to the lotus-hand's first touch,
They entwined in complete embrace.
Their red-petal lips united in a kiss
As they completed the foreplay of union.

She opened wide the gates of her thighs,
As white, firm, and round as plantain trees.
Then the prince, like a king of swans,
Entered her bliss-inducing lotus lake.

Her lovely body wrapped around him
Like a clinging vine entwines
An erect tree in beautiful full bloom
As they enjoyed this sexual embrace.

The lovely maid's face gazed upward,
As captivating to see as the beautiful moon.
Her husband's smiling visage seemed to
Drink the nectar of her fair charms.

Although cool moonlight shone upon them,
Perspiration beaded upon cheeks burning with lust.
The moist wind of passion blew strong,
But drunk with ardor their faces glowed like fire.

She moaned, completely prostrate
Under the heavy weight of the prince.

But still she danced with lavish movements,
Like a Champaka petal tossed by the wind.

Knowledgeable in all the arts of love,
They relished a thousand positions.
Yet lust immovably fixed their eyes
Half-closed, in the posture of samadhi.

The touch of her bliss-inducing lotus
Caused his hot ecstasy to erupt.
At the end of the raptures of lust,
They felt their bodies melt away.

Her mind pervaded by perfect joy,
The lovely young woman said:

"Lips never bruised by another's touch
Today open wide in a laughing smile.
The Utpala-scented portals of my mouth
Are now satiated by the nectar of bliss.

Adorned with tinkling bracelets, my soft hands
Never lusted to touch another for even a moment.
So today I have the marvelous good fortune
To unite in embrace with you, superb Kumara.

No other man had the chance to enjoy
The sight of my round, white breasts.
Today they are a fount of sublime joy
In contact with a handsome prince's body.

No man has ever ventured beneath
Garments covering my soft white thighs.
Yet today I have obtained perfect ecstasy
Thanks to the penetration of your lovely body.

No other man had opened my unspoiled lotus,
The source of mutual sensual bliss.
Today, noble prince, I am fulfilled
By the nectar of your ecstasy.

Ah ma ma la! O Lord of Men!
Your touch is the essence of pleasure,
Happiness superior to the immortals' rapture.
Please never suspend this festival of love."

She wove that garland of pleasant words
As an ornament to be worn on his throat.
Then, breathing the ties of their love,
He enchantingly whispered in her ears:

"Only you have a body like a supple lotus stalk.
Only you have a face as lovely as the full moon.
Only a glance from the corner of your eyes
Can pierce my heart like a sharp arrow.

In the vast expanses of the world's forests,
There are many astonishingly lovely trees.
But the best of all is the white sandal tree.
Who other than you is worthy of such sweet praise?

Because of the strong force of our prior actions,
Today we have the fortune to enter into union.
Once again our love is poured into one vessel:
Never shall I transgress this pure vow.

Because the pure customs of the well-bred
Last longer than rivers may flow,
My love, we shall enjoy in all our lives
The taste of the highest sensual bliss!"

Many other loving words were exchanged, until the harbingers of
dawn arrived at the summit of the eastern mountains. Finally, this joyous occasion celebrating the marvels of newly arisen sexual love came
to an end.

They obtained the essence of good fortune
To consummate their desire for each other.
Even the mindless, empty sky trembled
At that astonishing spectacle of desire.

To see this joyous festival of love,
Dawn's light arose in the eastern skies.
She only pretended to come to draw
Forth the jewel of the heavens.

The great lamp of the universe,
Gloriously blazing with rays
Of pure glittering light,
Came to illumine the entire world.

The sun came to wake them from sleep,
Doubting they could be in continual embrace.
But the lovers were in an unshakable samadhi,
Their minds entrapped in the joy of making love.

Then the maiden lotuses were
Liberated from suffering in darkness.
With happiness and a smile, their petals
Unfurled in a wealth of good fortune.

The prince and his consort, Manohari, lived happily together with their ministers in the great kingdom of Myriad Lights. For a long time they remained there, enjoying their sensual embraces.

24

In which Prince Kumaradvitiya's father is seduced into a second marriage

A

T THE SAME TIME IN OPEN LOTUS, the capital city of Gem of the
World, King Suryamati felt discontented working inside the
palace. To satisfy his desire to see the splendor of summer in full
bloom, the king took his entourage to the garden called Floating
Pavilion, in the eastern part of the castle precincts. There to pass the
time they amused themselves, frolicking like soaring flocks of sand-
pipers.

Imprudent members of the court ate and drank a fantastic array of
refreshments. The powerful liquors and honeyed wines they imbibed
made them extremely intoxicated. A few courtiers staggered when they
walked, while others danced and sang, some melodiously and some out
of tune. A few men shouted out abuse, attempting to instigate argu-
ments and disputes. Yet others' modesty was so overcome by alcohol
they publicly embraced slim girls, enjoying the honey of their kisses and
other sorts of amorous behavior.

All of the young men and women of the city secretively came to
view this exhibition from hidden corners of the lattice of vines and
trees surrounding the pleasure garden. Among these folk was Lavanya
Kamala, the lovely daughter of the minor official Padmankura. When
the king caught sight of her peeping like a forest nymph from a sheltered spot amidst the undulating trees and flowers, lustful designs
formed instantaneously in his heart. "Is she a goddess of the gardens, or
just a particularly beautiful mortal girl?" he wondered, and he went to
ask his ministers.

"A nymph, or perhaps a mere girl, is spying on us through an aperture in the hedge of trees surrounding the garden. Please find out what she really is. I command you to make these inquiries; tell me truly what is her lineage, what is her age, whether she has been taken in matrimony, and by what name she is known."

After listening to the king's orders, the ministers said: "We will do as you command," and they went off to question the girl as directed. The maiden cleverly bowed her head and said: "Please do not tease me! Why do you interrogate me about my family, age, and name?"

"We are not persecuting you. We merely follow the king's command."

"Well, in that case I will tell you the truth, please listen. I am a member of the family of the government official Padmankura: it is a lineage as worthy of praise as a stainless white lotus. As for my name, I am known as Lavanya Kamala. I am sixteen years old and so have not passed beyond cheerful play in my parents' home. I have not undergone the trial of being taken in matrimony to another's house."

The ministers reported exactly what she said to the king. He felt great joy. "If it is as they say, I definitely must have her for my pleasure!" This indecent thought arose unbidden in his mind.

That very day the joyful interlude ended, and the Earth Lord leisurely strolled back to the palace with the image of the maiden Lavanya Kamala engraved on his heart.

The next morning, the lowly minister Padmankura was summoned to the residence of the king. With a smile, his monarch said: "Kye, kye! O faultless servant Padmankura, there is a small matter you may help me accomplish." He continued, saying:

"In the mother-of-pearl womb of a faultless lineage,
An astonishingly lovely, shiny white pearl
Was nurtured by the heat of excellent virtue.
This fresh, incalculably precious pendant gem
Is a worthy ornament for the greatest of the great.
I have firmly vowed to dangle this jewel,
Found among the gardens of Floating Pavilion,
From the necklaces adorning my throat.

The lovely Lavanya Kamala has arisen
from the family known as Padmankura.
O best of my highest wise ministers,
You should send her to me as a gift."

Lustful desire, the heart of the king's words,
Shone like the sun, causing Padmankura to blossom.
His smile quivered like flower petals in the wind.
"O Lord, long may you rule!" he said.

Genuflecting, he further replied:

O Lord, you are the creator
Of all happiness and joy
For residents of the earth!
Please listen with love to my words.

My daughter accords with her name:
She is truly a gorgeous blossom.
Her face glows like a hundred moons.
Her eyes are a cluster of blue lotus petals.
Her limbs are like slim lotus stalks.
Her smile shows teeth like a range of snowy peaks.

Can even the maiden Manohari,
Renowned for her loveliness,
Sought for by our Prince Kumara,
Rival my daughter's amazing beauty?

Thus, if my swan Kamala has entered
The lake of my Lord of Men's mind,
How can I possibly question or object?
My body and life are yours to command.

However, where there is great excellence,
There are also extremely powerful hindrances.
Therefore, to obtain her for your lover,
You must take these promises to heart.

Even if you should enjoy my daughter's love
Just once, you must be as constant to her
As the moon is devoted to the night lily,
Even if Queen Kundaladhara becomes jealous.

Know that it would be impossibly wrong
To loosen the bonds of this new intimacy

Even if Manohari, royalty of Radiant Array,
Should hate her, unable to tolerate a rival beauty.

Some of your obstinate courtiers' minds
Are as hateful as jagged-toothed saws:
Even if they endeavor to cut you asunder,
Vow not to come under their influence.

In particular, even if superb Prince Kumara
Along with his skillful ministers
Should sow dissension and slanderous censure,
Your love must be as adamantine as diamond.

Pledge never to contradict her wishes:
Hold her words deep in your heart
And act upon all the secret desires
Poured into your ears by that captivating maid.

Now for the most important promise of all:
If there is male offspring of this superb union,
You will be bound to crown the child heir
To the marvelous wealth of the realm.

Thus, O gracious Earth Lord Suryamati,
Please repeat these unalterable promises.
These words will be like the sun shining
Clear light on the path to your goal.

When Padmankura finished speaking, the king thought: "Just as
I hoped! I have the power to take Lavanya Kamala into my hands.
However, two of the promises he is trying to exact are quite
improper. I cannot always heed whatever she should command,
nor can I treat with indifference the eldest of my line. My son,
Prince Kumaradvitiya, is adorned with so many amazing qualities, how could I make the progeny of this girl my successor?" So
he replied:

Your sensible words sprout
From wisdom broad as a lotus petal,
Flowering as bliss for my mind.
My wishes are about to reach fruition.

However, men discern their ruler's quality
As easily as traders separate baubles from gems.
So when victory drums loudly proclaim worldwide
The auspicious, compassionate, and judicious deeds
Of the peerless prince called Kumaradvitiya,
Would any clever man believe it to be reasonable
If I were to adorn another with the kingdom's crown,
Not placing this elder prince upon the throne?

I will attend to everything of virtuous purport
In the secrets divulged by the lovely maid.
But any ill-considered, hastily spoken deceits
Are not matters to be held as true.

Therefore, except for these two vows
Beyond the bounds of consideration,
I shall happily fulfill
Everything else you worthily requested.

The king's reply did not please Padmankura. With a black scowl he answered:

"Kye! Great King, I understand well the particulars of your intentions! Your equivocation may be illustrated by this example.

"We all would love to have a priceless, wish-fulfilling gem that grants all we desire or need. Nevertheless, we do not want to face the difficulties of obtaining it. To find such a jewel, we would have to risk setting out upon the vast ocean, placing ourselves in danger from demons and ill winds. Similarly, you want to hold in your hands Lavanya Kamala, a girl who is supremely beautiful. But you are unwilling to make these promises to obtain your object of desire.

"Therefore, I am opposed to your intentions. Because I am your servant, you may punish my disobedience with a fearsome edict and kill me. As for the girl, because she is so lovely, some ruler of a petty principality will fall in love with her. Her beauty and rank will enhance his wealth, power, and pride. Such a ruler will immediately agree to these promises, so my family's hopes will be realized. This is the true state of affairs."

After Padmankura spoke these words in a voice choked with tears, he bowed in supplication. The king's lust was so strong that his mind became hardened against rational thought. He was like a small boat tossed about on the powerful waves of the vast ocean. Nothing could stop him from obtaining his desire. So he thought:

"What Padmankura said is true. It strikes me as correct, for it is ignoble to dislike undergoing the difficulties that serve to accomplish a goal. In addition, it is unlikely that Lavanya Kamala would conceive a male who could become my heir. So for now, I can safely grant this minister's wishes."

"I promise exactly what you ask," he vowed.

The news that the king was about to engage in an indecent marriage, with all its attendant promises, passed quickly from one person to another. All the ministers came to know of it and were greatly distressed. The prime minister Parambhasvaramati's heart drained: he felt unbearably uneasy. He and all the other high ministers went to King Suryamati. They prostrated themselves before him without a glimmer of a smile, and with downcast demeanors, they said:

> Many times heretofore we have sincerely bowed
> Our limbs before your honorable lotus feet
> Worthy to receive the crown jewels of proud royalty.
> Now please listen to words motivated by pure intentions.
>
> Prince Kumaradvitiya was conceived
> In the womb of noble Queen Kundaladhara
> Thanks to the fortune of virtuous merit
> Held by Gem of the World, a realm praised
> As the most precious country in the world.
>
> From childhood, the prince was a master of scholars;
> He penetrated the depths of vast realms of knowledge.
> He is a fearless god among men: he has Brahma's wisdom,
> The glory of Indra, the martial prowess of Arjuna,
> Magnificent fame, and a mastery of all the arts.
>
> Now he has gone to the realm of Myriad Lights
> With a vast army to destroy our foes in battle.
> And we hear a report that his father, Suryamati,
> Wanders through the dark continent of ignorance.
>
> If Queen Mother Kundaladhara had borne no heir,
> It would be suitable to take a second queen.
> But we have appointed as your successor
> Prince Kumara, born thanks to our virtuous merit.
> So can it be true that you will take as a wife
> An object of scorn, the conniving, low-class Lavanya Kamala?

Kye ma! O Lord of Men! What are you thinking?
The world's censure will fall like rain upon us.
Prince Kumara's labors will be for naught.
This situation is extremely depressing and befuddling.
Please contemplate carefully! Act cautiously!
Do not go beyond the bounds of nobility!

Their thoughtful advice caused the king to hang his head. His face
wilted like a lotus placed in utter darkness. But despite his mortifica-
tion, he was not to be deterred. So he uttered these unpleasant words to
his ministers:

You host of ministers are called "wise ones,"
But you totally lack ability to discriminate!
You spout a long string of words
Akin to an echo, mere meaningless noise.

Kundaladhara's son is truly a vast
Ocean basin brimming with good qualities.
But even a hundred sons would not be too many
To rule peacefully, martially, powerfully, and prosperously.

An emperor of the universe has enormous strength
From the force of his powerfully virtuous merit.
He has hundreds of queens and thousands of sons.
Do we not consider him a lord worthy of praise?

Likewise, I am not striving for pleasure
Out of prurient desire for an object of lust.
I act in order to reproduce my royal line
For a kingdom rich with good conduct, society, and religion.

Use your precious wealth of intelligence
And cease improperly criticizing me.
Do not ignore the intent of my commands.
Listen properly and act according to your station.

Thus, based on self-deception and deliberate lies, the king took the
maiden Lavanya Kamala for his own. Although his ministers were
unhappy, they had no courage to say anything more. They sat mesmerized as figures in a drawing.

25

In which Prince Kumaradvitiya decides to return home

U NAWARE OF THE SCANDAL IN GEM OF THE WORLD, Prince Kumaradvitiya, Manohari, and their ministers were enjoying the opulence of the land of Myriad Lights. Finally, after some time had passed, the prince's memory, like a herald's exhortation, reminded him of his parents, court, and homeland. He decided to return to Gem of the World.

When the time for his departure for home drew near, he appointed the hero Bhavakumara to hold the kingdom of Myriad Lights to the path of righteousness and to protect its progress in that regard. He instructed the hero thus:

> O Kumara, you have the wisdom of your ancestors.
> You are a true friend who accomplishes my aims.
> With perseverance you perfected all the arts.
> You are properly famed as a master of all heroes.
> Son, fulfill my wishes and rule this land for a while.
>
> Memory's messengers again and again exhort me;
> The faces of my loving parents constantly arise,
> Reflected upon the clear mirror of my mind.
> My thoughts wander, and I long to go to them.
>
> My relations' loving eyes watch over me
> From the distant castle of Gem of the World

In the lovely parks of the city Open Lotus.
My thoughts are agitated with desire
To see the faces of my dearest parents.

Like a tender mother, I protected
My court and subjects as dear children.
They nobly wish to repay that kindness,
So I must fly to those respectful folk.

Therefore, along with much tribute,
I am prepared to mount a swift steed
To go to see that land of marvelous virtues
While you remain here to guard this realm.

Worldly wealth lacks any essence:
It is as impermanent as morning dew.
Its only use is to offer it with respect
To guides worthy of refuge: the Buddha, Dharma, and Sangha.
Give generously to all suffering hunger and thirst;
Without reluctance free yourself from miserliness
And open the doors to our treasuries of wealth.

If you act cruelly and with cunning,
Others will try to harm and thwart you.
So act compassionately and with control,
Holding in mind a love for all beings.

Refrain from black scowls of anger
And harsh words, which wound others' minds.
Delight others with pleasant expressions,
And they will be pleased to see your smile.

Now the people of this immoral land
Pretend to honor and respect you.
But it is not suitable to trust them yet;
Be cautious and prudent for a while.

Although shot on a bent bow of actions,
The arrow of honest intention is straight.
So without any confusion between virtue and sin,
Destroy the evil enemy which is wicked deeds.

Dismantle without any intimidation all laws
Discriminating unfairly between friend and foe.
With legitimate, straightforward actions,
Protect the populace with kind justice.

When noblemen engage in truly base conduct,
Drinking liquor and frequenting prostitutes,
They retain their titles but have fallen low,
So abandon desire for such insane play.

A mountain of particularly despicable deeds
Was the basis for this benighted kingdom.
Completely turning away from positive actions,
The people were totally involved in iniquity.

Ignorant of the Buddha, Dharma, and Sangha,
They lacked faith that actions bear results.
They disparaged their parents and elders,
Enjoyed fights, quarrels, and disputes,
And took pleasure in killing and torture.

These execrable customs arose from desire
To conquer the universe with weapons
Of deceit and improper, harmful deeds.
This type of behavior is disgraceful.

You must lead them along a good path,
Toward virtue in accordance with the Dharma.
These words are a few drops sprinkled
From the ocean of knowledge of proper conduct.
Use them to cool the burning pain of ignorance.
Partake of their triumphant nature worthy of praise.

After the prince spoke, Bhavakumara supplicated him:
"O lord! Hear me with love! I am a mere youth, ignorant of which actions should be done and which should be avoided. Therefore I am not worthy to be left here to rule this kingdom. Please excuse me from this task."

"O Kumara, do not worry! Be brave, and we will meet again soon," the prince replied.

Bhavakumara was not able to contradict this definite order. "I shall do as you command," he promised, and remained there.

Then the entire court assembled before Prince Kumaradvitiya; his consort, ministers, courtiers, and army, as well as King Chandramati, Devatisha, and their ministers came to the farewell ceremonies. It was as if the prince were Indra beautified by his entourage, or the moon embellished by the constellations. Then the prince, Manohari, and their army set out for the city of Open Lotus in the great land of Joyous Groves.

At the time of their departure, they sent a messenger quickly ahead to the castle of Gem of the World. The herald was instructed to prepare the capital to beat the great drums of good tidings and to hoist the banners of good fortune. When the messenger informed King Suryamati about the events in Myriad Lights, the king rejoiced. He was amazed and respectful of the excellent abilities of Kumara, and at the same time he felt ashamed of his own improper conduct. Embarrassed about his foolishness, the king felt uncomfortable as joy and regret vied for his attention.

Then King Suryamati and his court arranged a marvelous reception for the travelers. After all the sublime preparations for the welcoming festival were complete, the chief ministers, who loved and respected their monarch, rode a great distance out from the palace to greet the noble prince. They traveled for a few days as joyfully as a herd of elephants scorched by the blazing summer sun enters a cool lake covered by lotuses. They brought with them provisions worthy of this first welcome.

They felt great joy when they saw the approach of the prince surrounded by his great army that enveloped the earth. They rode as far toward him as they could. Then they dismounted and on foot forced their way through the crowd to Kumaradvitiya. When they reached him, they prostrated themselves before his lotus feet. Joy shone forth from their faces, and this glorious song burst from their throats:

> O emperor! Long may you rule!
> The blaze of your vast merit
> Ended the darkness of the devilish hordes.
> You are a treasure of glorious light
> Viewed insatiably, the sun for fortunate folk.
>
> Because of good actions in prior lives,
> At birth you were marked with signs
> Indicating your superlative qualities.
> In our view you seemed to shine like the sun.

In no time your tutors bowed to your feet,
Because you understood every object of knowledge.
You humbled the pride of all the world's warriors
As you successfully crossed the ocean of martial arts.

Your pacific actions, moist with compassion,
Refresh others like a drink of pure ambrosia.
But blazing like the fire at the end of time,
The fierce heat of your wrath burns away your foes.

You relied on harsh actions as skillful means
To give the fruit of happiness and peace:
You led to safety those dancing on the precipice
Of heinous deeds and about to fall into hell.

You successfully spread the light of the Dharma
Throughout the dark continents of ignorance.
We bow our heads to your royal, supramundane feet.
Please hold us within the bounds of your love!

They made many other joyful speeches in his praise. When they finally finished, they went before Manohari and said:

O seductive maid, your beautiful attributes
Cannot be rivaled in the least
By an amalgam of all the world's loveliness.
Your glance can conquer the universe.

In the gardens of the most exalted immortal gods,
The fruit of ambrosia grows on a wish-granting tree.
Merely seeing its flowers and fruit confers bliss.
You are just such a source of joy for gods and men.

Many sorts of precious things ornament
Your coiled and loose, shiny black hair.
Your eyes are the shape of a lotus petal.
Your jewelry is a feast for the eyes.

Your face glows like a lovely full moon.
Between your perfect lips as red as blood
Are teeth whiter than mountain snow.
Your sweet smile steals away the hearts of men.

Over your eyes shaped like a lotus petal
Are brows arched gracefully as a curling vine.
The lovely iron hook of your sidelong glances
Unimpededly summons men's lustful hearts.

We cannot express the true wonder
Of your charm, O vivacious lady!
You have the festival of good fortune
To be consecrated Prince Kumara's queen.

Today you come on your royal and holy feet
To a happy and prosperous great kingdom
As desirable as the essence of the god realms.
To welcome you here gives us great joy.

They made other speeches too to express their respectful pleasure
about the fulfillment of their long-held hopes. After this welcome, they
proceeded on to the city without delay. As they came nearer to the
palace grounds, the travelers could see that the castle of Gem of the
World had been ornamented outside, inside, and all around. It was like
this:

This land beautiful as a gorgeous peacock's throat
Was the perfect ornament of bejeweled Mother Earth.
There amidst the copses of many species of trees
Heavy with a burden of foliage, flowers, and fruit,
Was a palace constructed of gold and jewel bricks,
Very lofty and supported by pillars made of gems.

The light reflecting from its pure gold roofs
Seemed to fill all the surrounding space.
The eaves and balconies were girdled
With chains of gold and embroidered tapestries.

Enticing ornaments attractively outlined
The inside and outside of high, arched gateways.
Tiny bells tinkled on outspread pearl canopies,
Stainless moon-shaped ornaments gyrated in the breeze,
Pennants flew from jeweled shafts, and more.

Above the varied and gorgeous ornaments,
A priceless, white royal umbrella fluttered.

Then they hoisted a silk-fringed victory banner
On a precious base shaped like a half-moon and vajra.

Every other space was bedecked with wreaths
Of colorful silk ribbons and dangling gems.
It was all so incredibly captivating
It was hard for anyone to take it all in.

When they entered the city, they saw that the streets had been carefully prepared for their passage. The roads had been properly cleaned: the stones, dirt, thorns, and so forth had been taken to the rubbish sites. Sand had been spread, raked smooth, and sprinkled with sandalwood-scented water to keep dust from rising. Lining the boulevards were displays of various flowers that sent forth sweet fragrances.

All along their way and especially massed at the crossroads were young men, boys, youthful maidens, and girls dressed in fabulous garments and jewelry. They sang songs composed in the seven-tone scale: thirds, sixths, and tonics. Handsome youths, warriors, and other marvelous folk sportively played dice, danced, and made merry. Musicians played all sorts of instruments: some blew conch shells; others pealed iron bells; a few beat kettledrums, snare drums, hand drums, or bass drums; some took up stringed instruments with one to a thousand strings; and others played cymbals and small chiming bells. This unimaginably profound music of welcome sounded as if it were transferred to earth from the fairy realms.

Then through this lovely scene strolled the magnificent sovereign of the earth's wealth, Prince Kumaradvitiya, whom to see gives joy. With him was the sublimely seductive Manohari, a veritable goddess arisen from the essence of loveliness, a paragon of beauty. These two, surrounded by an entourage vast as an ocean, could not be outshone by the beauty of hundreds of full moons. Nor could their glory be rivaled by the concentrated light of a thousand suns.

The superb palace residence called Floating Wonder had been decorated with beautiful ornaments for them. High and expansive thrones worthy of Earth Lords had been set up for father Suryamati and Prince Kumaradvitiya. They sat upon them like paired suns adorning a golden mountain. On thrones suitable for precious queens sat Kundaladhara and Manohari as beautifully as moons rest upon the crest of Shiva. The petty kings Chandramati and Devatisha were placed on thrones deserving of them. The space in front of them was totally filled with ministers: those who were the highest of the supremely wise and those who were brave and heroic.

Desiring the wondrously lovely maid,
He had left his loving parents
And the kingdom's great wealth behind.
Immersed in battle, for a time he did not return.

Nobly he strayed onto the wrong path
Of neglecting to repay others' kindness.
To pacify the pain of separation,
He returned to show his parents a smile.

When the sun and the moon rise above the peaks
To shed their cheerful light to satisfy all,
The lotus and lily blossom and dance with joy.
Just so his return spread the light of happiness,
Dispelling the darkness of misery surrounding
His loved ones, court, and loving subjects
So multitudinous they filled the earth to its horizons.

The reunited family gazed insatiably at one another with love and affection.

26

In which the prince returns to a realm riven by dissension

THEN THE WELCOMING CEREMONIES BEGAN. Finally, after many joyful speeches had been completed, Father Suryamati's mind was filled with felicitous thoughts. So in front of the elegant celebratory throng he made this speech:

You have become a compassionate bodhisattva,
Taming beings with sublime wisdom and skilled deeds.
The sweet scent of great wisdom and virtuous merit
Wafts from the lotus of your strength and perseverance.

O son of noble lineage, you are fearless and brave.
When you heroically laughed in preparation for war,
I could not bear it and tried to keep you at home.
But nothing could stop you from leading the army.

The blazing fire of a great warrior's skill
Consumes inept adversaries as fuel.
They tried to douse your flame to no avail.
This is natural, so you renounced conceit.

You destroyed the vicious knaves' iniquity,
Illumining for them the path of virtue.
Then you took in your hands the royal maid,
A lovely moon, causing the lily of my heart to bloom.

Thanks to the power of our vast virtuous merit,
We easily accomplished all our hopes and aims.
Now with joyous and respectful delight,
Let us enjoy blissful songs and dances of rapture.

After this was said, Kumara got up from his throne and respectfully
bowed to his father. Planting one knee upon the floor, he said, "Long
may you rule!" And added:

Your great wisdom is difficult to fathom.
Your heart overflows with compassion.
I joyously supplicate my glorious father
Amidst this magnificent festival of wealth.

If a gentle man remains at peace,
Without exercising his power to subdue
Evil foes coming to fight with vicious intent,
Worldly men adhering to common customs
Will make him an object of disparagement.
So I trampled my enemies into the dust.

I took as my own a great kingdom,
A treasury of desirable objects.
I spared the lives and granted happiness
To its arrogant rulers of high lineage.

I entered the enervating stage of battle,
Killing many foes with skillful power
To obtain my companion in the pleasures of love.
My propensity to love Manohari is unbreakable.

Now that I have completed these deeds,
I have the good fortune to see my parents' smiles.

The prince told them about his adventures without leaving anything out or adding any fabrication. His father, Suryamati, found occasion to smile broadly. Some ministers put their palms together, raised
them to the tops of their heads, and prostrated themselves respectfully.
While a few discussed the amazing news among themselves, the throats
of others were too choked with tears of love to utter a word. The
excessive joy in some men's hearts burst forth into melodious songs,

whose harmonies delighted the fairies in their supernatural realms.

Queen Kundaladhara felt that this reunion with her son restored her to life. She felt great joy in her heart. But recalling her jealousy and unhappiness resulting from her husband the king's recent conduct she thought:

"Eh ma! I gave birth to a child worthy of the respect of all sons of similar kings. A son like this makes my heart glad. He has conquered our enemies and protected our kingdom with his courageous perseverance. Yet all his intelligence and good qualities are worthless now that King Suryamati has engaged in such indiscreet behavior. O how can I bear it!"

She let forth a long sigh and to alert Kumaradvitiya of this sad fact she said:

> Arising from the deep ocean of my body
> Is a son magnificent as the jewel moon.
> You are a treasure of nectar and goodness,
> Shedding the light of youth and compassion.
>
> O my son, glowing with great courage,
> You went away to conquer the evil enemy.
> Then a cloud of misery enveloped me.
> I saw no glimmer of joy or happiness.
>
> I could not force down my throat
> Ambrosia or food with a hundred flavors.
> I rested my cheeks in my hands;
> Sad tears accompanied long sighs.
>
> I clearly wailed loud cries, "O my son!"
> To the sky in the direction you had gone.
> But no news of you came to my ears.
> So I was tortured by unbearable sorrow.
>
> Here today you arise unblemished,
> Like the moon free from clouds.
> This fulfills my heart's desire.
> Seeing you I can die without regret.
>
> It is improper to speak of unpleasant matters
> During this particularly joyful festival,

But I cannot refrain from casting forth spray
From the turbulent ocean swirling in my heart.

I am debilitated by the constant torture
Of the manifold sorrows of this situation:
Your father was corrupted by improper lust.
Now if a son is born to Lavanya Kamala,
The daughter of our minister Padmankura,
Your father promised him the crown to rule.

Reports on the wind confirm this as true.
Upon consideration of this matter,
I wonder if he no longer loves you too.
Please break the chains of my misery!

The queen's words deeply shamed the king. He regretted his hurt-
ful actions. His face fell and withered like a flower struck by frost.
Kumaradvitiya stared at his father's face and thought: "Kye ma! My
honorable father was chaste and courageous. He had encompassing
wisdom and enduring patience. Nevertheless, despite his truly superior nature, he was swept away by the strong current of the karmic
river."
    With these thoughts in mind, he spoke:

O father, according to every hero
You are incomparably wise and brave.
If you are worthy of such praise,
Why are you following this improper path?

When men of pure, high, royal lineages
Engage in debased and decadent actions,
Will they not be attacked and destroyed
By the sharp weapons of men's curses?

Has there ever been a case where a girl
Of low caste would be a worthy queen
For a superb royal house esteemed by all
As a noble line before whom men bow?

A poisonous flower may have a lovely color,
But it shouldn't be an ornament in your hair.

Just so, a king of a line like a great Sal tree
Should not enjoy the charms of a common whore.

If you keep this wench unequal to your descent
As your companion in the pleasures of passion,
Then surely as the Ganges River flows to the sea
Your life and magnificent good qualities shall wane.

If you turn away from your long-term companion,
Kundaladhara, who is beautified by a special heritage,
To fall low and venerate a contemptible object,
Will not discordant, disparaging shouts fill the world?

Is it true that contrary to highborn
Custom you have cast out your former wife?
O father, someone has deceived your heart!
You carelessly deviate from noble behavior.

Kumaradvitiya's sharp words pierced the king's heart to the quick.
His face fell, his shoulders slumped, and he was unable to say anything.
Finally the king thought: "I must speak truthfully about this matter, for
I am unable to reverse my solemn promises to Padmankura. Yes, that is
the right thing to do." So, shamefaced, he replied:

O best of youths, eldest of my line, it is true!
I wander a dark path because I had no strength
To counter the powerful winds of former debased actions.

My sorrow and regret are not mere words.
As you can see, my self-resolve was weakened.
Either because of a loving connection in a former life
Or because I am possessed by an insuperable demon,
Doe-eyed Lavanya Kamala can lead me about
As if my mind were a corporeal thing.

Nonetheless, promises not made under duress
Are as unchangeable as those carved on diamond.
It is difficult to counter my edict, O noble son.

As the king spoke, the prince thought:
"My honorable father has fallen low; he is far from the conduct lov-

ingly adhered to by the noble. All men will speak ill of us as this infamy spreads before an unseasonable wind in every direction. I cannot bear to hear this!

"Yet, there is nothing one can do to obstruct the ripening of powerful actions created in the past. The results of prior actions must be experienced even though they do not accord with one's present intentions. If my father's karma is definite and irrevocable, how can I stop it? But I wonder if he has really cast my mother, Kundaladhara, out of his affections?"

So he said:

"Kye! You were known throughout the world as a praiseworthy, reliable Lord of Men who guided all beings. Yet now you are to be counted among low men who act despicably! If you ask why, well, it is like this example.

"You have loosened your grasp on a wish-fulfilling jewel, which effortlessly provided everything needed or desired. In its stead, you latched on to a colorful bauble of low-quality glass as if it were the essence of wealth. You have spat out like phlegm Kundaladhara, a woman born into a stainless lineage as high as your own. She is a mother to her servants and has ruled the country with love. All the good qualities of womankind make the sight of her an exquisite pleasure. Instead, you lust for a mere pretty face, which lacks even the scent of a single good quality. You have raised Lavanya Kamala up from a debased line of our own servants. You have made your own a woman with a crooked nature, who earns her livelihood through tricks and deceit. Please tell me how you can possibly think this to be right!"

The king responded:

"O Kumara, I beg you, do not be bound by such evil doubts! I know that Lavanya Kamala is notorious as a tigress, the enemy of life, and the source of manifold sorrows. Nevertheless, because my heart is stained by depraved propensities from actions in other lives, I am unable to cast her out. But how could I abandon Kundaladhara, my loving wife of many years, a woman of noble descent who gave birth to you, my particularly special son? I cherish both women; I do not hate one because of love for the other. They have the rank of first and second wives."

Kumaradvitiya was well bred and so respected his aged parent. He did not dare to disregard his father's words. He had to consider the two queens as equals, like elder and younger sisters.

27

In which Manohari returns to her parents' realm

THEN, IN NOT TOO LONG A TIME, Lavanya Kamala's womb was beautified by pregnancy. At the end of the term of months, a handsome and intelligent son was born. As soon as he was born, the baby was washed in saffron water and ministers tested the clarity of his faculties. After these rituals, the king lifted the child from his silk-swaddled cradle and asked Kumaradvitiya to use his skill in the divination of places, jewels, garments, trees, birth, women, horses, and elephants to find a name for the child. Kumara was quite astounded by the baby's qualities. He said:

> This noble child is amazing!
> He has every wonderful characteristic.
> He is the summit of a mountain of virtues.
> He is the equal of an emperor of the universe.
>
> When he fulfills my father's promise,
> I shall go to a forest hermitage
> To turn away from worldly concerns.
> This is a most marvelous chance for me.
>
> Empowered by the true words and practices
> Of the gods, ascetics, and wise tantric masters,
> May flowers of auspiciousness be scattered.
> Let all these virtuous prayers come to be.

May my wishes be fulfilled!
Let this child live long!
May he have great wealth and fortune!
Let him rule the kingdom religiously!
Let the banner of his celebrity be raised!

As he spoke these prayers, he sprinkled the petals of precious flowers over the child and named him Ananda Lalitasaras.

Then the baby was entrusted to the care of nurses who properly brought him up. From the time he was small, he made an effort to learn all the arts and sciences appropriate to his father's lineage. So in not too many years he became quite proficient.

During those years, the great city of Open Lotus was increasingly prosperous; it seemed like a pond of lotuses fertilely proliferating in the sunshine. Thanks to the force of their rulers' virtues, the populace obtained many boons; they were wealthy, prosperous, and happy, enjoyed good harvests, and were not quarrelsome. It seemed that the wonders of the golden age had spread to the horizons of the realm.

Kumaradvitiya and Manohari enjoyed themselves together, playfully partaking of the joys of embrace. Their sensual enjoyment of those sublime festivals of love was like the erotic delight of the gods savoring voluptuous heavenly pleasures.

Then there came a day when Manohari went to the dome atop their lovely palace residence. She gazed for a long time in the direction of her childhood home of Radiant Array. She minutely surveyed whatever there was to see and finally saw a group of traders slowly approaching, loaded down with valuable merchandise.

As soon as she saw them she thought: "These men are coming from my parents' realm. They surely have some news to tell." So she dispatched a maidservant to inquire. The maidservant understood her task. She went to the merchants and questioned them about tidings of their realm. An elderly trader with a cheerful countenance replied to her:

We come from the kingdom of Radiant Array,
Bringing valuable tribute to this realm
So that we may make offerings and honor
The son of the king, known as Kumaradvitiya.

We have heard that Manohari,
Descended of Dyutimat's line,

Was carried off to an unknown land
Like a Malika blossom blown before the wind.

Some report she definitely remains alive,
But others say that Death has claimed her.
We heard her parents and courtiers are in doubt,
Suffering the torture of unbearable sorrow.

The maidservant found these words depressing. She quickly returned
to Manohari and repeated the trader's statement to her. An image of her
parents tortured by misery arose clearly in the mirror of Manohari's
mind. Her distinct recollection made her ashamed of her neglect. So she
went to Kumaradvitiya and touched her head to his feet. She supplicated him unhappily with her face streaming with tears:

O superb prince! You are a vast tree of paradise
With a fruit whose nectar grants all wishes.
I have lived happily in the kind protection
Of your compassionate, cool shade.

When someone obtains pure joy for herself,
She may unwittingly cause sorrow to others.
Verily this is the nature of things in my case.

The lines of my parents' and courtiers'
Suffering were not written upon my mind.
While I enjoyed the taste of supreme bliss
In your embrace, I thought of no one else.

I was immersed in the swamp of desire,
But words which came to me via the speech
Of merchants have lifted me from that mire.

Since I have heard of my loved ones' sorrow,
My peace of mind has been stolen away.
So please let me go to my parents for a while.

A night lily always lusts to be with the moon,
So a short time after I leave to visit them,
I shall return to see you and request again
That you kindly grant me the joy of embrace.

As she beseeched him with many prostrations, Prince Kumaradvitiya thought:

"The true nature of all things in cyclic existence is change. All modes of being are impermanent, and being so, they are spurious. This lovely woman loved me so much she could not bear to be apart from me for a moment. But now memories of her beloved parents and friends arise and cannot be stopped. I will give her the opportunity she wishes for; she truly desires to see the faces of her parents.

"I too have been under the net of confusion cast by the lovely, deceitful maid of worldly desire. I have done many black deeds that were wholly on the side of nonvirtue. In order to keep the fruits of those sins from ripening, I must strive for the essential nectar of pure religious attainment."

So he said:

> Kye! O doe-eyed Manohari!
> You are the zenith of my sensual pleasure.
> Even for an instant I cannot let you go
> Outside the bounds of my thoughts of love.
>
> Whose mind would not be led away
> By the ropes of your sidelong glances,
> Your seductively lovely form, and
> Your behavior so pleasing to the heart?
>
> Thus, I who from my youth perfected
> Every sort of aesthetic analysis,
> Clearly perceive how wonderful you are,
> Ornamented by nobility and good qualities.
>
> You are the essence of all worldly happiness:
> Sights, sounds, memories, touches, and tastes.
> It is true that I cannot conceive of bearing
> Separation from one like you for even a moment.
>
> Because we grasp pleasant things as truly real,
> We have wandered in cyclic existence.
> The sins of lust and desire are a burden
> Heavier to bear than Mount Meru.
>
> Therefore, in order to dispel the dark clouds
> Of ignorance veiling the light of liberation,

I turn my mind toward religious practice,
To follow the footsteps of the great sage, the Buddha.

When you go you steal my heart,
But may your suffering be pacified
By a fount of medicine for sore eyes,
The pleasure of seeing your parents' faces.

In the samsaric ocean's turbulent waves of sorrow,
Even happiness is the nature of suffering.
See this clearly with no delusions.
Live purely, absorbed in virtues, with an aim
To gain liberation for yourself and others.

What was the young woman to think of these words, which in essence laid the basis for the peace and happiness of nirvana?

"Because this exalted prince loves me so well, I have never before heard such exhortations to renunciation. Surely he speaks of undertaking the path to liberation free from attachment now to stop me from going to my parents' home! Nevertheless, I will depart to see my parents' faces. But I will quickly return from there, brooking no delays, to obtain the pleasure of enjoying his smiles."

"I accept your commands," she said.

When the time of her departure neared, tribute of the most superior sort was gathered for her to take as gifts. Everything was the very essence of wealth: there were all sorts of jewels, lovely clothes, horses, cattle, buffalos, foodstuffs, beverages, and more. Manohari's eyes filled with tears at the pain of parting from her lover. She prostrated herself at Kumara's feet. Then, encircled by an entourage as vast as an ocean, she went off toward Radiant Array.

After the doe-eyed maid
Left the city of Open Lotus,
It seemed Lady Earth draped herself
In emerald green clothes to welcome
The blue rain clouds and fresh breezes
As her lovers in the festival of spring.

Lusty bees feasting on honey
Drunkenly hummed and danced

On the quivering stamens and petals
Of lotus, lily, and Utpala blossoms.

Southern breezes beckoned Manohari to
The copses of the precious shaded gardens.
Yet they fanned the pain of separation from her love,
So the pretty one sorrowfully sighed and yawned.

Her face looked toward her parents' abode,
But her mind went back to the superb prince.
Her feet readily went forward to her parents,
But her mind ran back to the prince.
Listless because of mental and physical discord,
She thought to turn back again and again.

At that time even her tiny belled ornaments
Seemed to play a mournful tune.
The wise lady was unbearably pained,
So she redraped her garments to mute them.

Then, as day after day went by,
The moonlike face of the prince
Arose often in the clear lake of her mind.
She grew impatient to return to him.

"My mind is pervaded by dark grief
While the moon, the lamp of the world,
Subsides in the west. But soon again
I shall enjoy its festive rising in the east."

Although this reflection was difficult to bear,
She set out again to repay her parents' kindness.
She went to her parents in Radiant Array,
But her thoughts were fixed upon the prince.

Finally came the time when she bowed to her parents' lotus-feet and satisfied their gaze with her smiling face. Afterward, when she told her joyful news, as worthy to hear as honey is to taste, everyone smiled broadly and laughed aloud. When she told of her tribulations, her tale was like a sharp thorn piercing their ears. Everyone wept and mournfully sighed. When she finished relating all that there was to tell, she set forth her presents like haystacks piled high. To her parents, relatives, and court she gave lovely things which combined the essence of wealth and fortune of both gods and men. These magnificent gifts fulfilled everyone's wishes completely. Contentedly and happily they remained there together.

28

In which the old king decides to abdicate and Prince Kumaradvitiya is prevailed upon to rule as regent

WHILE PRINCE ANANDA LALITASARAS GREW UP, his father, Suryamati, became aged. Now that he was an old man, he was weary of the work of governing. But the king was suspended upon the prongs of doubt about his heir. "Whom shall I anoint as my successor to the royal throne of the kingdom?" he wondered, so he requested that both his chief officials and the ordinary people give their opinions.

"O lord, I beg you to hear us. Please, O honorable father, do not be in a quandary about which son to give the realm. Because your elder son has all the marks of magnificence and good qualities of the gods, he is worthy of that offering. Do not look to anyone other than Prince Kumaradvitiya. No one will be able to censure that choice."

The king accepted their advice, for they had urged him all in one voice. But Padmankura became upset and confused as the time drew near to make the preparations for bequeathing the kingdom.

"Now is the time I should announce the solemn words of the king's promise to me," he thought. So he went before the king and reminded him of his oath.

The king said, "Kye! O great minister, please consider! I am not a man with a crooked nature. Nor am I one who leads others astray with lies. Neither am I like a cart drawn by a wild buffalo which runs amok! I know that the present situation is not in accord with the vow I made to you. Nevertheless, all the others have strewn flowery epithets in honor of the coronation of my elder son. It would be unsuitable for all of us if I make Ananda Lalitasaras, who is younger and less wise, the ruler of the kingdom. So to fulfill the wishes of the ministers of our court and the common masses, I will crown Kumaradvitiya my regent for a short time. Later, when Ananda Lalitasaras is more mature, I will have him presented with all the wealth and fortune of the realm in accordance with your desire."

"In that case, I accept your express command," said Padmankura.

Then the courtiers prepared every one of the wonderful articles for the enthronement of a monarch. They set out the crown ornaments of the brahmins: parasols, the lion throne, and so forth. His father went to Prince Kumaradvitiya and with a freshly scrubbed smile he said:

> As is the nature of all phenomena,
> I am caught in the noose of old age.
> My body and mind have lost their vigor.
> Because of senility I find it difficult
> To shoulder the burden of ruling the realm.
> Thus you, O noble, marvelous youth,
> A treasury of good qualities and actions,
> Should guard this realm with love from now on.

The king's words caused Kumara's mind great turmoil. His face clouded, and quickly, like a bee darting to a lotus, he bowed to his father's feet. He said:

> O Earth Lord! Honorable father and king! Please see me.
> I have degenerated because of my earlier craving
> For this kingdom adorned by a wealth of nonvirtues.
> I grow weary under a burden of sins difficult to bear.

> My brother has an abundance of good qualities.
> He has the signs marking an emperor of the universe.
> Please give the marvelous wealth of the kingdom
> To Ananda Lalitasaras, a boy adorned by great merits.

Again his father spoke:

> Son! You should not contradict me!
> If you lacked desire for the kingdom,
> Why did you strive so hard for Manohari?

Noble men know that vast waves of good deeds
Can be generated by using a kingdom's wealth well.
You are the sun, lord of the day who can dispel
The dark mists of sorrow shrouding our court and people.

Your brother is like the moon.
Unlike you, he cannot fulfill our hopes
To lighten this haze of misery.
So I place you upon my fearless lion throne.

After this, Kumara uttered this reply:

O honorable father! Please consider!
Yes, it is not right to reverse earlier intentions,
But can one enveloped in the incessant gloom of sin
Be able to help others as a guiding light?

Because of my striving for that lovely maiden,
I definitely shall have to experience
The inconceivably painful results of my evil deeds.
The only means to free me from that fate
Is to give up worldly affairs and rely upon austerities
In an infinitely peaceful place for meditation.
Then the seeds for liberation shall quickly multiply.

Absolutely all of these so-called virtues
Arising from the kingdom's plenty are tainted by evil.
They are like poison honey: sweet, but deadly to eat.
I shall have no opportunity for sensual pleasures
When tortured by excruciating agony after falling
Into the vast crevasse of the lower realms!
So, honorable father, support me with your kind views!

His father and the chief ministers were not pleased by this supplication. "We must express the drawbacks of a hermitage in order to dissuade the prince from his desire for the liberation of nirvana. We will
cause him to renounce that goal." They thought and so said:

O Kumara! Please consider!
From birth you lived in a pleasant realm,
Safe in a palace festooned with banners and fans.

How can you give it up for the wild jungle,
Where roaring carnivores, poisonous snakes,
And flesh-eating flies crave to consume your body?

You reject partaking a wealth of delicious foods
Beautifully served and made especially for you.
But will the roots and sprouts of trees and flowers
Be sufficiently nourishing to sustain your life?

You spurn the enjoyment of drinking
Delicious ambrosia to gulp tasteless water.
How can you bear to taste that beverage
In the company of birds and wild animals?

You despise the desire to drape yourself
In fine clothes, smooth and soft to the touch.
But how can you possibly wear the rough bark
Of trees, which will cause your body pain?

You exclude yourself from a carefree abode
And time spent pleasantly conversing with
Your dear parents, beautiful lover, and wise advisers.
But how will you live without companions or speech?

In this life fame and fortune arise
From the magnificent wealth of the kingdom.
But by ruling a vast, prosperous realm well,
A ruler can accumulate a great deal of merit.
So please protect well Gem of the World.

Do not disregard your parent's command.
Do not let your devoted subjects and ministers
Be without a leader or a safe haven.
O Kumara, we beg you to be compassionate!

Then they all prostrated themselves before him, tumbling down
to lie flat as felled trees. While they earnestly pleaded with him,
Kumaradvitiya thought:

"Such importunate faults have never endangered someone happily
living in a forest hermitage! This is definitely true. Nonetheless, I will
not cut the cord of hope clutched at by my parents and ministers: for a

time I will rule the kingdom according to the Dharma. I should proclaim now my firm vow about the tenor and short duration of my rule."
   He put his fingers together like a jewel upon his crown and said:

   Kye! Father and ministers, please listen.
   The wise are wary of reckless speech
   About subjects not to be spoken of so lightly.

   Sitting on this throne marshaled with much effort,
   I would be pained as if pierced by sharp thorns.
   But on a smooth and lovely leafen mat,
   My body and mind can be in happy unity.

   What use is a powerful king's castle
   Surrounded by the prison walls of samsara?
   I wish to be in a solitary grove
   Encircled by delightful flowers and trees.

   Common sense decays when you crave victuals.
   There is no better food and drink
   Than pure, clear water, sprouts, and roots,
   Easily enjoyed without cooking or work.

   We create many negative actions toiling
   And struggling to obtain pretty clothes.
   But even brutal men make offerings
   To those adorned with easily had tree bark.

   We die alone even if surrounded by friends.
   Even sweet words may be the root of misfortune.
   What better thing can there be in samsara
   Than contemplating religious discourses?

   O father, it is definitely true that
   Peace and happiness reside in the forest,
   But the realm may not be the basis of evil deeds.
   So I cannot counter your command
   To be crowned king upon the lion throne.

   I shall never stray from religious actions
   On the path praised by holy men hundreds of times.

I vow I shall make no efforts other than
To protect this kingdom with peaceful means.

It would be easier for me to leave this world
Than to rule this land by corrupt actions
Resulting from craving the trifling accouterments of life
Such as wealth, honor, possessions, and fame!

With these words, he fulfilled the hopes of the king and all his ministers. They said to him: "When you have been crowned the ruler of the kingdom, you can create virtue or sin as you please! O lord, we salute you!"

Afterward, Prince Kumaradvitiya, whom to see gives joy, mounted the lion throne and put on the precious crown. When the vast parasols of renown were hoisted, the fairies sang sweet songs and scattered an amazing rain of fragrant flowers from the heavens. They gave their benediction: "Long live the king!"

The prince vowed to himself, "Now that I have obtained my father's kingdom, I will never vary from the holy path. I will strive to make all people happy by making laws in accordance with the Dharma."

29

In which Prince Kumaradvitiya practices the perfection of charity

SOMETIME AFTER MANOHARI'S DEPARTURE, Kumaradvitiya thought, "From childhood I took great pleasure in proceeding along the path of virtue. Yet it is the law of the world that men act according to their families' caste and follow the occupation of their forefathers. It is like this example. When a leader of beasts sees a mirage in a sandy desert, he is fooled into believing it water and chases it to quench his thirst. All the other animals follow along behind him without question. In a similar way, ruling this illusory kingdom will cause my decline, for it is as difficult to halt the maturation of powerful actions as it is to arrest a flowing river! Even now, under the influence of unprincipled friends, I have done many frightful, unethical deeds. In addition, I have induced others to act iniquitously and rejoiced in the completion of those immoral deeds. Thus, I have done many things which will yield results so miserable they are hard to imagine. Where can I find a virtuous spiritual friend who can show me both how to purify these stains and the path to the greatest happiness?"

The young ruler sent out his emissaries to search in every direction for such a guide. In a delightful place secluded among rocky mountain crags, one messenger found the virtuous spiritual teacher Dharmeshvara. He had attained the state of an arhat and so was liberated from rebirth in cyclic existence. He had turned his back on wealth and honor; nothing in the entire universe—the desire, form, or formless realms—attracted him. Dharmeshvara was wise; he understood the ultimate reality of all phenomena. This knowledge had split open and emptied the egg of ignorance. He had the psychic power to see his own and others' former rebirths, to foretell beings' future births, to read others' minds, to hear their secret words, and to create miraculous displays. His body blazed like a golden reliquary stupa.

Just seeing the arhat made the messenger feel quite happy. He went and reported exactly what he had found to the prince. The news filled Kumara with expansive delight: he was happier than a peacock feeling the first touch of the monsoon rains upon his back.

He ordered the minister Jneyavan, "O admirable one, come here! I have heard that an arhat named Dharmeshvara dwells in a delightful solitary hermitage among the craggy peaks of my realm. Go to him and pay my respects. Say in my name that he is invited to the palace and that his presence here will fulfill all of my wishes."

"I will do as you command," said the minister. He followed the route of the previous messenger. When he arrived in front of the arhat, he bowed and supplicated him with the words ordered by the prince.

The arhat had turned his back on wealth and adoration. But he was an expert in knowing when gently to train those whose minds needed to be tamed. So he smiled broadly and accompanied the minister.

They were welcomed to the city with victory umbrellas, banners, garlands of flowers, chiming bells, and other sorts of offerings. Having ushered the arhat into the palace, they begged him to sit on a precious throne. Then Prince Kumara, his eyes brimming with tears, prostrated himself at the feet of this virtuous spiritual friend and prayed to him:

"Kye ma! A thick cloud of ignorance completely obscures my mind. I am ignorant of the law of cause and effect and the ultimate nature of reality. I have done this corrupt deed, and that one too. Please show me the means to purify them! In addition, I beg you to set forth the path to liberation and omniscience: please let fall the rain of nectar which is the Dharma!"

The virtuous friend Dharmeshvara was worthy of trust, for he had pacified his senses and subdued his mind perfectly. So, with a smiling countenance, he let forth the fearless lion's roar, enumerating the vast and profound Dharma. He taught in a way compatible with each of his listener's aspirations, inclinations, and abilities.

He instructed them that all samsara is a vast ocean of sorrow; even the waves of happiness are, in reality, suffering. It is like a sweet but poisonous drink. This ocean of existence is difficult to cross over, for it is deep and vast. He told them that if they desired to be free from it, they should view all its marvels as a blazing fire and nourish the virtues of charity, ethics, and meditation.

He said that they must abandon thinking of peace for themselves alone. Beginning with training in love and compassion, he taught them how to produce the precious desire for complete enlightenment in order to benefit all sentient creatures. First they learned that they should see all beings, as many as fill the boundless sky, as their kind, dear mother. These beings lack a leader and protector, so for their sake they were told they should be willing to enter the torments of hell as if they were a celestial park. They heard that they should put on the armor of this steadfast intent.

Moreover, he taught that from the first they must bear in mind that the nature of all phenomena is peace. Things lack any independent existence, they are empty of any inherent nature of their own, and so they do not independently arise or cease.

He taught these and other stages of practice with no contradiction between the profound altruistic method and the wisdom understanding emptiness. He gave the great gift of Dharma, which is free from attachment and peace for oneself alone. These teachings were the guide leading all seekers to the city of nirvana. They were the virtuous chariot of merit and wisdom. They were a vast ocean containing all the eighty-four thousand teachings of the Buddhadharma.

The arhat's instructions revived Kumara's dormant positive propensities for the attainment of Buddhahood. His virtuous mental continuum ripened. His bonds to samsara were loosened, so he turned away from samsara and toward liberation. The rain of holy Dharma washed the stains of ignorance from his mind. He obtained the holy eye, which perceives the nature of reality.

Then the prince thought: "I shall take the meaning of my virtuous spiritual friend's instructions to heart. I shall practice them to perfection. Therefore, I will first fertilize the roots of virtue, which grow from charity."

So within the city's bounds he had workmen erect great open halls for the distribution of alms. On the front of these buildings, he had this edict indelibly engraved:

My domain is the realm of a religious king.
Every lord, underling, and freeman who enjoys
This land ruled without corporal punishment
Must not disregard these noble, pacific laws.

If any angry, ferocious, and deceitful persons
Follow an improper, nonvirtuous path,

Acting with hateful intent to harm others,
Disrespecting and abusing their aged parents,
And denigrating the Buddha, his teaching and order,
Those persons deserve to be sentenced to punishment
Under my laws as heavy, firm, and righteous
As the mountains ringing the core of the world.
In this life they will endure the tortures of hell
Inside prison walls unbearable to see.
Finally they will be thrown to the Death Lord.

All renunciates, brahmins, and even laymen
With peaceful, tractable, and compassionate natures
Who practice virtue and act to benefit others
Are worthy of offerings, respect, and honor,
For they are in accord with my superior intentions.

To free from destitution men poor as hungry ghosts,
I will draw the bow of immeasurable compassion
And loose a rainfall of the arrows of alms.
I will vanquish hunger, thirst, and want.

Because of my love for those worthy of protection,
I will give them food, wealth, horses, and cattle.
After meeting their needs, I'll give what they wish,
Even be it my body, my life, or any of my limbs.

So that I may complete these acts of charity,
May all men come here with great joy,
Like bees desiring to see my lotus face.
I shall please them all with the taste of honey:
Offerings and presents given without miserliness.
Harken to these true words!

Evil men who had committed base deeds countering the path of
purity were terrified when they read this inscription. They were dis-
graced. All the monks, brahmins, renunciates, ascetics, and ordinary
laypeople who followed the path of virtue by adhering to perfect conduct
were honored and respected. They received magnificent gifts without having to beg. The masses of starving and destitute beggars received greater
quantities of alms than they asked for. It seemed as if their fortunes were
made equal to the king's, so that they could enjoy whatever they wanted.

Thus, even the word *poverty* was not known in that land. The realm as vast as the ocean was ruled without capital punishment. It was transformed into a wish-fulfilling festival of the golden age, with a complete complement of the perfection of all virtuous actions.

King Chandramati and Devatisha saw all this and so wondered: "This Lord of Men has taken the life histories of the bodhisattvas as an example to be followed. He is so dedicated to charity that he has cheerfully promised to give even his life without hesitation! So I wonder if he wouldn't return our kingdom of Myriad Lights to us?"

Therefore they went to Kumara and bowed so low that their topknots touched his feet. Then they supplicated him with this elegant poem:

> O Lord of Men! Bodhisattva! May good prevail!
> O conqueror! Kumaradvitiya, whom to see gives joy!
> We bow with body, speech, and mind to the supreme one
> Having the ornaments of deeds, fame, and good qualities.
> Your enlightened actions overflow with compassion!
> Please grant us what we wish!
>
> You have given the realm's bounty to beggars;
> Your wealth is now common to all.
> The sunshine of your famous, magnificent deeds
> Outshines the feeble starlight of others' repute.
>
> We are exceedingly amazed by your promise
> Compassionately to bestow whatever is asked,
> Even your life, a gift so difficult to give.
> O bodhisattva, please grant this wish to give us joy.
>
> Although it is not right for us to crave and desire
> The wondrous wealth, plenty, prosperity, and people
> Of our land, which you righteously took in war,
> Please return it to us in order to complete
> Your practice of the perfection of charity.
> With respect and joy we beg that our hopes bear fruit!

Kumaradvitiya felt great joy. He thought: "It is not at all right for me to enjoy utilizing property belonging to others. So I shall grant this boon just as they desire. However, in addition to granting that kingdom to their royal line, I shall bestow advice which leads along the path of virtue and reverses their rapt affinity for nonmeritorious actions." He said:

Kye! Earth Lords, it is true! It is true!
I shall grant your wishes exactly.
I know well that coveting the marvelous
Wealth of others is a cause for low rebirth.

The realm of Myriad Lights with its peoples,
Court, wealth, and prosperity is now given to you.
In addition, I present you with command
Over my treasuries, which lack no marvels:
There are superbly well-trained psychic horses,
Elephants with golden chain-mail headgear,
Precious chargers for the crafted chariots,
Milk cows, silken clothes, lovely jewels, and more.

O Earth Lords, father and son,
Following an evil path, you destroyed your own court
And slandered men of pure virtue worthy of respect.
Cast far away this manner of sinful behavior!

Distance yourself from all the nonvirtues:
Lying, jealousy, craftiness, coveting
Others' wealth or wives, a lack of compassion,
Harshness, pride, and great, ferocious anger.

By introducing crooked laws and disrespecting
Practitioners of austerities, your elders, and parents,
You will cause all beings to be tortured by sorrow.
You must abandon all this improper, sinful conduct!

Even a sparse scattering of the seeds of sin
Upon the field of life will produce a great yield
And ripen into their own unmistakable fruit.
Have faith in the nondeceptive law of causation.

Extremely evil, nonvirtuous deeds cause one
To be beaten by weapons on burning iron ground
And to freeze in miserable ice caverns.
Desist from deeds which produce such hells!

The result of a middling nonmeritorious deed
Is to be born a hungry ghost in a land of scarcity,

Eating only foul sustenance causing unbearable pain,
Hunger, thirst, heat, and cold. Forsake such deeds!

Even the most minor sort of nonvirtuous act
Forces one to take rebirth as an animal,
Tied and bridled to the unbearable sufferings
Of being stupid, killed, and belabored. Reject such deeds!

Thus, although you may be unable to go to the forest
To concentrate on abandoning craving for the world,
You must extract the precious essence
From the inherently worthless wealth of the realm.

So respect religious people worthy of being a refuge,
Give generously to relieve the sorrows and fulfill the wishes
Of beggars so totally debased by poverty and destitution
They seem to be nearly hungry ghosts.

Never abrogate the pure path of the Dharma.
Always protect the populace with good laws.
Continually make an effort to tame
Your wild minds with peaceful, compassionate means.

When the prince let forth these profound instructions in accordance
with the Dharma, King Chandramati and Devatisha became intoxicated
with joy and respect. They clasped their hands together, their tears fell,
and they vowed, "O Lord of Men, we will do as you say. We will abandon sin! We will practice virtue! We will desist from improper conduct!
We will be prudent!"

They also had the opportunity of obtaining the nectar of holy
Dharma from the virtuous spiritual friend Dharmeshvara. Thus, those
nefarious rulers and their ministers began to discipline and pacify their
minds.

Then they returned to Myriad Lights, taking with them all the valuable gifts given to them by Prince Kumaradvitiya. From that time
onward, they were famous as kings who ruled their realm according to
the Dharma, who preserved the Dharma, and who placed their subjects
in a state of happiness.

30

In which the prince's charity nearly bankrupts the realm and he is banished

BECAUSE KUMARA WAS SO STEADFAST IN GIVING ALMS, flocks of beggars came to him. They approached like herds of elephants plunging into a lotus-covered lake after being scorched by the sun. Other times they came like thick, black rain clouds gathering in the sky. On many occasions the prince set out great displays of things to give them, even more than they had imagined in their most hopeful dreams. He would bestow nearly as many precious clothes, foodstuffs, jewels, horses, cattle, and so on as the possessions of the northern gods of inexhaustible wealth. At last, even his treasuries containing mountains of valuable objects were close to empty. Kumara became extremely depressed when he saw this. "Now how will I fulfill the hopes of the beggars?" he wondered. In a state of confusion, his shining smile faded.

Padmankura and some others among his officials were hateful by nature. They were ignorant of the proper course of conduct. Some of those evil, baneful men were totally unsympathetic toward Kumara's virtuous deeds and so conspired against him. They went to his father, King Suryamati, and said:

> It is said the Earth Lord famed as Kumaradvitiya
> Was born as a jewel to be our Lord of Men.
> He has been crowned to command a great throne,
> And to him all men respectfully bow their heads.
>
> Yet his mind is disturbed by an evil demon,
> Or perhaps he is misled by another's treachery.

For we see that this realm is close to destruction
Because of his various ill-considered, injurious acts.

First with great effort we conquered Myriad Lights,
A land adorned with the wealth of gods and men.
How could he so happily give that land,
Back to our evil enemy and his progeny?

You may say that was because of his great compassion.
But, O lord, do you not see our treasuries
Are nearly emptied of their stores of wealth
Akin to the possessions of the gods of luxury?

The king felt it was improper for them to speak such words of slander in an attempt to create dissension. Kumara's father found his son's deeds to be quite amazing. So he said:

Eh ma ho! Such great perseverance!
Eh ma ho! What firmly rooted compassion!
Eh ma ho! Such waves of deeds!

The superb youth whom to see gives joy
Is ornamented with wonders and good qualities.
I sincerely rejoice and praise
The tidal wave of his actions.

Moved by the force of compassion,
Kumara became a superb master of giving alms.
His generosity is not motivated by desire
For worldly happiness, fame, honor, or wealth.

I find no fault in his generous deeds.
He firmly vowed to be compassionate like this
When he unwillingly assented to rule
Upon the lion throne of my realm.

Now I do not like your present attempts
To dissuade him from that direction
Nor your artifice to induce dissension.

He would give even his own life as a gift.
That very thought is unthinkable!

Those abominable officials became angry and displeased. So once
again Padmankura knelt down. He raised up his hands and reminded
the king of his former promises:

> O lord! Please see me!
> Kye! Consider whether it is right
> For an Earth Lord of high position
> Ruling a vast, magnificent kingdom
> To speak such rash, unreliable words!
>
> Great Earth Lord, if you so fear to see
> Any promises contradicted, do you not recall
> The time you were close to losing your life,
> As your mind twisted like a corporeal thing
> Painfully lusting for my daughter, Lavanya Kamala?
>
> When I gave her to you as you wished,
> You vowed that if a Kamala bore a son
> You would hold him equal to Kumaradvitiya
> And crown the younger brother king!

He reproached his lord in many ways. He even went to his daughter,
Lavanya Kamala, and urged her to try to foment discord between her
husband and his elder son.

But at this time his daughter was extremely attracted to Kumara. So
she thought, "If that youthful god will hold me close to his heart and
love me just as he does Manohari, then I will not cause dissension. Yet, if
that is not to be, I will sow calumny between father and son." So she
weighed thoughts of how to proceed.

One night when the honorable old king was snoring loudly, Lavanya
stealthily came out of her quarters and went to Kumara's residence,
Floating Wonder. Kumara was awake contemplating religious matters, so
he saw her coming. In alarm he queried, "Is my honorable father in
good health or not?"

"He is fine."

"Well then, girl, why do you come here?"

Tormented by lust, she had passed beyond modest and chaste behavior; her body shuddered and trembled like a mango blossom in the
wind. With a clearly lascivious attitude, she begged him: "Kye! O superior prince! I have sought you out of desire for your beauty. Please satiate me with a joyous festival of sensual pleasure!"

These words attempting to incite him to debauchery made Kumara feel weary with sadness. He thought, "Kye ma! The actions of dissolute women are scheming and shifty pretenses. All her thoughts are to deceive and swindle. Even while she disports herself as my noble father's consort, she leaves him to grovel before me out of lust. Although my lovely mistress Manohari seemed chaste, perhaps she is similar to this woman and behaving disgracefully. Her morals may have degenerated. I must turn my mind away from all sensual desire."

So he spoke these harsh words:

> Kye hu! You have an inferior form now
> As a result of prior indulgence in such perversion.
> I defame you! I censure you! Ogress!
> I do not desire you: you disgust and revolt me!
>
> Even while you enjoy being the consort
> Of my honorable father, the Lord of Men,
> You lust for an unsuitable partner;
> Myself or any handsome monk or brahmin!
>
> For aeons under the sway of your lust,
> You have taken many rebirths in samsara,
> Suffering the misery of aging, sickness, and death.
> Now yet again lechery misleads you;
> Your improper conduct will bear awful fruit
> As soon as you are born into your next life.
>
> In the fearsome and dreadful gardens of hell
> Is a platform of roaring fire emitting sparks.
> There the ferocious henchmen of the Death Lord
> Will pose as your husband and you will go to them.
> They will pour molten bronze into your womb
> And brand your vagina with a blazing iron hammer.
> I will not be able to help you then!
> Turn away from this and seek your future!

Lavanya Kamala was shamed and humiliated. Embarrassment made her perspire, hang her head, and sigh repeatedly. After she returned to Suryamati's bed, she thought, "I have acted badly and thoughtlessly. If Kumara tells anyone else how I was insane with lust, I will be an object of scorn, and my son, Ananda Lalitasaras, will not inherit the kingdom!

It all depends on his silence. I must have Kumara banished to another realm quickly!"

So she pretended to have had a bad dream and woke the king from sleep. Her face was covered with tears, as she dolefully said:

> O my lord! While I slept,
> A dream of evil omen came to me.
> Its sorrows seem so real!
> My heart palpitates with misery.
>
> The elder brother who obtained the kingdom
> Became ensnared by powerful poisonous envy.
> O sovereign, you and I were banished as enemies!
> His brother Ananda's throat and limbs
> Were bound by executioners' black ropes;
> He was subjected to the death penalty!
>
> This dream makes me shiver and be depressed.
> It is just as I have heard it said,
> In fear my hair stands on end,
> Sweat pours forth from my body.
>
> If that prince continues to be the regent,
> Please let me go somewhere else!
> Ananda Lalitasaras must be safely,
> Secretly ensconced in a hermitage elsewhere.
>
> If this is not to be, my Lord of Men's command
> Must shine forth like a pure, stainless moon
> Emitting the cool rays of the following promise
> To please the night lily of my mind.
>
> I beg you to send Kumaradvitiya to live
> In a delightful forest to absorb himself in religion.
> Then will it not be right to bestow the kingdom
> Upon his brother, ablaze with brilliant great virtues?

As she piteously spoke, her voice choked with tears, the king thought, "This woman is naturally intelligent. She understands the portents of unfathomable dreams and visions. O! May the evil prophecy of this dream never occur! Yet I cannot bear to banish that superb prince.

Nevertheless, I must undertake that difficult task, for I do not wish to contradict my earlier pledges."

Thinking thus, he became extremely despondent. His bright complexion dulled from depression, fading like a fresh green reed after it is cut. His eyes stared fixedly, and his lips blanched. The flesh of his body grew thin and gaunt. He had not a glimmer of a smile.

> Women are dishonest by nature.
> One whose very name is craftiness
> Completely deceived the kingly father,
> So he experienced unbearable sorrow.

King Suryamati was completely deluded by Lavanya Kamala's wiles. When the prince saw how his father's health had degenerated, his heart was greatly troubled. He went before his father and prayed with his hands together:

> "Honorable father! A source of fortitude,
> You engage in deeds of wisdom and virtue.
> What sort of unhappiness are you enduring?
>
> Your glorious health has decayed.
> The sound of your lyrical voice is dull.
> Your steady mind shifts like the breeze
> While your bright eyes stare fixedly.
> A smile never comes to your once red lips.
>
> Seeing this, I wonder if I cause you to grieve?
> If a minister be at fault, he should be destroyed!
> Perhaps your body's four humors are in discord?
>
> I beg you to speak openly, withholding naught;
> It is not right for you to remain silent
> About the reason you are so painfully injured
> Like a deer in the clutches of a carnivorous beast.
> I shall endeavor to accomplish whatever you desire."

His father bashfully replied to this supplication:
"Son, son, it is so. How can I not tell you,
So solicitous of your parent and so nobly behaved?

My lack of smiles and the decayed health
Of my body so unpleasant to see
Are not caused by a physical illness,
Nor is inimical conduct of the court at fault.

O magnificent son, the decline of my fortunes
Is due to your treasury of good qualities!
Also, I am enveloped in a fog of ignorance.
My mind is unstable, it shifts like the wind.

You ask how can that be? Well, when I lusted
For Lavanya Kamala's sensual good qualities,
I spoke some excessive words in a solemn oath
Because of a subtle stratagem of Padmankura.

I said that you, a magnificent wish-granting tree
Scented by the virtuous flowers of renown,
Would be banished to a peaceful forest
To bend under the weight of the flowers of religion.
Further, your younger brother, an ordinary tree,
Would be adorned by the highest rank of the realm.

I am afraid to counter my own utterances.
Yet, when I think that even thousand-eyed Indra
Could raise his jeweled lamp and search for aeons
Yet still be hard-pressed to find a treasure
Of good qualities like you anywhere in the world,
How can I banish you to a far-off forest?
The thought of the pain of even a moment's separation
Causes my health and happiness to wither.

You have an earnest, steadfast wisdom,
So you can alleviate my mental agony;
Please tell me what it is I should do
Without contradicting my promised words!"

So, lacking any idea of what he should do, the king entreated Kumara
to decide wisely. Kumaradvitiya thought, "Of all the deceits in the world,
the duplicity of women is the worst! They are the essence of insincerity.
Lavanya Kamala has surely misled my father through her craftiness.

"Eh ma! I have taken to heart the teachings expressed in the lion's

roar of my virtuous spiritual friend, Dharmeshvara. I have already accumulated much merit from the practice of giving charity. Now it seems I
am about to obtain time to promote the virtues of practicing ethics and
meditation!"

His face clearly showed his joy. He bowed his head to his father's
feet. He said:

Eh ma ho! It is most wonderful!
A father who so sincerely loves his child
Is as extremely rare and naturally pure
As the flower that blooms only at a Buddha's birth.
Do not grieve as if I were close to death!

As soon as a corporeal being is born,
It is afflicted by its impermanent nature.
Thus, the termination of birth is death.
All accumulation ends in consumption.
Togetherness finishes with parting.
This is the nature of existence.
So is it a matter for a father's pain?

Everything in the world is as impermanent
As lightning or a mountain waterfall.
Pleasures that instantly transform are undesirable.
Thinking of how long we've been oppressed,
Carrying a burden of a multitude of sorrows
Would shatter even an adamantine, patient heart!

Even if you find a high rebirth as a human,
Being in the womb is like the agony of hell:
It is an unbearably awful existence to live
In a foul amniotic ocean of ordure and blood.

Finally, squeezed like sesame in an oil press,
You emerge from the womb and are born.
Babies cannot speak about their discomfort.
They no know way to eliminate their misery
Other than to thrash about and cry.

Nurtured to maturity on our mothers' milk,
We know how to behave and avoid impropriety.

Yet pursuing pleasure we make others miserable.
The poison of our greed, hatred, and ignorance
Destroys our happiness: we are our own enemy.
Our nefarious behavior on a delinquent path
Renders purposeless our fortunate human life.

This life is like a fleeting afternoon shadow.
It quickly passes, and we are seized by old age:
Our bent bodies need the support of a staff,
Our hair turns white, and our faces wrinkle,
Fading like a lotus petal wilts with age.
We lose our teeth, so even our happy smiles
Become ugly, gaping holes unpleasant to see.
Even though we have many things of quality,
We have not the time or ability to enjoy them.
The decline of our youthful power and vigor
Binds our bodies and minds in ropes of misery.

Whenever the intolerable discomforts of illness
Harass us by internal or external causes,
We lie inert in the center of our sickbeds
And lose control of our bowels and urine.
We are served delicious, nutritious food,
But it will not go down our throats.
We can enjoy it only with our eyes.

When we are young, disease seems no danger,
So we pursue mastery of the arts and sciences.
But at the time of death, neither the illusion
Old people recount of their earlier prowess,
Nor medical advice, nor friends and servants
Can help us. They are all are given up.

At death we stare fixedly as a statue.
We abandon our inconceivably wondrous wealth,
Our dear friends, family, and attendants.
Alone we leave the herd wailing, "I am dying!"

As we die, we wonder what will become of us,
So we recall with inconsolable regret
The good and evil actions of our life.

We come to the end of this life tormented
By the fear of being reborn to suffer
The distress of the hell, ghost, or animal realms.

It is difficult to cross to the far shore
Of the samsaric ocean's turbulent waves
Of birth, aging, sickness, and death.
But the boat of bodhisattva deeds
Can carry you to the land of liberation.

These skillful deeds should be practiced
In a solitary forest hermitage,
With trees heavy with flowers and fruit.
There, on the tips of the lattice of branches,
Birds sing sweet melodies to wake one
From the deep sleep of ignorance.

Even ferocious carnivores peacefully venerate
With no enmity those who expound the Dharma.
As if showing respect to meditators,
Young bees dance and hum over the tips
Of gently swaying flowers, lotuses and lilies.

Its lovely, verdant meadows are moistened
By the emerald waters of twisting streams,
Whose sweet gurgling sound seems to teach
The fluctuating nature of all phenomena.

There I will stay on a mat of grass and leaves
In a house made of smooth reeds and foliage.
I will wear bark clothes, and take as my food
Tasty roots, sprouts, and pure, clear water.

Even if I were not exhorted, I would wish
To go quickly to that grove of austerities
Where firm and peaceful concentration
Complements the analysis of perfect wisdom.

Father, to free you from painful choice,
I cast off the kingdom's wealth like grass.
The feet of Ananda Lalitasaras should be placed

Upon the gem-encrusted, fearless lion throne.
Then I can enter the path which benefits all
By the pure ethics of the undefiled ten virtues.

Thus, honorable father, please attend.
This profound advice offers the means
For you to accomplish both your goals:
You will pacify your sorrow and keep your vow.

The prince's grief about the sufferings of samsara pained him so much that his face was covered with tears. While his son supplicated him, Suryamati thought:

"Kumara speaks of going to a hermitage as a means to free me from misery. Yet the pain of separation from him increases. But he is right; it is the nature of samsara that we part from our loved ones and meet with our enemies. We cannot obtain what we desire, and undesirable things befall us. The sordid components of our bodies and minds have only the nature of misery, thus we endure incurable anguish. Now Kumara intends to achieve permanent happiness. I should rejoice in this and not obstruct him."

So the king said:

It is true. Samsara has a hollow nature.
A creature's life is like a strand of froth
Upon the waters of sorrow and impermanence.

Marvelous youth is a fleeting rainbow.
This life's pleasures come and go like clouds.
Wealth is as unreliable as dew upon the grass.
Since I see this shifting nature of phenomena,
I cannot oppose your striving for nirvana.

Until you have attained liberation,
You may rely upon austerities in a hermitage.
But when you have obtained the path to freedom,
Please return to the kingdom to let fall the rain
Of doctrine, to train me and other sinful beings.

Long and loud sighs punctuated the king's speech. His eyes reflected the pain of parting from his son. His words filled the prince with the taste of joy, and he replied, "I will do as you request."

31

In which Prince Kumaradvitiya gives his kingdom to his younger half-brother and departs alone for his exile in the forest

A RUMOR THAT PRINCE KUMARADVITIYA was going to give away the wealth of the kingdom and dwell in a forest hermitage passed quickly from one person to another. As this news became widely known, his mother, Kundaladhara, his subjects, and the chief ministers who viewed their ruler with respect experienced great misery. Then Prince Kumaradvitiya handed the administration of the realm over to his brother, Ananda Lalitasaras. Making ready to depart, he went to bid final farewell to his mother. He said to her:

> From beginningless time I have taken countless rebirths;
> Hence, every living being has been my mother or father.
> Now I shall endeavor to repay the kindness of the mother
> Who gave me this meaningful life of freedom and fortune.
>
> I practiced giving away the marvels of the world,
> But I found no liberation from cyclic existence.
> So I go to a far-off forest to absorb myself in meditation.
> I vow to accomplish the superior aim of liberating
> All beings who have protected me kindly so many times.
>
> O mother, without distress arising from our parting,
> Rejoice that I engage in a bodhisattva's superior deeds!

Although she felt glad that Kumara was to lead his life engaging in deeds leading to pure enlightenment, the pain of parting from her cherished only child engulfed Kundaladhara. Her eyes fixed on him and streamed tears, wetting her face as she said these heartrending words:

> Beloved loveless son! Can you bear to part
> From your mother, who is as close to death
> As the sun is now to setting in the west,
> As you rejoice in entering the bodhisattva path?
>
> The fire of your good deeds burns away the passions,
> Yet at the same time it scorches my heart's joy.
> It is said that a mother without her adored son
> Does not live for very long. Pay you no heed
> To the meaning of our wise forefathers' homily?
>
> You say you wish to go to the forest depths
> To benefit all beings. But is it compassionate
> To inflict pain on your family and subjects?
> Can I not dissuade you from your desire to go?

His mother's words caused the mirror of Kumara's mind to reflect the intolerable pain of separation from a loved one. But his understanding that sorrow is the nature of samsara could not be shaken. So he spoke once again to his mother:

> I am not going away for my own peace and happiness,
> Casting off the superior love of the mother
> Who protected me with immeasurable kindness
> From the moment I took rebirth in her womb!
>
> Dear mother, your kindness to me in this life
> Is like my prior mothers', so many they fill the sky.
> Seeing this, I wish to repay all this benevolence.
> So I vow to attain enlightenment for others' sake
> And directly perceive the nature of reality,
> Thus accomplishing my own and others' aims.
>
> By training my mind in the three types of ethics—
> Eliminating vice, amassing virtue, and helping others—
> I shall free tormented beings from the three miseries
> Of ordinary pain, change, and afflicted existence.

When I put on the sturdy armor of courage
To lead all beings to the state of happiness,
All my mothers will rejoice in that action.
It is not right to cease striving for enlightenment
Because of the inability to bear slight discomfort.
So I give up desire for wealth, fame, and life itself.
I vow to free all beings from the ocean of samsara!

After this he thought, "If I listen to my mother's response, I may be obstructed from attaining enlightenment." So, not paying any heed to his mother's exhortations, he made three farewell prostrations. Although his mother spoke clearly and then wailed and fell into a faint, he impassively went out.

At this point, his younger brother, Ananda Lalitasaras, felt no happiness, even though he had obtained the kingdom as his own. He thought, "If my elder brother goes to attain the peace and happiness of nirvana, I shall follow him." So, crying and gesticulating, he addressed Kumaradvitiya:

Elder brother! You are the lord of light,
Causing the lotus of all people's hopes to bloom.
If you go to strive for blissful peace
In the western mountains' forest valleys,
A dark cloud of suffering will envelop the world.

My intelligence and courage shine weakly;
I am but a foolish firefly pretending greatness.
I assume the throne, but I have no power
To destroy the deep fog of our travail.

Without you, our Earth Lord and source of cool ambrosia,
Who will protect our people from suffering painful heat?
If we lose the wish-granting jewel of your life,
Who will let fall the rain satisfying those in want?

My lord, I vow that if you truly desire to go,
Then I too shall go in order to serve you.
And when you attain the sixth bodhisattva level,
Born in a pure land from a precious lotus bud,
May I be born there as your foremost disciple.

As you practice in accord with your vast, pure prayers,
Do not loosen the thick rope of your compassion for me!

Then Ananda Lalitasaras grasped the prince's lotus-feet in a vinelike embrace. His earnest devotion made the noble prince think, "His desire moves my heart with love. Yet it would not be suitable at all if he were to abdicate the kingdom to follow me." Stretching out his arm as elegantly as an elephant's trunk, he placed his hand on Ananda Lalitasaras's head and said:

Eh ma ma la! Dearest brother!
Your heartfelt words of desire
Are without deceit or pretension.
They pierce my heart to the quick.

However, you now have the opportunity to create merit,
For the coronation rituals for your rule are complete.
It is not the right time for you to go to live
In a distant forest of densely twining thickets.

Your youthful body is not yet fully mature,
So austerities would be difficult to bear.
It is not proper for you to follow me,
Abandoning your parents, a treasury of love.

Take hold of our honorable father's realm
Without becoming engrossed in sinful deeds
That ripen into the black fruits of sorrow.
Protect this great realm according to the Dharma
By acting honorably and following the path
Of goodness and virtue that I have laid out.

All men of exalted rank may make offerings to you,
But do not become haughty with pride and arrogance.
Always show deference and give respectfully
To those worthy of being a refuge: your parents and the wise.

When we are babes, our parents protect us
By any means, even killing if need be.
Never act like a despicable, unbred man
Who grows up to despise and malign his parents.

Without any favoritism, your firm and splendid laws
Should shine upon all as impartially as the sun.
Place our subjects ranging to the ocean's shores
Into the state of peaceful prosperity.

The mere rumor of battle with your army
Of fierce warriors may strike fear into your enemy,
But do not behave like an injurious thorn
Toward your court and retainers who serve you.

You must become a master of dispelling the darkness
Of your enemies' hatred by emanating the white light
Of a fine wise man's smile of bravery and patience
And skillful speech which contains little deceit.

A face black with anger is unpleasant to see.
Fiery, harsh words scorch your own and others' minds.
Do not enter into a course of action
Deceitful, dishonest, or crafty by nature.

Although you have vast holdings of land,
High status, and great wealth, do not be vain.
Carefully investigate the natural dispositions
Of those who speak sweet words and false praises.

In desperation, some men bow to their inferiors,
But when prosperous they ignore their ruler.
Your behavior should not swing up and down
Like a balance scale responding to mere trifles.

If an Earth Lord takes pleasure in evil,
Others will follow his sinful example.
If he delights in virtue, his people will too.
So carefully discern what to do or avoid.

Because we are naturally full of hatred,
We view virtue incorrectly, of course!
Exhorting or rejoicing in others' sins
Leads to lower rebirth, so avoid such deeds.

Those who give charity will never be poor.
Those who hoard riches like honey may lose their wealth.
Always nourish the poor as your loving relations
With extensive bounty given freely from your hands.

Because of the force of our selfish desires,
We cannot give even a sesame seed of our own.
Covetousness makes us seize others' affluence.
Untie the knot of selfish miserliness.

All mundane and transcendental good qualities
Arise in reliance upon a spiritual friend.
The mist of nectar of his religious instruction
Ripens the sprout of virtue in your mind.

Clouds of ill-spoken words block the light
Of the path to liberation and open the door
To low rebirth. So vow not to be influenced
By wicked companions for even a moment.

You know that nobles resting on high thrones
Often come to grief pursuing an object of lust.
So take as a basis of your happiness a wife
With all woman's good qualities and no faults.

Adulteresses eager for handsome men
Fall away from the conduct of pure deeds.
Gross lust decreases one's wealth and life;
Its consequences are hard to bear, so give it up.

Relish the nectar of the superb beverages
Respectfully served to noble classes:
Sandalwood-scented liquids, pure milk,
And curd the color of moonlit night lilies.

Drunkards are not prudent, proper, or tranquil:
You lose your reputation in a drunken dance,
And even your parents seem to be your enemy.
So do not imbibe intoxicating liquors.

The wise will gather and value your instructions
When you speak wisely about religion and polity.
Be wary of uttering the sins of speech;
Flighty gossip and deceptive lies expose
One's truly base nature without disguise.

Countless satraps bow their heads before
The fearless lion throne of this high position.
Always place your feet firmly without wavering
Upon the throne beautified by their crown jewels.

Because of strong craving for foreign places,
Men roam the roads of cities and towns
And clearly display careless behavior.
Abandon all places that destroy your reputation.

The way to guard both the Dharma and the realm
Is to lay out a path of virtuous worldly conduct
That is in accord with religious principles.
This, I tell you, should be your first act.

You may be able to enjoy marvelous wealth
In lives throughout hundreds of aeons.
But those things are all deceptive and impermanent.
What wise man grasps them as lastingly real?

Understand that all rebirths conditioned
By the impure stains of karma and the passions,
From the highest god realms to the depths of hell,
Have a nature of only pervasive suffering.

Ananda Lalitasaras! Holding to the Dharma,
Protect this realm filled with good, virtuous people.
Be a wish-granting treasure for the populace.
Afterward, renounce desire for this life's work
And engage in deeds leading to enlightenment.

   Immediately after instructing his unhappy brother, Kumaradvitiya
departed from the palace. When he reached the outskirts of the city,
the prince disposed of the panoply of parasols and jewel-handled yak-
tail fans which fluttered everywhere about him. He walked off on his

own two feet, having abandoned all of his thousands of horse-drawn chariots, his elephants with golden chain-mail chamfrons, and his horses fitted with jeweled saddlery. He went forth alone; only his inseparable shadow followed him. No longer surrounded by his ministers, close retainers, court, or servants, he was as solitary as the sun in the sky.

32

In which his subjects unsucessfully attempt to prevent Prince Kumaradvitiya from going to a forest hermitage

T HE MINISTERS AND MEMBERS OF THE PALACE COURT who respectfully held their ruler close to their heart gathered together to see
the prince depart. Their loud laments were like the disconsolate
cries of magpies and crows.

A few embraced the prince. And their eyes brimmed with tears as
they worried aloud: "Here in the kingdom we have an abundance of
wealth and happiness. In contrast, the forest is a terrifying place: wild
beasts, poisonous snakes, and even tiny insects will injure you there!"

Others seized his feet and queried, "Have you no compassion for us?
You are going away and so abandoning your parents, whose kindness is
so difficult to repay, your relatives, and your subjects, who love their
king. Is this the conduct of a bodhisattva?"

One man placed the prince's hands upon his head and said, "The
wealth of the kingdom satisfies those in need far better than the practice of austerities in the forest. Of all the results of virtue, the merits
which come from giving alms are the best. So please act accordingly."

Yet others grasped parts of the prince's clothing and blocked his
path, uttering: "O Lord Kumara! If we do not do any wicked actions,
there will be no reason for you to abandon us and leave!"

When they saw how Kumaradvitiya was going off alone, a few
pleaded with him: "Please do not go to the vast expanses of the forest!
Even the road which leads there is perilous. Surely enemies, wild beasts,
or some other such things will destroy you!"

People clamoring their various thoughts covered the land. The
prince could not make his way through them. Then, arising from the

strength of his renunciation, Kumaradvitiya had this compassionate thought:

> "Kye ma! Those who dwell in the world
> Usually turn away from virtue.
> I see that they are trying
> To tie me with insignificant bonds.
>
> They unite to devise plans to obstruct
> My approach to the practice of the Dharma
> By displaying attitudes of concern,
> Execration, affliction, and sorrow.
>
> Because I have accumulated bad karma,
> My future lives will be in incessant hells
> Where one is burnt on red-hot iron ground
> Or frozen in cold crevasses of ice.
>
> In general, my companions were degenerate:
> They never obstructed my destructive deeds
> When I went to conquer the enemy.
> In fact they were in the forefront
> Of my powerful four-division army.
>
> Yet today, when I go to practice the Dharma,
> I have no chariots, elephants, or chargers.
> Nor have I any foot soldiers or ministers.
> Where are those dedicated friends today?"

Once Kumaradvitiya thought this way,
He uttered the following profound secrets
More loudly than the deep dragon thunder
Of rain clouds or any of Brahma's songs:

> "Fools do not fear the forest of samsara,
> Yet that is proper abode to fear:
> For there is no escape from that place
> Engulfed in a fiery pit of suffering.
>
> In a solitary and delightful spot
> Of the peaceful wooded forests,
> The wish to attain enlightenment thereby to benefit others

Will be my friend and succor.
I fear not the approach of vicious beasts,
For there is no greater gift than one's life.

Courageous men may quickly conquer
A powerful, contentious enemy realm,
Coming to engage in all-out warfare.
You cannot defeat the Death Lord: him I fear.

Bandits and robbers may try to kill you
On the dangerous road to a hermitage,
But a generous bribe will protect you.
The Death Lord cannot be so appeased: him I fear.

The forest's poisonous snakes and carnivores
Bare their vicious fangs and threateningly roar,
You can be saved by destroying them or fleeing.
The Death Lord cannot be countered: him I fear.

There are profound antidotes to evil magic spells.
Wicked ministers can be countered by good laws.
Skillful pacifying speeches can divert bad men.
The Death Lord cannot be opposed: him I fear.

The ignorant say they fear the roads, forests,
And lonely places good for religious endeavor.
Those fools are extremely confused: unhappy,
Turbulent samsaric abodes do not frighten them.

O ministers and people whose Dharma eye is blind,
How can you obstruct my pursuit of religion?
Consider matters well: earnestly guard
Yourselves from sin and obtain merits.

I ceased acting heartlessly toward
My relations, court, and subjects.
I began the bodhisattva's waves of practice,
To absorb myself only in accomplishing all men's aims.

Therefore, your attachment to me is improper.
You know what deeds to do and what to avoid,
So respect your ruler and honestly do your duty

In a wise, well-bred, and contained manner.
A religious realm prospers thanks to the actions
Of wise men with good and stable natures.

As soon as all creatures are born,
They want to be happy and avoid pain.
Since we are all the same in this way,
Try to generate the wish to help others.

Like a single lightning flash illuminates
An overcast, dark night for a mere instant,
We have a human life of freedom and fortune.
Rejoice in extracting its essential purpose!

"Furthermore, listen to this! Without our own volition we are born with afflicted, illusory physical and mental continuums. Old age comes to us like the shadows of evening. We know of no way to reverse that process: like a flower that has begun to fade, there is no way to revive its bloom. Sickness arises like a wind: we cannot foretell when it will strike. Even the conditions which sustain life can become a cause of death. Thus, the supports of life are few, but the causes of death are many. Death is always close to life; life is like a flower carried away by a river or a water bubble instantly destroyed by the slightest touch. Think about these things properly and then absorb yourselves in the practice of Dharma. Moreover, it is like this:

"All phenomena exist as mere imputations,
Like illusions they depend on causal conditions.
Not thinking, we accept their appearance as real,
But examine them and you find no inherent existence.
To exist as an imputation without a true nature
Is not a contradiction, as the wise know.
Join this wisdom to the method of loving-kindness
To partake of the nectar of the religious path.
Strive in this way to benefit all creatures!"

His profound advice in accordance with the Dharma filled their minds with respect. So when they saw that there was no doubt that the prince was going to leave, they realized it was not fitting to block his path. But their suffering over his departure was difficult to bear, and they uttered loud cries of tormented sorrow:

Kye hu! O marvelous Kumaradvitiya,
Lord of Men with compassionate means,
And a treasury of love for all beings,
We are ignorant of where you will go.

When we lack a lamp for our people,
Who will overcome our dark sorrow?
If we give away our wish–granting gem,
Who will fulfill our needs and desires?

We will decline like a child
Who has no dear loving mother.
Now your people and court lack
A ruler: upon whom can they gaze?

Suryamati is a heartless king:
He has caused his subjects
To endure this pointless sorrow.
Are we punished for breaking his laws?

Even if he is not ruled by love
For his dearly cherished son
Who bears the lineage of succession,
Why does he make us suffer so?

Today masses of undesirable vicissitudes
Are falling all at once upon our heads.
It is the ripening of nonvirtuous actions
That were accomplished during other lives.

Kye ma! O heartless father
And royal prince Kumara!
How can you bind your faultless
Subjects to such unhappy sorrow?

While they uttered these and other disconsolate laments, the prince
passed beyond the last of the city's crossroads.

33

In which Bhavakumara joins his lord in exile

JUST AT THAT TIME, the hero Bhavakumara arrived at Gem of the
World after returning the wealth of Myriad Lights to King
Chandramati and Devatisha according to Kumaradvitiya's command.

As he rode toward the palace quarter, he heard the doleful sounds of
weeping and the words "Prince Kumara! Prince Kumara!" He became
alarmed and in a panic galloped up to the others. All he could see was
that they were pained by unhappiness and misery. "Kye ma! My protector, lord, and comrade-in-arms! Prince Kumaradvitiya, born thanks to
our fortunate lot of merits, and whom to see gave joy, must have passed
away!"

The fierce pain of this woeful thought seemed to cause his heart to
break. With a crash, his senseless body fell from his horse. He lay on the
ground unconscious. Then the ministers and servants sprinkled him
with cool, scented water and fanned him. Slowly he regained consciousness. He rested his cheeks in his hands and questioned them in a
hoarse, weeping voice: "Kye! How did our protector, the singular Prince
Kumara, so unfortunately pass away?"

"King Suryamati was corrupted by others and came to prefer
another," they said.

"What! Did he have Kumara killed under the insidious influence of
others?"

"No, that is not the case," they replied. "He has gone to the forest
valleys of boundless peace."

From their recapitulation of the events, Bhavakumara was freed from his fear that Prince Kumara had gone on to his next life. This gave him a bit of relief, but he was sad that the prince was no longer in the kingdom.

"Kva ye! O ministers, all of you, not missing a one, are gathered here. So who has gone to wait upon Prince Kumara?"

They said, "He is without a servant: he has gone without a companion."

Hearing this made Bhavakumara very disgruntled. He spat in their faces and said, "You are unworthy of being held close to anyone's heart! It is unthinkable that such a wonderful Lord of Men should leave without a companion! If you lack the inclination to follow and serve him, your wailing and thrashing about here is but a sham!

> When he wielded power over this realm,
> Magnificently wealthy and powerful ministers,
> Like constellations gathering round the moon,
> Adorned him like a clearly auspicious sign.
>
> Today, when he departed to dwell in the forest,
> He began the difficult journey in solitude.
> Not one of you wished to follow his dusty feet.
> Are all of your hearts made of stone?
>
> Kye hu! This court is shamelessly naked!
> You have cast off the clothes of modest propriety.
> You weep, "What a pity to be without Kumara!"
> But your wails are counterfeit, merely for show.
>
> When that ocean of marvelous good qualities
> And treasure of compassion ruled as our lord,
> Countless ministers and servants ringed him.
> It would be easier for me to die seized
> In the fangs of the forest's ferocious beasts
> Than to see him go alone as he does today!
>
> I shall follow his footsteps!
> When I meet him I shall honor him.
> How can it be right for his servants
> To abandon him in his time of need?"

Bhavakumara had no attachment to his home, parents, loving mistresses, or retainers. He left them all to hasten along the path traversed earlier by Prince Kumara. In a wide plain which lay beyond the cities and towns, he found Kumaradvitiya walking alone like a blazing solitary light. He was like a deer who had gone far ahead of the rest of the herd. Bhavakumara's sorrowful tears fell like handfuls of pearls. He thought, "Kye ma! My lord is without an entourage or any mount. He is impoverished. He goes alone into difficult, deserted places. How can I bear it!" He ran up to Kumara and grasped his feet. He cried:

> Eh ma! Lord, you engage in waves of pure deeds,
> Seeing the marvels of the world as a fiery hell.
> But how can you bear to travel totally alone,
> Without the surging waves of your court and wealth?

Kumara smiled radiantly at him and replied:

> Son! It is amazing that you follow me.
> You are worthy of being a peerless comrade.
> However, to create the causes of happiness
> It is easier to be without a companion.
> For when the fearsome Death Lord arrives,
> No friend other than the Dharma can free you.
>
> O Bhavakumara, do not follow me!
> In the forest vicious carnivores threaten.
> We will lack food, drink, and clothes to wear.
> There will be no lovers or pretty maids to see,
> And your friends and relations will be far away.
>
> Engaging in the practices leading to enlightenment
> Is for those who make vast waves of prayers.
> They are not practices meant for ordinary men.
> Do not attempt them for me; return to Gem of the World,
> Where Ananda Lalitasaras rules on the throne.
> Respect him, for he is indistinguishable from me.
>
> Make noble customs increase like the waxing moon.
> Men with bad natures waft about like cotton fluff,
> They may appear to be your friends at first,
> But eventually their evil character will manifest,
> So abandon all sinful, nonvirtuous associates.

In the world many things seem pleasurable,
But they arise dependent upon afflicted actions.
See that they are solely of the nature of suffering
And put on the courageous armor to practice the Dharma.

Your parents and loved ones will suffer without you.
Relieve their pain and make them joyful.
I shall make prayers that you will be reborn
As my disciple wherever I enjoy my next life.

Bhavakumara pondered the prince's words: "If I cast away this loving ruler, on whose face could I possibly gaze?" So again he prostrated himself before him. Getting up from touching his head to the prince's feet, he supplicated him:

You are a strong wish-granting tree,
Your deeply planted roots are compassion,
Your boughs are heavy with the fruit of charity,
Your fame's sweet scent wafts through the world.

If you go to be the ornament for the forest,
I shall come too and rely on your bounty.
I shall be a young vine entwining myself
Among the spreading boughs of your faith
And the blossoming flowers of your wisdom.

Wherever a royal prince may go,
It is easier for an ordinary man.
Even if there be fearsome dangers,
No food or clothes, and very cold,
I would rather die than not go!

If you are not the beautiful ornament
Of the lovely palace of Gem of the World,
Upon whose face could I gaze there?
How could I call out another's name?

You say a peepul tree has amazing qualities,
But it is not an object that attracts me.
How could I gladly leave a wish-granting tree
Whose powers fulfill all my needs and desires?

If your honorable father the Earth Lord
Treated even you, his dear son, without love,
If someone like me should counter him slightly,
I can hardly imagine the fearsome repercussions!

O Kumara, I followed you when you went to war.
Now you go the lonely forest to practice religion.
Since I too carry a heavy burden of intolerable sins,
I'll happily follow you so I can eliminate them
And accumulate great collections of merit and wisdom.

So please gaze upon me with your far-seeing eyes
Of compassion, which desire all beings' liberation!

When the prince saw that Bhavakumara's resolve to accompany him
was firm, he gave the hero permission to follow. Practicing austerities as
they went, they proceeded in stages to the forest.

Prince Kumara saw all worldly marvels as a river of blazing fire, so he
was not under the sway of attachment. Nevertheless, because he had so
many powerful karmic propensities in relation to Manohari, a little possessive clinging to her remained in his heart.

At one point on their journey, near the edge of the forest, the two
men came upon the corpse of a young girl. She must have wandered off
the main road and then been hunted down by fierce wild beasts. Soon
after her death, they came upon the terrible scene. The prince, sad at
heart, said to the hero Bhavakumara:

"Kye ma! All composite phenomena are impermanent: without their
own volition they come to naught. My beautiful love Manohari still
steals away my mental fortitude, but in the end she will die and no
doubt be just like this.

For the most part, worldly men are like this:
To them the body and mind do not seem different.
In her glorious youth this maiden was attractive.
Today she is a corpse, no longer with any life.
Now not even her family will find her desirable.
When they see her, they will run away in disgust.

Her tresses of curly, shiny black hair
Were draped with garlands of unblemished flowers

And beautified by precious jeweled crowns.
Now they flap in the wind like a yak's tail.

The sidelong glances from her wonderful eyes
Were a source of sensual pleasure for lustful men.
Now they are repulsive, blood-stained crucibles,
For crows and vultures have pecked out her eyes.

When her red lips opened in a rosy smile,
You could see her flawless, pearly teeth.
Today it is revolting to see her tongue
Between her gaping jaws bared in horror.

Her white, round breasts were worthy of caress
By the lotus-hands of a devoted first lover.
Now bloodied by the strike of vultures' beaks,
All desire for these horrors ceases.

Her limbs were enticingly smooth and soft
And adorned with lovely precious ornaments.
But today her limbs are but ugly stumps;
Jackals and other beasts devour her flesh.

Intercourse with her was unalloyed bliss.
Her touch was the essence of sensual pleasure.
Now a host of beasts, maggots, and crows
Enjoys her fresh lotus that gave such joy.

This stunning, lovely, youthful maiden
Captivated the firm hearts of desirous men.
Now who can bear to see the waterfall of pus,
Filth, and stench pouring from her orifices?

This maiden gave joy when she lived:
But dead she is offensively ugly.
Now how could anyone lust for her?
Even to recall this scene makes me retch.

Because of that unsuitable emotion called desire,
I too could be led into hell in an instant.

Now my mind will not stray for a moment,
Even toward a woman who knows all love's arts
And is a thousand times lovelier than Manohari."

The last flicker of desire for the lovely Manohari was extinguished in his mind. Then they slowly proceeded along the path.

34

In which Manohari learns the prince has gone into exile and follows after him

NOW DURING THIS TIME, Manohari was relishing her visit to her parents in Radiant Array. Eventually she learned that Prince Kumaradvitiya had ascended his father's throne and was ruling the kingdom according to the Dharma. She was extremely glad to hear that and returned to Gem of the World as quickly as she could.

When she approached the city of Open Lotus, which usually was so lovely to see, she found its appearance had deteriorated. It was dry and dusty, and the populace seemed greatly reduced in number. The sorrowful demeanor of those who were there made her wonder what had caused such ill omens. She proceeded on toward the palace filled with doubt; not one of the city folk dared tell her the news, because she and noble Kumara had been such a loving couple. As she went on, it seemed that the lovely greenery and sweet smells of the summer gardens had been touched by an autumn frost: all the leaves had wilted, and the flowers drooped. The peacocks and other birds let forth no songs; they seemed mute, unable to emit a sound. She went onward increasingly worried.

The delightful palace of Gem of the World used to glow with magnificence. Now it too, inside and out, was completely covered by a thick layer of dust. The precious gold of the pinnacles, balconies, and doors had lost its luster. The bells on the silk-fringed curtains still moved in the breeze, but they were soundless. All this was appalling to her.

As she came into the palace, she saw that the ministers and retainers were in the grip of deep sorrow. Their complexions were dull, their flesh was thin and diminished, and their tight-lipped faces were covered with the lines of tears. When she began to question them, they fled from her like frightened deer. Now she became quite disturbed.

"What! Marvelous Kumaradvitiya, the Lord of Men, could not have died!" In distress she went from the top to the bottom of the palace, begging someone to come and quell her doubts. But no one replied to her cries. Then she thought, "Kumaradvitiya surely must be in his residence, Floating Wonder." But she found that joyful suite also was covered by dust and as empty as a lake from which all the birds had flown off at once.

"I have no doubt, the noble prince has died!" she thought. In anguish she began to thrash convulsively and weep like a doe struck by a poisoned arrow. Finally, like a tree cut at the root, she collapsed by the side of the palace portals.

The prince's mother, Kundaladhara, heard her and came running to her there. With the customary scents and cooling fans, she helped Manohari regain consciousness. Manohari tore her hair, ripped off her ornaments, and piled them on the floor. Like an insane woman, she stared fixedly at his mother's face, unable to question her coherently for quite a while.

The prince's mother also was choked with tears. She said to Manohari, "Kye, my lady! Do not be so distraught. Prince Kumara has not died from an illness that was a disharmony of the four humors. Nor did his enemies find a chance to kill him. He was such a skilled sportsman that a fall from his elephants or steeds could not cause him to pass away. However, he has turned his back on the world. He saw even the wonders of this kingdom as a pit of hellish fire. While his closest ministers' and retainers' tears flowed, he left us to reside in a forest hermitage. As there is no doubt about this, clear your mind and cease this insane behavior."

Manohari was freed from the fear that Kumara had passed into his next life. But the pain of not being with him made her weep aloud. She cried out Kumaradvitiya's name. Sighing and gasping, she lay pressed against the doorsill for support. Like a dove struck by a stone, she was weakened and had no will to rise. She grasped his mother's feet and said:

Kye! Supreme mother Kundaladhara!
From his birth you protected him with love.
Comprehending this awful situation,
My heart trembles with evil visions.

The superb city of Open Lotus has become
Like a city of ghosts without bright luster.

The palace which shone like the gods' abode
Is unpleasant to see, covered by dusty dirt.

The smiling ministers so skilled with words
Scowl blackly and cannot say a thing.
The flowers and leaves of the gardens' copses
Are wilted, and birds no longer sing there.

My heart is broken, shattered all to bits.
In sorrow my sentient body is like a corpse.

He is a treasure trove of all good qualities,
The benefactor who loves all people as his kin,
Even perfect recollection of his seductiveness
Cannot equal him really. O where has he gone?

Even the deep dragon thunder of the clouds
Or a rain of Brahma's songs cannot compare
To his voice, which sounds like perfect music.
O where has the expounder of gentle Dharma gone?

Like an unfathomable, deep, and wide ocean,
Rippling with waves of practice for enlightenment,
His heart is moistened by love for all beings.
O where has this noble bodhisattva gone?

Like a feather blown before a strong wind,
I am unfortunate and know not what to do.
I have no home, no place to call my own,
No lover to confide in, nor any position.
How can I remain here in this empty realm?

I rejoice that the prince has begun great deeds
Thanks to the kindling of his propensity for virtue.
Kumara has seen the many faults of desire,
So I too no longer wish to be his consort.
But though I fear for my life, I shall follow him,
For he is worthy of offerings and refuge.

Dear mother, you may not have the fortune
To be with him again before you pass away.

So pray that you will meet as close friends
In the vast pure lands in your future lives.

King Suryamati and his ministers heard this doleful lament. They became concerned and so came to Manohari and said:

"Lady goddess, know you well! Our single refuge, Prince Kumar-advitiya, has renounced samsara. He went to the forests quite a while ago, vowing to liberate all sentient beings. Your resolve to follow him is marvelous, but we cannot tell you where to go. And should you attempt this, there is no doubt that fearsome robbers, wild beasts, or some such thing would kill you.

"Therefore, because the noble Kumara and his brother are like possessors of a single body and soul, stay here as the noble queen of the wonderfully handsome Ananda Lalitasaras."

These words were extremely distasteful to Manohari. "O foul king and ministers!" she thought. "Today they turn their faces away from Prince Kumaradvitiya, a master of glory and good qualities, to make his younger brother ruler of the realm. In addition, they have no feeling for my piercing sorrow. They fear that I will try to follow Kumara and so try to obstruct me. But offering Ananda Lalitasaras and the kingdom to me is like serving bloody meat to a fawn who desires only sprouts of green grass to eat. I have no passion for them, they are but dust." She said to them:

O Lord of Men! You and your ministers
Pretend to offer me beneficial advice.
But the blazing fire of your crooked words
Scorches my mind, inflaming pain anew.

There are many radiant orbs in the sky,
But none compares with the sovereign sun.
Many Lords of Men rule over the earth,
But who can compare with Kumaradvitiya?

In the faultless gardens of the god realms,
There are marvelous flowers whose virtuous scent
Is the fount of life for the entire universe.
But they are not wish-granting trees like the prince.

Like fronds of grass, many petty kingdoms
Cover the earth's plains and valleys.

Those places do not give me any pleasure.
What is Ananda Lalitasaras to me?

Without the marvelous sovereign Earth Lord,
This kingdom seems as empty as the sky.
Its wealth of pleasures have vanished
Like moonlight when the moon has set.

If I am without Prince Kumara so worthy of refuge,
No one and nothing can make me experience joy:
Not even if I should obtain Indra as my lover
In a realm with the riches of the northern gods.

What use is it to eat? How can I drink?
What good is the kingdom's wealth or another lover?
What can I do with clothes or precious jewelry?
I have no desire for any worldly, mundane marvels.

Thus, I will face the direction he has gone.
I shall enter the dense forests after him.
I would rather perish in the jaws of snakes
And wild beasts than not fulfill this desire.

So with only a few provisions and a pair of maidservants, she left the superb city. Her feet followed the path Kumara had gone. She questioned anyone and everyone she came upon, even animals, if they had seen him and could tell her which way to go.

That most beautiful woman with a perfect manner
Gave not even a fleeting glance of desire
For the kingdom's wealth or the marvelous charms
Of the Lord of Men's son Ananda Lalitasaras.

Her mind was firmly fixed upon Prince Kumara.
She followed him, risking the life-threatening
Hardships of the lonely roads and forest.
But she heard no news of him at all.

Her body tired and her mind became confused.
Her seductively lovely beauty deteriorated.
Her face became lined with rivers of tears.

Her bracelets could slide up to her shoulders
Because the flesh of her limbs was so emaciated.

Her eyebrows were rigid. Her eyelashes trembled.
Swollen eyelids obscured her sidelong glances.
Her ruby red lips and rosy cheeks paled.
Her sweet voice cried out hoarse laments.

That transcendentally flawless beauty
After a while became so thin and wan,
Even her charming form came to resemble
The body of an ordinary pretty woman!

Worldly people's desires are never satiated.
They know the results of accumulating karma,
But they carelessly lust again and again,
Acting like thirsty men drinking salt seawater.

As rivers continually pour into the sea,
Most women always act for a fruitless end.
Although they have pursued a hundred husbands,
They have not reached the limit of desire.

However, from the pearl garland of Manohari's former lives,
The light of former prudent actions shone forth.
Even in her dreams she desired no lover
Except the noble prince. How amazing!

By this time, Prince Kumaradvitiya and the hero Bhavakumara had been going deeper and deeper into the forest for quite a while. Finally, in one part of the jungle, they found a place suitable for their hermitage.

The earth was covered with grass so green it seemed like the outstretched wings of a parrot. There were large trees garlanded with rings of vines. The heavy weight of the many leaves, flowers, and edible fruits made it seem as if the trees bowed down to them. On the tree boughs thousands of cuckoos, parakeets, parrots, and other birds sang sweetly and frolicked in a lovely dance. Some trees had bark that was smooth to the touch and peeled off in large pieces. This bark was very fine and light, and so it was agreeable to rest upon and wear. This area was quite extensive. There was no path made by men, but groups of

stags, does, and elephants came and went at will. There were pristine
streams, whose fresh, flowing water made sweet, gurgling sounds.
Nearby was a large, deep lake. They named it Perfume Lake, for the lovely
scent of its water lilies and lotuses wafted everywhere on the breeze.
Young bees softly hummed over the multicolored water flowers.
Geese, red ducks, and many other waterfowl beautified the area with
their intrepid flight.

In that isolated spot, the two men built a pleasant hut of leaves. Then
they absorbed themselves in austerities and meditation.

At this point in time, Manohari and her maidservants entered the
jungle. It seemed to them that the forest was as large as the universe and
totally uninhabited. They searched in every direction but could not find
Kumara. They became physically and mentally fatigued. Tears of anguish
covered their faces. Their flesh became thin and lost its healthy glow.
Finally, when their provisions were just about exhausted, Manohari
wearily slumped down upon a large, flat boulder to rest. She propped
her cheek on her hand and said these pitiful words:

> I heard that earth's magnificent sovereign,
> Prince Kumaradvitiya, who gives joy to all,
> Had gone to the forest to practice religion,
> Abandoning ill-fated me, an object of pity.
>
> Could others have deliberately misled me?
> If so, ferocious beasts surely will kill me.
> I am tormented by a multitude of sorrows.
> Who can save me now and keep me from death?
>
> I searched the dense jungle for a long time
> To no avail. Now I do not know what to do.
> Woe is me, I have no refuge or lord! Kye ma!
> Kye hu! O Buddhas, view me from your heavens!

Then she fainted. At this time, perverse thoughts came to the maidservants. "Our provisions are now almost gone. How can people live
without food and drink? We have come into the fearsome forest even
though we cannot be sure that the prince came here. And if he has
wandered here, no doubt fierce wild animals have killed and eaten him.
Now this is our chance to go back to our own country."

So they abandoned their unconscious mistress to return through the
dense forest to their homes. But almost as a rebuke for their disgraceful

thoughts, they lost their way. Wild beasts killed them and enjoyed eating their flesh and drinking their blood.

> Particularly good or evil thoughts
> Have unmixed and clearly distinct results.
> Good never ripens into suffering by mistake.
> The law of cause and effect is amazing.

> With thoughts black as the night of the new moon,
> They pretended to be the light that makes flowers bloom.
> It is a fact that all the misery which befell them
> Was the result of their despicable thoughts and deeds.

> The pair of maidservants acted deceitfully
> Because of the evil thoughts in their minds.
> So wild beasts seemed to kill them in anger,
> Tearing their bodies to shreds for food.

> At that time even the spirits of the trees
> With baneful intent wished those women harm;
> They seemed to scatter vile odors in the sky.
> So we see the astounding results that occurred.

Then a breeze arose from the south. On its way through the jungle, it picked up dewdrops infused with the scent of flowering vines. This refreshing breeze revived Manohari from her faint.

> She was the quintessence of worldly beauty.
> So of course clever men desired her
> Wonderful, youthful, feminine charms.
> Yet even inanimate objects seemed to love her.

> Even the foliage could not endure it
> When she seemed about to die from sorrow.
> The boughs shuddered and trembled,
> Leaves seemed filled with teardrops of dew.

> The sweet southern breezes seemed to sigh
> And brought moisture to revive her form.
> Swaying branches reached down like hands
> To lift her head and exhort her to rise.

Gradually Manohari regained consciousness. She looked all around but did not see her two maidservants, who had been sitting in front of her. She grew so frightened her hair stood on end.

"Kye ma! Could ferocious wild beasts have eaten them? Oh no, perhaps they have gone in search of water to revive me from my faint. Or maybe they thought I had died and went to search for a suitable burial site."

Her love for her two attendants was so strong that she disregarded her terror of the forest's creatures and wandered about in all directions calling out, "O friends!"

Despite her search, she did not find them. She grew tired. As the sun was about to fall into the watery wastes of the west, the shadows bent to the east as is their wont. The heat of the day lessened as a cool wind picked up. The birds ceased their twittering and returned to their nests. Because she was without her companions, there was no way to insulate herself from the ferocious roars and grunts of the beasts. She had no means to leave the forest.

"Now I shall die. There is nothing I can do but sit down and wait for death. But I will pray that the merits that come from satisfying the hunger of the beasts, birds, and insects with my body will result in Prince Kumaradvitiya's loving me in another life," she thought.

She sat down on the same boulder she had rested upon before. As her tears dripped, she joined her palms and recited these verses:

> I prostrate myself before the Buddhas who are our guides,
> To their teachings and superb religious community.
> They never abandon their vow to watch all beings
> With compassion all through every day and night.
>
> A human rebirth is a wish-fulfilling gem:
> It is a seed that can ripen to Buddhahood.
> Ignorance drowns us in the ocean of samsara.
> If one relies on a spiritual friend's guidance,
> Perfect liberation will top one's victory banner.
>
> A human life is hard to find and easy to destroy.
> The iron grip of the idea of "I" and "mine"
> Hauls us away from the bliss of liberation.
> O Buddhas of the ten directions, please save me!
>
> Although I experienced much adversity
> Following the dusty footprints of Prince Kumara,

I have not attained the fruition of my hope.
Please may I be with him in another life!

I cast off this lowly female form, a focus
For suffering desire, ignorance, and hatred.
May I be his virtuous friend or first disciple,
To respect him and accomplish what he teaches.

This body is as beautiful as reflected moonlight,
But it is an obstacle to the practice of Dharma.
May I complete the accumulations of merit and wisdom
By giving it to beasts, birds, and vermin to enjoy.

When I have given up this body, in later lives
May I perfect the four ways to gather disciples:
Offering wealth, speaking sweetly, teaching ways
To tame the mind, and practicing what I preach.

May I complete the six perfections of training:
Joy in giving, consummate moral conduct,
The armor of patience, irreversible perseverance,
Unshakable concentration, and profound wisdom.

May I reach the state of complete enlightenment
Motivated to engage in these superb practices
Just as all noble bodhisattvas courageously
Strive to complete great deeds to benefit all.

She recited these verses imagining that there were Buddha fields filled with Buddhas and bodhisattvas surrounding her. She prostrated herself before them and earnestly made other profound prayers all through the night. At dawn she continued to chant erudite prayers, whose sound drifted through the woods like a distant cuckoo singing, "koo hoo."

35

In which Manohari finds the prince's forest retreat and joins him in the practice of religion

THE HERO BHAVAKUMARA ROSE AT DAWN and went in search of some roots and sprouts. He heard the strains of that profound song and thought the singer's voice sounded remarkably like Manohari. So he went toward the sound, carefully searching all the hidden spots of the jungle. The instant Manohari saw him, joy overcame her. She felt as if she had caught hold of a rope rescuing her from a fall into a vast chasm. Meeting him was like being drawn out of the jaws of death. Her hair rose up on end she was so happy. Shedding tears of relief, she ran and seized hold of him.

"Kye ma! Is Kumara well and happy? Has he met any misfortune? Please take me to where he dwells!" she said.

Bhavakumara was astonished that the lady was in the forest without any companions. But he did not dare to reply in detail.

"I shall go ask the noble prince for his permission," he said.

Then he left her and supplicated the prince: "O lord, please consider! Your loving wife has braved the terrors of the forest and come here without an escort. She begs permission to pay her respects."

Kumara thought, "Women are well known to be demons! There can be no doubt, she has come here to destroy my chaste ethics, ruin my concentration, and wreak havoc on my austerities. Did she not come to satisfy her lust?"

But he further thought: "While this is true, since my mind is now strong, I cannot be corrupted by anyone. Even if thousands of beguiling women came here together, what could they do to me?"

"Just as she wishes, let her come here happily," he said.

Having been granted leave, the hero Bhavakumara showed Manohari the way to the hermitage. The exhausted young woman staggered there, trembling like a reed in a hurricane. She grasped Kumara's feet and petitioned him:

> O great bodhisattva, son of the conquerors!
> You are a stainless source of love for all.
> You are alive and well in your hermitage today
> As a result of practices leading to perfect enlightenment.
>
> O superior prince, you have made ill-starred
> Me undergo many difficult travails.
> Because I never thought of anyone except you,
> In sorrow my body has degenerated to this state.
>
> O lord, formerly you gazed on me with loving eyes
> And laughingly let forth wide smiles of joy.
> But today there is not a glimmer of a smile.
> Your face is clouded, and you utter no loving words.
>
> Did you see me do anything foul?
> Did crafty attempts to part us disturb you?
> Please tell me clearly of this matter.
>
> Without you, a white royal sunshade,
> I have suffered the hot pain of misery.
> My lily-flower heart was engulfed in darkness
> Outside the radius of your smile's nectar-light.
>
> If you are not moved by the force of compassion
> When you see how my body's splendor has waned
> As a result of sorrow worse than that of a widowed swan,
> To say you act for all beings is mere verbiage!

Kumara had unremitting love for her. But despite her pitiful and reproachful supplication, he thought, "I will not have her jeopardize my concentration and contemplation." So turning away from desire, he held his body straight. Seating himself in meditation posture, he said:

> From beginningless time, because of lustful craving,
> We have drowned in the turbulent ocean swells

Of the misery of birth, aging, sickness, and death.
Relying on someone like you causes this pain.

Women are crafty masters of deceit,
Forcing all men down improper paths.
This is illustrated by Lavanya Kamala
Acting indecently in regard to me.

I fully comprehend the faults of desire;
It is the basis of lust, hatred, and spite.
It is the sword edge cutting off happiness.
Its nature is the root of all misery.

Thus, even if every magnificent goddess
And beguiling demoness were to come here,
Their flower arrows could not sting
My heart to lust even in my dreams.
So what could any ordinary woman do?

Thus, it is a grave error for you to be here
In the fearsome forest, following me out of lust.
May you find whatever little happiness there is
In sensual pleasure. May you get what you wish.

This speech made her sorrow increase. "Now the superb prince is
casting me out like spent fuel." Pained by his severe reproaches of her
difficult endeavors, she sobbed like a swan caught in a snare. Then she
said to him:

Today I hear a heartless speech from someone
Famed as a bodhisattva and treasure of compassion.
Lord, if you have pity for even part of my pain,
Caused by love, how can you cast me out?

Those engaging in noble deeds give up selfishness
And take up the burden of liberating all beings.
To abandon even one creature is not in accord
With a bodhisattva's great waves of conduct.

So when you can obviously see that my pain
Is greater than the misery of burning in hell,

What sort of a vow is your promise to work
For all beings if you won't protect me?

Because it is extremely difficult to distinguish
Women of good conduct from those leading to evil,
You impugn all women as objects to be cursed.
But it is untrue that all women are so base.

If you can say all women are corrupt
Because one is immoral, then can I say
Superb Prince Kumara so worthy of praise
Is like Chetadasa because they are both men?

You abusively denigrate all women
As having crafty, deceptive natures.
Give up these wrong thoughts about me.
Please protect me, for I come as your disciple.

After she spoke, the prince thought, "Women are always contradictory. Their words are not worthy of trust." So again he spoke:

Listen, pretty one! Do not obstruct my practices.
This forest is not a place for your cravings.
Women are always in pursuit of lustful desire,
But I reject it to travel the path to peace.

In the fearsome forest, wild beasts threaten life.
We have no provisions to sustain us other than
Roots and sprouts to eat and pure water to drink.
There are no soft garments to keep out the cold;
We wear only the bark of trees and never speak.
We are always absorbed in meditative concentration.
Do you think you could possibly do this?

So return to Joyous Groves in order to savor
Pleasures like those enjoyed by the gods.
In the precious palace of that superb realm,
You will be honored by the court and populace.

Endlessly thirsting for sex, we fall into samsara.
You are one who would lead me to lower rebirths.

In particular, nonvirtuous deeds ruin concentration.
Captivating woman, I will not let you do this to me!

We cannot bear to be without sensory pleasures.
Women are the root of that enjoyment and craving
Which force men to take future suffering rebirths.
So it is not right for me to stay with them.

Men competing to obtain pretty girls
Fight and threaten each other's lives.
Insane with hatred, they act iniquitously.
All of this occurs because of women.

A lot of sexual activity causes the senses to fail.
Also, women are the source of ignorant confusion
About the Buddha's teaching of cause and effect
And the qualities of the Buddha, Dharma, and Sangha.

Men become conceited, proud, and very vain
When they obtain a pretty girl as a lover.
Women are the basis of all the passions;
Love them and you fall into samsara's deep chasm.

Do not lust for me! If your attractive body
Craves the pleasure of sensual arousal,
Take a lover equal to the gods, better than I.
Rely on those who are involved in this life!

No doubt you shall obtain what you wish.
Live in bliss with a lover who accords
With all your inclinations and desires.
Enjoy all of the pleasing sensual pleasures
Surrounded by all your friends and court.
O Manohari, may you be happy and carefree!

He had renounced cyclic existence. His clear expressions showed he chose to extinguish his passionate attachment, even toward his life's companion, Manohari.

Manohari thought:

"There has never been anyone other than this superb prince in my thoughts. Before, because the flower of fate was cast upon me, I endured so many difficulties for him they cannot be recounted.

"Now noble Kumara has abandoned affairs of this world. His intention to reside in the forests of peace is clear. So it was right that I had let go of my hope that we live together as man and wife. I wandered long, deserted pathways that were difficult to traverse because I hoped to have the good fortune to wait upon him until my life would end. If I could remain here to reverence this noble being, my lowly body, which heretofore collected only evil karma, could be used to obtain liberation from the chasm of the lower realms. I followed his footsteps assiduously, heedless of any hunger, thirst, fatigue, or terror of wild beasts. But I have been set outside the bounds of his love."

Pained by sorrow impossible to endure, her weakened body tumbled down headlong. Her braided hair fell loose and tangled upon her shoulders like crows chancing there to roost. She sighed, and her tears fell thickly. Her eyes became completely round, as if she were facing death. The force of her misery made it difficult for her to breathe, yet she prostrated herself before the prince and weakly supplicated him again:

> You are right. Because of desire
> Most beings follow a path leading
> Over the edge of an immense abyss.
> I will never disrupt your religious practices.
>
> I flew like a bee to your lotus-feet.
> But my coming here is not out of lust,
> Nor to deceive you, nor to achieve fame.
> Isn't it impossible to destroy your austerities?
>
> I endured many difficult trials
> Following my prince's dusty footprints,
> For I too take delight in the practice of Dharma.
>
> I was drawn here by attraction
> To your wondrous and good qualities,
> But it is not right to call this lust.
>
> How could I be in search of that now,
> When that has joined unfortunate me
> To unending sorrow for many lives?

O lord, here in the peaceful forest
You vowed to work for all beings.
But you shame me with many rebukes.

You show me no loving compassion.
Yet it would be far easier to die
Than to leave the bounds of this place.

Like a field where poison grows,
This ill-fated body is my lot.
Crushed by sorrow and grief,
It bears a heavy burden of sins.

Now if you bind me with ropes
And start to lead me away,
I vow that the continuity of my life
Shall end right here in this place.
Even if my prince doesn't smile upon me,
I cannot be diverted from my noble intent.

When you were a Lord of Men, ruling
The entire earth to the far ocean shores,
I was crowned your precious queen.
Then with unfailing love and devotion
I revered, honored, and respected you.

Now you are finished with conjugal love.
As a beggar lacks absolutely everything,
You are without food, drink, or clothes.
You are solitary as a rhinoceros in the wilds.

Where can I go if I leave you living here?
Even if I am to die, I shall do so right here.
If I live, it shall be nowhere other than here.

O prince, you shall either preserve me
Thanks to your compassion or cast me off.
The power of my karma is fixed;
I experience no pangs of regret.

When she uttered those verses, a strong feeling of pity arose in the hero Bhavakumara. It was so unbearable that he spoke:

"O god, please attend to me! The lovely lady Manohari has perceived the many disadvantages of desire. She has agonized over them and so not come here for lustful ends. She has come out of admiration for your excellent qualities and great waves of practices. How can Manohari be compared with the ordinary run of women? She has virtuous characteristics far superior to others: not for a moment did she consider taking a lover other than you. Her fortitude and perseverance are sublime. And she has displayed a desire to practice religion. So now surely you should entertain her wishes!"

Prince Kumaradvitiya deeply considered Manohari's aspiration again. In order to relieve her misery, he smiled at her. In the clear, deep tones of Brahma, he said:

It is so! It is so! O noble lady.
You have all the signs of a wish-granting tree:
The roots of superior thought are firmly planted.
The boughs of perseverance are widespread.
There are the variegated flowers of compassion.
It is amazing for a woman to have such courage.

Because your mind is attracted
To meditation and austerities,
Live carefree in this hermitage.
In accordance with your abilities,
Partake of the nectar of the Dharma
By absorbing yourself in contemplative practices.

Even a perfect wishing jewel
Lifted atop a banner of victory
Fluttering over all worldly foes
Cannot compare with the value of this human life.
A life like this that can fulfill your goals
Is difficult to obtain in hundreds of aeons.

Continually viewing all beings as your mother,
Master the essence of the six perfections
And four ways of training your disciples.
Thus you will attain the state of enlightenment
And be able to bestow happiness upon all.

However, this life does not last long.
Even the clever are easily destroyed.

Everyone reborn because of karma and the passions,
From the depths of hell to the highest god realms,
Is under the sway of the Lord of Death.

Moreover, each person collects his own karma:
Virtue causes happiness and sins yield sorrow.
Although you may petition the Lord of Death
To save you from the fruition of your deeds,
He cannot bestow virtuous results after you sin.

He cannot be fooled by dissimulation and lies.
Even the powerful cannot fight with him.
The wealthy may offer him precious riches,
But no one can be snatched from Death's jaws.

Deluded by ignorance, we are born in samsara.
The Death Lord doesn't care if we are young or old;
His lasso will haul us out of the play of life
Unerringly, according to the nature of our deeds.

At death the best and only means to aid us
Is our practice following the holy Dharma.
There is naught but that which can help.
So you should make an effort to practice now.

Thus, even if you become a universal emperor
With dominion over all seven great possessions
And an army that rules over four continents,
You will not be free from the vicious Lord of Death.

Thus, a powerful realm, inexhaustible wealth,
Incalculable friends, servants, and lovers
Are like the pleasures in a dream: suffering
Is their true nature, so who would crave them?

You may rule a kingdom for a hundred aeons,
But the work of the world will never end.
Who doesn't revere the practitioner of religion
In the forests, free from clamorous distractions?

Beautiful lady, may your hair stand on end
With joy, having cast off the bonds of misery.

> Absorb yourself in accomplishing your own
> And others' aims in this life so difficult to find.

"Now I have obtained just what I hoped for!" thought Manohari. She was so joyful that the small hairs on her body did stand on end. She feebly staggered to her feet, and then she prostrated herself before the prince.

> Their solitary hermitage for contemplation
> Had verdant meadows green as a peacock's throat.
> These were totally blanketed by beautiful wonders:
> Precious trees bowed under leaves and fruit,
> And lovely flowers fluttered in the breeze.

> Cuckoos, swans, and other birds sang
> With sweet, carefree voices that made
> One laugh with a joy free from misery.
> The peacocks let out their jagged cries
> And fanned their tails in dance.

> The pure, pristine streams prettily gurgled,
> Casting forth strands of smiling bubbles.
> The entire sky seemed to be reflected
> In the mirror of the vast inland ocean lake.
> Its boundless waters held jeweled treasure:
> The surface rippled like molten sapphire
> And wafted forth an amazing sweet scent.

> On the profusion of multicolored lotuses,
> Bees happily cavorted, drunk on honey.
> The swan king and other winged creatures
> Flew and soared, sounding their drumming call.

> Wild creatures free from the fear of attack
> Could come and go in a carefree manner.
> Even the fierce fanged carnivores behaved
> As if their viciousness were pacified.

> The hermitage in the wood damp with nectar's dew
> Was filled with auspicious, praiseworthy signs
> And free from the three distractions: commotion,
> Nonvirtue, and ordinary mistaken appearances.

There the three desiring to free themselves
From worldly bonds and attain the bliss of liberation
Lived in leaf huts supported by their endeavors
In meditation unruffled by the winds of passion.

Many times they enjoyed the good fortune
Of absorbing themselves in deep concentration
On renunciation arising from seeing samsaric suffering,
Bodhicitta, which endeavors to liberate all beings,
And wisdom comprehending reality free from any extreme.

36

In which Prince Kumaradvitiya is liberated from samsara and engages in a miraculous bodhisattva practice

DURING THE MIDDLE STAGE OF PRINCE KUMARADVITIYA'S LIFE, he stayed in his hermitage, working single-mindedly to perfect his austere ethical conduct; the meditations on immeasurable love, compassion, joy, and equanimity; the four trancelike absorptions, and so forth. At last he obtained consummate control of the five sorts of worldly psychic powers: his divine eye could perceive others' past lives and their next rebirth; his divine ear could hear even secretive speech uttered near or far; he could read others' minds—apprehending their greed, hatred, ignorance, or the lack of those passions; his recollection of prior rebirths led him to understand the working of his own and others' virtuous and nonvirtuous karma; and he could perform miracles such as making fire blaze forth from his upper body while water gushed from below.

Then the prince thought: "I have accomplished this. But despite my efforts to practice every virtue and doing just as much meditation, I have not yet freed myself from the cycle of repeated rebirths. These rebirths are compelled by attachment, the other passions, and karma as unyielding as armor. So what use are these trances and the psychic powers common to both the Buddhist and non-Buddhist paths?"

So he sang these words in a pure song of Brahma to Manohari and Bhavakumara:

"The basic cord binding us to cyclic existence is grasping at a truly existent self. In order to escape it, we must first rely on analysis that considers the essential nature of every object. If we cannot counter our mistaken manner of conceiving reality, we will not be able to extirpate the root of all samsaric suffering. I now know that the source of all misery is desire: an ignorance which grasps the self as real.

"Everything actually exists without its own nature in the ultimate sense. But in addition you must be able to establish that conventionally things arise in dependence upon causes, conditions, and their parts. These two paths of thought are not contradictory.

"We must find the way between the extremes of nihilism and absolutism. We must obtain a powerful conviction that although nothing has an independent nature of its own, things do exist in reliance upon our positing them. It is of primary importance that we consider this, familiarize ourselves with it, and actually make it an integral part of our mind."

The prince had no faith in any good quality of seemingly desirable objects. Eliminating skittishness and slothfulness from his mind, he strove to follow this path perfectly. Finally, with no object able to cause his mind the slightest disturbance, he attained a direct perception of the ultimate nature of reality.

He became a trustworthy guide to the city of nirvana. He had come to his last rebirth caused by karma and the passions.

Then he thought: "Because I now enjoy the nectar of nonconceptual wisdom, I should engage in great waves of deeds that will free all beings who are not yet liberated." And he stayed in meditation on these things in the forest.

After some time the prince recollected his promise to his father. "Now that I have obtained liberation, I should go back to Gem of the World to teach the holy Dharma to my kindred, subjects, and loving friends. I will instruct them in accordance with their aspirations, abilities, and subtlest obscurations, so all those limitless beings will turn away from actions that lead to falling into the lower realms."

When he stated his intention to return to the city, Manohari and Bhavakumara had great misgivings. "O son of the Buddhas, treasury of omniscience! Ever before you said that the kingdom would cause you to degenerate in so many ways. So why do you go there now?

"This forest grove for the practice of austerities is delightful to see. It is not besmeared by disruptive commotion. Grasses, fruits, clear water, and the bark of trees spontaneously become our food and clothing. We have no anxieties and engage continually in concentration.

"There is neither happiness nor peace in the prison of samsara! If we leave this hermitage, we will nourish egoism, pride, anger, and deception, because the kingdom's very nature is nonvirtuous sin. How can it be right for you to go there?"

When they queried him, Kumara announced his plan to strive joyfully for the sake of others:

> It is true that for the unliberated
> The kingdom's bounty is the basis of sin.
> However, I am now free and completely apart
> From all torment caused by craving for existence.
> It is not right for you to doubt this.
>
> If I am unable to engage in purposeful deeds
> For the sake of my parents and limitless beings,
> How can I repay their kind protection of me?
> I will douse the kingdom's fire of suffering
> With the cool water of my enlightened deeds.
>
> Worldly endeavors are as hollow as bamboo:
> Who bothers with such flimsy, useless reeds?
> The Dharma explained with pleasant words
> Subdues greed, hatred, ignorance, and the passions.
> I shall set down a mountain of precious advice
> So they may partake of the glories of liberation.

Because those two were unable to disregard his words, they followed
wherever the prince might lead them. And so they left that place which
had nourished concentration.

They traveled on and on. When they reached the halfway point of
their journey, they were in the middle of a dense forest. They stopped
and separated to search for provisions. Not too far off, Bhavakumara
found an extremely tall fruit tree with luxuriant branches and firm roots.

Drawn toward the tree by desire, Bhavakumara climbed all the way
to the top. After plucking some fruit with a marvelous color and scent,
he began to descend.

The hot rays of the sun and years of rain had roughened some of the
tree's branches. In places there were splinters as stiff and sharp as nee-
dles. When Bhavakumara stepped down heavily on those cutting spikes,
his feet were badly cut. It seemed as if he had created the karma to
experience a razor-sharp hell. He fell from the tree like a ripe fruit!

He writhed on the ground in agony. His body sweated profusely, and
his eyes stared fixedly. The ground became red with his blood.
Kumaradvitiya and Manohari found the hero Bhavakumara there in this
extremely pitiable state. They trembled in fear, for it seemed as if the

image of his death appeared in front of their eyes. They knew of no way that they could help him. So Prince Kumaradvitiya thought:

"Kye ma! I cannot abandon in distress this friend who regarded me with such heartfelt respect. We cannot return to our hermitage or proceed to Gem of the World. But here, without a doctor skilled in saving lives, Bhavakumara will surely be caught in the Death Lord's noose! I have absolutely no means to relieve him of pain."

In sorrow and with unhappy hearts, they remained at the foot of that tree all night.

At dawn Manohari and Kumaradvitiya discussed what they should do. Blinded by ignorance, Manohari had no doubt that Kumaradvitiya was an ordinary being, so she said: "I dreamt that Bhavakumara would recover if the marrow of a bodhisattva's bones were rubbed on his wounds. But this dream is pointless. Where could we ever find the marrow of a bodhisattva's bones!"

Prince Kumara tasted the same joy as when he first drank the nectar of the wisdom of directly perceiving reality. He thought, "Those who are called bodhisattvas care for others more than for themselves. For many lifetimes I have tried to train myself to think and act under the influence of this sort of love and compassion. Thus, with the marrow of my bones, I will give him life!"

Then he said:

> It is so, O wise one!
> Lady, your dream was fortunate.
> Relying firmly on deeply rooted compassion,
> Bodhisattvas cherish others more than themselves.
> Once I remove the marrow of my bones,
> I shall save my companion from death.
>
> From beginningless time, times without count,
> I have taken a body like this again and again.
> But my lives were wasted; never used to any purpose.
> Here today I shall strive to extract
> The essence of the purpose of a human life!

"Go and bring me some sharp stones to crush my foot!" he ordered Manohari. Trembling with fear, Manohari begged of him:

> Kye! O glorious master of enlightened actions!
> Please do not do this ill-conceived, improper deed.

There is no truth in that hallucination I saw.
Dreams are illusory and deceptive phenomena.

Lord, there is no doubt that hordes of demons
Unable to bear seeing your great waves of deeds
Possessed my mind in order to deceive me.
Dreams are known as paragons of lying duplicity.

I have never seen in any medical text
Nor heard our elders or wise men say
It is salutary to apply the marrow
Of a bodhisattva's bones to a bodily wound.

Even if there truly were to be some benefit,
If we are overcome by this servant's pain,
How could we possibly bear it, O lord,
If your foot were smashed to bits?

Thus, this dream was a delusive chimera.
Who places faith in something like that?

Although she begged him to desist, his vow of powerful compassion
was irreversible. So again he spoke:

Although nowhere in the world does anyone
Say dreams and illusions contain the truth,
Nor does ancient lore urge this cure,
This method does have the power to succeed.

The strength of my wish to help others
And my powerful love for Bhavakumara
Act together to form this solemn vow:
I will definitely relieve him from distress.

Formerly with unfeigned courage, this child
Never hesitated in risking his life
To accomplish any worldly or religious deed
Required in order to realize my goals.

Now, when he is in such adversity,
Surely I transgress the noble path

If I am disinterested in helping him
Through inability to cut off my lowest limb.

A shameless person who has little gratitude
For others' kindness will go down the road
To the three lower realms in later lives,
Following the indubitable law of causation.

Lovely lady, when you came in search
Of the perfect Dharma, you promised
You would not obstruct my practice
When I engaged in great waves of deeds.
Today you must recall that irrevocable vow.
O fine-featured lady, it is not proper
To create an impediment to my virtuous deeds!

Still Manohari was not relieved of worry. How could she search for any stones? Apprehensive that Prince Kumara was going to do his foot some harm, she attached herself to him and would not leave him alone for even a second. But his intention to do this deed to benefit Bhavakumara could not be deterred, and he realized that there was nothing stopping him except Manohari. So at one point, with feints and dodges, he tricked her. Slipping behind her, he caught her and tied her to a tree with sturdy willow fronds. Manohari was unable to move.

Then the noble prince went to Bhavakumara's side. There he wedged his foot between two stiff roots as a brace. But as soon as he began to cleave his foot, despite his terrible wounds, Bhavakumara hauled himself hand over hand to Prince Kumara. He seized his leg and prayed: "Kva ye! This deed of yours will cast me into hell! Please desist from this exceedingly great act!

Your body is a treasury of wonders and good qualities.
When touched, its sweet scent diffuses everywhere.
Although your vow to act for my lowly sake is amazing,
This deed will not place all beings in blissful liberation!

Although your intention is inconceivably kind
Because you care for all, how can it be right?
If you act just for my sake, you will deprive
Limitless creatures of a leader and a refuge.

Your feet are like lotus roots: firm and round.
Their smooth soles are marked by a wheel design.
If you destroy them, my stumpy feet and legs
May recover their health, but what use is that?

Out of pity for my state of misery,
You would destroy your wonderful legs.
But if you relieve my physical torment so,
My mental anguish will be like unto death!

If someone merely were to prick
Your lovely body with a needle,
Surely the ripening of such a deed
Would cast him into the lower realms.

The vast heavens of the universe are filled
With countless celestial garlands of stars.
But only the princely sun can alleviate
Creatures' sorrow. There is no other like you.

Karma that must be experienced is hard to reverse.
So a lowly being like myself may die like a dog.
But so that you, a bodhisattva who leads all beings,
May live and prosper a hundred aeons, I shall die!

Not only with words did Bhavakumara supplicate him. But the prince disregarded his pleas. The power of his superior thought to benefit others overrode every objection.

His legs were like lotus stalks: smooth and round, they evenly slimmed toward his ankles. He had walked majestically as a swan: merely seeing his gait women became oblivious to all else because of lust. The prince made sure that his right foot was tightly wedged between two large aboveground roots. Then, with great force, he hurled his body to one side, thereby shattering his leg.

The supreme way a bodhisattva creates virtue
Is delight in acting for others without self-concern.
The heavens, highest mountains, and deepest oceans
Shuddered and quaked in agitation and amazement.

The sun seemed to shine even into the night,
Pervading all space with white light.

The faultless, full autumn moon glittered,
Sending forth light rays bright as the sun.
A misting rain of flowers of paradise
Fell from a cloudless sky to cover the earth.

On the boughs of the trembling precious trees,
Flowers of unbreakable faith burst into bloom.
The branches came together and bowed their tips
In homage to the bodhisattva many times.

In the vast voidness of the heavens,
Immortal ladies clad in godly raiment
Performed dances and songs as offerings
To waft into his ears as a musical treasure.

The profuse flowers on the refreshing ponds
Let forth saffron dust and sweet perfumes
To pervade all the space with the essence
Of scent that satisfies the olfactory sense.

An ephemeral rainbow appeared in the sky
As water sprites and river goddesses
Garlanded with necklaces of pure white foam
Took delight in offering clouds of spray
Scattered from the waves to cool his foot.

Thus, the bodhisattva prince clearly showed
He was an unparalleled master of concentration.

When Manohari perceived these astounding miracles, she became extremely agitated. "Kye ma!" she thought. "When one sees visions like this, it means that even the gods are amazed. Prince Kumara must have done injury to his leg!"

Sick with terror, she struggled with great force and managed to break the willow fronds binding her to the tree. She hastened to the tree where they had left Bhavakumara.

There she saw Prince Kumara. He had shattered his lovely limb into fragments as if it were but a tree stump. Now, without any regret, he was calmly removing the marrow from his bones.

Amazement and sorrow vied with each other in Manohari's mind. In a pained, hoarsely weeping voice, she expressed her sorrow:

O wonderful Kumara, Lord of Men and bodhisattva!
You are a paragon of glittering brightness
Like the light of a thousand suns reflecting
Off the vast snows of incredible Mount Kailash.

Your two legs, like fresh lotus roots,
Were pure white, firm, and round.
Now one is fit only for deerflies to enjoy.
How will I bear even to recollect this sight?

Through destroying your leg like this,
It seems the possibility of leading all beings
To liberation was cut off by one blow.

O lord, because you destroyed
Your foot marked with a royal wheel,
There is no way for your life to continue.
Thus, all creatures will lack a refuge
And will wander in the dark land of ignorance.

You are someone who rejoiced in the resolve
Even to give up your body for another's sake.
You are unlike others, who rejoice merely
To live on after being near to death.

Because of your great, supremely enlightened actions,
Ill-fated I must inhabit a house of sorrow.
I have fallen heir to inconceivable misery.
Anything I think of is perverted and purposeless.
Never shall I have any chance of happiness.
How many nonvirtues from earlier lives have ripened!

Although the noble prince found his pain difficult to endure, he sent
forth the white light of his smile like streams of ambrosia to pacify her
anguish. Then he said:

O my lady! Do not be grieved!
Rejoice in my superior wish.
I did not do this to gain fame or honor
Or to obtain a kingdom or high rebirth.
Nor did I act desiring my own happiness.

Bhavakumara viewed his ruler with love,
And his nature and conduct are pure.
So I did this to free him from torment.
By thus relying on the life raft of
A bodhisattva's deeds, I will rescue
Limitless beings from the samsaric ocean
And place them in the land of liberation.

Because I feel no pain in giving up
My body, life, and all my wealth,
It is the means of giving all beings happiness.
You should rejoice that with such a small deed
I have accumulated a vast amount of merit!

The hero Bhavakumara's wounds were large and deep. They had festered and opened as wide as full-blown lotuses. His limbs were so
swollen there was no way to distinguish his ankle from his thigh. The
prince carefully rubbed the marrow he had removed from his own
bones onto Bhavakumara's shattered limbs. While he did this,
Kumaradvitiya made prayers that this action be conjoined with his wish
to free other beings from misery.

After three days had passed, there was no longer the slightest bit of
pain in Bhavakumara's limbs. He had completely recovered. They all
were extremely glad.

His slightest breath was to benefit others.
He accepted the holy bodhisattva vows
Just like saints of countless former aeons:
I shall not hesitate to act for others' sake
And so will become enlightened to benefit them.

A bodhisattva has the power to dry out an ocean
Or to transform a desert into the essence of moisture.
Thus, the afflicted man who lacked a means to live
Was made well through the bodhisattva's power.

37

In which the prince performs a second bodhisattva deed

PRINCE KUMARADVITIYA SEEMED to have transferred Bhavakumara's torment to himself. Although the prince experienced unbearable agony, he felt no sorrow, for he had freed Bhavakumara from illness and accomplished a bodhisattva's deed without any obstacle.

He gave Bhavakumara and Manohari pleasant instructions in accordance with the Dharma. He taught them, beginning with renunciation. Then he spoke of how difficult it is to obtain a human rebirth of leisure, how easy it is to die, and how necessary to take up the essence of the human life once one has obtained that extremely purposeful basis. By explaining these and other topics, he pacified the minds of his two followers.

Quite some time passed this way in the deep forest. Kumaradvitiya's two disciples offered him fruits and sprouts, but he had no desire to eat because of his pain. The youthful complexion of his attractive body went into serious decline. His lovely, large eyes became shot with red, and his gaze froze like a lotus petal touched by frost. A river of pus, blood, and yellow fluid oozed continually from the wound on his shattered leg. Each day his pain increased.

"There is no way he can continue to live!" thought both Manohari and Bhavakumara. "I am suffering greater sorrow than I would at my own time of death! I cannot see the end of the suffering of cyclic existence. Sometimes, bodhisattvas appear to enter nirvana in order to teach their disciples about the ultimate nature of reality. These students mistakenly grasp at themselves as truly existent, hold other people to be inherently real, and believe phenomena are permanent and exist just as they appear. Perhaps that is what will happen now!"

They were so depressed that they hung their heads and could not utter a word.

At the same time Prince Kumara was thinking: "Here in this forest I have perfectly accomplished a bodhisattva's deed: I have given my body and life without expecting anything in return. I have perceived the three spheres of charity—the gift, the donor, and the recipient—as ultimately empty of inherent existence. Now, I no longer have any wish to live.

"However, if I do not properly point out the route out of the forest, after my death my two companions will wander onto the wrong path. Then the fierce beasts of the forest will surely take their lives.

"Now they live without mishap, for they are in the shade of my wish to attain enlightenment for others' benefit. Although they are attached to me, it is dangerous for them to stay in the woods any longer. I must send them to the city."

So he said to them:

> May the Buddhas and bodhisattvas of the ten directions
> Always protect you with their compassionate blessings.
>
> If you piled up the bones of every body
> I have been born into and cast off at death
> In samsara caused by karma and ignorance,
> Those bones would surmount the mountains.
> The ocean basins would be too small
> To contain the blood from those lives.
>
> I was born so many times to no avail.
> I wasted my chances and obtained no benefit.
> Here, with this body that lacks an essential nature,
> I have accomplished a perfect bodhisattva's deed.
> I have not the slightest regret or pain,
> And now I shall sleep in the realm of peace.
>
> Dear ones, know this well!
> You two must leave my side.
> This dense, boundless forest is thick
> With ferocious beasts with gleaming fangs
> And poisonous snakes to take you in their jaws.

All those beasts blaze with fires of hatred;
They wish to destroy you and consume your flesh.

Now you live happily in a place like this
Because you are protected by the power
Of my selfless striving for enlightenment.

But as soon as I depart for death's realm,
You will be without any protector or refuge,
Like small, weak animals in a crocodile's jaws.

If you remain here, you will surely come to ill.
Give up your attachment to me and go happily away.
To liberate your parents and all other creatures,
Practice the perfections with great waves of deeds
And do not forget the right view of reality.

Our time of companionship in this life is over.
Today is my last, but I pray that together
We will enjoy the blissful good fortune
Of a pure land free from karma and ignorance.

No matter what road you two may roam,
May gods, fairies, and spirits protect you.
May you be happy and reach all your goals.
By this benediction may all blessings be yours.

The hearts of those two fell when he pointed out the path and
exhorted them to proceed homeward. "Now our noble prince will pass
away!" they thought. They cried out as loudly as peacocks caught in a
snare. Waves of tears cascaded from their eyes as they touched their
heads to his feet and entreated him once again:

"Kye! O Lord Kumara, please view us kindly! A bodhisattva is a
lordly guide who takes pleasure in striving to perfect his own and others' goals. Such a being should not think like this! Where could we
find another home, realm, or trustworthy teacher? If you, a great
being, enter the sleep of the realms of peace, we shall end our lives
right here!

"In addition, please consider this. These are ignoble instructions
for a lord to give. The disintegration of your body for our sake
deprives us of joy; so is your heart not moved with pity for us?

Kumaradvitiya thought about their words. "Because I have courageous bodhicitta and understand that all phenomena are empty of true existence, this is surely the time to display one of the marvelous deeds of a bodhisattva." He held his body upright and projected his voice with the deep tones of Brahma's song to utter this inconceivably profound prayer:

Those with feeble minds cannot rejoice
Even in the accomplishment of a single
Marvelous deed of a great bodhisattva.
This well-known statement is obviously true.
Thus, abandon your wrong views and doubts.
Listen to this song of my word of truth.

May all of my prayers be fulfilled effortlessly
By joining the power of my pure superior wishes
To the blessings of all the Buddhas and bodhisattvas
And the words of truth of gods and ascetics
Who dwell in the boundless heavens and earth below.

My endeavors like this were not done to obtain
High rebirth as a god or a universal emperor
Nor for worldly happiness, wealth, or reputation.

The forest of samsara is densely thicketed
With suffering caused by karma and ignorance.
As many beings as could fill the sky
Wander there, lost since beginningless time.

In order to fulfill my promise to lead them all
To the happy state of liberation free from rebirth,
I will put on the strong armor of enthusiastic,
Irreversible perseverance for the Dharma.

My body had extremely marvelous qualities.
It was superior to a superb wishing jewel.
I shattered its limbs to benefit another:
By becoming medicine for the hero Bhavakumara,
I experienced great happiness in his recovery.
I feel no regret, sorrow, or sense of loss.

> Because this is true, for the increase of the Dharma
> May my leg be cured! May it be better than before!

As soon as he uttered his words of truth, his foot became more beautiful and attractive than it had been before! The power of his great honesty completely healed him. Like a knife slicing through water, you could not find where the fatal cuts had been.

When he proved himself to be such a master of miracles, the gods and all others who took pleasure in good deeds were amazed. A great clamor and joyful hubbub arose in the heavens. Bhavakumara and Manohari were so happy they wondered if it were but a dream. They experienced the taste of happiness that knew no end. They clasped their hands together like lotus buds before sunrise and placed them at their crowns. They bowed down to him with pure faith and trust.

> Eh ma ho! All praise to our lord,
> Who is a wish-granting tree with boughs
> Weighed down under the fruits of charity,
> Whose firmly established roots are great
> Compassion and powerful perseverance!

> Ordinary men may be rich as the gods,
> But desiccated by greed they cannot bear
> To give away even a tiny sesame seed.
> If they give even the slightest amount
> Of their enjoyable riches or provisions,
> We consider it to be quite amazing.

> O Lord of Men, you gave up your attachment
> To the marvelous resources of the kingdom.
> You made yourself equal to a pauper
> By bestowing all your treasuries' opulence:
> Horses, elephants, chariots, food, and garb.
> So what need is there to mention your gift
> Of the kingdom which has the nature of sin?

> In a great action you perfected giving
> Even your lifeblood, so difficult to bestow.
> When you perceived an unfortunate creature
> Pained by misery, you reflected the agony
> Onto yourself, magnifying it like a mirror.

When any embodied creature achieves
A feeling of supreme joy by giving up
Its cherished life for another's sake,
The universe is too small to contain it.

Eh ma ho! Our poor feeble minds
Were unable to rejoice sympathetically
In the great waves of this magnificent deed.
Today we confess and recognize this before you.

In this life and later rebirths,
There is no better leader than you.
Procuring the good fortune of meeting you
Is like realizing the profits of our virtue.

Eh ma ho! O lord, you are a fount
Of nirvana's desirable nectar: even
To see, hear, recollect, touch, or taste
You grants satiation to all fortunate beings.

Their words made Prince Kumaradvitiya happily smile, showing his pearly teeth. Then he replied:

"Dear ones, yes, that is the case! Bodhicitta, the desire to obtain enlightenment for others' benefit, is difficult to obtain even if one meditates for hundreds of aeons. Gods and men pay homage to this precious object. Thousands of Buddhas in the midst of their vast entourages in each of the ten directions extol its glory. When a pitiful creature in the prison of samsara generates bodhicitta in his mind, all the Buddhas call him their child. The good qualities of what is thus praised are beyond anyone's calculations."

Then, without any delay, Kumaradvitiya and his entourage of two proceeded toward Gem of the World. Without further trouble they passed through the jungle, where wild beasts and fearsome poisonous snakes dwelt. They left the dense forest that had never been penetrated by the light of the sun or moon.

38

In which Prince Kumaradvitiya returns to the city and spreads great joy with his teaching

THEY PROCEEDED IN LEISURELY STAGES to the distinguished capital city where they had lived in great prosperity, happiness, and leisure. There in the past the prince and his consort had draped themselves in celestial raiment and precious ornaments. Wherever they strolled, parasols, yak-tail fans, and tall banners had preceded them.

They felt quite joyful when they finally saw the city Open Lotus. Now, however, they were clothed in scanty garments of tree bark, without a single piece of lovely jewelry. They looked like the paupers who wander the outskirts of towns. When the three travelers entered the metropolis, not one of the populace thought to ask who they were. They made their way to the palace without being called upon to explain their business and parentage even once.

They found the prince's parents, his brother, and the ministers together in the palace residence Floating Wonder. They had gathered there to assess revenues and collect taxes. Their minds were all in turmoil over this work.

When the three of them entered, the king and all the ministers leapt up from their seats, forgetting all the lovely objects that were before them. They looked all around, wondering if their presence was an apparition or mirage tricking their eyes. When they were sure that the three were really there, tears of astonishment and joy choked their throats. They stared at them fixedly. Finally some came forward to embrace them. A few prostrated themselves and touched their feet. Others grasped bits of their garments. A happy clamor arose, filling all space.

Then Prince Kumara, his queen, and his minister sat down comfortably. The old king and his ministers saluted them in one voice:

"Kye, Kumaradvitiya! You are a great being and a treasury of wisdom! You were never overpowered by desire, not even for the marvelous wealth of our kingdom. You spat it out as if it were phlegm! You fearlessly went to the dangerous forests filled with fierce beasts and poisonous snakes as cheerfully as if you were going to a celestial palace.

"The road you traveled was so very long, and there were so many dangerous ravines, deserts, and storms! Were you not debilitated by these difficulties? Were you not even a little scared? Were you anxious? Were you able to live comfortably? Were you homesick or not? Did you find liberation by following the perfect path?"

Prince Kumara had attained the state of a superb leader. He had an encompassing understanding of the profound and vast ocean of Dharma. He had no fear in regard to explaining it properly. So, in a voice thundering like the rain clouds' dragon roar, he said:

> We discriminate between friends and enemies,
> Hating one group and loving the other.
> This partiality produces the three poisons:
> Greed, hatred, and ignorance are the chains
> Tightly binding us to cyclic existence.
>
> So, I no longer say I adore this and hate that:
> I love every being in the universe equally.
> With this superior thought I took on the task
> Of liberating all from the miseries of samsara.
>
> There is nothing better than practicing the Dharma
> To repay the kindness of my loving parents
> Of this wonderful human rebirth in particular.
> Thus, now that I have attained the liberated state,
> I shall not reject my earlier vow to come here,
> Wearing the armor of courageous compassion, to teach
> The holy Dharma in order to relieve your suffering.
>
> You said the road was difficult and long,
> And the forest is a place of danger and fear.
> However, no matter how much they frighten you,
> They can do no more than destroy this life.

Conceiving the self as real is the true enemy.
It gives rise to the passions that yield
The manifold sorrows that have crushed us
Again and again from beginningless time.
They force our rebirth only to destroy us again.

The best means to triumph over the passions
Is to join the compassion of a bodhisattva
With wisdom comprehending the nature of reality.
Karma and the passions can oppress you no more
When you know that emptiness of inherent existence
And compassion for all are not contradictory in the least.
With this assurance, what chance can there be
For fear of the road or the forest to harm you?

When I said I will attain liberation,
It was not to eliminate my suffering only.
My purpose is to liberate all the beings
Dwelling in the ocean depths to the sky above.

If I had desired to rule this realm
Because of its bounty of marvelous wealth,
The sinful deeds of my rule would ripen
Into miserable, long-lasting experiences.

Immediately after this life, in my next life,
Surely I would have been led to the hells.
There the hideous hordes of the Death Lord
With fangs bared in anger thunderously roar,
"Strike! Kill!" like thousands of dragons
As they make you suffer burning wounds.

Fear hell, not the pleasant hermitage grove
Where bees flit over a paradise of flowers,
Trees bow down under their weight of fruit,
And the refreshing touch of a southern breeze
Moves the willow boughs in a playful dance.

There are no obstructions to concentration there:
The brooks gently fall, and the birds sweetly lift

Their throats in song, making music for the ears
Delightful as the tinkle of celestial cymbals.

A hermitage like this is hard to find,
Even if you search for a hundred aeons.
There, by enjoying infinite times
A concentration free from ecstasy and oblivion,
You will free yourself from suffering rebirths.

Your subjects toil hard to amass possessions.
But if your taxes squeeze them like an oil press
So they cannot enjoy what they so painfully gained,
You will fall into a bad rebirth as a hungry ghost.
As such you will have a gray complexion, weak eyes, and
A long, skinny neck leading to a cavernous stomach:
You will suffer the pangs of extreme hunger and thirst.

Therefore, be satisfied to consume the food
Easily and effortlessly found in the forest.
Through enjoying the delicious roots and sprouts
And perfectly clear, cool water to drink there,
You will imbibe the nectar of undefiled wisdom.

If you are sunk deep in oblivion and ignorance
About actions and their results as well as
The right view about the nature of reality,
You will instantly take rebirth as an animal.
Then in a dark cloud of stupidity you will suffer
Harsh beatings and drudgery, and be led to slaughter.
It will be hard even to hear the words *holy Dharma*.

The light of profound wisdom that comprehends that
All phenomena exist without being truly existent
Eliminates the dark mists of ignorance
And blocks the path to the lower realms.

We all have a human life of freedom and fortune,
But, like a lightning flash, it lasts just a moment.
When you see it is the mirror reflecting liberation,
Why would you waste this valuable opportunity?

O father, ministers, and people, things appear
Pleasant, but they are sweet only in name.
Really they are like a poisonous flower:
You crave its abundant beauty, but eventually
It kills you, causing much suffering to arise.

Because you are attached to things like this,
You are confused about how to free yourselves.
Worldly things vanish like ripples on water.
Why tire and exhaust yourselves for them?

His parents, brother, and all the ministers were happy to hear this speech, containing the essence of helpfulness in accordance with the Dharma. Moved by powerful faith, they touched the crowns of their heads to his feet many times.

At this time the sweet news of his return was drummed far and wide: "Kumaradvitiya viewed the bounteous riches of the kingdom as a blazing pit of fire, so he went to a hermitage in the fearsome forest. However, he was not quashed by any harm or hazard! He has perfected the great deeds of a bodhisattva and attained the holy state of peaceful liberation! He has returned to Gem of the World on his lotus-feet, vowing to free all limitless beings from suffering! He will let forth the torrential rain which propagates the boundless Dharma!"

When this was announced in the three provinces of the kingdom, people everywhere felt the urge to partake of the nectar of the Dharma and desired liberation. Uncountable numbers of people proceeded toward the palace of Gem of the World. King Chandramati with his son and ministers came from the great satrapy of Myriad Lights. King Dyutimat, Manohari's mother, Chandraprabha, and their ministers came from Radiant Array.

At this time Kundaladhara had the good fortune to be reunited with her cherished son, Kumaradvitiya. His attainment of the nectar of wisdom and discourse upon the purpose of the holy Dharma satisfied her every wish.

"Now I have not the slightest regret," she thought and was filled with joy.

In general, human life is fraught with peril; it is quite easy for the body to perish. It is like this example: in the ocean there are many sharks, killer whales, and barracudas. These carnivores do not live together harmoniously: they compete to feed on living beasts. When any creature of the watery deep falls into their jaws, there is no

chance it will live long! It is just the same for the body: when its elements of fire, water, earth, and air are in conflict, this illusory body
breaks apart instantly. No one in the world can maintain his body permanently.

Mother Kundaladhara was in mortal danger from a disharmony of
the four elements. Just as the forests are bereft of their beauty when the
snows and strong winds of winter topple the trees, so her body had
been robbed of its form and vitality by this illness. She had become very
weak and had no desire for food.

The holy prince extended his right hand toward her with the graceful movement of an elephant's trunk. He took his mother's hand in his
own and asked, "Mother, are you suffering from illness? Are you in
pain?"

In reply she said, "O bodhisattva prince, I have fallen ill and am quite
close to death! Nevertheless, I have no regrets, for I have obtained my
heart's desire."

Even while sorrowful thoughts figured in Kumara's mind, he
recalled, "There is no way to counter the ephemeral nature of composite phenomena: there is no cure, for this is the way things are." So he
said to his mother:

O mother! Please do not grieve!
Inexpressibly many times we have been reborn,
Wandering in samsara since beginningless time.
Primarily we are lost in the deep lower realms,
Lacking knowledge of the way to a pure land.

Thanks to many merits, we are born as humans.
But just once; this life does not last long.
It is like a lightning flash on a cloudy night
Or the crest of foam formed by a crashing wave.

Even Buddhas free from samsara and nirvana
Cannot grant life to pitiable beings like this,
Even though they wish to shelter and support us
In their endeavor to lead us beyond sorrow.

Thus, honored mother, the flower of youth
Wilts at the touch of winter's old age
And is destroyed by the frost of illness.
Then, one can do naught but be reborn.

So at death completely extirpate desire
For your relations, possessions, and even
The illusory body you have had in this life.
Focus upon the good qualities of a pure land;
Pray to be reborn there in a jewel-lotus womb.

Constantly bear in mind the profound essence
Of the instructions I have given many times:
All phenomena always lack any inherent nature!
May you be absorbed into the stainless Dharmadhatu!

These profound instructions gave her hope, closed the door to the lower realms, and pointed out the path leading to liberation. Kumara poured into her ears profound praises of the qualities of the Buddhas.

Kundaladhara's relatives and entourage gathered around her, knowing that she was about to die. They were immobilized by ardent grief, for there was nothing they could do to save her. They all stood about as if they were lines in a drawing. His mother stared fixedly at Kumara's face. Then, she smiled slightly and gave up her life without any anguish at all.

All composite phenomena eventually change,
For they lack any definite inherent nature.
At death we give up the components of our bodies,
Only our consciousness wanders on alone.

Her oceans of friends, relations, and court
Gathered around and shed rivers of tears.
But like a deer who has strayed form the herd,
His honorable mother had to suffer death alone.

At death you cannot take with you any food,
Drink, or abode, nor any friends or relations.
Not one person can follow you out of regard,
Thinking, "I love you too dearly for us to part."

Kye ma! Samsara is a poisonous tree:
Any person who deludedly desires to enjoy
Like a bee the sweet honey of its flowers
Will surely come to ruin in the end.

In this case, her dear entourage gathered there
Were completely blinded by a deep fog of misery.
The sound of their dismal wails filled the air.
The smooth floors seemed to become cavernous pits
Into which they fell and lay still in a faint.

To revive them, the bodhisattva prince fanned them
With refreshing instructions. He helped them see
That all composite phenomena are impermanent;
Like illusions, everything lacks true existence.

Then Prince Kumara made many offerings on behalf of Kundaladhara. In this way the marvelous wealth of the kingdom was used to create merit for his mother. The force of these deeds released Kundaladhara from the lower realms. She climbed the staircase of these merits to the city of pure liberation.

39

In which the prince's teacher, Arhat Dharmeshvara, preaches the Dharma, thereby helping all beings

A FTER HIS MOTHER'S DEATH, Prince Kumaradvitiya thought about all the people who had braved the difficulties of the long journey to come and see him. "It would not be right if those who came in search of the nectar of the Dharma continued to wonder if they have come here in vain."

So he gathered around him King Chandramati, King Dyutimat, and all the others who had flocked like bees to his lotus-face. With respectful reverence, they paid homage to him. Then he gave them extensive advice in accordance with the Dharma. This should have fulfilled their wishes to learn how to strive for liberation.

However, the situation was like this: although all rivers flow into the great ocean, the ocean's thirst is never quenched. Similarly, although the prince proffered a feast of Dharma hundreds of times a day, they were insatiable.

"Since they are still not satisfied, I will ask my spiritual friend, Arhat Dharmeshvara, to offer them the nectar of the Dharma," he thought. So he went to his spiritual teacher and supplicated him:

"O guide of the universe! Please consider this small matter with love and compassion. Kings, queens, monks, brahmins, ministers, and countless others have come here in search of liberation, for they fear the suffering of bad rebirths. Please give them a feast of the ambrosia of the Mahayana Dharma, which lacks any attachment to solitary peace!"

The saint gratified him with a happy smile. "Holy prince, I shall do as you wish and teach just as you have done. Please have those people

who have come in search of freedom told that the arhat Dharmeshvara
will let fall a rain of instructions containing the nectar of the Dharma.

"Thus, whosoever desires liberation from the fiery pit of samsara;
whosoever craves to understand that the nature of composite phenomena is impermanent, changing, and like a dream; whosoever wishes to
abandon this abode of totally defiled suffering; and whosoever yearns
for freedom having considered the pure, cool peace of nirvana should
come here. Attend to this well!"

"I shall do as you say," said the bodhisattva prince. Just as he had been
commanded, noble Kumara sent messengers in all directions to ring out
those words.

Then, like flocks of geese gathering upon a lotus pond, people came
to enjoy the fortunate occasion of hearing the holy Dharma. They set a
precious throne upon a lion pedestal. When the arhat Dharmeshvara set
his lotus-feet on the high, plush cushions of this seat, he was like the
sun beautifying a mountain peak. The great bodhisattva Kumaradvitiya,
at the head of countless seekers of liberation, prostrated himself and
placed offerings in front of his teacher.

The arhat straightened his body. He could not be overcome, for he
had obtained every type of fearlessness: he could guarantee that he
had abandoned all the obstacles to liberation and could express his
intuitive understanding about what other beings needed to abandon
and how to do so before all sentient beings, including enlightened
ones. He was without anxiety, for he had the four types of analytical
knowledge: he knew the meanings of words, the structure of language, how to communicate clearly, and all aspects of phenomena.
So, with the roar of a lion, he sang this profound song of the
Mahayana Dharma:

> I respectfully bow my head and prostrate myself
> Before the Buddhas, bodhisattvas, and their disciples
> Dwelling in the boundless space of the ten directions
> And the all-encompassing expanse of the three times.
>
> I teach the holy Dharma, free from attachment
> To solitary peace, to pitiable sentient beings
> Sunk deep in the fearsome samsaric ocean
> So they may attain complete enlightenment.
>
> Everyone's mental continuum is naturally pure.
> However, adventitious stains have obscured it;

Always acting under this clouding influence,
We have taken rebirth in samsara throughout time.

All those who take birth as sentient creatures
In the interwoven pattern of high and low rebirths
Are the same: they all desperately crave happiness,
And they all wish to avoid experiencing sorrow.

Beings whose nature is all-pervasive suffering
Do not know how to achieve what they wish:
Craving deceptive pleasures, they turn away
From the bliss of attaining the ultimate good.

Thus, those who are bound by karma and the passions
Cling to mere appearances and hold them as real.
They have no chance to free themselves from samsara:
So, break the chains of grasping at "I" and "mine"!

All the good qualities of samsara and nirvana
Grow as sprouts from a single supreme field:
Proper reliance upon a perfect spiritual master.
So follow him with seemly thoughts and deeds.

Waves of actions to accumulate merit and wisdom
In many former aeons resulted in your human rebirth.
It is unrivaled by hundreds of priceless jewels,
For you have the fortunate chance to hear the Dharma
And lack nonhuman obscurations and human disabilities.

When you carefully consider the causes, nature,
And rarity of a human life, you realize that it
Is hard to find even once in a hundred aeons.
So you should nourish the sapling of this life,
For it can mature to be heavy with beneficial fruit.

High rebirths arise from charity and morality.
The practices of ethics, meditation, and insight
Motivated by a wish to attain nirvana oneself
Yield personal liberation or solitary enlightenment.

Reliance on the practice of the six perfections
And four ways of gathering and training disciples

For the sake of innumerable mother sentient beings
Quickly results in reaching unsurpassable enlightenment.
What can compare with the good qualities of this?

This body has no permanent, inviolate nature:
It is definitely a perishable phenomenon.
It does not last long and changes in an instant,
Like a random lightning flash among surging clouds.

We are like animals led to the slaughterhouse
By butchers whose arms are stained with blood.
Without any pause our every step and breath
Takes us closer to the Death Lord's domain.

When we die and go on to our next rebirth,
What use are family, jewels, or wealth?
Even our much cherished body is left behind.
There is no other refuge than the Dharma then.

The body is extinguished like lamplight.
Cast off like a shell, it does not transmigrate.
Only the fruits of sinful or virtuous deeds
Follow you as a shadow stays with a form.

Consider what you will experience as the result
Of deviating onto a path of degenerate action:
A miserable rebirth, unpleasant circumstances,
And a propensity to act heinously again.
Strive to avoid even the subtlest evil deed!

Then contemplate that supremely virtuous deeds
Are the causes that mature into pleasant results.
So take up such actions, for there is no other way
To achieve your own and others' desirable aims.

Those who wander in the forest of samsara,
Which is like a blazing pit of fiery sorrow,
Cannot accomplish their heartfelt goals
And always lack what they most desire.

The womb is an agonizing, hellish mass of filth.
After a long time there you are pressed out;

Squeezed and crushed at the time of birth,
Our skin seems to be flayed as we come out.

As we age, our old bodies weaken.
Even our desire for objects lessens.
As our faculties dull, even our children
Heartlessly say, "Old man, just die"!

When the four great elements are in disharmony,
Our pitiful bodies suffer grievous pains,
Like a sheep set upon by a pack of wolves
We face the unbearable, unlimited misery of death.

Finally even skilled doctors give up hope.
Although we are surrounded by our families,
The Death Lord inexorably seizes us in his jaws.
How can you bear to continue to suffer death?

Moreover, our bodies, life, and possessions are like
A tree of paradise rich with leaves and fruit.
Its roots may be severed by the ax of sinful deeds.

Our dear friends whose behavior seems delightful
At death become a burden as heavy as a mountain.
For we suffer the pain of separation from loved ones
To whom the bonds of love are tight and long held.

In short, the defiled components of body and mind
Which we have cherished throughout our lives
Are the door to all our samsaric rebirths
And the basis giving rise to all misery.

It is totally unsuitable to have any faith
In samsara, for nothing in it is definite:
Fathers and sons can become mortal enemies
And enemies become your most valued friends.

The mothers' milk we drank in our rebirths
And the tears we have wept in exhaustion
Would overflow the four great oceans' basins.
Yet even now we have not been satisfied.

Every sentient being dies and is reborn
Into a defiled, impermanent, and illusory body.
If you piled up the bones of all your lives,
They would be higher than any mountain.
What use is there in finding a body again?

Blown by the fierce winds of karma,
Your consciousness transmigrates to a new birth.
If the mothers of all your births lined up,
The vast extent of space could not contain them.

Even if you become an emperor of the universe,
In samsara you may become a slave once again.
The sun always sets, plunging us into darkness:
Who can be sure they will obtain and retain wealth?

At death you give up your body to be reborn
As a god, human, animal, hungry ghost, or hell being.
None of your helpful friends can go with you:
Only your sinful and virtuous deeds are carried on.

Immersed in samsara, essentially an ocean of misery,
You suffer birth, aging, sickness, and death over again.
Things seem pleasant, but they become painful after a while:
Samsara involves the suffering of constant change.

Reborn because of the power of karma and the passions
From the highest heavens to the lowest hells,
We live, to die and be reborn into misery,
For suffering is all-pervasive in samsara.

Thus, all-pervasive suffering is hard to bear.
Knowing the miserable nature of the bad rebirths
Should impel you to strive for liberation.
If not, you must be possessed by a demon.

Amid roaring fires on a burning iron ground,
Hell's denizens dismember one another with weapons.
Then a voice from the sky says, "Arise again,"
And they revive to suffer that same agony anew.

In that fiery place, the Death Lord draws lines
Upon our bodies according to our evil deeds.
Then sharp weapons saw us into that pattern.
My hair bristles merely to think of this agony!

Then, running in search of safety, we are crushed
Between stone mountains shaped like horses and sheep.
How can we bear the misery of being pulverized,
Ground up, and beaten by clubs of strong iron?

Then the winds of karma drive us into a house
Of iron indistinguishable from a fiery inferno.
Instantly the exit disappears; it is no refuge,
And we howl with the pain of unbearable burns.

We finally escape from that existence
To a similar iron house encasing the first.
We're tortured by even greater searing burns than before;
Our agonized shrieks fill all the realms of hell.

A sharp, red-hot skewer will impale your body
And lift it into a caldron of molten metal;
Your flesh and bones will be boiled away,
But the excruciating heat will not cease.

Born again, blazing tridents pierce your body;
Flames burst forth from every orifice and pore.
Encircled by flaming iron, your body ignites
Like a lamp wick. This suffering is incomprehensible!

The inferno's conflagration envelops every direction.
Creatures indistinguishable from the flames howl
As molten metals are poured into their mouths.
This is a place where unceasing torment is endured.

Outside the iron fence encircling the hells
Are indefinite realms that are minor damned states.
In the fire pits near the gates to the great hells
Are putrid, odorous swamps with scorching hot bottoms.
You are enticed to stony mountainsides to climb
Fearsome trees, whose sharp iron thorns and
Razor-sharp leaves slice you like a knife.

A great hell denizen's life is not short.
You stay an aeon in the first intolerable hell,
And each one hotter is half again longer.
Or it is said you will suffer inconceivable misery
For as long as your evil karma has not been exhausted.

In the cold hells, one falls into an extremely steep
And deep ice cavern in a plain of dense snowdrifts.
Terrifying darkness pervades every direction,
And an extraordinarily cold wind gusts all around.

We shiver like thin reeds in the freezing gale.
Feeling cold, we long to wrap up in warm clothes.
But our flesh is covered only by goose bumps,
Like ice-crystal rosaries offering no warmth.

The cold causes our goose bumps to blister,
Unbearably tormenting our pathetic bodies.
The irresistible power of our own evil karma
Creates all these wretched conditions and traumas.

We cannot tolerate enduring these hardships:
We suck in our lower lips three fingers deep,
And like geese in a snare we loudly cry, "Achoo!"
This is the result of enjoying nonvirtuous deeds.

To whom can the wretched go for refuge
When caught in a maelstrom of ice, snow, and wind?
Our plaintive cries are caught in our throats:
We sob only the muffled lament "kye hu."

Enveloped in this cold so hard to endure,
Our words and voices are weak and unclear.
We shiver and our teeth chatter loudly;
We hold our cheeks but cannot stop quaking.

Then our bodily complexion degenerates
Like a lotus faded and wilted by the cold.
The Death Lord slices us into five petal parts;
Carved into bits we are in a miserable state.

Our skin, hair, and complexion seemed pleasant,
But when we perceive the agony of being splintered
Into sections like a ten-petaled red lotus,
How can samsara's miseries seem pleasurable?

Born there once again, our bodies crack open
Along lines like a hundred-petaled lotus.
Our inner organs and bones are clearly exposed;
The cold seems to penetrate our very life force.

The duration of the cold hells is immeasurably long.
Life in the first cold hell lasts as long
As it takes to empty an eighty-bushel granary
If only one sesame seed a century is removed.

Each hell colder is said to last
Twenty times longer than the first.
Once you fall into this tragic place,
You suffer until your evil karma is finished.

Those who come to be born hungry ghosts
Suffer the pangs of hunger wherever they go:
It's hard to find even pus or excrement to eat.
Their merits are so minimal that even trees
Heavy with fruit seem bare when they are near.

For many long years, you are tortured by thirst:
Even the word *water* is rarely heard by ghosts.
You may see a large river and go there to drink,
But your poisonous mouth evaporates every drop,
Leaving nothing to drink there at all for you.

A hungry ghost has a mouth small as a needle's eye
And a throat as narrow as a horse's tail hair.
So even if you find a morsel to eat or drink,
You cannot eat, and your huge stomach is never full.
You are reduced to consuming your own flesh,
And blazing fires scorch your throat and stomach.

Hungry ghosts live to suffer freezing and burning
In alternation for more than fifty million years.

Even moonlight and cool breezes burn them in summer.
In winter, fires and sunlight chill like ice water.

Taking birth in a miserable animal realm is anguish.
Countless creatures trying to eat one another
Pack the ocean as tightly as a seedpod.
The strong squeeze the weaker ones between them,
And even in the ocean you can die of thirst.

Some animals are slaughtered for the minimal
Qualities of their flesh, skins, bones, or wool.
Others are exhausted but are forced on by beatings
To carry loads while their wounds ooze pus and blood.
Stupid and dumb, not knowing what to do or avoid,
Some animals suffer as if they were in hell.
Some creatures live an aeon while others only an instant.

Avoiding the chasm of the fearsome lower realms,
You may obtain an excellent human rebirth.
But if you do not use this superb chance properly,
A human life can be a door opening to suffering.

The rich are miserable protecting their wealth.
The poor endure agonizing muscle aches and pains
Searching for wealth and never finding what they want.
Worldly riches are nothing, merely ripples on water.

When the desire-realm gods perceive the signs
Of their own degeneration leading to death,
They see their past, present, and next rebirth.
This causes mental agony a hundredfold worse
Than the tortures endured in the lower realms.

The demigods wound one another, filled with hatred,
And are weakened by pervasive disputes and quarrels.
Despite their intelligence, they never see the truth
Because of karmic obscurations, so suffer this anguish.

Thus, only this priceless human life of quality
Is the foundation for obtaining enlightenment.
Compared with all the dust on earth, this life
Is as rare as the dirt caught under a fingernail.

Moreover, this life does not last long:
It is as fleeting as a winter evening's shadow.
It is over as quickly as a precipitous waterfall.
You should realize you have no time to spare.

The fault of fancying life's appearances
Is overcome by the ambrosia of renunciation.
When you are convinced about the law of causation,
You will endeavor to engage in proper conduct.
When you contemplate the endless pervasive misery
Of the particular and general sufferings of samsara,
You will strive for liberation with more than words.

If you do not persevere in these contemplations,
Whatever you do is motivated by karma and passions,
Causing the wheel of suffering existence to cycle.
Thus, always desire only liberation, never crave
To be Brahma or an emperor, even in your dreams.

If you do not hold to the special pure thought
Of striving for unsurpassable enlightenment
Only out of desire to benefit other beings,
Your own and others' aims cannot be fulfilled.

Thus, it is proper flawlessly to produce
The precious desire to reach the ultimate state
Of Buddhahood, perfect in wisdom and compassion,
Focusing on limitless mother sentient beings.

Regard every creature to the ends of space
With equanimity, not labeling them friend or foe.
Then recognize each one as your mother;
Recall her kindness and endeavor to repay it.

How can you obtain undefiled pleasure in this life
When even contaminated happiness is not to be had?
Do not rely on transitory things although you now feel
That things with the nature of misery are pleasurable.

Desiring happiness, but not knowing how to attain it,
People vanquish their foes and cherish their friends.

So they continually suffer in this life and create
The causes to be without pleasure in future lives.

Without artifice you should learn to produce
This loving thought: "Wouldn't it be wonderful
If all mother sentient beings could be happy?
I shall cause them to experience great joy."

My mothers are bound tightly by the ropes
Of contaminated good, evil, and neutral deeds.
Trapped in the prison of samsara, they are reborn
In the desire-, form-, and formless-realm states.

Streams of desire, hatred, ignorance, and wrong views
Sweep you away continually, without any cease.
They are the cause of the turbulent waves
Of the river of birth, aging, sickness, and death.

The eye that can see what to do and avoid
Is completely covered by a thick blanket
Of ignorance about the law of causation,
Fastened by the iron chains of grasping
"I" and "mine" as inherently real.

Think how wonderful it would be if all beings
Who have endured without cease all types of misery
On the long samsaric road since beginningless time
Could be free from suffering and its causes.
Decide: "I will free them from their sorrow."

That noble thought of great compassion is the sun,
Drawn forth by the chariot of love and kindness,
To shed the pervasive white light of bliss
And permanently dispel the dark clouds of sorrow.

The only one in the universe who can accomplish
The aim of liberating all mother sentient beings,
Who have protected us with kindness again and again,
Is renowned as a fully enlightened Buddha.

Thus, consider all the vast good qualities
Of a Buddha's ineffable body, speech, and mind

And make dauntless prayers to attain that state
Which accomplishes your own and others' aims.

Learn to desire enlightenment for others' sake,
For this is the path followed by all Buddhas.
Practice the three ethics of accumulating virtue,
Keeping your vows and working to benefit others.

So, concentrate with great effort to produce
This supreme, expansive thought of love.
Meditate on the pith of bodhisattvas' practice:
Cherishing others far more than oneself.
Emulate the exemplary life of Kumaradvitiya,
For he joyfully gave away his body and wealth.

Pure morality is the fertile ground
From which all good qualities grow.
Strive to abide in positive practices
So you may harvest their virtuous fruits.

Despite your many acts of helpful kindness,
Noxious beings forget and like butchers
Threaten your life; but do not be angry,
Put on the sturdy armor of unruffled patience.

In order to liberate all pitiable creatures
From being tortured by hundreds of sorrows,
You must perfect a bodhisattva's practices,
Persevering enthusiastically, without laziness.

Nourish a peaceful concentration free from
Sluggishness and flightiness that never strays
From a diamondlike, single-pointed absorption
In the profound nature of ultimate reality.

The wisdom which subtly and precisely analyzes
Ultimate reality is the stainless sword
Hewing down every point held by an extreme view.
Right understanding of reality lacks any extreme.

Because you are attached to the taste
Of seeing others experience well-being,

Grant every wish of every creature,
Giving them what they desire and need.

Out of love for those whose Dharma eye is clouded
By total ignorance of what to do and avoid,
Sweetly explain whatever will train them,
Thus giving a lamp illumining the path to freedom.

The best of all holy beings' waves of deeds
Is to unfurl the banner of compassionate courage
To act in a way leading to accomplishment of
The temporary and ultimate happiness of all beings.

After setting out whatever training is needed
To tame each being according to its nature,
Engage in marvelous deeds for others' benefit
That will lead them to supreme enlightenment.

Those engaging in deeds leading to perfect enlightenment
Are thus worthy of the homage of worldly gods and men.
They are the restful shade tree for those beings
Tired and lost wandering on the long samsaric road.
They are the cupped hands which rescue beings
From the deep and fearsome chasms of the lower realms.
They are the Dharma-sun that clearly illuminates
Areas enveloped in thick, dark clouds of ignorance.
They are the jewel-moon that bestows cooling liberation
To pacify all those scorched by the pain of the passions.

The backbone of unsurpassable enlightenment,
And the cause and effect of both Mahayana paths,
Is this uncommon cause known as bodhicitta.
It is extremely fortunate even to hear that term
Meaning the desire to obtain enlightenment
In order to benefit all sentient beings.

No matter how familiar you are with virtuous practices
Such as renunciation, repentance, and bodhicitta,
Without the sharp sword of wisdom analyzing
The selflessness of phenomena, you cannot be freed.
So in order to cut out the roots of cyclic existence,
Rely on the methods to comprehend dependent origination.

By combining analytical and placement meditation
On the ultimate nature of reality—all phenomena
Exist and are empty of any truly existent self—
You realize the essence of supremely peaceful union
Pervaded by the suppleness of great bliss,
And uproot the wrong view that considers emptiness
And dependent origination to be incompatible.

This wrong view arises in your mind
Because of not differentiating between
"Totally nonexistent" and "not inherently existent,"
Thus clutching at the extreme of permanence.

Falling to the extreme of total annihilation,
You say nominally imputed phenomena do not exist
Because they cannot be found in samsara or nirvana;
So the relationship between causes and their results
Is a mistake not establishable by valid cognition.

When you believe that is the nature of reality,
You destroy the law of causation; so for disciples
There is nothing to practice nor actions to avoid.
This web of extreme views anchors you to the depths
Of hell, for you carelessly commit evil deeds.

When not under analysis, all phenomena
From forms up to omniscience are nominal imputations;
Therefore you understand that causation can function.
Then, when you analyze phenomena with supreme reasoning,
You find that there is not an iota of inherent existence.

When you are skilled at seeing no contradiction there,
You identify the object of the conception of true existence
As the object of refutation which lacks inherent existence,
Just by knowing the meaning of dependent origination
Without needing the slightest glance at other proofs.
Thus, you become convinced about the dependent origination
Of all phenomena which exist as mere nominal imputations.

This conviction is the sign of completing the analysis
By study and contemplation on the profound object

Of the view that is free from all extremes.
This is the path praised as perfect by the Buddhas.

Generate the fortitude to overcome the enemy—samsara
Produced by ignorant grasping at a truly existent self—
With the king of reasoning about dependent origination,
The perfect view that is beyond extremes of elaboration.
Therefore, train your mind by faultlessly accomplishing
This path common to both supreme Mahayana vehicles.

Those who wish to practice the adamantine vehicle,
A pure path noble as a victory banner's pinnacle
And hard to find even in a thousand lifetimes,
Should rely on a master of the supreme vehicle,
Mature their mind streams with the four empowerments,
And even risk losing their lives to protect the vows
And pledges that are the basis for all mystic powers.

Relying on the perfect spiritual instructions
Of the profound path of the tantric systems,
Persevere in the yoga of the two stages of practice.
In one lifetime you can easily reach the state
Of enlightened Vajradhara in union with consort,
Thereby leading all sentient beings to that state!

With this and other speeches, he opened infinite doors to the vast
and profound holy Dharma. His explanations were clear, correct, and
well and variously composed.

To those suitable to be practitioners of the supreme vehicle that
quickly leads to enlightenment, he explained everything that should be
practiced by intelligent disciples to lead all beings across the ford to the
shores of freedom.

Some of the people who listened to this explanation of the holy
Dharma attained the state which spontaneously accomplishes their own
and others' aims. Others obtained the fruit of arhatship. Some entered
the city of liberation. Others dove into the ocean of the pure land
realms. Some generated precious bodhicitta in their mind streams and
became sons of the conquerors. Yet others came to understand that the
nature of samsara is suffering and so went to a hermitage desiring liberation: there they experienced the bliss of samadhi. The remainder of the
incomprehensible numbers of folk there entered the path and were lib-

erated from suffering rebirths in the lower realms. Their minds were washed clean of all the pervasive stains of the passions.

Thus, by lighting this great lamp of the Dharma, the pure light of liberation reached every being enveloped in the unbroken darkness of samsara.

Then Prince Kumaradvitiya and all the others in the assembly scattered fresh flowers and made prostrations before their spiritual friend, the arhat Dharmeshvara, with respect and joy in each others' achievements.

Then, to laud him, they uttered these praises three times:

"O lord of the Dharma, you are a virtuous spiritual friend. You are the guide for those in samsara. No one but you has ever protected us so kindly through offering us the Dharma. Our king did not do so; neither did the gods; nor did our dearest friends and relations ever offer it so. You have dried up the oceans of our blood and tears. As if we were a herd of deer, you have freed us from traps. You have shut the door to the lower realms and opened wide the door to high rebirth and liberation. You have severed the root causes for us to be born as hell denizens, hungry ghosts, or animals. You have placed us in the marvelous state of liberation, the god realms and the purposeful human realm!"

EPILOGUE

I offer the Buddhas streams of perfect music,
Expressing pleasant ideas with melodious words.
Their vast and profound religious discourses
Are the stairs leading into a precious palace.

To explicate the four aims of men customarily found
In poetics—love, virtue, wealth, and liberation—
Herein I described love as many beautiful maidens
Causing the flower of lust to bloom joyfully.

By my churning the ocean of deeds which create merit
Through giving ordinary riches and the special Dharma,
The resulting vast wealth of merits shone
Like the sun and moon vanquishing dark poverty.

The holy Dharma difficult to find in a thousand aeons
Is the path to achieve the four bodies of a Buddha.
Its essential points were completely, accurately,
And clearly explained in language easy to understand.

The good fortune to enjoy the bliss of liberation
Is the auspicious sign that one took to heart
The essence of the peerless Dharma instructions,
Thus completing a description of the four aims of life.

In the great tradition of poetics, poetry and prose
Clearly describe the arena of the composition's tale.
The cities of Open Lotus and so forth were depicted
As more praiseworthy than the immortals' abodes.

The sweet-scented ocean with rippling waves was portrayed
As a precious lake whose far shore could not be seen.
The nature of the mountains was described as humbling
The pride of eagles exhausted trying to ascend the peaks.

Two seasons were specified in particular: spring's
Spreading glory and summer's auspicious abundance.
During the play of supreme sensual bliss, I depicted
Even the sun and moon as rising because of lust's force.

There were superlative praises of the sports
Of lovely maidens in lotus-covered ponds
Set amidst the artful copses of sweet trees
In the pleasure gardens of Radiant Array.

The character of a festival of joy was recounted
As the pleasure of drinking, singing, dancing,
And obtaining union with a captivating youth
During the enjoyment of a great marriage festival.

First they were tortured by inconceivable agony
As a result of not obtaining their heart's desire.
But later, after the marriage rituals,
Pleasure in sexual bliss was recounted.

From the time of his birth, Kumaradvitiya
Had all the good qualities of a high rebirth.
Matured thanks to the care of his loving mother,
His qualities were praised as waxing like the moon.

The way to rule a great realm peacefully or forcefully
Was clearly exemplified through entering the councils
Of the wise many times, and by the skillful emissaries
Traveling swift as birds among the three kingdoms.

Noble Kumaradvitiya was described in battle
As the general of a great four-division army.
The enemy was destroyed like hoarfrost in the sun.
Thus, the prince's might spread like summer's bounty.
This completes all the poetic representations.

Filling the vast heavens over the religious Land of Snows
Are roiling blue clouds heavy with the moisture
Of adepts' discrimination of all objects of knowledge.
By the raining down of the essence of precious advice
That increases everyone's harvest of beneficial happiness,
Their own and others' aims were brought to fruition.
I recall their kind deeds and give faithful thanks.

Bound by the chains of karma and the passions,
Sentient beings suffer in the darkness of misery.
Out of habitual ignorance of what to do or avoid,
They are led into the chasm of the lower rebirths.

Now pitiful beings lacking discriminating wisdom
Have obtained the fortune to enjoy effortlessly
An ocean of nectar ruffled by waves of helpful advice,
A precious treasury of the Dharma given by the guides
Who unerringly lead us along the noble path.

The well water of words created by my ignorant mind
Is muddied by wrong views and briny trivialities.
Some question the benefit of completing this work,
But every object of knowledge can be reflected
On the pure mirror of conventional knowledge.
This wreath of poetry and prose tells a story
That can increase the understanding of its readers.

Many words clearly express the poetic themes
Of love and war, but in essence it is a tale
Of renunciation loudly drumming the Dharma,
Awakening others from the sleep of ignorance.

The author is sunk deep in the mire of carelessness,
Weighed down by a heavy burden of samsaric misery.
Enveloped in clouds of laziness, he lacks the Dharma eye.
Thus, because he is ignorant of what to do or avoid,
Whatever he writes is akin to a mere echo.

Nevertheless, my superb intention was virtuous:
I clearly explained the marvelous qualities of the

Four aims of men so that religious instructions
Would arise from a tale enjoyed by ordinary beings.

I wrote, drawing from the works of former scholars,
Intending to change a bit but not contradict them.
No gossip, slander, or strings of lies appear here.
My intent was to write a conventional story of love
To draw forth the glittering sunlight of the Dharma.

May the virtues arising from this work
Be as shining white as the snows of Mount Kailash.
Just as Kailash's great rivers will flow
To the jewel sea until the end of time,
May whatever merit these instructions have
Be a river carrying all beings to the ocean
Of totally omniscient Buddhahood.

This composition of poetry and prose titled *The Tale of the
Incomparable Prince* was written according to the tenets of dramatic
composition joined to a presentation of the four aims of men according to the tradition of poetics. The plot and manner of composition
were intended to lead others' minds from renunciation and the
impermanence of all phenomena to the essence of the Dharma and
liberation.

A so-called pearl garland like this was requested of me many times:
sometimes poetry lovers entreated me with euphonious words, while at
other times people sent poetic letters exhorting me to write. I wrote
this book in response to their requests.

I am the lowliest of the lineage of Kazi. I waste all my time, for I am
flighty and lazy. I am the slothful creature known as either dByangs
chen dga ba Tshe ring dbang gi rgyal po, or by the name of Tshangs sras
dgyes pa'i blo lden.

This work was begun when I held the post of district commissioner and judge of Gri gu bkra zhis mthong smon, a part of Yar
'brog near the large lake Dang ra gyu mtsho. It surrounds the venerable temple bSam 'phel nor bu, which grants all wishes for high
rebirth and liberation via the sounds of the kettledrums in songbirds'
throats.

sGrol lha gang dkar Mountain is a high, white, crystal dome surrounded by rocky crags. There in an eagle's aerie is Padma gling, where
the master of wisdom Padma Sambhava lived. At the foot of this peak is

mDo mkhar bkra zhis rab brtan. Two large rivers wend through the valley encircled by stands of trees. At harvest time there is no danger of
hail or inclement weather. The inhabitants of the land have turned away
from killing ignorant creatures and are naturally inclined to virtue. It is
there that I completed the text.

May this work be of benefit to all!